SO · FAR · FROM · SPRING

Happy Birthday, Guys!
Love from us,

Ben, Anita, Bud + Rachel

(Peggy Simson Curry was raised
on the Boettcher Ranch, one of the
4 ranches of the Big Horn.)

Also by Peggy Simson Curry

NOVEL

Fire in the Water

POEMS

Red Wind of Wyoming

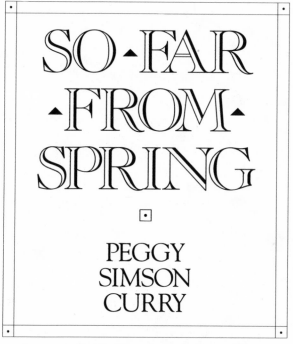

SO·FAR ·FROM· SPRING

PEGGY SIMSON CURRY

A novel of the American West

PRUETT PUBLISHING COMPANY
BOULDER, COLORADO

First published by The Viking Press in 1956;
first Pruett Publishing Company edition 1983,
second Pruett Publishing Company edition 1993.

Printed in the United States

10 9 8 7 6 5 4 3 2 1

Library of Congress Cataloging-in-Publication Data

Curry, Peggy Simson.
So far from spring.

Reprint. Originally published: New York: Viking Press, 1956.
PS3505.U826S6   1983   813'.54   83-21179
ISBN 0-87108-840-1

For my husband, Bill

PUBLISHER'S NOTE

In late May of 1983, my wife and I were returning from California to our home in Boulder, Colorado in our small plane. After we left Grand Junction, the weather worsened and we turned north at Kremmling, hoping to skirt the storm. But as we tried to fly over the Medicine Bow mountains toward Laramie, the clouds thickened and we turned back, landing under darkening skies at Walden in Colorado's North Park. Although the runway had been cleared, there were many snow drifts around. Fortunately, there were two hospitable Walden school teachers, A.M. Swenson and Mary Rupp, taking a hike on that windswept plateau, and they gave us a ride into town. The next morning we awoke to a steady snowfall, and after breakfast at the Coffee Pot restaurant, we set out to pass some time. We found a haven right next door in the Bifocal book store. To my further surprise, I found that the owner, Jane Larson, was an old friend from Boulder. As we talked books, I mentioned that we were republishing *Red Fenwick's West*, as I knew Red's work was popular in ranch country. She countered with the suggestion that we consider Peggy Simson Curry's novel, *So Far From Spring.*

Looking out at the May snowstorm, I thought it was certainly an appropriate title for a book set in North Park, and shortly after we returned to Boulder I wrote Mrs. Curry, received a copy of *So Far From Spring,* and, after a brief consideration, decided that this fine novel of turn-of-the-century ranch life deserved to be revived. Later, at the Leanin' Tree gallery in Boulder, we found a Ted Blalock painting among their fine collection of western art, and it, too, seemed appropriate to the title, and the setting, of *So Far From Spring.* We think it is a book that you will want to read and that you will want to keep.

Fred Pruett

CHAPTER I

Kelsey Cameron stood alone on the prairie in the pale noon sunlight. It was late April in 1898. He set his cheap straw suitcase in the sagebrush and straightened to face the wind that came at him out of the west, blowing off the snow-capped mountains. It was a vicious wind that pasted his trousers to his long legs, sent his suitcoat flapping behind him, and tugged vainly at the coarse, forward-growing hair that jutted down the center of his forehead in a rough red V.

So this was North Park, Colorado, the place his cousin Tommy had written about; this was the wonderful country where a man could go into the cattle business, get rich, and live as he pleased. "God," Kelsey muttered, staring at the monotonous gray landscape.

The vast loneliness of the earth crowded into his mind and formed a cold knot. There was desolation here he could never have pictured in his wildest imagining. All around the big valley were mountains, white and cold and aloof, like the jagged waves of some giant winter sea that had hurled itself savagely against the sky and been frozen there forever.

Between the mountains was the prairie, a rolling, drab earth, covered with the gray sagebrush. Southward a lone butte lifted like a strange island out of the lower land. And to the north, close to him, was an ugly, rounded mountain that faced him like an enemy, the lower slopes barren and gray, and a dark stubble of trees on the summit. And there was nothing

1

anywhere—no gull to sweep the clean blue arch of sky, no house standing firmly on the earth, no human being walking toward him on the dusty road. Only the wind kept him company, battering him, nagging him, thrusting through his clothing to his shivering bones.

He tried to tell himself that all of North Park wasn't like this part where he walked; he knew there was a town away there to the southeast where a haze of blue smoke lay in the air, and there were ranches and rivers hidden from view by the rolling plains. But he could not rid himself of the sharp disappointment that had been with him ever since he got off the train at Laramie, Wyoming. Vividly now he remembered the jolting ride across the Laramie Plains in the spring wagon with the crude canvas covering to shut out the weather, and the slower ride over the mountaintop on the sled, for snow still lay deep in the high timber. And today, in another wagon, he had come down out of the foothills and into this valley—the Park, his companions on the stage had called it.

What a wrong and foolish notion he had carried in his mind of North Park. When his cousin had written of it, Kelsey had pictured many trees and little towns with cattle ranches between them. Once, crossing the mountain from Laramie, he'd tried to explain to one of his companions what he thought about North Park. The man had grunted, looked at him pityingly, and said nothing. And when he'd gotten off the stage, two hours ago, the same man had leaned out to say, "Better change your mind and ride on into town with us. It's a long walk to the Red Hill Ranch—maybe sixteen miles." When Kelsey hadn't answered, he'd added, "Well, fella, take it easy. You'll get used to it."

How could any man get used to anything so big and empty and lonely? And it was more than the way the land looked; it was the way it felt—overwhelming and forbidding. Here he was nothing, nothing at all—a speck in distance, a stranger. For a moment Kelsey felt so bewildered and alone that panic came over him, sending him running up the narrow road, stumbling over the sagebrush that grew in the center of it. Then panic left him as quickly as it had come, and he slowed to a walk, panting, feeling sweat under his arms although the cold wind rushed against him and hammered at him like a thousand padded clubs.

"Damn the wind!" he said to the empty blue sky and the gray earth. "It's worse than the winter gales in the old country." And the familiar Scottish landscape rose in his mind, green and beautiful and so far away. He halted and dropped the straw suitcase as terrible homesickness washed over him, leaving him shaken and desperate. If I could see my mother, Taraleean, and her garden, yellow now with daffodils . . . What madness had possessed him that he'd left his home, his mother, and the lass he loved?

A look of bitterness settled over his rugged young face with its bold, thick nose and wide mouth. Anything was better than staying in Scotland, even this bleak, unfriendly land so far from spring. He stooped and picked up his bag and walked on, the stiff new shoes rubbing his heels raw, his stomach cramping with hunger, his mouth hanging open as he gulped the shallow air of the high mountain valley.

As he trudged on he tried to forget that he was disappointed, tired, and broke. Somewhere ahead, maybe over the next rise of ground, lay his cousin Tommy's ranch. He called to mind exciting lines from Tommy's letters—"Acres of land for the taking . . . hundreds of Hereford cattle . . . country fit for a king . . ."

A king. Yes, anybody could be like a king in America; a common man could become president. And was such a thing possible in Scotland? Never! Again the bitterness was in him, bringing to his mind the thing that had begun when he was a small boy at school, for there he had punched a playmate in the nose for saying the Camerons were only common folk and could never own land like the lairds. And that night he had gone to his father and said, "Is this ground our house sits on not yours, Father?"

"The land belongs to the laird's estate, as does all the village. But the house is mine, and the things in it."

"And why is that?"

"It is the way in Scotland, lad. Some are born of the nobility and some are not. I pay no taxes on the ground where this house sits, but I must pay rent to the laird's factor. That's how the laird lives—on the rent from his land."

"And is there no ground that isn't the laird's?"

His father thought for a while and then replied, "Well, there is the high-water mark along the shore, the place where the sea has washed up on the earth. That is part of the sea and belongs to no man. Why do you get such a frown on your face, lad? What is it that troubles you?"

"I'll build me a house on the shore someday; I'll make it from old boards—pieces of broken boats—and I'll take no orders from the laird or his factor, and I'll pay him no rent."

"What daftness is this in a lad not yet old enough to know his own mind?"

Then Kelsey's mother, Taraleean, put her hand on the boy's head and said, "Leave the lad be, John. It's no daftness in him, but only the wild dreaming such as is in myself. Many a time—before I knew you, John—I asked myself why I was born to be an Irish tattie howker and pick potatoes while others rode in fine carriages." And she pressed Kelsey close, hiding his face in her skirt, saying, "Be careful, lad, for the wild dreaming leads to hurting."

The wild dreaming. Kelsey paused and shifted the suitcase to his other hand. What a dreaming they had done, he and his lassie! The things he'd promised her—how he'd own his father's shop someday and they'd go once a year to London, where she'd buy herself all manner of fine things to wear! And what had come of all his hopes and plans? An ugly country, no money, and himself walking like a beggar on a lonely road.

He shook his head, trying to put his rising anger from him; he mustn't think on Scotland, for such thinking tore him apart. The bloody gentry! Let them keep their land and be damned! Here he would have his own bit of earth and no man to give him orders as if he were a stable boy. And here, as soon as he had the money, he'd have Prim Munro, his lassie.

Kelsey walked slowly now, forgetting the sagebrush that shuddered in the wind, forgetting the whole of North Park. He saw only Prim, a pert bit of a lass with a tiny waist he delighted to span with his big hands; he saw her clear green eyes, her smooth black hair, and her mouth so full and smiling. What was it folk at the village always said of Prim? "A wee breath of a lass, but with a look in her eyes that says there's iron in her."

His arms ached to hold her again as he had held her before he left Scotland; there, in the hut he had built on the shore— *his* hut—he had loved Prim Munro and made her his own. Ah, what a night that had been!—the smell of the sea around them and the plushy sound of it breaking against the shore. He stopped in the narrow road, drew a handkerchief from his pocket, and wiped the moisture from his eyes. More than the wind does this to me, he thought—more than the wind, for what is a man until he loves a woman and makes her his? Surely nothing but an empty shell waiting to be filled. I should never have left Prim back there—not after what we were to each other. Some way I should have brought her with me.

Then he was angry. God in heaven, could any man reason with Prim's mother? Could any man talk sense into the stubborn and selfish mind of that old sow Big Mina Munro? Certainly he had tried hard enough; he had explained that Prim must come to America with him, that they were married in the eyes of God if not before men, and that to leave her was a cruel thing and not fair to either of them. But Big Mina had cursed him and ordered him from her house. And Prim had only wept and cowered in a corner like a demented child.

"Stand up to your mother!" Kelsey had cried. "Don't let her do this to us."

But there had been no answer from Prim, and no comfort from anyone that night until he went home to Taraleean to pour out the whole story of his love for Prim, the words torn from him in passion and sorrow. "Oh, Taraleean, Taraleean, my mother, what is this thing between a man and a woman, that an ugliness is put over it? What is so wicked about the thing we did, my lassie and me?"

"Hush, lad. Hush and sit here by me. Take the stool there at my feet. Put your head in my lap." And he had felt the gentle touch of her fingers that had so often dug in the earth to fit the curve of the new potatoes when she was a tattie howker, before his father found her and loved her and married her. And her voice with its clear, singing sound spoke quietly to him. "All things are ugly or beautiful as a man sees himself and the way of his heart. It is what some folk make of a thing that puts ugliness on it. Make what happened with you and Prim Munro a good and beautiful thing; make it so if it takes a lifetime. And what is the meaning of life, anyhow, but we lift our ways above ugliness into beauty, that we make honor out of dishonor and good from evil? Big Mina is wicked. Don't let her hurt you or Prim. You must rise above Big Mina —and above the world."

Again he wiped his eyes, staring over the strange, barren country. His mother's words had been good; they had been with him like a warm cloak in the days before he sailed for America. And she had kept her step light and her head high, even when all the Camerons gathered to bid him farewell with weeping and drinking and the tossing off of their little poems that were so poor in meter but strong in feeling.

Now he felt the need of his mother, and the need of all his people with their warm, deep voices and their quick way of talking and doing. And he wanted Prim. Damn Big Mina Munro! Surely here in America there would be ways to deal with Big Mina. He would write Prim every day, pouring out his love, and Prim would become weary of listening to Big Mina's talk; Prim would cease to believe that, because Big Mina had borne a daughter late in life, she, Prim, was to blame for the asthma and rheumatism that plagued Big Mina. When he had a job and money, then Prim would come to him; for what could really separate them now? Not an ocean or Big Mina or the world!

He was comforted by this thought and walked more lightly toward the west. He came at last to a place where the rising prairie dipped sharply and the road wound down a steep hill. Then a smile came over his face, for there, at the foot of the hill, was a rider. Kelsey hurried down the road, eager to meet whoever it might be.

The rider had pulled up his old black horse and sat slackly in the saddle. He was a small man with wisps of white hair sticking out from under a dirty black cap. His face was brown and wrinkled, and his crooked neck was set deep in the thick shoulders. As Kelsey came close and stopped, he looked into eyes the color of faded blue cloth.

"Afternoon, son," the stranger said. "What you doin' out here on the flats afoot?"

Flats, Kelsey thought. What kind of name was that for the rolling country? Before he had time to answer, the little man swung down from the saddle in such a free, smooth motion that Kelsey could only stare.

"Hell of a big country to be walkin' over, son. Come far?"

"From across the Platte River. I left the stage there. I'm Tommy Cameron's cousin, and I'm looking for his ranch."

The faded eyes opened wide. "Whadda you know!" And the man stepped forward, thrusting out a chapped, dirt-lined hand. "Glad to make your acquaintance, son. I'm Jediah Walsh."

Jediah Walsh was very close now, and Kelsey could smell the strange rank odor that came from him. Didn't this little old man ever wash his clothes?

"I know Tommy real well," Jediah said. "I take care of the headgate up at the mountain lake, and I walk the big ditch. That ditch waters the meadows of the Red Hill Ranch. Yep, I chase water when I'm not runnin' trap lines. You might say I'm a man that's just part employed, for I only work in irrigatin' season—and that don't get goin' good until May and ends about the first week in July. Trappin', that's not work; it's usin' your wits and havin' fun at it. Takes a right smart man to outwit foxes and coyotes, mink and martin, to say nothin' of beaver."

Talkative old bugger, Kelsey thought, restraining a smile. And then he thought of the empty country. It was no wonder men had a lot to say when they met other men.

Jediah spat on the ground, and a brown river of tobacco juice ran down his gray-whiskered chin. "And I betcha Tommy never opens his mouth to you about me bein' responsible for the water he uses. Most ranchers gotta blow about their fences bein' in good shape, about the hay they're gonna cut, or about the cattle and the markets. Hell, son, they wouldn't have no grass, no cows or nothin', if it wasn't for water. Yep, water controls everything in the West—and don't you ever forget it."

"And a fine place Tommy must have," Kelsey cut in, eager to hear about the ranch.

"Hmm. So Tommy's told you all about his place, eh?"

"He's written to me since he left Scotland six years ago." Kelsey's face broke into a smile. "I haven't seen him since I was fourteen. It'll be a great time when we meet again."

Jediah scratched under one arm. "Gotta get me some new clothes; been wearin' these so damn long they're ready to drop off. That's why I'm headed for town. Tell Tommy I'll be back soon."

"How far is it to the ranch?"

"I dunno—maybe five or six miles yet. See that ridge over there—the long one runnin' north and south with the peaks lookin' over its shoulder? Ranch is right at the foot of it. We don't measure distance out here; we just take a look and guess at it. All you have to do is follow the road."

Kelsey looked at the long ridge. "That's close."

"Nothin's as close as it looks in this country, son. You see a mountain and it's so sharp and big you figure you can hop right over to it. Instead you walk until your belly's up against your backbone." Jediah shifted the chew of tobacco, making a bulge on his cheek, and looked across the land. "Great country, ain't it? God's own. Ain't another like it on the face of the earth."

Kelsey didn't answer. One place like North Park was enough. If Jediah Walsh had ever known the green fields of Scotland . . .

"Grows on you, this country," Jediah went on. "And it ain't the way it looks on first acquaintance. Most good things don't shine up fancy on first meetin', whether it's a man, a woman, or a country."

He was quiet for a few moments and then added, "The Park's more than a place; it's a way of livin', son. And you're gonna fall in love with it or you're gonna hate it the way a man can hate another man's guts. Nobody I ever met has an in-between feelin' about the Park." Then he smiled a sudden warm smile that made his face startlingly young. "I gotta hunch about you. A big redheaded fella with eyes to match the sage-brush belongs in this country." He swung into the saddle, looked at Kelsey for a long moment, and added, "So long, son. Come up to Big Creek Lake and see me—if Tommy don't work the tail off you."

Kelsey watched him ride up the hill, sitting so carelessly in the saddle. He drew a deep breath of the fresh air. Was there ever a man lived had such a stink to him as this Jediah Walsh? And he chuckled to himself as he moved on.

In the late afternoon Kelsey limped to the top of a low hill and stopped. There before him, maybe half a mile away, lay the ranch. Around the buildings the earth was vivid red, as though a big barrel of red paint had rolled down the ridge and broken open at the foot of it. And when he looked around he saw that all the land before him had the red color. Then he noticed the cattle; they were everywhere—on the brown meadows south of the ranch buildings, in the open land north of him, and on what appeared to be pasture there below him. He had never seen so many cattle, and there was something about them he found hard to describe. They seemed to belong to the earth; they were somehow a part of the grayish-red country with the wind blowing over it.

He went down the hill, wincing from the pain in his heels, opened the pole gate, and closed it carefully. He started following the road that led across the pasture toward the house, filled with impatience to see Tommy. And then his steps slowed, and finally he came to a stop, for the cows were close to him, their white faces lifted curiously as they looked at him. The sunlight touched their dark reddish-brown hides; they snorted and ran and then turned to study him, all the white faces toward him. How many were in this bunch—a hundred, two hundred? For a moment they made him think of a mass of enormous white daisies. He laughed at himself; it was a notion such as a woman might have. Then an excitement stirred in him. If all these cows were his he'd be a fair toff; he'd be like a laird in the old country! And suddenly he knew he liked cattle and wanted them for his own, and it was more than the money they would represent; it was a feeling deep in him as he looked at them. For the first time since he had left Scotland he felt right inside himself. And he left the road, walked into the sagebrush, putting out a hand toward the cows, saying softly, "Here, you lassies with white faces—don't run from me."

But they snorted loudly and fled, stirring up a fine red dust behind them. A distance away they turned once more. He smiled and limped on toward the ranch house, forgetting the pain in his tortured heels. There was no doubt about his future; as soon as he had any money to spare he'd buy a cow.

CHAPTER II

The two-story ranch house was sunk in the earth; the logs were bleached silver-gray from time and weather and chinked with the vivid red mud. A sagging fence surrounded the house, and the yard was choked with dead brown grass that hissed in the wind. Kelsey walked to the door and knocked. It swung open with a scraping sound and a man stood there, a stocky middle-aged man with a stubble of graying whiskers and mild blue eyes. He wore a dirty floursack apron tied around his middle and carried a big spoon in his hand. "Ya?" he said. "What you want, young fella? Boss ain't hiring no men this time of year."

Kelsey wet his parched lips. "I'm Tommy's cousin from the old country."

"Come in, come in! Hilder Larson, that's me." And the man thrust out a big red hand. "Pleased to meetcha. Tommy, he ain't come in from chasin' water yet, but he will soon. And Dalt, he ain't in either. Sit here by the stove, young fella. You look plumb fagged."

Kelsey lifted the tin dipper that hung over the washstand in the corner and plunged it into the water bucket. He drank, the water trickling over his chin. Then he sat down and took off his shoes. The blisters on his heels had broken and were bleeding.

Hilder made a clucking noise in his throat and got a basin of water. "You shove 'em in here. You get poison from them broke blisters if you ain't careful."

11

Kelsey lowered his burning feet into the cool water. Then he sat, looking around the kitchen, while Hilder cut up potatoes for supper. The log walls were smoked almost black and had been covered here and there with old newspapers; some, hanging almost free of the wall, rattled when a gust of wind struck the house. The place smelled of stale food, manure, and sweat. A milk bucket sat near the stove, stained with dried milk and dust; a thin crust of manure rimmed the bottom. Ashes were spilling out of the stove, and the woodbox was covered with grease. The floor looked as though it had never been touched by soap and water. My God, Kelsey thought, I've seen better places for pigs in the old country!

The door banged open. Kelsey looked up. A big man stood staring at him, a man with the broad Cameron nose, sharp black eyes, and thin black hair with a shine of red in it.

"Tommy!" Kelsey said, his heart filled with sudden gladness. "Tommy Cameron!"

The black eyes blinked. Then the thin lips spread in a smile. "It's John's boy, by God! Kelsey!" And he came forward and grabbed Kelsey's shoulders with both hands, shaking him and shouting, "Lad, what brought you to this country? And how is the harbor? And were the snowdrops in bloom when you left? Did the braes have the bright green look to them yet? And how's Old Crow that used to sit by the harbor tellin' stories to the lads? And your handsome mother, Taraleean—how's she?" Tommy paused for breath, suddenly laughing. "By God, I didn't expect to see you."

"I've had my troubles," Kelsey said. His hands began to tremble. He burst out, "Tommy, I've left Scotland for good. I'll never go back! I've come for a job."

"What about your father's shop?"

For a moment Kelsey couldn't speak. He struggled to control the bitterness and anger that filled him.

"He always wanted you to carry it on," Tommy said. "He

planned things that way from the time you were old enough to walk down the village street with him."

Kelsey spoke then, his voice shaking. "The shop's in strange hands. The manager for the Duncan estate—he wouldn't let me take it over when my mother decided to give it up."

Kelsey bowed his head, trying to get control of himself. Tommy said nothing for a moment, then walked toward the door. "Gotta go up to the bunkhouse. Back right away."

There was silence in the kitchen, and while Kelsey waited for Tommy's return his thoughts went back to the bitter scene with the laird's manager. He lived again the bright cool day when he had walked joyously down the village street, saying to Prim Munro, "Today's the start of big things! I'm off to see the factor, Captain Morrison, and ask for the shop in my name."

The factor was having a walk up the shore, and they met just outside the clipped hedge that surrounded the laird's big house. Kelsey remembered to hold the excitement within him long enough to ask after the laird's health.

"He's off to the South of France," Captain Morrison said, pulling at his long nose, which was turning blue in the cold air, "and I'd not mind being there myself. It's the devil's own weather we have here in February."

"But good for business," Kelsey said, "for herring are running thick in the sea and all the fishing folk spend their money in my father's shop."

"The shop, eh?" The captain's face became wary.

"It's what I've come to talk about. You know how my mother and I have run it since my father died—how I got her to cut down on the spending and finally paid off all her debts. Bless her, she was never a businesswoman. But the books are clear at last, and Taraleean is ready to give it up. I'd like to take over." Kelsey's hands gripped hard behind him, and he could feel the thump-thumping of his heart.

There was a long silence while the gulls screamed away from

the steep cliffs along the shore, while the whole sea danced with sunlight. Then the factor's voice came out steadily and impersonally. "You can't have it, Kelsey."

"Can't have it!" The rough red head came up. The wide gray eyes were unbelieving. "Can't have it, you say?"

"You're not twenty-one."

"What's that got to do with it?"

The factor shrugged. "It's a rule the laird has: no one under twenty-one can run the shop."

"But I've tried to prove—" A pain was in Kelsey's heart. A mist blinded him. "I've paid my mother's debts. My God, man, I've had no young life. I've given up everything for the shop!"

"No matter of proof," the captain said, clearing his throat. "Just policy—the laird's policy."

"But it's my father's business. It was his for years, and you can't—"

"Oh, we've a man in mind. And he'll keep you on. I'll speak to him about it."

"I'll work for no man in the shop that was my father's! Listen, my mother—let her keep it. I'll go on helping her. I'll—"

"Your mother," the factor said quietly, "should give up the business. I've been noticing things; the way she's run the shop hasn't suited us. There's no need to stand here talking, Kelsey."

"Goddamn you! Goddamn all of you!"

"Hold that tongue of yours, Kelsey Cameron. You've given us trouble enough—putting up that ugly shack on the shore right under the laird's nose, and—"

"You—" Kelsey's voice broke. He turned and walked quickly away, the whole bright day blurring before him. So this was the answer to years of work to pay Taraleean's debts, to months of planning the future with Prim. For a moment the boy in him rose above the man, and tears stung his eyes. He stopped then and stood, breathing deeply, staring toward the sea until it came clear and clean again, stretching away to the far horizon. Then he spoke passionately to the empty water. "I'll leave Scotland! I'll go where a man can become more than a thing to be stepped on by the lairds and their factors! I'll go to America, the place my cousin Tommy wrote about. Yes, America!"

And here I am, Kelsey thought, raising his head in the smelly kitchen. And things have to work out; they've just got to.

He waited nervously until his cousin came in the door again. Tommy had a whisky bottle in his hand.

"Tommy," Kelsey said, "do you know what that bloody factor did? Just before I sailed for this country he had the gall to come to my mother's house and offer me a job as game-keeper on the laird's estate. Gamekeeper—a servant to the laird! That's when I told him to go to hell and take the laird with him."

"Well, kiddo," Tommy said, "you made a fine ass of your-self—let your fool Cameron pride run away with you, the way it always has. Jobs don't grow on bushes, y'know. And beggars can't be choosers."

Kelsey stared at him, confused and shocked. He'd crossed an ocean; he'd borrowed money to get here; he'd been certain Tommy would understand, would say to him, "You did the right thing. I'll see you get a new start here, Kelsey." Now, thinking of the money he had to pay back, Kelsey felt sudden fear. He wet his cracked lips and said, "You can surely use me —I mean, I'm a good worker, and I thought—" He stopped, for there was a strange expression on his cousin's face.

"Sure, sure," Hilder interrupted. "We use him, eh, Tommy? He's had bad trouble and he's come a long way to see you."

Tommy said nothing, set the whisky bottle on the table, and went to the pantry for glasses. Kelsey's confusion mounted.

"Your letters," he began, "about all the chances for a young man—"

Hilder knelt before Kelsey, a flat tin of salve in his hand. "I fix them feet. Bandage them tonight. Rubbed raw. Jesus Christ, son, you sure walked hard!"

"Walked?" Tommy looked intently at him.

Kelsey's face flushed. "Oh, it wasn't so far—just from where I got off the stage. I—I was out of money. You see, I borrowed what I thought I'd need from Big Mina Munro, Prim's mother. She was the only person in the village had the money to give me."

"I got an old pair of slippers you can wear tonight. Rest your feet. You want a drink of whisky?"

"My stomach's too empty, Tommy."

"Hell, it's good on any stomach. Here, have a shot." He poured two glasses half full and handed one to Kelsey. "Help yourself, Hilder, but for God's sake don't burn the potatoes again!" He took his drink in one quick gulp.

"Big Mina, huh?" Tommy said, smacking his glass on the table. "Is that old sow still running everybody around the harbor?"

"She is."

"And what about that bit of fluff you fancied so, her daughter?"

"Prim? Prim's there with her."

"And not likely to leave, either. Big Mina put the sign on the girl when she was hardly old enough to walk or talk—bellered and carried on about Prim tearing her apart and how she'd never be the same again. Hell, Big Mina was crippled and too fat before she ever had Prim. People used to say only the devil could have seen to the fact that Thomas Munro got Big Mina pregnant at such an age. Prim came along years and years after she'd had the two boys—and she was no spring chicken when Thomas married her." Tommy began to laugh.

"I remember once when I was just a lad and up there with my mother. Thomas was about to take off for sea again, the way he always did to get away from Big Mina. Well, the old girl threw herself on the floor and moaned and groaned that she was about to die. Thomas just stepped over her and said, 'Go in peace, then.' "

Kelsey chuckled, the whisky hot in his throat. "He's the only one who could ever trim her sails."

"And say, does Crowter the rag-buyer still hang around after Prim? When I was back there she was only a wee lassie— maybe thirteen—and Crowter was just getting a good start in his business. He must have been twenty or more, and he was always following Prim around like her shadow."

"Prim never fancied Crowter and never will. Besides, if she'd wanted a lad she'd have found something better. Crowter, why he's—"

"Beneath her? Oh, I dunno, Kelsey. What's Prim Munro but Big Mina's daughter? Remember how Crowter liked to whistle to Prim? He could fashion up the damnedest tunes— outta his head." Tommy turned to Hilder, who was standing listening to all their words. "Get the meat cookin' for supper —and see it ain't so raw it bawls when I stick a fork in it."

"Go to hell," Hilder said.

Tommy laughed. "Worst cook east of the Continental Divide, but nobody else'll stick in the Red Hill Ranch kitchen."

Kelsey was feeling lightheaded and talkative. "If it hadn't been for your letters I'd never have had the courage to face Big Mina and borrow the money from her. I carried one right in my fist the day I had to see her, and it put a stiffness in me. She's always hated my guts because of Prim. She talked right up to me, told me the only reason she was letting me have the money was to get me out of Scotland and away from Prim." Kelsey took a drink from the glass Tommy had filled again. "She said"—he snickered—"she said, 'The Indians will fancy that red hair of yours.' I let her think it; I wouldn't spoil it by telling her the Indians were gone and the big cattle herds— How many cattle you got, Tommy?"

"Cattle? I don't own no cattle. I'm foreman for Monte Maguire. Monte Maguire owns the cattle."

Kelsey blinked, sobering. "But I thought— When you first wrote and said you'd taken up the homestead and started a cattle herd—"

"Oh." Tommy cleared his throat. "Well, I did take up a homestead and I had a few cows. But I decided to sell. Monte bought everything from me. And I got a job here for the rest of my life and no worries, so—"

"I was sure you owned cattle—and this ranch."

"Good God! This is a big ranch. It costs to have a ranch like this. And I'm not burnin' to set the world afire like you always was, kiddo. A man lives and learns it don't pay to go broke. And I want to tell you something: you'll be lucky if you get a job in this country now. Spring work's started, and ranchers ain't hirin' extra men until hayin' season. Thirty dollars a month, that's what you'll get—if I can talk Monte into letting you stick around."

"Thirty dollars a month!" Kelsey stared at him. "I did better at the harbor!"

"What'd you expect, kiddo—a foreman's job to start?"

The door banged again, and a boy walked in, a thick-shouldered boy who might have been sixteen or seventeen. Although his face was young and smooth, his pale brown eyes looked older, as though a lot of living lay behind them. His hair was thick and straight and yellow-brown.

"Long Dalton," Tommy said, introducing Kelsey as his cousin from Scotland. "If you want to know anything about horses—or women—ask him."

Long Dalton grinned. "Glad to see you, buddy."

Hilder began setting the table, tossing plates and silver on it in a haphazard manner. "Jake here tonight?" he asked.

"Hasn't come in yet," Dalt said. "He was ridin' the upper pasture where we got the two-year-old heifers. The early calves oughta be starting to drop."

"If he's found a heifer havin' trouble," Tommy said, "he might not be in until midnight. Jake won't leave a cow havin' her first calf until he's sure everything's hunky-dory."

"I didn't see anythin' showin' yet when I was along the ditch today," Dalt said. "And the water's comin' through fine. Guess we're done shovelin' snowdrifts for this spring."

Then Kelsey remembered the little man he'd met on the prairie and said, "I saw Jediah Walsh. He's off to the town. Said he'd be back soon."

"Fat chance! He'll be on a three-day drunk over town. Hell, he ain't been out of the hills since last fall. One of us better go up to the lake tomorrow and check the headgate to be sure everything's all right."

"Jediah's a great guy," Dalt said. "Finest fella I ever did know. I heard two preachers talk in my life so far, and Jediah's got more to say about religion and all sorts of other things. Jediah's words make sense—even to a cussed kid like me."

"Well," Kelsey said, smiling, "he's really got a strong smell to him."

The men laughed. Dalt said, "That's beaver castor smell. He baits his traps with stuff made outta the castors. He'll get aired off good by the Fourth of July, and then he won't smell no different from the rest of us."

"Set up to the table," Hilder said. "Food don't taste so greasy when it's hot."

"Jake's the best cow foreman in the Park," Dalt said, dragging a chair to the table. He glanced at Kelsey. "Jake takes care of all Monte Maguire's cattle, and Monte's got three ranches. There's this one, the North Fork Ranch across the hogback, and the home place over on the Platte River."

Three ranches, Kelsey thought wonderingly, remembering that Tommy had said a place like the Red Hill cost a lot of money. He reached for one of Hilder's soggy biscuits. "What kind of man is Monte Maguire?" he asked.

The men looked at one another. There was a silence, and then Tommy said, "You'll find out."

*   *

Late that night Kelsey took the kerosene lamp and went upstairs to the small bedroom Tommy had told him was his. It was a narrow, stall-like place; the hay-filled bunk was covered with soiled blankets and a stained tarpaulin; an overturned wooden box served as a table; and rows of spikes shone along the walls. Hay, old magazines, crushed cigarette butts, and a few crumpled handkerchiefs littered the floor.

Kelsey set the lamp carefully on the low box, went to the one small window, and opened it. The air inside was very stale, and the blankets on the bed smelled of men and sweat. He took the blankets to the window and aired them, shaking them carefully, and then remade the bed. After that he opened his suitcase, feeling a need to see and to touch the few belongings that were part of home. He folded and unfolded the heavy sweater Taraleean had knitted for him before he left Scotland, and he took out his father's old Bible, a small one John Cameron had always carried in his pocket. Kelsey held it tenderly in his hands, stroking the worn leather. He found a shirt Prim had given him. In the pocket was a postcard she'd once sent him from Edinburgh while she was on a trip. He peered in the dim light to read the brief, neatly written message: "Be home in a fortnight—your loving lass, Prim." For a long time he sat with the postcard in his hand, staring at the log walls of the bedroom with a sense of unreality. At last he closed the suitcase, undressed, blew out the lamp, and got into bed.

The bunk was very hard; his sore heels burned like fire, and his legs kept twitching. His mind began to work feverishly with thoughts of the past and the future. He figured again the amount of money he owed Big Mina and tried to guess what would happen to him if Monte Maguire didn't let him stay on at the Red Hill Ranch. And when he thought of his meeting with Tommy a sense of distress filled him; although Tommy had been pleasant at the supper table and during the rest of the evening, there had been something lacking. It's like there's no warmth left in him, Kelsey thought. Had this strange, cold country changed his cousin from the easy, big-hearted lad Kelsey had known around the harbor? Or had he never really known Tommy well enough in those early years to understand what kind of person he was?

Kelsey's eyelids closed. He dropped into deep sleep and began to dream of the day his father died, the day he had been a lad of thirteen, walking down the village street with his mother. Taraleean had a little basket over her arm; she'd fried a fresh fish and baked scones for her husband's lunch. They came into the shop and saw his father slumped forward in the old chair, his chin resting on his chest. Taraleean put down the basket and tiptoed forward, bending over John Cameron to cover his eyes with her hands and whisper, "Who is it?" It was so quiet then, and Kelsey heard her voice change as she said, "John—John!" And the sound of her sorrow began, drifting out to the quiet harbor street. The women of the village came running, their long full skirts fluttering like frightened birds. They pushed past him, saying, "Oh, dear God! It is the sound the Irish mothers make when their sons have been drowned at the sea! Taraleean has lost her man!"

Kelsey wakened, shaking, and felt the strange bed under him. And he thought that grief was a thing a man was never free of, for it came back from some far place in the mind to live again when least expected. He lay in the darkness, remembering the night he had sat with family and friends by the casket of his father in the front parlor at home. All that night his sisters had combed their black hair, weeping and using the new tortoise-shell combs an uncle had given them. And toward morning he had cried to his mother, "Make the lassies leave their hair be!"

Then Taraleean had put her arms around him and said, "Steady, lad. You must be strong. Who is to help me run the shop if I can't count on you?"

He turned over in bed, punching the lumpy pillow that smelled even more rank than the blankets, and he longed for his room in Taraleean's house, the big clean room with the fireplace in the corner. I mustn't think on it, he told himself. That's all past. He heard a cow bawl on the Red Hill meadow. Cattle, that was what he must put his mind on. And the cow foreman, the man Jake. Jake could tell him what he must know.

CHAPTER III

Kelsey wakened early. He stretched his aching legs and tried to go back to sleep. Finally he got up, dressed, and went down to the kitchen. There was no one around; the fire hadn't been started in the coal range. From one of the main-floor bedrooms came the sound of Tommy's snoring. Kelsey found an old jacket hanging on the kitchen wall, slipped into it, and went outside. It was a cold, clear morning; a faint red showed in the east. He walked toward the barn, looking curiously at the corrals. He was leaning against the fence when a man came out of the barn—a tall, stooped man with wide hips like a woman's. He was leading a saddle horse, walking mincingly in high-heeled boots and wearing wide, flapping leather pants. A black handkerchief was tied around his neck. He saw Kelsey, shoved his hat back from his forehead where a line of white lay above the tan of his face, and grinned.

"Mornin', Kelsey." His voice was low and soft. "Heard you'd blown in when I come home last night. I gotta ride the north pasture—coupla heifers are on my mind." He moved on up to Kelsey, pulled off a glove, and thrust out his hand. It was a smooth white hand, but the grip was firm. "I'm Jake, Monte's cow boss."

Everything about Jake was neat and immaculate, from the creased trousers to the top of his big dark hat. Kelsey tried to keep from staring at him, finally blurted out, "Man, how can you have hands like that and work?"

Jake smiled. "I keep 'em that way. Cowpunchers got a rep-

23

utation for havin' pretty hands. That's why the women like us; we don't rough 'em up too much. I see what I gotta see from the saddle, and most of the work I do can be done with gloves on. Punchin' cows ain't like fixin' fence or shovelin' manure, kid."

"I'd like to go with you to see the heifers."

"You would, huh?" Jake blinked. "Well, I never could figure out a man who wanted to get outta bed until he had to, but you're welcome to string along. Hold this nag and I'll fetch you a horse." He started toward the barn and turned. "Ever been on a horse before?"

"No."

"It's a damn good job I asked. You mighta been kissin' the sagebrush. Don't worry. I'll get you an old cowpony that knows more than both of us put together. Say, you don't have any boots or chaps—well, it won't matter, for we're not travelin' far. North pasture's only a step." He looked Kelsey over for a moment. "Reckon you'll do, kid." A little later he came out of the barn with the horse. Kelsey stepped eagerly forward.

"Hold it, kid! Even an old horse ain't gonna tolerate that. You're on the wrong side. Start over. Take the reins and the horn in one hand—like so. Now reach for the stirrup, and up you go." And he laughed as Kelsey pulled himself awkwardly to the saddle. "Them stirrups is long, but you won't be runnin' no races."

They rode slowly through the pasture Kelsey had walked across the day before. The cattle were scattered and quiet. There was no wind, and to Kelsey the earth seemed more remote than before, for it had a darker, bleaker appearance.

"We always keep the heifers here," Jake said. "They been bred as long yearlings, so they'll calf early, for first calves don't always come easy. We gotta watch 'em, and we don't turn 'em out on the flats as soon as the older cows. Older cows can calf by themselves."

"I don't know anything about cattle," Kelsey said. "I couldn't ask a question that made sense."

Jake gave him a sidelong glance. "Well, there ain't much to say about it. You can put the whole shebang in a few words —feed 'em and breed 'em. That's all of it, kid." Jake yawned and then straightened in the saddle, staring ahead. "Just the way I had it figured; them two have dropped their calves, but trouble's started. Well, I'll be damned. One of 'em don't want her calf; she's tryin' to steal the other heifer's." He kicked his horse into a lope, heading toward two young cows standing off by themselves. Kelsey's horse plunged after Jake's, and he clung to the saddle horn while the saddle smacked him briskly on the backside.

He saw one cow cleaning off her calf, licking it with her tongue and nudging it to its feet. Near her, the other heifer ignored the calf on the ground, lifted her head, and let out a bellow. Then she ran to claim the standing calf.

"Crazy bitch!" Jake was out of the saddle and running to the deserted calf. He yanked off his shirt, bent over the dark heap on the ground, and began rubbing it, wiping away the membrane. The calf gave a feeble gasp. Jake tipped the head back and thrust his hand down the throat, pulling out mucus. He lifted the calf to its feet, shouting at Kelsey, "Here! Hold him up! I've got to head that wild one off!"

Hurriedly Kelsey dismounted, went to the calf, and put his hands on it. The calf felt warm and damp. He watched Jake ride after the heifer, which ran in circles around the other heifer and her calf. She kept bellowing, and the long bloody afterbirth dangled from her. Then Jake's horse was right on her flank, darting to head her off, swerving with incredible speed, anticipating her every move, working her farther and farther away from the calf she wanted to claim. Kelsey saw that Jake was taking the wild-eyed heifer toward the barn. He looked at the wobbly calf and didn't know what to do. Then he gathered it in his arms and started walking toward the corrals, the old saddle horse following. The calf bawled weakly. From it rose the humid, rank, yet strangely sweet odor of birth. It was a smell could turn a man's stomach, Kelsey thought, but it was the smell of life. The sun came over the east mountain range of the Park, and its light and warmth fell over him and the new calf.

Around him the cattle stirred, some getting up from where they had lain among the sagebrush, some taking a step or two and stretching, some appearing to notice him for the first time and moving away. The pinkish-red light of the sun touched them and stained the tops of the mountains behind the long ridge back of the ranch house. And a small wind came out of the south, bringing the fragrance of woodsmoke, telling him that Hilder was up and had started the cookstove in the kitchen. He saw Jake waiting for him at the corral gate, and he shifted the calf in his arms and walked faster.

They put the calf with the heifer in a box stall in the barn. "If she don't claim him," Jake said, "we'll have to feed him skim milk." Then they walked toward the house. Jake's hand rested for a moment on Kelsey's shoulder. "You got a good initiation, kid."

Kelsey looked at the stains on his clothes. He remembered the feel of the calf and the way the hair had curled on the top of its head. And he thought how quick was the beginning of life—out of darkness, like the sun bursting over the mountains. "It was fine," he said, more to himself than to Jake.

The men were at the breakfast table. There were beads of water on Dalt's thick, slicked-down hair. Hilder's face was redder than usual from bending over the hot stove. Tommy looked up from his place at the head of the table, and Kelsey felt the coldness in his small black eyes. "If you expect to stick around here," Tommy said, "don't let me catch you actin' the cowboy. You get on the end of a shovel where you belong—and stay there."

Hilder and Dalt looked down at their plates. Jake took off

his hat and smoothed the top of his bald head. "Shucks," Jake said mildly, "it's no skin off'n your nose, Tommy. Work day ain't even started. What's wrong with the kid givin' me a hand?"

"You run the cattle," Tommy said shortly. "I run the ranch, see? I'll decide what he does and when."

Jake shrugged. "Some people act like they been hit in the ass with a sour apple." He reached for the tin washbasin. "Come on, Kelsey. Let's clean up."

Kelsey's face was hot. Did Tommy have to speak so sharply to him before all the men?

*   *

Two weeks later Kelsey sat in the bunkhouse with Dalt and Jake; he spent every free moment in the bunkhouse, for that was the only place he could see Jake and talk with him and be free of Tommy's curt tongue and sharp eyes.

The rain made no sound on the dirt roof, but Kelsey could see it streaking down the fly-specked window. Jake had taken off his yellow slicker and was shaking it. "Keeps on rainin', a man'll have web feet," Jake said.

"It won't," Dalt replied. "It'll turn to snow. Now's the meanest time in this country. A man's sick of winter and achin' clear down to his guts for warm weather. And what kind of summer we got here anyhow? Not much, I'll tell you. Like an old-timer said, North Park's nine months winter and three months late fall. And spring—I haven't seen any of it."

"Up here at eight thousand feet," Jake said, "spring's bound to be mostly a notion a man carries in his mind." He eased his feet close to the round black heating stove. His boots were wet, and they began to steam. A roaring sound came from the stove, rising and falling with the gusty wind. "Got a few more calves this mornin'," he added. "Hell of a day for those young cows to be havin' 'em."

Kelsey stopped whittling on a match. "Jake, if you were starting a cattle herd what would you buy?"

"She-stuff. It multiplies fast."

"A man can't get anywhere working for wages," Kelsey said. "I've got to get cattle."

Jake squinted at him and smiled. "You got the curse of ambition, kid. All depends on what a man wants, I guess. Now me, I wouldn't own a cow for love or money. Oh, I like 'em. I feel good bein' around 'em, but let somebody else worry about the market, how many are gonna die with blackleg, and if there's enough hay to get 'em through the winter."

"How much hay does it take to winter a cow?"

"A man oughta figure roughly two tons in this country."

Dalt got up and stood with his back to the stove. "These ranchers in the Park been cuttin' that short by a damn sight. They'll end up with too many cattle for the feed they got."

"They've got by," Jake answered, nodding in the heat.

"Yeah? Well it could happen right here; if Monte Maguire keeps buildin' up the cow herd, we could lose half of 'em in a tough winter."

"Ah, hell," Jake said. "I won't buy that."

"Ranchin's tough up here," Dalt went on. "Ask some of the Laramie Plains men what they think about raisin' cattle in North Park. They'll tell you it's a lot easier out their way. They don't put up much hay; the plains bare off with the wind, and a cow brute can rustle most of the winter. They don't get the snow we get, and it don't stay on the ground; a cow can find grass."

Jake sat up straight. "Just because you think the Laramie Plains is a banana belt compared to the Park, don't figure Wyoming's foolproof, either. Parts of that country are just as tough as here, and they've had some blizzards would curl your whiskers."

"It's still an easier way of ranching."

"Yeah? And what cattle top the markets? The Park cattle.

And you know why? Because they're heavier; they weigh more at market. And another thing, when a cow has to rustle grass she's a weaker cow, and her calf's weaker and gotta be tailed up when it's born instead of standin' strong."

"Don't get your dander up, Jake. I wasn't figurin' on tellin' you anything about cows."

"The trouble is," Kelsey said, frowning, "a man would have to go deep in debt to own a ranch and cattle."

"Shucks, kid," Jake said, grinning, "a man ain't livin' till he's in debt. Never really get out myself. Come spring I always fall in it all over again."

"It's the cat wagons that come in from Laramie that keep him broke," Dalt said, winking at Kelsey.

"Well, it sure is a nice way to go in debt," Jake murmured.

The gong rang, announcing the noon meal, sending a clear *ping-a-ling* across the wet day.

"Hurry up," Dalt said as they walked toward the house. "Hope Hilder had better luck with his pie today. Last one was all fruit and one before was all crust. Looks like he could strike a happy medium."

"I want to take another look at that calf his mama wouldn't claim," Kelsey said. "Then I'll be in to eat."

"He's fine," Jake said. "A man'd think he was related to you, the way you fuss over him."

Kelsey hurried on to the barn. The calf was in the back stall, fenced off from the rest of the barn. It thrust a wet, cold nose through the bars. Kelsey smiled and put his hand on the white face. "Now, young Robin O'Dair," he said softly, "you look better than you did two weeks ago when I carried you in— and you can't be hungry again!" The calf sucked at his hand. He fondled it a few minutes longer, wishing it belonged to him instead of to Monte Maguire.

When he left the barn he saw the storm had broken and tatters of cloud were streaming over the shoulder of the hogback, drifting between the aspen trees like smoke. "The creepin' Johnnies are with us," he said to himself, and thought suddenly of his mother, Taraleean, who always spoke of the fogs and mists as the creeping Johnnies. How close she seemed! And he stared at the long cloud-wreathed ridge and tried to hear again the sound of her voice. It was at night that he missed her most, drawing the rough, smelly blankets close to warm his loneliness. And it was at night too that he remembered his sisters with a closeness he had never felt for them when he was home. When he thought of them and of his mother, he missed also the Reverend Angus McCullough, who had been his father's close friend and who had treated him like a son after John Cameron's death. In the garden of the manse he had spent many pleasant hours with Reverend Mr. McCullough.

And what have I come to? he asked himself now, hurrying toward the house. What has this land to offer but cold and no green and a man's back breaking from shoveling manure to build dikes in the meadows?

When he walked into the kitchen Tommy said, "You ride the upper ditch this afternoon, Kelsey. The big boss, Monte Maguire, oughta show up tonight. Gotta have everything checked and in top shape. But before you ride the upper ditch, fix that broken dam below the barn—in the upper part of the meadow. Take the sodboat and a load of manure from the corral."

"And be sure you get it off'n your rubber boots when you come in for supper," Hilder said. "We want things to smell good when the boss comes."

As Tommy walked to the barn with him after the noon meal, Kelsey said, "I been talking to Jake. Jake says the only money's to be made in cattle."

"Well, he damn sure better talk that way. He's cow foreman, ain't he? That's what he's paid for, makin' money with cattle."

"If I could start a cow and calf—"

Tommy stopped and stared at him. "You got a debt to pay Big Mina Munro. You got a job—at least at the moment. You got a bed to sleep in and food to fill your belly. And, by God, you're eatin' your heart out to get a cow and calf! If you didn't happen to be related to me I'd send you down the road talkin' to yourself, so help me!"

"What's wrong with a man dreaming and planning? Do you think I borrowed money and left Scotland just for a job? I've a right to have cattle, just as much right as any man."

"Not here, you don't. It ain't Monte Maguire's policy to let hired men run stock." Tommy shook his head wonderingly. "Who the hell do you think you are, anyhow? Now, you listen, kiddo. Hook a team to that sodboat and get to spreadin' manure. And then ride the upper ditch. Get the lead outta your pants or you won't have a job at thirty bucks a month!"

Tommy brushed on past him. Kelsey stood for a moment outside the barn door, angry and a little puzzled by his cousin's words.

Kelsey hooked the team to the sodboat, which was a long low contraption with a frame of two poles with the ends slanted up like sled runners. Over the poles boards were nailed to form a floor for carrying manure from the corrals to the meadow. As Kelsey drove up to the big manure pile at the corner of the barn, a movement caught his eye and he saw a muskrat come out of the slough. The slough was trickling with water that came from the springs in the willow clump above the house. The muskrat curled up in front of the manure pile, which was steaming in midday sun and warmed the muskrat's back as a stove might have.

Kelsey leaned on the pitchfork, smiling. "Fancy that," he said. Then he remembered Long Dalton had told him a man could pick up extra money from the pelts of coyotes, beaver, and muskrat. He took a step toward the animal, lifted the pitchfork, and then hesitated. "Go on with you," he muttered. "I'll not knock the life from you when your eyes are closed in sleeping and your back warm and not a care to trouble you. But I'm making you no future promises, mind you. And tomorrow you'd better stay in the willows."

When the sodboat was loaded he put a shovel and a pitchfork in the pile of manure and drove down the meadow, standing up front, his feet set wide apart and braced. Water sloshed up between the boards and drained off brown with manure stain. He came to where the small dam had broken and mended it carefully, tramping down the manure with his rubber-booted feet.

Then he turned toward the hogback; on its lower slopes was the glitter of the outlets from the main ditch, where water spilled down at intervals. Below and parallel to the main ditch was the spread ditch, shaped shallow so that water poured over all its edges, sparkling like scattered diamonds in the sunlight. Farther down, below the spread ditch, furrows and laterals caught up the water again and spread it over the meadow. The whole system of irrigation fascinated Kelsey, and now another thought struck him. There was the way the cattle came onto the meadows in fall and were fed hay all winter; their manure fertilized the spring earth, bringing up new grass to become hay and feed them the next winter. "The wonderful economy of nature!" he exclaimed to himself.

Whistling, he stopped by one of the outlets of the main ditch, where the flow of water was controlled by sod and rock. He got off the sodboat and went to examine the outlet, which seemed to be spilling too much water. After digging sod, he packed the sides to prevent washing. Then he bent over the stones that were in the mouth of the opening. He started shifting them, as he had seen Dalt do to hold back some of the water.

His ear, always sensitive to sound, caught the change in the noise of the water; he moved a big rock, and it babbled forth in a different key. A smile came over his face and, forgetting his work, he began to play with the stones, arranging them this way and that, his head bent to catch the music. And suddenly, when a fine note struck his fancy, he burst out singing, tilting his red head back.

> *"Ye banks and braes o' bonnie Doon,*
> *How can ye bloom sae fresh and fair?"*

He was back in Scotland. He was walking in the heather with Prim beside him and his arm about her, holding her so close they walked as one person. He closed his eyes and sang again, his heart reaching across the big valley, the mountains, and the far ocean, his singing saying the things he could never say in the letters he'd written at night by the feeble glow of the lantern.

He played with the stones and sang until he felt light and mellow and at peace with the world. Then he went back to the barn, saddled a horse, and rode the ditch above the ranch house.

It was suppertime when he got back. He noticed the gray team in the barn and the buggy standing outside the corral. He hurried toward the house, then paused by the watering trough, which was just outside the yard. He dipped his face deep in the trough, scrubbing the sweat from it with his hands. He dried himself carefully on a worn handkerchief. He didn't want to look dirty when he met Monte Maguire. A man who owned three ranches and two thousand head of cattle was important, and Monte Maguire might be the key to his future.

He pushed open the kitchen door, took an automatic step toward his place at the foot of the table, and then stopped and stood, staring at the stranger who occupied the place of honor at the head of the table. From a distance he heard Tommy's voice. "Monte, this is my cousin Kelsey, from the old country. Thought maybe we could use him for the spring work."

The eyes looking at him so sharply were a cold sky-blue. The hair was smooth and blond and swept severely back from the tanned face with its high cheekbones and pointed chin. But the mouth was full and wide, and against the faded wool shirt the firm, swelling breasts were plainly outlined.

"Sit down, young fella," she said. Her voice was curt and husky.

He was too stunned to speak. He fumbled for the backless chair, sank into it, unable to take his eyes from her as she got up and moved to the stove and poured herself another cup of coffee. He saw with shock that she wore men's rough trousers; her hips strained against them. Below the knees her legs were wrapped with gunnysacks that extended down into the worn high-buckled overshoes. As she walked back to the table he was sharply aware of the bigness of her. And he thought, Only a tramp along the shore in the old country would wear such shabby clothes.

"If you want any grub," she said, looking at him with amusement in her eyes, "you better get it while it's still there."

He reached automatically for a biscuit.

"So you rode the ditch this afternoon, eh?" The amusement had gone from her eyes now, and the cold, probing look was in them again.

How old was she—twenty-five, thirty-five? There was no way of knowing. And was it Miss or Mrs. Maguire?

"Yes, sir—I mean, Miss—"

"Madam," she corrected and glanced around the table, the full mouth quirked in a smile. Long Dalton snickered.

"Yes, madam." He heard Tommy laughing softly now and looked at his cousin angrily.

"And what did you see when you rode the ditch?"

Kelsey's hand paused midway between his plate and the platter of meat that oozed blood. "See?"

"Why, yes." Her voice was impatient. "Were there any holes in the ditch bank?"

"I—uh—I didn't see any."

"Then where did the water come out?" she asked dryly.

The muffled sound of stifled laughter swept around the table. Kelsey's face burned.

"And was there any cattle along the ditch, young fella?"

It annoyed him that she addressed him as "young fella." Who did she think she was—his grandmother? "I didn't notice any," he answered.

"See any cow tracks?"

"Tracks—I didn't look for cow tracks."

"Did you notice if the south slopes of the hills north of the ranch were greenin' or still brown?"

He swallowed and said nothing.

"See any cow manure up there, young fella?"

He shook his head, torn between humiliation and disgust. A woman, a woman talking about things like cow manure! It was—well, not proper at all. And he disliked Monte Maguire intensely. A big bold piece of brass, that's what she was!

She put down her fork and leaned forward. "Listen, young fella," she said, "a cattleman's life depends on noticin' things. When you ride anywhere on a ranch you see everything. You gotta see if a ditch is runnin' high or low, if the outlets are washed or plugged. You gotta look at cattle and see what shape they're in—thin or fat or ailing. You gotta see fences— if they're up or down or about to fall. And you always check the grass, notice if it's greenin' or still hung over from winter. Young fella, you gotta learn to keep your eyes open if you expect to work for me!"

Kelsey sawed at the tough steak, his face smarting. The meat tasted like sawdust. Then he heard the curt, husky voice again. "I come in from the flats this afternoon. I seen three cows, two of 'em dry, up in that country you were supposed to be ridin' over. By lookin' across the upper meadow, I could tell by the shine of water the ditch was carryin' a full head and the outlets filled. I seen green showin' on the hills north of the ranch and lots of green under the spread ditch. Those three cows bound to have been along the ditch where it was green-est and left their tracks and their manure plain for anybody with eyes to see."

He felt miserable; he felt smaller than he'd ever felt in knee pants when the schoolmaster laid the strap to his hand. There was the sound of chairs being pushed back from the table, and then Monte Maguire said, "Jake, I seen lots of dry cows in the meadow."

Kelsey looked at the boss puncher. Jake fingered the black silk handkerchief at the throat of his clean wool shirt. Now Jake examined the nails of one hand.

"That so, Monte? Didn't figure there were any more drys than usual."

"Well, there are. What happened?"

"Couldn't say," Jake said in his soft, slow voice. "We run the bulls with 'em like always."

"Some of the cows are pretty old, ain't they?"

"About eight years, I figure."

"Ship 'em come fall. I can't afford to keep cows that don't calf. We got enough cost in this country, having to feed hay all winter. How are the two-year-old heifers? I question if it's smart to breed them as long yearlings."

"Well, they're comin' along. We'll have some loss, as usual. They don't calf easy when they're so young—gotta pull lots of 'em, too. Most places in Wyoming ranchers don't try to breed long yearlings."

"It's different here, though," she replied. "Costs us to carry a cow through the winter. In Wyoming they don't put so much into a cow—not when she can rustle most of the winter. Be-sides, the way we have to feed heifers in this country, they get too beefy if they're not bred young. Still, I wonder if it's prac-tical, breedin' 'em the way we do. Now, about so many cows showin' up dry this spring—"

"I tell you," Jake said, clearing his throat, "I handled things the same as all the years before. But it did get terrible hot last July when we turned the bulls out with the cows. Wasn't like this country at all. Cows was layin' around in the aspen shade with their tongues hangin' out. Might be that had something to do with 'em showing up dry."

"Christ a'mighty," Monte Maguire said, "wasn't that hot, was it?"

Kelsey pushed back his chair and left the table. If a woman wanted to use such language, he wouldn't listen to it.

Her voice stopped him. "Wait a minute, young fella. I've something more to say to you—when Jake and I get through talkin'."

Kelsey stood by the stove, hearing Jake go on talking about the dry cows. "Well, Monte, I've heard of it happenin' in lower country than the Park. Cows just don't breed when the weather's too hot. But if you want the truth, I'd rather lay the dry cows to them old bulls you oughta shipped. I told you when we culled the herd last fall that you needed to ship three or four old bulls and replace 'em with young bulls. But you got stubborn and put your foot down."

"Did I? Well, I was too damned optimistic. See many slinkers this spring, Jake?"

"A few—and maybe some more comin' up. And, as always, we had some abortin' in the heifers in January and February. But these cows, the mature ones that slink a calf, ain't worth a damn. If they start doin' it, seems they do it again the next year. And ain't it a funny thing how you can't let a slinkin' cow run in a pasture next to the young heifers havin' their first calves? Seems they'll slink their calves too."

"I know. An abortin' cow's got to be kept clear of the heifers. Seems there's a sympathetic understanding between 'em. Can't be explained—like a lot of other things about animal life, Jake. Well, we'll ship all the slinkin' cows this fall. Fatten 'em up on summer range, and they'll weigh in good when they hit the market. Now, one more thing, Jake. I see Tommy's got the irrigatin' started and you still got cattle on the meadows. You know I like the meadows cleared of cattle before the water starts pouring across 'em. How come?"

"They just got the water goin' good the last few days, Monte, and I didn't think the grass was quite ready on the flats. I figure on kickin' the cows onto the flats tomorrow."

She nodded. "That's good enough."

The other men walked out. Kelsey stood nervously by the stove, moving his feet restlessly. He watched Monte Maguire roll a cigarette with neat quick motions of her hands, put it in her mouth, and light it. The sight revolted him.

She looked at him through the drifting smoke. "Don't think much of me, do you, young fella?"

"The name's Cameron," he said shortly, "Kelsey Cameron. No, I don't think much of any woman who wears men's clothes and smokes tobacco."

"I see you speak your mind like I do. But you don't need to get huffy. The worst I ever say to you will be to your face, Mr. Cameron. And what I oughta do is kick you off the place —dreamin' along up that ditch—but maybe I expected too much, you being strange to the country."

"I don't have to stay here," he said angrily. "I'll be glad to leave."

"Didn't say you had to leave, did I? What did Tommy say I'd pay you?"

"Thirty dollars a month."

"I'll make it forty. And let me tell you something: there's a lot to learn about ranching and cow business. Don't expect to soak it all up overnight. Be a little patient. Now get the hell outta here. And the next time you ride a ditch, open your eyes."

CHAPTER IV

His pride smarting from the sting of Monte Maguire's words, Kelsey set out to learn the cattle business. During the two and a half months that followed his first meeting with her he sat late in the bunkhouse, throwing question after question at Jake. Sometimes he used pencil and paper, trying to make clear in his mind the cycle of grass and cows and weather. At every opportunity he observed at first hand some small detail of a complex business—a calf being born, a cow being doctored for disease, a bull being marked for discard and shipping because of age. And as he began to understand a little about the cattle he saw their relationship to the land.

Grass controlled where they would go at what time of the year. When cattle became restless on the spring meadows, pacing the fences, that meant the flats were turning green. Cowpunchers had only to open the gates, and the cows drifted naturally and easily to the spring range which lay between the ranch and town. In the brownish meadows they had just left, more grass came on, greening later than the flats, where the prairie sagebrush held moisture. And in June, when the flats had been grazed clean, cattle moved on to the fresh, close-to-the-snow grass of the high summer range in the mountains. As old snow melted they moved higher, and as fall came on, with the first flurries of new snowfall, cattle drifted back down onto the flats and meadows.

"I've got to get it right in my mind," Kelsey would say to

39

Jake. "I've got to understand more than weather and grass and where the ranges are. There's the business of keeping calves and bulls and cows separated at the right time."

And Jake would answer, smiling, "It's simple, son."

And after a while Kelsey saw that this was true. Bulls were with cows only at proper breeding time—a time that guaranteed a calf wouldn't be born in a snowbank. Bulls went out of their tightly fenced pastures to the mountain ranges in July, and ran with the cows until fall. Rock salt was placed in grassy parks, where cows would gather and the bulls would find them. Steers were pushed on the higher slopes to keep them away from the cows. Steer and heifer calves were kept in separate pastures after their first winter. "Because a steer is cut," Jake said, "that doesn't change his notions when he reaches a certain age."

June was branding time; fall was weaning and shipping time. Summer was for making hay, and winter was for feeding from the cured haystacks.

There were two kinds of cattle: range cattle, and purebred stuff. Purebreds were used only for breeding purposes. Range cattle went to the beef markets. In the Park most of the cattle were Herefords, commonly called "white faces" because of their white markings.

"Purebreds are full-horned, Kelsey," Jake explained patiently, "and got numbers burned in the horns to match numbers on their pedigree. They gotta be kept in tight pastures all the time. Full-eared, too. You never see a purebred with an ear mark."

Everything about cow business cost money, Kelsey concluded—especially bulls. All bulls were purebred, and a good bull meant good calves. How long would a man have to work at forty dollars a month to buy a bull? His figuring gave him a sense of mingled impatience and futility, but neither feeling lasted. With each new day he went about his work, eager to learn more. And this fine June morning he wished he were helping with the branding and cutting, but Tommy had sent him to town for rock salt.

The lumber wagon rattled along the narrow road. Kelsey, holding the lines lightly in his hands, looked over the backs of the team to the rolling country. One of Taraleean's letters was in his pocket, but he had not heard from Prim, although he had written her two or three times a week. A paragraph in his mother's letter stood out vividly in his mind: "Prim Munro's gone for the summer—to the highlands, some say, but not a soul seems to know where. . . . Before she left, Crowter the rag-buyer was seen with her along the highroad and in the town of a Saturday night. Maybe I shouldn't be telling you this, but I think you should know . . ."

He had written Prim again last night, an angry letter with words crossed out and then put in again. What did she mean, running with Crowter after what they had been to each other that night on the shore? And why hadn't she answered his letters? What was he to think of her, anyhow?

He felt foolish, remembering the words he'd so painstakingly put down the first weeks at the Red Hill Ranch—"Prim, my dearest one . . . Prim, my very own . . ."

Before him now was the wide river he had crossed the first day he was in the Park, and the ranch house south of the pole bridge was the home place of Monte Maguire. As Tommy had directed, he turned in at the gate and followed the rutted road along the river bank to the ranch house with the dirt roof that sprouted grass and weeds and small tomato-red flowers. He tied the team to the hitching post, walked across the bare yard, and knocked on the front door. A middle-aged woman with thin gray hair drawn tightly back from her high bulging forehead opened the door, looking at him questioningly, her pale lips pursed.

"Is Monte Maguire in?"

"You'll find her at the corral. She's not often in the house, except to eat and sleep."

He drove the lumber wagon to the corrals. Back of the barn was a smaller corral, and it was there he saw her. She was bending over a bull that lay on a pile of hay in one corner. She held a bottle of whisky in one hand, and Kelsey could hear the heavy, rasping breathing of the bull as he walked toward her. She bent lower, setting the bottle aside, trying to force the bull's mouth open.

"Let me do it," Kelsey said.

She straightened, wiping sweat from her forehead. "He's got pneumonia, I figure. One of those Missouri bulls I bought this spring, and the altitude's hard on 'em. I thought I ought to drench him."

Kelsey forced the animal's head back and the mouth open. The bull was feeble. Slobbers ran from his mouth and a yellow discharge from his nose. Monte poured the whisky down the throat. The bull snorted and choked, but he made no attempt to rise. He was gaunt, the ribs showing under the yellowish-brown hide. He closed his eyes, making an ugly sound.

"Hell," Monte Maguire muttered, "he's gonna die anyhow. I just as well have drunk the whisky and rubbed the bottle on his belly." She glanced at Kelsey and added dryly, "It was good whisky and wouldn't have hurt me—though I see it pains you to think of me, a woman, having a taste of whisky."

A thin smile quirked his lips. "I no longer think of you as a woman, Mrs. Maguire."

A flush spread under the tan of her skin. He was surprised to see anger in her eyes. Her words came out cold and steady. "A lot of men have, Mr. Cameron. And what's your business here this mornin'? Speak up! I'm not goin' to stand around all day."

"Tommy said I should mention I was after a load of rock salt."

"Get it at Faun Gentry's. That's where I do my trading."

She picked up the empty whisky bottle and walked away, leaving him standing beside the sick bull.

He drove on, hearing the meadow lark's clear, sweet notes from the willows. The town of Walden lay on a rough plateau above two rivers. The scattering of log and frame buildings stood lonely and windswept. Approaching the single block of main street, Kelsey felt again a sense of shock and disappointment. There were no trees or shrubs, only the buildings, naked and bold and yet with a sense of unreality about them, as though they had been hastily dumped there on the gray land and might be gone tomorrow. Over them stretched the sky, high and blue and clean, curving down to rest on the tented peaks to east and west.

A woman was hanging out washing before a small log house, her long full skirts hitched up at the waist, showing the men's boots she wore to wade through the mud, for the earth was soft from a recent rain. The wet clothes whipped in the wind, startlingly white in contrast to the shabby buildings.

The main street was wide, a stretch of mud rutted by the tracks of buggies and wagons. It was splotched with piles of horse manure, some old and some fresh and steaming, a few rusting tin cans, pieces of wood, and sodden fading newspapers that lay against the bleached uneven wooden sidewalks.

To Kelsey's left a low dirt-roofed log building carried a crude wooden sign with the rough letters BLACKSMITH. Next to it was a similar log cabin, but the sign on the front was so faded he couldn't make out the words. Beyond these was obviously a hotel, a double-story frame structure painted pale buff and sporting a square balcony facing the street. Beneath the balcony a porch was trimmed in brown scroll and flanked by pillars painted chocolate-brown. Next to the hotel was what appeared to be a sort of town hall, a grayish-white frame building with a cupola and bell on top. Farther on, Kelsey glimpsed a water tower and windmill.

Opposite the hotel was a store building; a faded red-and-white-striped awning jutted out to shade the wooden sidewalk: GROCERIES & HARDWARE. On up this side of the street were saloons and hitching racks and another large frame store building with the word GENTRY'S painted in large black letters across the board front.

As he drove toward Gentry's store the street scene was one of slow activity. Men talked in groups of twos and threes, and occasionally a woman made her way up or down the street with groceries in her arms. But the town was dominated by the men. Cattlemen and cowhands stood in front of the saloons, talking markets and cows. Their hats rested low over their eyes or far back on their heads, showing the narrow strips of white forehead. Other men moved up and down the street, mingling with the storekeepers and saloon owners. As Kelsey got out of the wagon, tied the team to the hitching rack, and looked around, he noticed the small white frame church east of the main street. It had a sharp, thin steeple pointing up toward the blue. He felt a sense of satisfaction when he looked at it, and a part of him applauded those who had made a church possible in this isolated, crude country. He remembered that Jediah said preachers had the hardest time trying to make a living in the Park, for ranchers made up the larger part of the population and didn't often drive twenty or thirty miles by buggy to attend church.

"That don't mean they've got no religion," Jediah had said. "Man can't live in this country, with the big peaks and seein' life all around him every spring, without havin' a humble and grateful feelin' toward something. Don't matter what you call it, son; you'll know it's there when you been in the Park a while."

Kelsey walked across the wooden sidewalk, looking at the half-dozen men lounging in front of the building. Their friendly, curious faces were turned toward him in frank appraisal. One of them was talking. ". . . and the judge, he come out dressed like he was ready to hold court and he looked at that cow dead by the meadow fence. Then he turns to Shorty, his hired man, and says, 'I presume she must have expired during the night.' "

The men burst into laughter, and Kelsey smiled as he walked into the store. The air smelled of dust and cigar smoke. Confusion lay over everything, as though all the goods brought into the valley had been tossed here and there with no thought of arrangement. Counters lined the walls, and big wooden tables in the center of the store were covered with all manner of materials—bolts of dress cloth, kegs of nails, harness, shoes, canned goods, horse liniments, saddles, boxes of candy.

Kelsey walked between the tables, brushing against them, trying not to knock things onto the floor. He saw a little bald-headed man behind a counter, a man with a tuft of sandy-colored hair above each small pink ear, and he knew that this must be Faun Gentry.

Faun was smoking a cigar. It hung in the corner of his mouth, the black stub moving up and down in the yellow skin of the thin sagging face. The sunken brown eyes peered from wrinkles of flesh, making Kelsey think of a bloodhound. Faun was waiting on a tall, rounded woman who held a baby in her arms. A shabby coat partly covered her faded calico dress, and a man's hat, old and crumpled, was jammed over her untidy brown hair.

"That be all, Miz Plunkett?" Faun asked, the cigar moving with his words. "You want me to charge it?"

She shifted the baby to her hip. "We can't pay you till Harry ships come fall, Faun."

"Sure, sure, I understand. Cowman's always broke till shippin' is over. You stop and see Dolly 'fore you go home. She's ailin' again. It's because she won't go out in the sun—claims the sun's too strong in this country and leathers a woman's skin. I tell her I'd rather she'd get tough skin than be like the stiff I've got laid out in the back room."

The woman nodded, smiling. Then Faun took the cigar from his mouth and leaned across the counter, lowering his voice. "Did I tell you 'bout Ellie Lundgren last week? Y'know how she is, pretendin' to be so damn prissy. Well, she ain't satisfied with the meat Vic's got out on the ranch, whether it's a cow he's butchered or a buck he shot in the pasture. She comes in here and sniffs everything, her nose in the air like always. And she says, 'What kinda meat you got, Mr. Gentry?' I names everything from ribs to roast, and she just shakes her head. Then I says, 'How about some nice tongue, Miz Lundgren?' 'My,' she says, 'how could I eat anything come outta an old cow's mouth?' And then I says, 'Well, Miz Lundgren, you just bought five dozen eggs.' "

Mrs. Plunkett's laughter rang out, hearty, catching laughter, and Kelsey joined in. They turned to look at him then, and Faun came around the counter and held out his hand. "Howdy, stranger."

Kelsey grasped the slender, nicotine-stained fingers. "I'm Kelsey Cameron, Tommy's cousin, and he sent me in after rock salt for the Red Hill Ranch."

"Well, well, so you're the fella from Scotland. Want you to meet Amie Plunkett. She's your neighbor to the south—runs the post office for the west side of the Park."

Amie smiled at him with warm brown eyes. "It's high time I've met up with you. I've been sorting those letters from Scotland and wondering about you."

But no letters from Prim, Kelsey thought, only from Taraleean. What was Big Mina Munro doing to his lassie while he was away here in a far country?

"You tell Tommy," Amie went on, "he isn't treatin' you right. You oughta be gettin' around and meetin' some people. What's he up to, keepin' your nose to the grindstone? And I'll bet you've been lonesome, too." Impulsively her hand touched his arm. "You come see us real soon—and stay for supper. Harry's been wantin' to meet you. Every time Hilder rides down for the mail he talks about you and we ask him how you're gettin' along." She gave his arm a little shake. "Don't let Tommy get you down. Everything's going to be fine." The baby began to whimper, and she started rocking it gently in her arms. "I've got to get home now. I'll expect you down. We'll be lookin' forward to it."

Kelsey thanked her and watched her walk from the store.

"Helluva fine woman," Faun said, "but don't make much of herself—always looks 'bout the way she did just now. When she come into the Park—a few years back, it was—she was some fancy chicken. Dressed to make a man turn his head and look, I can tell you. Don't seem to care any more, though. Maybe because Harry's got her pregnant all the time. And folks say she never gets around to fixin' herself up because she's too busy readin' books. Why, I even heard she takes a book to the privy with her—in winter, too, when it's cold. Now, would you think a person'd get anything through his head when his other end was freezin'?"

Kelsey laughed. He liked Faun Gentry.

"But I'd take Amie any day, books and all, before I'd have any truck with Ellie Lundgren. Vic Lundgren's one fine fella and about as good a cattleman as there is in the Park, but Ellie—little dried-up wisp with a pinched-in mouth like she'd been suckin' on a sour pickle. Vic's cross, that's what people call her. Ain't it hell how a good man can get stung?" Faun sighed and then added, "What'd you say Tommy wanted?"

"Rock salt."

"Well, we'll get around to that all right. Listen, it's slack time in the store right now—must be gettin' close to noon. Come on in the back room, and I'll set us up a drink. Dolly, my wife, she's agin liquor—agin sin too. The new preacher's got her wound around his finger. Why, hell, she's up there singin' hymns in the new church damn near every night, and worst is, she can't carry a tune. Sour as cat piss, Dolly's singin'. Well, let's go back now before somebody comes in."

The back room was small and littered with empty boxes. Against the far wall was a long table with a sheet spread over it. A form lay under the sheet. Faun waved a hand toward it and said, "Fella drifted in here 'bout a month ago. Been hangin' around Bill Dirk's saloon, takin' the boys in poker. Got himself shot last night. Had it comin'. Was him or Bill. Forced Bill into it. Didn't find no letters or anything on him, but I gotta fix him up a little and bury him. I don't like the job, but nobody'll take it on but me, and you can't let a man stay on top of the ground for the magpies and coyotes to tear him apart." Faun reached under a box and pulled out a whisky bottle. "Drink up, son. It'll put hair on your chest."

When Kelsey handed him the bottle, Faun nodded and murmured, "Thanks, don't mind if I do." Faun took a quick drink, made a face, coughed and said, "God, that's good whisky! Listen, you can't go home this afternoon."

"I thought I should."

"Stick around. We'll have a poker game at Bill Dirk's tonight. Have some fun, son. You'll need it if you expect to stay in this country and be happy. There's nothin' to equal a good poker game—not even an accommodatin' woman. Tell Tommy I was outta rock salt and you had to wait till the evenin' freight wagon got in from Laramie. And I'll tell you what, I'll pay you to help me bury this fella this afternoon. That way you won't feel you're pinchin' yourself to sit in on a few hands."

Kelsey thought about it. Faun went on, "It spooks me, buryin' a man alone, and the minister's gone outside—that's anywhere outside this valley, son. And you could eat supper with Dolly and me. She likes company, and she's a good cook. Only don't mention the poker game. I'm comin' down to work in the store, see? I'd take it as a real favor if you'd help me, Kelsey."

"Well, all right, then."

They buried the stranger at five o'clock that afternoon in

the shabby graveyard at the edge of town. It was a lonely place on a little hill, and clumps of sagebrush grew around the wooden markers. Kelsey thought of his father, laid to rest in a fine grassy plot a mile from the village. It was like a lawn, that graveyard, and not a weed in it. The stone on his father's grave was the finest marble and carefully inscribed. And there was a high stone wall to keep cattle and horses from walking over the graves.

But did it matter? he asked himself, leaning on the shovel, looking beyond the graveyard to the vast open country and the far mountains standing over it. What was the end of man but dust the cows might walk through in the evening, when the last blue flower had closed before the dark? Ah, the pity of it!

"Don't seem right to leave him with no Scripture said over him," Faun muttered. "But the preacher's gone." He leaned on the shovel, staring down at the fresh dark earth.

"I'll speak over him," Kelsey said. "I want to." He took off his wide-brimmed, mud-stained hat and bent his head. And words his father had said to him as they walked the shore came back to him. " 'Man . . . cometh forth like a flower, and is cut down . . .' "

Yes. And myself to come to this, and Taraleean—dust and the sun going down, and the names to be blown away and forgotten. And even Monte Maguire to come to this, big and strong as she is, and the life beating up like a high sea in her body . . .

He went on into the Lord's Prayer, feeling the earth solid beneath him and the wind against his cheek. He finished, put on his hat, and turned to go.

"You did good, son," Faun said gravely. "A man oughta know the Scripture. There's a time it fits when nothing else will." He shouldered the shovel, and they walked to the waiting wagon.

Faun's home was a four-room log cabin two blocks from the

main street. The walls inside the house were covered with printed cloth that was tacked at the ceiling and stretched tight and tacked again at the bottom log. Everything was so clean it brought pleasure to Kelsey. "It's like being home," he said.

Dolly Gentry was pleased to see him. She was plump, had a small pale face and little soft hands that glittered with rings. She patted her hair, which fascinated Kelsey, for it was an odd shade of black with no shine to it, and because of the way it fitted her head he wondered if it might be a wig.

As they sat at the table she said, "You must find the Red Hill lonely, and no pleasure or good comes to any man who works for Monte Maguire. She's nothing but a—"

"Dolly!" Faun scowled at her.

"Well, it's true! Why shouldn't I say so?"

"You've no proof, Dolly."

"Ha! Proof! Does a woman need proof when one of her kind spends all her time around men? And how'd she get hold of all that land she's added to her holdings since old Flit Maguire died? Why did Tommy Cameron give up his good homestead, turn it over to her and go to work for her? And what about the cowpunchers who worked for her, got fired, and left the country broke? What happened to their money? You know as well as I do that lots of them never spent anything in town."

"Dolly," Faun said, "all you say is gossip. Monte's the best customer I have, and I'd thank you to keep your mouth shut."

"That's it," Dolly said peevishly, "stand up for her. Men always do. But she can't pull the wool over a woman's eyes! Why, she hadn't been married to Flit Maguire any time when she was chasing all over the country with his hired men."

"And why not? Flit got so he wouldn't even bring her over town when he came for groceries. And he was a lot older than Monte. I never liked Flit Maguire, Dolly. He was a hard, cruel man, and I'd not have blamed her if she'd left him."

"Ha!" Dolly laughed shortly. "She wouldn't leave him, not

when she knew he was old and ailing and owned a ranch and cattle. She knew he'd die and she'd get it. And no wonder he wouldn't take her anywhere—a girl he picked up in a cathouse!"

"Shut up!" Faun shoved his chair back from the table. "And she was only dealin' cards at the house, in case you didn't know the truth."

"Dealing cards! Well, that's the fanciest name for it I ever heard!"

"Come on, Kelsey." Faun turned at the door. "I'm working at the store tonight. Won't be home till late."

"Is that so? See you don't drift into Bill Dirk's saloon, close as it is to the store."

Faun's brows lifted. "Bill Dirk's? How would I have time to get over to Bill Dirk's?" He walked with Kelsey into the soft June night. The wind had gone down, and a stillness hung over the town. When they got to the street they angled across it to where a wooden sign hung creaking in the wind—BILL DIRK'S.

"Looks like a few o' the boys got in," Faun said, jerking a thumb toward the horses tied at the hitching rack.

Inside the air was smoky and close. There was a crude wooden bar at the far end with an oil painting of two naked women hanging on the wall behind it. Bill Dirk came forward. He was short and fleshy, with thin black hair parted in the middle and slicked down, but the ends stuck up like spikes. His features were fine, almost feminine, and he wore a big diamond on his little finger. He shook Kelsey's hand and said, "I know Tommy. Good man, but no poker player. We don't ask him no more. He's afraid of money—pains him to lose and damn near scares him to death to win, for fear he won't be able to keep it. Man oughta leave poker alone if he's afraid of money. Come in the back end. We got a game ready to go."

They went past the bar and through a narrow doorway into a small room with a window set high in the wall. Around a bare table four men were waiting: the Swedish rancher, Vic Lundgren; Jed Posser, who ran the hotel; Slim, a cowhand from the south end of the Park; and Jediah Walsh.

Jediah peered at Kelsey with his faded blue eyes. "Shucks, boy, if I'd known you was comin' in I'd have rode with you instead of on horseback. I come in late this afternoon. My ears was plugged with wax again. Friend of mine come up yestiddy, and I got him to watch the headgate while I was gone. Old Doc Bingham said it wasn't any wonder I was deaf as a post. Sit down, boy. Y'know how to play this game?"

"Dalt and Jake played with me a couple of times in the bunkhouse."

"Dalt, eh? Well, that young fella knows his cards. But Jake never did have any card sense. Born without it. Always havin' to ask who bet and who raised and if it's stud or draw. And he wants to stay in every pot because he can't stand to be out. Holds his cards up close like he hoped to read new spots onto them. Now, Vic there, he's the one to watch. He's been suckin' us dry all year."

The blond middle-aged Swede nodded. "Yup, yup," he said, clicking his false teeth. "You want to start now, Dirk?"

"What we come for, ain't it?" Posser said, his pale eyes shifting nervously. His hand trembled as he stroked down his thin iron-gray hair. He began to cough and finally put a soiled handkerchief over his mouth.

Slim said nothing. He was tall and thin and moody-looking.

"Deal 'em. I come to play." Faun rubbed his tobacco-stained hands together. "And bring in the bottle, Dirk. I'm thirsty."

"Open for two bucks." Vic's teeth clicked.

"Raise the openers. Up two," Kelsey said.

They looked at him. Jediah smiled, his old lined face beaming. "That's tellin' 'em, boy!"

The game settled into silence except for the placing of bets and the clanking of chips and silver. The air got heavy and stifling with smoke. Faun Gentry took off his tie and then his coat. Jediah Walsh sat in his heavy underwear and the stench of sweat and beaver castors came from him. The bottle passed from hand to hand. The cowboy, Slim, looked more gloomy. Posser twitched nervously. Periodically Vic Lundgren's teeth clicked and he muttered, "Yup, yup!" Faun Gentry smoked constantly; as one black cigar burned away, a fresh one replaced it. Only Jediah Walsh was relaxed.

Kelsey won pot after pot. He began to feel expansive. Why, hell, he thought, I'm on top of the world tonight. I can't lose. I'm like a damned blood in the old country!

This was the life! This made a man forget a girl in Scotland, a girl who didn't write him as she should; made him forget the lonely nights at the Red Hill Ranch, and his heart crying for the green land far away. And God, the fun of it!

He looked around the table, filled with affection for all these men who had welcomed him to their game. "Since I left my mother, Taraleean, I've not spent such a wonderful night," he said, his voice rising with excitement. "But I'll be no hog with my money. From now on the whisky's on me!" And he tilted back in the creaking chair, shouting, "Hey, bar-lad! Set them up on Kelsey Cameron! Wet the gentlemen's whistles, please!"

The men laughed, and Vic Lundgren said, "He ain't like Tommy. And did you ever see anything like the hot streak he's had? Beginner's luck, yup, yup!" Vic stood up a little unsteadily and lifted the fresh bottle. "Here's to you, Scotty. May you live long and have a good woman to sleep with!"

Again the game settled into silence. They played harder now; the money was shoved from hand to hand, but most of it stopped before Kelsey. Daylight was showing against the narrow high window when Vic stood up and said, "Breaks me. And I still owe you fifty dollars, Scotty. You want a check, huh?"

Kelsey rubbed his eyes, which were bloodshot and smarting

from the smoke. He was drunk, as much from winning as from the whisky. "No," he said, getting to his feet, standing tall in the little room, his red head thrown back, "not a check, but a cow—a cow that'll have a calf in spring, a good cow with a straight back, short legs, and just enough white showing in the right places, a cow out of a good bull. That's what you owe me, Vic."

"You pick her or I pick her, come fall?" Vic asked.

"You pick her, Vic. I trust you."

"I give you this cow, then, when we bring the cattle off summer range. Any cow Vic Lundgren has is a good cow, Scotty, and don't let nobody tell you no different. I give you my word on it, and my word is better than gold in the Park—eh, men?"

Faun Gentry nodded, belching loudly. The man Slim slipped quietly out of the room. Bill Dirk began to gather up bottles and poker chips. Posser just sat, staring down at the table, reaching in and out of his pocket, looking at the empty hand and then putting it back, as if he couldn't believe the pocket was empty.

Kelsey walked out of the saloon, swaying from side to side. He pounded Faun on the shoulder and told him what a noble gentleman he was, by heaven, and that great blood ran in his veins and he was proud to know him, by God! Faun responded in the same mood and then went slowly toward his store, pulling a big key from his pocket.

As Kelsey started across the street Jediah Walsh fell into step beside him. In the middle of the street Jediah pulled a pistol from his pocket and fired it into the air, shouting, "Hurrah for the Fourth of July!"

"It's not," Kelsey said, hiccuping. "It's only June."

"Well, hell, it still starts with J, don't it?" Jediah looked all around as though he expected to see some activity on the quiet street, sighed, and pocketed the pistol. "Come on, son, we'll go to the hotel. And I'll bunk with you!" He linked his arm through Kelsey's. They wove across the empty street and up the creaking wooden steps into the hotel.

In the lobby a fat woman sat behind the desk, picking her teeth with a hairpin. Her little eyes bored into Jediah. "Where's my man?"

Jediah bowed awkwardly. "Possy, ma'am, he's just delayed collectin' his winnin's from Mr. Dirk." He bowed again and urged Kelsey toward the stairs.

"He better be," she said dryly. "We got no money to lose, and him coughin' his head off every night."

They got to the room, which was bare-floored and had a torn green blind flapping at the window. When Kelsey lighted the lamp a fly began to bump monotonously against the ceiling. Jediah squinted up at the fly. "Crazy son-of-a-bitch. Thinks he can break right out into the sky. Like some people, I reckon."

"Watch the lamp," Kelsey warned. "We don't want to set fire to the place."

"Listen, son, I been drunker than this more times than I can count. And I've started all over again the next mornin'. How much'd you win?"

"A hundred dollars and some—that's besides what Vic owes me. I'll send that hundred to Scotland." And he stood thinking of Big Mina and suddenly said angrily, "That's why Prim's not got my letters. Big Mina's got them first. I ought to have known."

"You did good, son," Jediah said. "What you gonna do with a cow, though?"

"Start my own cow herd, that's what."

Jediah started taking off his shoes. Then he got into bed, fully clothed, and pulled the covers to his chin. "Some folks ain't gonna like it, you havin' a cow," he said, yawning.

Kelsey pulled up the blind and looked over the buildings to the land, big and fresh in the first light of morning. "Ever hear of Bobby Burns, Jediah?"

"Can't say as I have."

"He was a poet—wrote about real things, like men drinking together of a Saturday night. Listen, I'll tell you about them. . . ." And he began to quote Burns, his heart quickening to the lilt of the words. He turned to the trapper and shouted, "My God, isn't it wonderful? To think it and feel it and then say it like he did!"

"It is," Jediah Walsh said. "You turnin' in, son, or you gonna sleep roostin' on the side of this bed like a damn chicken?"

"I was thinking of Prim, my lassie. I was thinking how long it's been since I saw her face and heard her voice. I was remembering the way she felt in my arms, and her tears. I should have married her, Jediah. It wasn't right I should leave her, not after what we'd been to each other."

"You can send for her," Jediah said. "And never be sad for havin' loved a woman. Just be grateful you had the chance."

"But the sadness is in it, and I can't help it. It runs in me like a streak of darkness, Jediah."

"In all of us," Jediah said, "but don't be sorry."

Kelsey got up, walked to the washstand, where the big white bowl and white pitcher were sitting. He poured water into the bowl and tossed it against his face. He blew out the lamp and moved toward the bed, a music moving with him, whirling in his head with the words of poetry and with the thought of Taraleean and Prim. He tossed his shirt and pants on the floor and got in beside Jediah. The smell of the beaver castors, rank and overpowering, swept over him. But then he slept suddenly, plunging into darkness as though he had fallen over a steep cliff.

CHAPTER V

September. A few early snows had dusted the peaks with white. The cattle began their slow drift to lower country, wandering along the creeks, moving through the open gates into the meadows and onto the flats. It was an inevitable and unhurried homecoming.

The lush green feed of summer range was now cured and had a greenish-brown color. This was the feed that hardened the fat on cattle and put them in shape for the long drive to shipping points. The hair on the cattle was long and in bloom, shining darkly as though it had been oiled, for maturity came early in the high country where any summer night might carry the breath of snow.

By the middle of the month it was roundup time at the Red Hill Ranch. On a clear, still morning, before daylight, Kelsey sat at breakfast with Monte Maguire, Jake, and the other punchers. Outside the yard fence other cowpokes were gathered around the chuck wagon of the Big C outfit from Wyoming, for the Big C ranch cattle drifted onto the summer ranges of the Park. In turn, some Park cattle made their way to the grazing grounds of the Big C. In the meadow below the ranch house the Big C cavvy mingled with the horses of Monte Maguire's riders, feeding on the short second crop of grass that came up following the haying season.

"You got any chaps?" Monte looked at Kelsey, the yellow lamplight shining on the tan of her face.

It was the way she always threw a question at a man, he thought, giving him no warning.

"There's an old pair of angoras in the bunkhouse," Jake said. "I don't wear angoras any more. Like the batwing leather ones better."

Tommy Cameron frowned. "What would he want with a pair of fuzzy pants? They'd look like hell on a man fixing fence. Our fences gotta be tight for the weaning."

"Any fool can fix fence," Monte said. "I want him to learn cow business."

Kelsey's heart quickened with pleasure. Then he saw the red come up in Tommy's face. "It's your money," Tommy said to Monte. "If you want to throw it away so's a hired man can play cowpoke it's no skin off my nose."

"I don't throw money away," Monte said curtly. "I invest it." She pushed back her chair and stood before the kitchen stove, methodically rolling a cigarette. The men looked down at their plates. It was quiet in the kitchen. Then the still morning was broken by the clear sound of bells.

"Wrangler's bringin' in the cavvy," Jake said. He smiled at Kelsey. "Always bell a few horses so's the wrangler can find 'em in the dark. You come to the bunkhouse and we'll try those chaps. I got an old pair of boots you can have. What about a saddle?"

Kelsey turned to Tommy. Here was a man with a fine saddle, and never using it, for Tommy ran the ranch and let the cowboys handle the cattle. Kelsey wet his lips. "I'd appreciate it—" he began.

Tommy's fork paused midway between the plate and his mouth. He gave Kelsey a long, cold look and then went on eating his breakfast.

Kelsey's face burned. Then he heard Hilder speaking. "Yust take mine," Hilder said. "Is not so fancy, but it will do. You take it, Kelsey, and welcome to it."

Light was breaking when Kelsey left the bunkhouse with

Jake. He felt happy in the worn yellow angora chaps and the run-over boots. There was excitement in him as they walked past the Big C chuck wagon, where the air smelled of smoke and bacon and a few punchers lingered over an extra cup of coffee.

At the corral men were already flipping the wide loops of their lariats over the heads of milling horses. Beyond the toss-ing heads and the clouds of dust a faint streak of red lay in the eastern sky.

"Cowpokes take off in pairs to gather cattle," Jake said. "That way a man can ride a green colt by snubbin' him to the saddle horn of the other fella, who's ridin' a settled-down horse. If a horse gets used to goin' along beside another horse, he soon quiets. Each rider's got a string of six or seven saddle horses, and he's got to break out two or three colts every year to keep his string in top shape."

As Jake said this Kelsey saw two punchers mounting horses outside the corral. The horses went wild, rearing up to paw the air and then come down hard, ducking their heads between their front legs and humping their backs.

"No snubbin' for them," Jake said, chuckling. "They're gonna do it the hard way. You always see a few fellas ridin' their damnedest come roundup time."

As they rode onto the flats the sunrise met them, drenching the white-tipped west peaks in red. And the stillness held, with no wind rising up from the floor of the Park to nag at them in their riding. Cowboys from neighboring ranches came across the gray land, some already pushing a few cattle before them.

"Gatherin' goin' on all over the flats this mornin'," Jake said. "East cattlemen are working the east side; south-end ranchers are ridin' the south flats of the Park. We work the north and northwest."

All morning he rode with Jake, giving the cowpony its head, letting it move around the straying cows and calves they found in the ravines and on ridges of Independence Mountain. By early afternoon a milling, bawling herd of cattle was bunched against an old fence on the flats, and ranchers cut out their own and hazed them toward their home places. Dust and the smell of crushed sagebrush filled the air.

"They don't need to look too close for brands," Jake said, sitting easily in the saddle at the edge of the herd. "If you notice, Kelsey, you'll see the big outfits got other marks to go by. Some of 'em got ear marks and some got wattles. Wattle's a small piece of hide that's been cut and let hang loose on the animal. You can see 'em danglin' on jaws or necks or briskets. Monte don't use no wattles. She's got an ear mark besides her brand. Swallow-fork ear mark is what Monte uses—a V on the end of each ear. We ear-mark 'em when we brand. All big outfits like to use ear marks. Makes it easier to cut out their cattle when the hair's long and brands get hard to see."

Monte, who had ridden up, rolled a cigarette and said, "I don't need any mark to tell my cattle from the rest of 'em. Maybe all cattle look alike to a greenhorn like you, Kelsey, but those of us who breed cattle try to get a certain type. We've all got out own ideas about the kind of bulls we want, and the kind of calves. After you been in the business for years, your cattle stand out from the other fella's cattle. Hell, I can look at that stuff they got bunched and tell you every cow that's mine without giving a thought to brand or ear mark. And Jake's just as good."

Jake was pleased but tried to look modest and said, "I ain't quite that good, Monte."

"Well, damn near it." She shifted in the saddle, looked at Kelsey, her eyes narrowed to cool blue slits in the cigarette smoke, and added, "We figure to ship while the bloom's still on. Mostly we start the drive to Laramie around the first of October."

"There's a steer from the Davis outfit in the south end," Jake said, pointing. "He sure enough drifted from his home range. Musta come fifty miles."

"Well, we'll work the flats today, and when we have the field roundup tomorrow we'll kick anything that don't belong to us toward Walden, have the jackpot for unclaimed stuff there, as usual, and turn those mavericks over to the brand inspector for him to sell."

"If nobody gets a chance to claim them mavericks and slip 'em into his herd," Jake said, grinning.

"Nobody'll get the chance," Monte said. "We got too many sharp cowmen from different outfits. Nobody's gonna lay claim to an unmarked calf and get away with it."

In the early dusk Kelsey and Monte and Jake rode toward the Red Hill Ranch. Before them and behind them riders from the Big C slumped in their saddles, quiet coming over them now that the day's work was over and the long night was ahead. For Kelsey the free, wonderful day of gathering cattle had ended too soon. He wished that he might be beginning all over again, with the horse under him, the sunrise in his eyes, and the wide gray plains ahead.

Weariness settled on him at the supper table, but after eating he went to the bunkhouse, where the punchers had gathered; some were playing poker, and others rehearsing in detail this roundup and other roundups.

"It was easier gatherin' than last year."

"Maybe. I sure hope I make the drive to Laramie this time. I ain't been there since last year. Wonder what's new at Corinthia's place."

"It won't be new; it'll just seem that way to you."

"Say." Jake stirred from his customary place in front of the stove. "Remember the time old Frank Blutcher was with us when we shipped that trainload of steers to Omaha? We were all in the caboose, waitin' for the train to start, and this girl comes in sellin' *The War Cry*. We all gave her a buck. She hit us just right. Then old Frank, he follows her out of the caboose. A little later he comes back with his face all scratched to hell."

The men burst into laughter. "He oughta known better than try to make a Salvation Army girl."

"Well," Jake said softly, "you never can tell about a woman until you try. Wonder what happened to old Frank?"

"He went to Texas. Said he couldn't take cold country no longer."

A momentary silence fell over the men. From the poker table came the clink-clank of silver and chips. "Don't any son-of-a-bitch check a cinch into me. What you so proud of, son?"

"Whores over fours. Can you beat 'em?"

"Shucks, I only got treys over deuces. Shake out something, Hank. I want to peek at a good hole card."

A Big C puncher raised up from the tarpaulin-covered bunk where he had been half asleep. "Say, that little buckskin I was ridin' threw me higher than a kite up in Ruby Gulch on Independence Mountain today."

"How come?"

"Slim and I run onto a black bear in the strip of willows at the spring below the aspen patch. We tried to rope him. Every time I got ready to spill a loop on him, my horse would jump sideways. He finally spun away, and I was usin' the spurs on him when he flipped his tail over the rope. Jesus! I didn't have a chance. He tossed me halfway to heaven. Then he bucked all the way to the willows, with me tearin' along right behind him. A fella can run like hell when he's on foot and thinkin' a bear is about to snort in his flank with every jump."

"I'd like to 'a seen it. Your horse was lucky he didn't bust a leg among all them prairie-dog holes."

"Most of our punchers was wearin' their forty-fives. I could have shot him. Y'know, Jake, you oughta carry a gun when you're ridin' rough country. If a good horse breaks his leg, only kind thing a man can do is shoot him."

Jake nodded. "I know, but I just don't take to packin' pistols. A man should, for if he gets throwed and hung in the stirrup, havin' a gun to kill a horse might be the thing would save his life. But I guess I'll go on takin' my chances with myself and my horses. I figure the only men who oughta pack guns are the men who really know how to handle 'em. Y'know, when the West opened up and wagons was crossin' to California and Oregon, they had more damn fools kill people by accident just because men had guns and didn't know how to use 'em. Hell, you're always hearin' about Indians killin' people on wagon trains, but you don't hear much about people killin' each other because they got careless with guns or was plumb ignorant about usin' them."

Again there was a lull in conversation. No sound came from the poker table, where the men held their cards close, studying them carefully.

Jake yawned. "Must be a flock of full houses and flushes out in that hand of draw. Well, boys, tomorrow we do the field roundup here, cut the stuff for shippin', and any strays that go into the jackpot. Suppose the Big C figures on shippin' about next week."

"Yep. More ridin'. A man spends half his life in the saddle."

"Far as I'm concerned," Jake murmured, "it's as good a place to spend it as any."

Kelsey moved away from the stove, into the frosty fall night. He walked slowly down the worn path to the ranch house and stood for a moment, looking up at the stars. They were big and close and very bright. He thought of Prim and of the harbor, where the night sky was soft and the sound of the sea was always with a man.

The yard gate creaked, and he saw Monte Maguire walking toward him. She came to stand beside him, saying nothing, looking out across the land. He wondered what thoughts ran in her mind. Did she think only of cattle on a night like this—or of the man who had been her husband? Did the enormous silence of the world here, so close to the sky, make her lonely; was a part of her crying for things the mind could never define?

She turned her head and looked at him, and he knew she tried to see into his face. His heart suddenly felt big and crowding to his throat. Then, quickly, she brushed past him and went into the house.

CHAPTER VI

Kelsey rode into the yard of the Plunkett ranch with the cold fall rain drifting over him. He'd come for the Red Hill Ranch mail. After tying the horse to a fencepost, he walked through the muddy yard, which was pockmarked where the chickens had dusted themselves in summer.

To Kelsey the house had an easy, slipshod appearance that matched Amie's character. Built of logs, it had settled on one side, listing toward the east. In many places the mud chinking had fallen from between the logs and been replaced by rags. There were no curtains up, for Amie never got around to ironing them until they were so mussed it was time for another washing.

Beyond the house he could see the river, running high from the heavy fall rain. Yellow leaves clung to the willows, made brighter by the wetness of the day.

He stepped onto the sagging porch. Sodden chickens huddled under it. A clutter covered the gray boards of the floor. There were old tin cans, worn coats and shoes, toys, a wooden washtub, a rusty boiler, two pitchforks, shovels, and a soggy crust of bread a child had dropped half-eaten. He knocked on the door, which was sticky from jelly-smeared fingers, and heard Amie's warm voice lifted in a shout. "Come in if you can get in!"

Harry Plunkett was sitting at the kitchen table, drinking coffee. He wore no shirt, and his long gray underwear was stained at the armpits with sweat. Opposite him sat Amie, her dark hair wound carelessly on top of her head, loose strands clinging to her plump cheeks. She was wearing a soiled pink wrapper; the hem was stained black from trailing across the kitchen floor. The baby, a little girl, cooed to herself where she lay in a clothes basket, her pink toes thrust in the air above her. From another room came the noise of the three small boys playing.

"Coffee's hot," Amie said. "Sit, Kelsey, and take a load off your feet."

Harry looked sour—in one of his brooding moods, Kelsey thought; Harry was either away up or away down in his mind. He was big and fair-skinned and heavily freckled, much younger-looking than his wife. Now he stuck a finger in his ear and worked it back and forth. "Got them head noises again."

"Oh, hell," Amie muttered, setting a cup before Kelsey, "he gets them every year this time. When haying's over and he starts thinkin' about winter, then he's got wheels in his head."

"By God, you wouldn't think it's so funny if you had 'em," Harry said, scowling at his wife. "You gonna get Kelsey his mail, or are you gonna sit here and run off at the mouth for an hour?"

Amie thumbed her nose at him, and a brief smile lighted Harry's face. The dirty hem of the wrapper flipped behind her as she went from the kitchen to the small bedroom which was the post office.

Harry poured coffee and shoved a cream pitcher toward Kelsey. A hard yellow river of cream curved from the mouth of the pitcher and down its bulging front. "I dunno if this country's worth what it takes out of a man," Harry complained. "Man tears his guts out chasin' water and shovelin' manure all spring. Then he runs himself thin after the cattle until they're ready for summer range. After that it's put up hay, and every time a cloud rolls over the range a man worries for fear he's gonna get his grass wet, and then it'll burn and maybe have to be put up damp, and after that it can sweat in the stack and cause sickness in the cattle come winter. And winter—what's before a man in winter but shovel hay until his back's broke down and—"

"It's not shovelin' hay that's broke down your back," Amie said tartly, putting a pile of mail on the table before Kelsey. "And any time you want to take over the kids and the house I'll be glad to pitch hay. I'd just like the chance—no kids to fuss with, no meals to cook, no house to clean."

"You oughta been a woman like Monte Maguire," Harry said, his eyes narrowing as he looked at his wife. "She run right out of the house and onto the range—like a man."

"And more power to her! I like Monte Maguire. She's the only interesting woman in this damn snowhole of a country. What's more, I don't care what the other women say or think about her."

Harry shrugged, a glint in his eyes now. "Well, she sleeps around, they say. Only trouble is, them that are supposed to get it don't keep it long."

"You talk dirty, Harry Plunkett! Didn't ever see it, did you? Got no proof, have you? And what if she has slept with a few men? She's human and lonely, and no man or kids to hold her down. Maybe I'd do the same thing—if I was free."

Harry laughed. "Now, Amie—"

"You think because I've been pregnant and spread out until I'm two ax-handles across the rear that I couldn't find a man?"

"Now, look here, Amie, there's some things men can do and it's figured to be their right because they gotta, but—"

"Got to, my foot! Men been gettin' away with that idea since heck was a pup. Trouble is, women let 'em and never put up a fight." She turned to Kelsey. "You got two letters in that pile of mail—both of them from Scotland."

"Amie." Harry glared at her. "You're not supposed to fiddle with other people's mail."

Her dark eyes opened wide. "Am I to sort letters with my

eyes shut? How could I help seeing they were from Scotland?"

"Don't forget one day I caught you holding a letter of that kid Long Dalton's up to the light," her husband accused.

"I was only tryin' to find out if he got that girl in a fix—the one was waitin' table in Posser's hotel. He didn't. Found out since he can't get nobody in trouble. He's got something wrong with his—"

"Amie!"

"Oh, all right! He's sort of sterile, you might say—and a good thing, or this country would be full of Dalton bastards."

Kelsey burst into laughter. A man never knew what Amie would say next. It was one of the pleasures of being in her company.

"Be quiet," Harry said. "Let Kelsey read his letters in peace, will you?"

"Be quiet yourself. Pass the cream." There was a sound of ripping cloth as she stretched an arm toward the pitcher. "Damn, there goes that seam again! What's the matter with the thread they make nowadays?"

"Haven't noticed you usin' any," Harry replied.

Kelsey turned his attention to the stack of mail before him. He sorted through the catalogues for Hilder, Dalt, Tommy, and the cowpunchers. He went through the ads. Then he came to the two letters. One was from Taraleean, and the other— His hand trembled and his heart was suddenly full. Prim had written at last! Prim had found courage to defy Big Mina. He laughed softly back in his throat. Did Big Mina really think Prim would forget him because an ocean lay between them?

It was only a small page of a letter, and very wrinkled. He smoothed it impatiently, thinking, Not long enough, my lassie —not nearly long enough, and I'll be telling you about that when I write. Then he bent close to the blurred page, his breath quickening.

Words leaped up at him, smudged and shocking. "I may as

well tell you before somebody else does. . . . I'm back from the highlands, and it's as I feared all along. . . . It can't be kept from the harbor folk any longer. . . ." He read on, a sickness growing in the pit of his stomach, a numbness creeping over his mind. And when he finished he put his head down on his arms and made a groaning sound in his throat.

"Kelsey—what is it, boy?" He felt Amie's strong hand gripping his shoulder. "Bad news?"

"Yes," he said stupidly, "bad news, Amie."

She shouted at her husband, "Don't sit there like a bump on a log! Get him a drink! He needs it."

"No, Amie—no, I don't want any whisky."

"Get it anyway, Harry. He can use it."

Moments later Harry thrust the glass into his hand. Kelsey gulped the whisky.

"Cut some wood, Harry," Amie said. "We're out, and it's cold in here."

Harry raised his voice in a bellow. "Andy! Jimmy! Dick!" But his three small sons continued their playing. He shoved back his chair. "For hell's sake! Were they born deaf?" Muttering, he banged the kitchen door behind him.

"Is it a death in the family?" Amie asked.

Kelsey didn't answer. He sat thinking, No, not a death, a life, a life beginning that's my own—a wee one that's mine and Prim's. And me here in this far country, and the lassie with no husband to stand by her side and stop the wagging tongues.

Harry came in and dumped an armload of wood on the floor by the stove. He looked at Kelsey and at his wife. Then he put on an old jacket and went out into the wet day.

"Nothing's ever bad as it seems," Amie said. "Another drink, boy?"

He shook his head, and then, because the whole thing was too big and painful for him to hold in himself, he looked into Amie's kind, plain face and blurted, "The lassie I have in the old country—she's to have a child, and it's mine."

Amie Plunkett lifted her broad shoulders. She put her hand over his and said slowly, "Well, what about it? You love her, don't you? It might be something to fret over if you didn't love her. Listen, boy, lots of good people have started off in the world not marrying because they wanted to but because they had to. Take it easy, Kelsey. You can send for her. You can meet her outside—maybe in Denver—and get married, and who's to ever know you didn't marry her in Soctland?"

He got up and began to pace back and forth. "I've got to get the cow—today," he said, talking to himself. "I've got to have more than wages to take care of Prim and the wee one. And I better write a letter—now."

Amie found paper and pencil. "I'll see it gets to town tomorrow," she promised. "Harry's got to buy groceries. We're down to our last bean."

For a time he just sat at the kitchen table, staring out at the fall landscape. There was a wet and muted sadness over the whole big country, the like of which lay in himself. Then he turned to the paper and began to write quickly and passionately. He loved her, and she surely knew that. She was his own before God, and there was nothing to be ashamed of. He couldn't come for her, not now, but she must come to him. He'd send his check for this month's work—it was all he had —and surely her brothers would let her have enough money to book passage. She must come quickly. . . . He glanced up, a mist before his eyes, wiping quickly at his nose. Again the pencil moved across the paper. "As long as I live, I'll make it up to you, Prim. What a glory I'll have in loving you, in making the world right for our bairn. You are my own, my dearly beloved, my wife."

Early that afternoon, after eating the noon meal with Harry and Amie, he rode on toward Vic Lundgren's ranch. Now that the cattle were all back on the meadows, he would get the cow that Vic was holding for him. He'd take her home to the

Red Hill Ranch. Time enough later to worry about what Tommy or Monte Maguire might say.

He saw no sign of Vic around the corrals and went up the slope to the ranch house. Ellie Lundgren answered his knock. "Oh, come in, Mr. Cameron. Vic, he be here pretty soon. He go to town after wire. Starting to use wire on his fences, he says. When a thing is new Vic, he thinks he wants to try it, but he never likes anything new."

Kelsey followed her into the kitchen and saw the table was set with linen and fine china. But there was only one place, and it was obvious that she had just finished eating. A bottle of wine was on the table with a fragile glass beside it.

"Sit down. I give you a drink of my wine, Mr. Cameron. I eat alone. Never with the hired men. I serve them, but I do not eat. It is my right to eat alone if I want."

She got a small glass from the cupboard, filled it with wine, and handed it to him. "People talk because Ellie Lundgren, she eats alone and has a bedroom to herself. I don't care. You think I have known only a man like Vic Lundgren? Well, I tell you something, Mr. Cameron. I was married before—handsome man who reads good books, takes me to hear the music in New York."

She picked up her empty glass, stroked it, murmuring, "Yes, we eat out at places where there is fine dishes and glasses, like this."

Kelsey shifted uncomfortably, wishing Vic would come in.

She looked up, and her faded eyes were sad. "Oh, he tires fast of me, this fine man in New York. It almost kills me when I have to leave him. But I'm not sorry, Mr. Cameron. He gave me so much! And what have I in this cold, lonesome country? Vic, he is clumsy and work with the cows so long he don't know how to touch a woman—ach, it sickens me! But I give him a daughter, and she is like him exactly; they both care only for cows. It is that way with most men in this place. They forget a woman is not like the cows, not ready for love any time. They think she is like the animals."

He was embarrassed and wanted to get away from her. Her voice grated on his nerves, for it was high and thin and sounded ready to break. He drank his wine in a quick gulp.

"I get along, I live," Ellie went on, pushing back the graying strands of her hair. "I get all the papers from New York. I see what play is there, and the music. Maybe it is foolish that I sit here and pretend Ellie Lundgren sees the play and hears the music."

Vic came in then, to Kelsey's relief. "You come for the cow, eh?" Vic shoved his hat back, glanced at Ellie. "Nice, huh? Eat by yourself without me." There was bitterness in his voice.

Ellie got up and began clearing the table.

"Come on to the corral, Kelsey," Vic said. "I got that cow in. Figured you'd be along this week."

The heavy feeling lifted from Kelsey's heart when he saw the cow. She was beautiful; she was fat from summer range, and her reddish-brown hide had a richness to it, and the white on her was cleanly marked in the right places.

"Best damn cow in the country, yup, yup," Vic said. "You like her, Scotty?"

"Like her! Man, she's glorious!" Kelsey went forward, humming under his breath. The cow lifted her head, blew through her nose, and began swinging her tail from side to side.

"She is wild yet," Vic explained. "She don't want you close, not till she's sure about you being her friend."

"Bonnie Jean," Kelsey said, his eyes shining. "That's what I'll name her. How old is she, Vic?"

"She is yust three-year-old. She is bred as two-year-old and has her calf fine. Don't need no help. I want you to have the best to start. I spend three days pickin' this cow. And in spring she gives you one dandy calf."

"Bonnie Jean," Kelsey said softly. It was the beginning of

his dream, and as he looked at her he saw her multiplied by ten, by hundreds.

"The old woman," Vic said, dropping his tone, "I don' know what to do with her. She is worse than she used to be. Doc Bingham, he say she is in the change. Oh, I can't tell about a woman, Scotty! You think if it is change that works on her, maybe she be better someday, huh?"

Kelsey looked into the rancher's brown, troubled face. "It's a thing they go through," he said, remembering vaguely talk he had heard around the harbor. "She'll get over it."

"Amie—I talk to Amie about it, and Amie say with some womans it is all in their heads, this trouble with the change. Amie say too much has been made over it by old womans tellin' tales to young womans until young womans can't think about it without bein' scared. Amie, she say to her it will be a blessing." And then Vic's face lighted and he laughed. "Amie, it is right for her, yup, yup. No more kids, huh?"

In the damp, quiet afternoon, with the smell of the earth around him, Kelsey drove Bonnie Jean toward the Red Hill Ranch. He wouldn't put her among the other cattle, not yet. He wanted her in the corral, where he could get acquainted with her.

As they moved parallel with the meadow he looked across the brown stubble that had a shine to it after the rain, and he thought of the haying season behind him. It was the time of noisy men in the bunkhouse, the poker chips clanking at night, and the time of the early beautiful mornings when a man felt good and as if he had been born all over again and no weariness or sadness in him. It was the time of the hot noons, the smell of hay dust thick to the nose and the green-headed horseflies plaguing the horses, and the stink of sweat on the men when they stopped to eat the hot noon meal Hilder brought to the field in the lumber wagon. And there were the afternoons—the cooling breeze dropping over the hogback, and the shadows long on the mountains, and the sound of the mowing machines far down the meadow like the purring of big cats. And the going home at last, riding in from the field in the evening light that took the sharpness off everything as it rounded the hills and the peaks, filling the hollows with dusk —home, and the supper waiting, and a man gulping the food and going to bed, and quiet at last with the cool night wind playing over him in a silver caressing that was like the touch of a loved one.

Now the cattle were on the land that had once been green, and the green was heaped in browning stacks for winter, and the poles of the stackyards were dark from the rain. Quiet was over everything—a waiting quiet, as though the earth were caught between summer and winter.

"It's like myself," he said aloud. For the earth had aged from spring to autumn, and surely he had aged. Ah, yes! Sometimes, he thought, I believed I had never been a lad, but now I know that I was. It was this morning that those days were gone forever and I was suddenly a man, with a woman and child to think of. How quickly it comes upon us, then!

Dusk was dropping over the hogback when he came to the corral. He put the cow into it and stood there, so enraptured at the sight of her that he fell into dreaming again.

The voice cut sharply through his thoughts. "Is that a Christly camel I see in this corral?"

He turned and saw Monte Maguire come through the gate, walking with the long free stride of a man. The silvery light of her pale hair stood out in the gathering dusk. She paused beside him, almost as tall as himself. "Where'd she come from?"

"Vic Lundgren's."

"What's she doin' in my corral?"

"She's mine."

"Oh, is that so? You figure she's better than Two-Bar stuff?"

"No, Mrs. Maguire. But she's almost as good."

"Almost?"

"Well, you might have a few better—not many, though."

There was a long silence, and then Monte Maguire said, "And what did you figure on doin' with her?"

He put his hand on the corral fence to steady himself. The wood felt rough and strong and cool-wet from the rain. He thought of Prim and the child that was his, the heart of it beating there in Prim's body. "Mrs. Maguire," he said, forcing his voice to be steady, "I have to make a start in the cattle business. Wages aren't enough. I thought you might agree to cut some of my wages so I could run a few cows. I'd make more that way. And today—today I found out I had to make more than just a wage."

"Why?" The word was frosty. It would have withered a strong man.

Her still, composed face was suddenly sharply clear to him there in the few feet of dusk that separated them. And he knew that she was not a woman a man lied to. He told her the truth then. And when he had finished there was such an ache in his heart he could no longer face her. He walked a few steps away and stood by himself in the corral with the wet-manure smell rising around him.

Beyond the corral, on the side of the hogback, he could see still the muted scarlet of the aspens, and he was touched with sadness. The night was coming down, night that blotted away everything, all the color and shifting light of day. Only the mind and heart kept alive what was gone. The aspen fire didn't die with the darkness, not as long as he was there to remember. It was in him, Kelsey Cameron, that the world lived and died. And when he was gone there would be the child that was his and Prim's—the child to speak his name when that name was no more. That child would remember him through its whole life, even as he would remember Taraleean in the silence of himself long after she had gone.

Would this strange woman never speak? Why must he stand here waiting for her temper, for the curt tongue that would tell him he must move on and find another job? And then her voice was there, with a softness in it that had been unknown to him before this moment, and her fingers were hard and strong on his arm, giving him a little impatient shake. "A hell of a man you are, going to Vic Lundgren instead of to me if you needed help. And as for cattle, Vic's not dry behind the ears yet when it comes to learnin' cow business. Keep your cow. Run her here, and I'll make the cut in your wages. As soon as you have enough money, buy another cow. But get the rest of 'em from me—you hear?"

Weakness swept over him, making his knees tremble. He tried to thank her, but the words wouldn't come out through the tightness in his throat.

"A tough break doesn't hurt a man," she said. "Sometimes it makes him what he is. I've had 'em. I know. And I can look the whole damn world in the face and tell it to go to hell and never miss it." Her hand came away from his arm, and he heard the sharp catch of her breath.

"I'll make this up to you, Mrs. Maguire. I'll— Some way I'll show you how much I—"

"There's nothin' you have to prove to me, Kelsey. And I'm not giving you anything, either. You'll earn what you get. Better yank the saddle off your horse and come to supper. That cow'll keep till mornin'. She won't look any different come daylight."

After he had unsaddled the horse they walked to the house together. Hilder was dishing up supper. Tommy sat on the bottom step of the stairway, and Long Dalton lounged in the doorway to the living room. Three cowpunchers and Jake were sitting at the table, waiting for food.

"Evenin', Monte, Kelsey," Jake said.

Monte nodded and went to wash her hands. She thrust a loose strand of the blond hair into the knot on top of her head. When she sat down at the head of the table the others moved to pull up chairs.

"Ready to start weanin', Jake?" she asked.

" 'Bout the end of next week, I figure."

"Well, keep 'em in till the bawlin' stops inside the corral and out. Keep 'em shut up until the cows stop pacin' the fence and the calves get hungry enough to eat grass."

"Think I need to be told that?" The boss puncher grinned at her.

She smiled. "Just makin' talk—like a woman, I guess." She turned to Tommy and added casually, "Kelsey's brought in a cow he got from Vic Lundgren. He's gonna run a little stuff here. I'll handle his wages so you won't have to figure how much to take out."

The men all looked at Kelsey. Long Dalton was smiling, and there was a glint of interest in Jake's mild eyes. Silence grew heavy in the kitchen. Tommy shifted in his chair. His sharp glance moved around to Monte and back to Kelsey. "So you got in cow business, eh? What brand you got?"

"KC—Kelsey Cameron."

"That so? When'd you tend to that?"

"This summer—wrote to the brand office in Denver."

Tommy gave a short laugh. "And kept it all to yourself, eh? Work fast, don't you?"

Monte Maguire reached halfway across the table to spear a biscuit with her fork. "Think we ought to ship the culls next week when we get through weanin'. Another thing, Jake—how's the count? Miss any when you got 'em back on the meadows?"

"Well, I figure we're short about forty head, Monte."

"Forty! Where the hell are they?"

"Pocketed in the pinnacles somewhere."

"Then you damn well better roust 'em out before a big snow comes and shuts 'em off in some canyon."

"I'm goin' to, Monte. Give me time. I already spoke to Jediah about keepin' an eye out for 'em when he's stringin' his traps."

"Well, that's good. Jediah'll find a stray cow if she's any-where in that whole west range. And now he's through watchin' the ditch for me he's got nothin' to do but run the hills like an Indian. Guess he is part Indian, at that."

"He claims to be," Dalt said. "He told me his grandpappy got next to a squaw one cold night in the Wind River Moun-tains of Wyoming."

"If the winters there take after our winters, can't say I blame him," Monte said.

The men laughed and began pushing the big bowl of stewed prunes around the table so each man could spoon a few into his sauce dish. "No cake?" Jake asked.

"I made one," Hilder said, scowling, "but the damn thing miscarried. I look, and she is puffed up fine, and I look again, and she's flat. It's them damn white eggs. I never could make a cake with white eggs. Jesus Christ, why don't we get more chickens that lay brown eggs?"

Long Dalton snickered and winked at Monte. She said, "Why don't you try duck eggs, Hilder?"

"I ain't cookin' with no ducks' eggs, Miz Maguire. And I ain't bakin' with none of them white eggs any more. Brown eggs, or I am striked, you hear?"

Kelsey pushed back his chair. He hurried to the corral and satisfied himself that Bonnie Jean was there. He could hear her soft breathing as he stood near her in the starlight. He could see the dark shape of her in the corner of the corral. He stared at her until his eyes ached and the cold wind whipping down off the hogback made his teeth chatter.

When he went back to the house Monte Maguire had gone to bed in one of the downstairs bedrooms. Hilder was sitting at the kitchen table, reading the local paper. Tommy stood be-fore the stove, a cup of warmed-over coffee in his hand.

"Smart as hell, ain't you?" Tommy said.

"I don't know what you mean, Tommy."

"Suckin' in with the boss behind my back!"

"You leave Mrs. Maguire's name out of this. And I didn't say anything to her about the cow until tonight, when I got back from Vic's. Why are you sore at me, Tommy? I didn't ask anything of you—or take anything from you."

"And by God you better not! I'm not playin' nursemaid to your cow or tellin' the punchers to look after her. I'm paid to see to the Two-Bar stuff. Another thing—don't think you're set up with Monte Maguire. She'll kick your butt off the place any time she takes a notion. Let that sink into your fat head, kiddo!" Tommy turned, plunked the empty cup down on the table, and walked out.

Hilder glanced up from the paper. "You do yust fine, Kelsey. Don't pay no heed to Tommy. He is always one sorehead about somethin'. Only reason I stay here or Dalt stays here is we like workin' for Monte. Monte, she maybe give no favors to most men who work for her, but she is fair and square, and that's good enough for me. Tommy, he get mean as hell sometimes, but we yust act like we don't notice it. He is good enough man, and Monte knows that. He sees things run in top shape on the ranch and don't drink too much like some hired men."

Kelsey went up the narrow wooden stairway to his bedroom. The wind rose with a mournful wailing around the corners of the house. Be snowing by morning, he thought. He got into bed and pulled the rough blankets close around him. He thought of Monte Maguire there in the room below him, feeling again the bigness of her beside him in the corral, hearing again the surprising softness that had been in her voice for a moment. What would it be like for a man to hold a woman like that in his arms? How would it be to feel that strength against you and the blood beating up warm in answer to a man's need?

He turned impatiently, thrusting his face into the pillow that had the heavy man-scent of himself. God forgive me! It's of Prim I should be thinking—Prim, the finest lass that ever walked the village streets, and now the mark of shame on her and me the cause of it. Ah, the cruelty of it—Prim and the old women staring at her and the sly words on their lips.

But Prim would be free of it soon. Surely she would come to him at once. Even Big Mina wouldn't try to hold her now, not when a child was coming, a child to be born without a name. A confusion of emotions broke over him—sorrow, anxiety, protectiveness toward Prim, wonder at the thought of his child. A son to carry his name? Or a lassie? Let it be a lad, he prayed, closing his eyes and feeling the healing cold of the night wind on his hot eyelids. The world was easier for a lad.

He slept at last and dreamed of Monte Maguire. He dreamed of loving her in the naked sunlight in the corral, and in the midst of his loving he knew Tommy and the men watched him, but he could not stop himself. And behind their faces he heard Prim's weeping, a sound that was Prim but had no body or face to hide behind. He wakened wet with sweat and shaking. He got out of bed and stumbled to the window and threw it open wider. Wind-driven snow swept in on him, cold and clean.

CHAPTER VII

The letter lay before him in the December morning that was lighted by the glow from the kerosene lamp. Downstairs Hilder was cooking breakfast, and the smell of frying steak came up to the bedroom. Soon, when breakfast was over, he would go out to feed the cattle with Dalt. But now, in this little time before going to work, he would read the letter again.

No, Prim had written, she would not come to him. Big Mina was very sick. A doctor came to the house every day now, and Big Mina was in bed all the time. If he wanted her, Prim, and the child that was his, he must come back to the old country. Her brothers would give him work in the fishing boat. They had promised her that. Her father had come home from Africa and was drinking every night in the tavern, and it was a terrible time for all of them, with the herring-fishing slack and herself not able to be seen on the streets now that she was so big with the coming child.

He turned the letter over, and more words were waiting for him: "Many's the time folk come to this house to ask after my mither's health and I run from them and hide myself under the stairway and wish to be dead and folk never to see my face again. . . ."

Oh, my God! he thought, putting his head in his big work-roughened hands. Have I brought her to this? But then remorse gave way to anger. Big Mina was not likely to die. Big Mina had taken to her bed to hold Prim by her side. Even the

81

child's future didn't matter to Big Mina, selfish bitch that she was!

He heard the jangle of the breakfast gong. He hid the letter under the hay in his bunk and went down to eat. There was a surly mood on the men this morning. They'd had their fill of heavy snows and cold.

"You get your team harnessed before breakfast?" Tommy asked shortly. "Or can't you get outta your bed in the mornin'?"

Dalt spoke then. "I put the harness on the team before I did the milkin'."

"What are you?" Tommy asked. "His nursemaid?"

"Between me and Kelsey, the harnessin', ain't it?"

Hilder shoved a plate of pancakes toward Tommy. "Eat. Keep your mouth full and you don't spout off so much. What difference who puts harness on a horse or not? Jesus Christ, everybody is touchy around this place."

The lamp on the table flickered. Wind roared down the chimney. Dalt looked at the window. "It's blowin' so a man can't see his hand in front of his face. Better just open a stackyard and let the cattle get what they can."

"Like hell," Tommy said. "I don't want no hay tromped into the snow. We might need it before spring. You feed."

Dalt shrugged. "So-so with me, if a man can keep it on the hayrack. Come on, Kelsey."

Kelsey buckled on overshoes, pulled the thick Scotch cap over his ears, and fastened the heavy coat. Tommy watched him warm the tattered mittens over the stove. "You tryin' to freeze your hands off? So damned anxious to hang onto your money you won't buy a pair of decent mittens? Christ, I hate to see you sittin' here eatin' and blood runnin' outta your hands!"

"You take my mittens, Kelsey," Hilder said. "I don't use them much. They almost like brand-new."

"No, Hilder. I—" He had started to say he had a reason for saving every dime.

"You ready, buddy?" Dalt asked.

"I keep the coffee on the stove," Hilder said. "Man needs hot coffee any time he comes in when the weather she is like now."

They went into the morning that was still dark and filled with the roar of wind. Snow stung Kelsey's face, like a million needles pricking his skin. Snow hissed at the lantern Dalt carried. Pale light was coming in the east as they drove down the meadow, the lines hooked over the front of the rack, their backs humped against the wind.

"A man's crazy," Dalt muttered. "No country's worth it. This is my last winter." Wind sucked the words from his mouth.

They came to the stackyard and opened it, floundering in the snow, laying aside the heavy poles so they could drive close to the stack and load the rack. They climbed on the stack and began forking hay. It was hard work, but even so they couldn't keep warm. From time to time they stopped, crossed their arms, and beat their mittened hands, *slap-slap,* against their shoulders. Kelsey's stomach curled with sickness, for severe cold always made him feel like vomiting. Sometimes the world around him turned purple instead of white, and then he'd hang his head down and finally thrust his face into the hay. There was a fragrance there in the heart of the stack where green lay under the brown topping, a faint fragrance of summer. It tortured the heart with longing; it made it harder than ever to straighten and look into the driving snow. The earth was small, mornings like this, for it had no horizons. It was like a white, smoking cave from which there was no escape.

They got out five loads of hay, stringing it along the feed trail that was hard-packed from the hoofs of the cattle. "Enough!" Dalt coughed and gasped for breath.

Kelsey blinked, staring at him. "Your nose, Dalt—it's turning white!"

Dalt jumped off the rack, scooped up a handful of snow,

and rubbed it against his nose. "Throw on a little jag for the barn and let's go! To hell with freezin' to death!"

They put on a light load, closed the stackyard, and burrowed down in the hay as the team moved toward the barn. Slowly warmth began to seep back into Kelsey, but his head ached from the cold. He lay quietly, grateful for the shelter. He began to compose another letter to Prim, shaping it in his mind. He must tell her he couldn't come back to Scotland now, not when the debt to Big Mina wasn't completely paid off, not when he'd have to borrow more money to make the trip. He tried to think of ways to help her understand that there was nothing to do but come to him, even if she had to wait until after the baby was born.

They unloaded the hay in the barn after scattering some in the corral for a few sick calves that couldn't be on the feed ground. "Got to break the ice in the watering trough again," Dalt said.

Kelsey scarcely heard him. He was still writing to Prim, telling her about Bonnie Jean and how the cow would have a calf in the spring, and how everything was going to be fine if Prim would only come to him.

That afternoon, when he put the letter in an envelope, he enclosed ten dollars, a Christmas gift. Then, though the wind was still blowing, he saddled a horse, took the old rifle Jediah Walsh had given him, and went out to hunt coyotes, riding the lee side of the hogback.

Toward evening the wind dropped and he came across two coyotes chewing on a carcass at the far end of the meadow. He got off, pulled the mittens from his hands, propped his elbows in the snow, and, with his breath steaming before him as his mouth hung open, he drew a bead and fired. One of the coyotes jumped in the air, its tail twisting, and then crumpled down on the snow. The other coyote ran, streaking from the meadow toward the flats. Kelsey fired again and again, but the second coyote went free. Jediah would have known what was wrong with his shooting. Maybe he hadn't led the coyote far enough.

He got slowly to his feet, walked to the horse, which had sidled off fifty yards and was trailing the bridle reins. He thrust the gun in the scabbard. He'd traded Jake a sweater Taraleean had knitted him for that scabbard. When he rode up to the coyote he saw its tongue hanging out. The coyote made little bucking jerks, the blood pumping from its mouth with every jerk. Its urine stained the snow yellow.

He got off the horse and prodded the coyote with the toe of his overshoe. The eyes were glazing over. The movement in the body was slower now, the jerks coming farther apart. After a while he turned it over, and it lay limp in the snow. He picked it up and tied it behind the saddle while the horse looked back at him and blew through its nostrils. Ten or fifteen dollars, he thought. Money to pay on his debt.

A sense of isolation settled over him. It seemed he had always been here, plodding up the snow-packed trail toward the ranch house, alone and lonely in his heart.

He took the coyote to the house and began skinning it out in the corner of the kitchen while Dalt and Tommy looked on. "The damn fleas are jumpin' on everything," Tommy complained, scratching himself.

"The sooner a man skins 'em the less they stink," Dalt said.

"How'd you know?" Tommy demanded. "You never shot any."

"Jediah said so, and Jediah knows."

"That's right enough. That old bugger knows everything. Honest to God, Dalt, sometimes I think Jediah's got coyote in him. He smells things out like a damn animal."

Kelsey got a stretcher from the woodshed and pulled the coyote skin over it. He tacked it tight, took it back to the shed, and set it against the wall. Then he went in and washed the blood from his hands. He felt the fleas on him and began to strip off his clothes, letting them fall to the kitchen floor.

"You want fleas in the soup for supper?" Hilder shouted. "You get outside when you shake them fleas off yourself."

"All right, Hilder." He gathered the clothes and went out to the cold woodshed and shook them hard before he put them back on.

At the supper table Hilder said, "Y'know we got an invite for Christmas dinner—all of us?"

"Where?" Kelsey looked up from his eating.

"Amie's. Amie Plunkett, she say last time I pick up the mail, she say, 'What you boys doin' for Christmas dinner?' And I say, 'Well, Amie, I put on a big roast like usual.' Then she shake her head, that good woman, and say, 'Christmas we have lots of roast chicken, and you boys all come help us eat.' Now, what we take her for present, eh?"

"Well," Tommy said, "I was figurin' on goin' to town."

"There's candy at Faun's," Hilder said. "Only be sure he don't give you some he spills coal oil on like he did me once."

"Candy!" Dalt said. "That's nothin' for a Christmas present for a woman. Women like things like—well, underwear and nightgowns."

Hilder and Tommy looked at him. "How do I know what size she'd wear?" Tommy said.

"You try 'em on," Dalt said. "I'd say your butt is about as big as hers."

"I say it ain't," Hilder said. "I say she is maybe two inches wider."

"Shucks," Kelsey said, laughing, "you ought to buy her some jewelry. Faun's got a pendant with a blue stone in it—if it's not sold. Maybe something like that—"

"Good!" Hilder nodded. "Better taste than pants or nightgowns. You buy it, Tommy. We all ship in on the cost. And another thing, you bring some good whisky. We all get happy at Amie's, and I sing like I used to in the old country."

"If you do it'll curdle the gravy," Tommy said. "Hell, you can't sing."

"Is that so? In the old country I have brudder who plays
organ. Ya, I do. You think my people yust dumb farmers?
Not. This brudder is smart and make good music. When I am
young I sing with him while he is playin'. I sing in the church
choir. I sing tanner."

"Tinner!" Tommy snickered.

"Tanner, damn you! I sing like birds. When I get that
whisky I am singin' for Amie."

"All right. I'll get the whisky."

"We ship in payin' for that, too. And you don't forget to
pay your share, Tommy Cameron."

"Me? I'm goin' after the stuff. I get a commission, don't
I?"

"Commission, balls!"

Tommy laughed. "All right. It's settled, then. You want
to sit in on our poker game tonight, Kelsey?"

"No, not tonight." Kelsey got up quickly and went to his
bedroom. He wanted to play. He wanted to play so badly it
was like a thirst in him. And the nights were so long. The
darkness lasted and lasted. And what was there to do? Nothing. There was nothing but to play poker, and that he
couldn't do. He wouldn't let himself, not now, not when he
had to have money.

He paced restlessly back and forth in the narrow room. If
I could shoot in the dark, he thought, I'd hunt coyotes. It
would be better riding with a rifle than shut up here in this
house. Then he saw the three books on the box at the end
of the room: his father's Bible, a copy of Burns's poems
Taraleean had sent him, and the big book Tommy had let
him bring upstairs—*The Diseases of Cattle*. He read from
all three, but they didn't still his restlessness. His mind wandered from the printed pages to the window. Frost lay across
it, so thick he could scrape it off with his thumbnail. In a
little while now this year would be ended, and a man could
look forward to spring. Spring . . .

*   *

It was in early February that the news of the child came.
Kelsey returned from feeding cattle at dark, for the wind had
blown too hard to get any work done in the morning. When
he and Dalt got to the house lights were already burning and
Hilder had built up the fire for cooking supper. A pile of mail
lay on the kitchen table. Tommy sat by the stove, reading
the paper.

Kelsey picked up his letters, three of them; two of them
were from Taraleean and Prim. He saw the name in the corner of the third letter and was afraid. The Reverend Angus
McCullough. Wasn't a minister often the one who passed on
bad news?

Quickly he tore open the letter and read: ". . . and I
have baptized your child, Kelsey, though some are not
pleased that I have. And I saw to it that Prim had no need to
go before the church board and make a confession of her sin
and have them throwing questions at her like a fistful of
stones. . . . I have baptized your child 'Heather.' It is my
wish that you and Prim may soon be together. . . . Your
daughter is a beautiful child and has the best of both of you
in her. . . ."

Mingled pain and wonder filled his heart. Heather, his
daughter! He looked around the ugly kitchen, at Hilder and
Tommy and Dalt. He said, having a need to share the news,
"A lassie—I've a wee lassie in the old country. They've
named her Heather."

And then such a mist came over his eyes that he brought
his big hand up and wiped it away, half laughing and saying,
"It stirs a man, it does. It makes him feel something he never
felt before." The letter shook in his hand. "This, it's from
the minister, and he—he baptized her, he gave my lassie a
name, before God and the whole village. May God bless the
Reverend Angus McCullough! A man, a prince of a man!"

And he stood with his head thrown back and his face filled with pride and sadness and glory.

It was Hilder who broke the silence that drew out in the dull and grease-stained kitchen. "We drink, then," he said softly. "We drink a blessing to Kelsey's little daughter. We drink to her and to her mudder. Get the bottle, Dalt. Is hidden in the bunkhouse in my suitcase—under the bed you find it. It is some I have left from Christmas. This is more Christmas. Get that bottle quick, Dalt. This time we kill him, leave nothing."

It was a strange and wild night for all of them. When Hilder's bottle was empty Dalt produced one. And when that was gone Tommy went into his room and brought out a bottle. They forgot about eating. They drank and talked. Kelsey read his mother's letter aloud and said, "See what a woman she is! See the love of her and the music of her!"

Prim's letter he did not read aloud but only to himself while Hilder got very drunk and sang in Swedish. It was a very short letter from Prim. "I wanted to die—but now I want to live. I have seen my wee lassie's face and it has changed my life. I can bear anything now."

After a while Tommy quoted Burns, and Kelsey quoted Burns, and Dalt recited a smutty ballad about a woman who peddled her butt on the Big Goose Range. Then Kelsey stood up and drank to each of them and told them they were the finest men he knew—God had made no finer on the face of the whole bloody earth. He sang a song of the tattie howkers that Taraleean had taught him. When he had finished this singing he stood up and raised his right hand and swore to God he would give his child, Heather, the best life a lassie could have. After this he sat down with the tears pouring over his cheeks, drank more whisky, and said over and over, "It's life—my God, it's life! Will there ever be another night like this? Drink up, Hilder! Drink up, Tommy, man! Drink up, Dalt!"

They were up until dawn broke, and then Hilder went to sleep on the kitchen floor. Tommy got sick and vomited on the kitchen table. Long Dalton helped Kelsey up the stairway and into bed and got in with him, holding the rough red head against his shoulder as he might have held the head of a woman and saying softly, "It's all right, buddy. You're damned right, it's all right. We'll make it that way, you and me."

They slept into the middle of the afternoon, when Tommy wakened first, soaked his aching head in a bucket of cold water, and then bawled at the top of his lungs, "Get the lead out! There's cattle to feed!"

CHAPTER VIII

Four years had brought some changes, Kelsey Cameron thought, riding down from the mountain's shoulder with Monte Maguire and Jediah Walsh. He had got a start in the cattle business; he had cows and calves of his own. But the situation with Prim remained the same. Month after month, as the seasons turned and one year drifted into another, he had kept up the patient, pleading correspondence with her, but she had not come to him. Always her answers were the same—beseeching him to come home, filling pages with talk of Heather's growing, and telling Kelsey how much she needed and loved him.

He had driven himself almost beyond endurance, working as one obsessed to pay off his debt and buy cattle. Sometimes a terrible desperation took hold of him, and he told himself that tomorrow he would sell his cattle, quit his job, and go to Scotland. Then a hot pride would rise in him, and he'd vow never to face Big Mina without money in his pockets to care for his child and Prim. And always, while these feelings mixed and struggled in him, there was work to be done, his cattle to worry over, and the need to acquire more cows.

Now, in the sundown of the late fall day, he sat easily in the saddle, a bigger and tougher man than he had been during his first year in the Park. For a week they had been searching for lost cattle, but hadn't found them. Up in the country of the Seven Lakes they had seen only signs of cattle, their marks on the trails and on the grass.

"It beats all hell where they've drifted to," Monte said as they came to a wide opening in the timber and rode three abreast.

"Maybe into Wyoming," Jediah said. "Anyhow, we sure had a nice trip." And he turned to jerk the rope on the pack horse that trailed behind them, loaded with bedding, food, and cooking equipment.

Kelsey lapsed into dreaming over the days just past, days in the pale autumn sunlight in a country where no other human being crossed their path. He thought of the mountain springs where the clear icy water bubbled, and where the ground around them was covered with the chalk of blue grouse until a man could say it looked like a chicken yard.

There was the time they had rested on a slope, looking across a steep canyon to the side of a peak where mountain sheep were playing. Through Monte's heavy fieldglasses he had watched the sheep; their thin legs were graceful above the neat dark hoofs. Every motion they made was light and easy, as though their hoofs contained springs that allowed them an effortless bounding into the air. And while they jostled and jumped around one another, tossing their rumps to left and right, a ram had come to stand on the canyon's rim, easy there on the edge of space, the sunlight shining on his great curving horns. For a time he stood looking over the world—magnificent, self-contained, beautiful in his isolation.

And there were the evenings by the campfire, the simple meal of beans and bacon, bread and coffee finished. Then it was as though he sat with Monte and Jediah in a special time and place. At times they talked, and as often they were silent. Jediah and Monte seemed to sense when a man wanted the silence kept, when one small word would have been an intrusion. And because of this he felt closer to them than ever before and wished for nothing to happen that might spoil this time.

It was on such an evening, when they sat listening to the play of wind along the pine branches, smelling the smoke of the fire, that Kelsey said, "Where else could a man live as he lives here? Where else could he feel so small and yet that so much is expected of him?"

Jediah answered, "The whole of the Park, son, gives a man that feeling. In a way, the Park's a sort of symbol of the whole country—so free, so big, yet askin' that a man give the best that's in him to live up to it."

Kelsey saw the firelight on Monte's face and the way she held her head to the side, listening carefully, her eyes thoughtful. In the firelight there was a softness about her that a man didn't see during the day; after sundown she became a woman.

Now he came from the past into the present as Jediah pulled up and said to Monte, "You want a buckskin to take in with us? This is as good a deer crossing as any."

"Sure." She nodded. "Fresh venison steak would taste fine."

They had come out of the timber, and a sagebrush-covered park lay before them. They rode to the fringe of pines and aspen on one side of the park, tied their horses back in the timber, and went to sit behind a big willow bush, their rifles ready.

"Little more red be runnin' in the west before they drift into the clearing," Jediah said, squinting at the salmon-colored streaks in the sky. He looked around him and added, "It ain't gonna be such a bad winter."

"How can you know?" Kelsey asked, smiling.

"Man always knows come August and September, when the field mice and the beaver start showin' their signs. Deer can tell too. No bunches high-tailin' it over the hills to the lower country in Wyoming. Winter's gonna come late this year—and not too hard."

A grayness hung in the shadowy corners of the park, and dusk was sifting among the trees. They sat quietly, waiting for the gray shapes of the deer to draw away from the dark fringe of pines and the pale trunks of the aspen.

Jediah will see them first, Kelsey thought. Jediah always saw the deer first, and would lift his hand in a small, unhurried motion. Then any other man had to look and look, finally to make out the bucks and does standing by the smudge of purplish willows.

A bluejay scolded, back in the timber. Jediah's head turned. "Somethin' troublin' him?" he murmured. Again there was silence and the almost imperceptible darkening of shadows. Red was spreading in the sky, creeping into the flat gray strips of cloud. A squirrel chattered.

"Not deer causin' that," Jediah whispered. "He's used to 'em."

There was the quick brittle sound of breaking brush, and a fawn bounded into the clearing, running wildly through the sage. Before Kelsey had time to move or think, a coyote streaked after the fawn, gray and fast and skimming the sagebrush. The fawn wheeled sharply, gave a terrified bleat, and raced again for the protection of the timber.

A high, shrill squeal came from the darkening pines. There was more crackling of brush, and then the pitiful broken cry of an animal in pain; a brief pause, and a weakened, hoarse sound that broke off. Silence claimed the earth and sky.

Kelsey wet his lips, shaken, seeing the thing that had happened all too clearly; the panting, racing fawn and the coyote closing in on it, making the quick slash at flank and shoulder, and then the fawn staggering as the coyote lunged for the throat, the knifelike teeth sinking deep and wrenching back to stop forever the feeble cry, and the warm red blood pouring onto the earth to darken and cool.

Monte Maguire got to her feet and stood motionless, staring at the timber where fawn and coyote had vanished. The long moments drew out, and then the coyote appeared, trotting easily now.

Her rifle came up. The coyote leaped as though it tried to climb the air, and crumpled down, its front legs folding under it. As it fell, Monte Maguire shot again, and the coyote jerked and a tuft of fur flew from it. She walked quickly toward it, and when she was close she began to shoot, throwing bullet after bullet into the mangled body. Kelsey ran to her and jerked the gun from her hands. He dropped the rifle and grabbed her shoulders, shaking her. "Monte! Are you crazy? He's dead."

Her eyes were angry and brilliant. Her full lips drew back. "Damn him! Damn him!"

He felt the firmness of her flesh under his fingers, and in that moment his legs trembled and his chest was tight. Her breath was warm and quick against his face, her mouth half open, and the big breasts rising and falling under the tight woolen shirt. The strange purplish-red light of after sundown fell over them, caught in her hair and on her skin.

Jediah's voice came, strange and startling. "You didn't have to blow him all to pieces, Monte."

Kelsey stepped away from her, and he saw her hands move up to cover the places where his fingers had been. Slowly she turned her head to face Jediah. "I'm glad I did it!"

"Funny thing," Jediah said, "you come here to kill and you take it out on an animal for doing the same thing."

"It was cruel," she said. "There's ways of killing—some decent and some not."

"Nature's cruel sometimes," Jediah said gently. "We won't get a buckskin tonight. That shootin' has scattered 'em all over these hills. Might as well go home."

They rode into the gathering dusk, and after a while the owls began to hoot out of the darkness. Kelsey looked into the chilling night and thought, When summer comes I'll go for Prim and my lassie. I've waited too long now. No matter what happens, I've got to go.

CHAPTER IX

$\backsim \quad \backsim \quad \backsim \quad \backsim \quad \backsim \quad \backsim \quad \backsim$

No one in Big Mina's house had slept much but Heather, the child. Now, on the morning of Kelsey Cameron's homecoming, Prim Munro stood before the bay windows with her hands pressed over her ears. Would the noise of her mother never stop? Could she stand for another minute the tirade of Big Mina's words, beating against her? Months of it had gone on, ever since Kelsey had written that he was coming back.

Prim remembered the day Kelsey's letter had come, and how she had taken it, as always, down to the shore, where she could be alone with his words. That day the summer sea was calm, the tide out, and the reek of seaweed in the air. She smoothed the folds in the page, her heart pounding, trying to read at a glance all his pencil-smudged words. And then the wonderful meaning of one line stood out; that sentence was large and clear and alone. *"I am coming for you and the lassie."*

Tears began to run down her face. She read the words again and again. She looked at the sea and the sky and went back to the letter. She put her hand on the green brae and pulled up grass and held it hard. She read the letter once more. Then she got up and walked miles along the shore, her face lifted to the sun, sometimes weeping and sometimes laughing. What a strange sound there was to laughter! And at last, tired, she stood with her back to the cool, hard surface of a rock and watched the tide come in with a slow murmuring that was like plaintive music. And she thought, Och aye, what kind of lassie am I to love a man so much his words can mean life or death to me? And always it's been that way, for longer than I can call to mind. But the torture of it—oh, the torture of loving and never knowing for sure you're loved as much in return! And then she saw that the tide had covered the offshore rocks and was creeping over the sand to her feet. If love could come to me like that, smoothing over all the doubt . . .

That night she held Heather in her arms, whispering as she kissed the sleepy child, "Kelsey's coming back to us. Your father's coming at last!" And when Heather slept Prim brushed her own long black hair to shining and arranged it first one way and then another on top of her head. Would this style or that suit Kelsey Cameron? She washed her fine clear skin and lightly massaged above and below her wide green eyes. And at last she stood naked before the mirror, staring at her body, seeing with relief that her waist was still small, that her stomach was flat with no scars from the stretching of the skin while she had carried Heather, and that her breasts were firm and smooth and beautiful. I am the same as when he left me, she thought, and surely that will please him. Then her eyes went back to the studying of her face. Hadn't it changed? Wasn't there a sadness on it? And she tried a stiff smile, quickly telling herself that she had a more interesting face now. Who wants to look like a lass instead of a woman? It's a woman Kelsey will expect to hold in his arms.

And what would Kelsey be like? Had the faraway country changed him?

Big Mina's words rose, strident and emphatic, pushing away all memory of the day the letter had come. "If you go with him to that place, you've no stiffness in you. Any time I'd lower myself to take a man who forgot me for years—for years, mind you!"

Prim whirled to face her mother. Her eyes were swollen from weeping, and her face was gray from lack of sleep. "The years have nothing to do with it, so they haven't. He loves me." She said this with a conviction she didn't really feel; back in her mind was the nagging doubt that Big Mina might be right, for Big Mina had said over and over that Kelsey Cameron wanted only Heather—"And to do his duty by going through a marriage ceremony," she'd added scornfully.

"God knows what a daftness is in you," Big Mina said, her puffy hands gripping the cane, tapping it impatiently on the floor.

For a startling, clear moment Prim saw her mother objectively—a big feather pillow of a woman, all bulges and softness, settled in the sunken chair where she always sat. Only Big Mina's eyes were hard, small and black and set deep in the purplish wrinkled face with the big hairy mole on the upper lip.

"You poor fool." Big Mina looked at her pityingly. "Does it make you happy to throw yourself at a man who doesn't want you at all?"

"Stop it! Stop it!" Prim began to cry. "Is it so wrong I love him? Is that daftness?"

"It is when he'll never feel the same about you, when he hates your mither, when his damned Cameron pride kept him from coming back to work the fishing with my sons. No, there's no love for you in Kelsey Cameron. There's only his pride and wanting to take the wee lassie."

Prim went to Heather, who was playing on the floor, stooped and gathered her into her arms, holding her close. "My lassie!" And a rush of tenderness filled her as she remembered the long years of waiting for Kelsey, when every day she had given her love and attention to the child. Then her mind leaped forward, scurrying frantically for a good strong thought to cling to. Everything will work out, she told herself; everything will be wonderful when I'm with Kelsey.

If he'd only stay here, she thought, putting the child down and beginning to move nervously around the room. Scotland's my home, our home. I don't want to leave it. And my mither—

Oh, the confusion of it! Hadn't some of the village said that she, Prim, was weak and had no strength because she didn't leave her mother and go to Kelsey? But it was just as true that others had shared Big Mina's point of view that Kelsey should come back to Scotland and stay, because surely Big Mina was a cripple—and my fault, Prim concluded; there's no doubt of that.

Big Mina's voice cut into her thinking. "Kelsey Cameron just as well marry any loose lass; it would mean as much to him."

For this Prim had no answer. She could only stand shaken, a cold knot forming in the pit of her stomach. And then the fear was on her, fear that in Kelsey's arms would never again be the love she had known that night on the shore. "No, no," she cried, "I won't think that! I won't ever think it." And her mind made a wild attempt to conjure up a picture of the future with Kelsey.

*   *

To Heather it was a morning of weeping and slamming of doors. And Big Mina's voice was loud even to the little girl, with whom she had always been gentle and soft-spoken. It was as though the house had been entered by some unseen and evil thing. Even the sea was disturbed, roaring over the rocks at the harbor mouth. The wind carried spray to the windows, and it ran like tears down the glass.

Heather was frightened and fled upstairs and crawled under the bed. It was there, with a fuzz of lint on her cheek, that the Reverend Angus McCullough found her and coaxed her out to sit on his knee, giving her a piece of pink candy with a sharp taste to it.

They sat in a chair by the bedroom window, where they could see the storm-tossed water and the village streets. The minister's face was pointed, like the face of a mouse, his skin blue-splotched and brown-patched. His hair was rough, for the

wind had been at it all the long walk from the manse to Big
Mina's house.

"Lassie," he said, "you are a big lass now. You will be five
years old when winter comes again. You mustn't tremble.
What is it that frightens you?"

She brought her hands up to cover her mouth and spoke
through her fingers. "A big thing I canna see, but it's in this
house and has horns like the devil!"

"So Big Mina has filled you with her talk of the devil, has
she?" He sighed. "I gave you your name, wee lassie, when
your nose was no more than a pink flower in your face and
your eyes closed in sleeping most of your days. Aye, yes, I
gave you your name—though it nearly cost me my kirk, and
some said I consorted with the devil. What is the name I gave
you, lassie?"

"Heather—Heather Cameron!" The sound of it purred off
her tongue like the song of a kitten.

"Aye, and it suits you well enough—not only your black
hair with the shine of red to it, but your gray eyes, like the
eyes of your granny Taraleean. Do you know who it is that's
coming to see you this day?"

"My father!"

"Aye, and I loved him like my own."

"There's to be a wedding," she said. "I've a dress my Uncle
Murdo and my Uncle Sammy brought me from London."

"Fancy that! And do you know whose wedding it is to be?"

"Aye! My father and mither."

"And all the village will be there—all but a few old harpies
we'll not miss."

"And my granny, Big Mina, will she come to the wedding?"

"As to her, I couldn't say."

"And I've a gold chain to wear around my neck!"

"Of course," he said, nodding his tousled head.

She jumped from his lap and ran to the window then, and

pressed her nose to the pane, standing on tiptoe. "Will he come soon? Will a tree fall doon and stop the hack?"

"Nothing will stop your father now," the minister said. "He has worked so hard and waited so long to come for you. Keep watch, now, and you'll be the first in this house to see him when the hack stops there at the head of the street."

"Lie doon, lie doon, you west gale, and leave my father be!" And then suddenly she saw the hack with the horses trotting before it. When it stopped at first she could see nothing, for it seemed as if the whole village surrounded it. And then the crowd parted and a tall figure was walking up the road by the side of her grandmother Taraleean. His head was bare, and his hair so bright the whole of the wild gray day seemed to fall back before it. She watched him until he came to the gate of Big Mina's house. There he stood, speaking with Taraleean, who kissed him and then went on up the road. Heather whirled and ran toward the bedroom door.

"Careful," the minister warned. "Do you want to fall and split open your bonnie head?"

The stairway seemed so long it might go on forever, but at last she reached the room. She saw her father standing with her mother in his arms. His face was against her mother's hair, and his eyes were closed. She could hear her mother weeping. And because in that moment she felt so left out of things, Heather ran forward and tugged at the skirt of her mother's dress.

They looked at her then. Her father dropped to his knees beside her, and his eyes were close and gray and misted. "What a wonder this is!" he said, and his voice was so low Heather scarcely heard it. His hands touched her gently and slowly.

"You're Kelsey," she said. "You've come home!"

Then he caught her close and held her so hard it hurt. His face pressed to hers, and she felt it suddenly wet.

"Poor Kelsey," she whispered. "You're weary this day." And she lifted the hem of her skirt to wipe his cheek.

It seemed they rushed her away to bed when her eyes were full of waking and before she could finish her supper. The rain had fallen harder at sundown, and now it ran from the roof, filling the night with sound. Her uncles sat by her bed, fat Uncle Sammy and thin Uncle Murdo.

"Now go to sleep," Uncle Sammy said. "I'll not move a step from this room till you do. If you won't sleep, then you canna wear the new blue dress."

"Aye, shut your eyes, you wee wiggler," Uncle Murdo added. "Here, you can keep my watch under your pillow all this night so you'll have it if you waken."

Heather took the watch and put it to her ear and pretended to sleep. After a while her uncles went away, whispering and walking on their toes. Then she got up and crept down the stairs and opened the door just a crack. She could hold her eye to it, and it was fine then, for she could see everything and hear. It was for her father's voice she listened.

Big Mina sat in her chair. Grandfather Thomas walked the room with his hands behind him.

"So you're back, Kelsey Cameron," Big Mina was saying. "You've aged in that wild country—aged, but not lost your damned Cameron pride. It still sticks out all over you."

"I've had a hard time, Big Mina," Heather's father said. "I told you I'd make the money to marry Prim and take her with me."

"Big talk, when you hadna a sixpence in your pocket."

"And what of it? What of it, I say?" shouted Grandfather Thomas, turning on his heel to spit in the fire.

"I'd be rich now," her father said, "if I hadn't had to sell my cattle so I could come after Prim and the wee lassie. And I'm not here with empty pockets, Big Mina. Did you think I'd come crawling and begging as I once did?"

"Well, I'll say this for you, you paid what you borrowed."

"Yes, by God! Every bloody penny!"

"Oh, Kelsey, Kelsey!" Heather's mother went to him and put her arms around him, pressing her cheek against his shoulder. "Don't talk of it now."

"Yes! And I'm taking her back to America with me, Big Mina. This time you won't stop her, for I'm marrying her as soon as it's possible."

Big Mina began to cough and choke; her face turned purple. "Then I'll die this night! I'll die afore your very eyes, Kelsey Cameron, and my soul haunt you the rest of your days!" She started wailing and rocking herself back and forth.

Then Grandfather Thomas walked to Big Mina. "Close your mouth! Close it now! One more bleat out of you and I'll wring your bloody neck, so help me! Prim's got a life to live, for herself and her bairn, and you'll not stop her from leaving this village. You've got to the end of your rope, Mina."

"Oh, you drunken bugger! You that ran off and left me to raise my wee ones by mysel' while you went sailing around the world and lay up with women in strange ports and filled your guts with whisky!" She turned to Kelsey, panting, tears on her cheeks. "And you—I thought the Indians would get you!"

He laughed. "Some foolish hope, Big Mina."

"And you'll not take the wee lassie, not Heather. The boys and I want her. We raised her, so we did. And now, when it suits you, you come back to claim her. I'll not let you have her, Kelsey Cameron. Never!"

Heather slipped through the doorway then, ran to her father, and put her arms around his legs. She held hard to him while Big Mina's voice rose in swearing, while her uncles shouted at their mother to mind her tongue, while her mother started weeping, and Grandfather Thomas bent close to Big Mina, his fist doubled, saying, "I'll let you have it! By God, I'll shut you up!"

Heather began to tremble. Then she felt her father's arms lifting her and holding her tight. "She'll go with me this night to my mother's house," he said. And he snatched up a shawl, folded it around her shoulders.

"Kelsey!" And there was her mother, looking strange and blocking their way to the door. Words that had no meaning came from her mother. "Not to Taraleean Cameron's . . . talk spread over the village . . . me and Crowter . . ."

"Get out of my way, Prim." Heather's father took a step. "You had her all the years. I never felt her warm in my arms." And then he was walking past her mother, through the kitchen, and at last to the door that opened into the darkness.

*   *

Kelsey Cameron walked through the wet night with his daughter and heard the mournful calling of a foghorn far out over the sea. When he came to the quiet of Taraleean's kitchen she looked up from where she sat by the fire, the little whisky glass in her hand. " 'Tis only for this night," she said. "Tomorrow I won't need it." Then she smiled the sudden warm smile that reached out and touched him with love. "Ah, if it isn't just like John Cameron walking into my house again! How I wish he could see you now—a man."

He sat down, holding Heather in his lap. "I'm sick all through me," he said. "My stomach's churning and my head aching. I couldn't live with that shouting and fighting."

"Who could? Not the blessed Lord himself."

He quieted himself there by the fire, holding his small daughter close to him, thinking, Oh, the blessed peace of this house! The gentleness of my mother! And he looked lovingly at Taraleean, who was so tall and straight and carried herself like a queen. Streaks of gray lay in her thick black hair, and in her eyes was the dreaming expression he had often seen when he was a lad. And he remembered how she would stand at the head of the village street, swinging a strand of ivory beads in her hand and looking to the west, for that way lay

Ireland. Once she had let him hold the beads, saying, "These are not what most folk think, for I knew no religion but that of the potato pickers. The beads were given me by an old man who came home from a far port across the world. They feel cool and smooth to the fingers—and even a tattie howker needs something to hold in her hand when she talks to God. It brings Him closer."

And now he thought too of how she had always been in spring when he was growing up—a restlessness upon her in the season of the new potatoes. Then she would sing the strange wild songs of the Irish potato pickers, and when his father came home from the shop she would run to him and throw her arms around his neck, saying, "It's time for loving me, John." And his father would send him to visit a friend or to the village on some foolish errand.

Kelsey smiled, shifting Heather in his lap. And I knew, young as I was, that my father loved Taraleean while the light still lay bright on the land. And how that would have shocked some in the village!

He said, "Tell me how it was when you met my father."

"You heard it many times as a lad."

"But I want to hear it again now."

Then she moved about the room, dramatizing, as she always did when she told a story. "Here I was in the potato field—like so, and all my skirts tucked up for fear they'd trip me while I was picking." And with a deft twist she fastened skirt and petticoat high while Heather sat up straight and stared. "And the other tattie howkers were singing and packing the potatoes into the little round wooden barrels. I began to sing too, and maybe I had good wind that day, for I looked up and there was John Cameron, leaning over the stone wall that fenced the field and staring right at me." Taraleean hummed a few bars of lilting music. "And I stopped singing and stared back at him—like so!" She cocked her head to one side, and Heather glanced up at Kelsey and smiled. "Then John Cameron beckoned to me and said, 'Come here, lassie, and let me have a close look at you.'

"Now, we were a rough-looking lot, I can tell you—our clothes old and stained with earth, and our hands rough from picking potatoes. But I went to the stone dike, and John Cameron said, 'And what is your name, lassie?'

"And, mind you, I acted like I had no thought of telling him. 'It's only one I picked up on a lone road of a misty night,' I said, 'and you could never pronounce it with your thick Scotch tongue.' But he replied, 'I must know it.' Then I answered, 'It is Taraleean—and I think a farmer once gave it to his horse.' And the two of us went off into gales of laughter."

Taraleean took a few quick turns around the room, laughing, and Kelsey heard the high, clear sound of Heather's mirth joining in. "Then," Taraleean continued, "he says to me, 'I'll buy you meat cakes and scones for your supper.' I told him we liked to steal our suppers, and you should have seen the look on his face.

" 'Is it that you get paid so little for your work?' he says, his face very serious. 'It is,' I answered, 'and there's great pleasure in outwitting the safe, sober folk of the world. And I see a bulge of a Bible in your pocket. Are you a minister who'd like to convert us from stealing?'

" 'I am no minister, lassie,' he says, 'but I like the Book with me, and I often read it with my friend, the Reverend Angus McCullough.'

"The other tattie howkers started to leave their work then, for night was coming on. They got in the old cart pulled by the big gray horse and called to me to come along and be quick about it. And what did that sane, sober-looking John Cameron do but reach over the stone dike—he was a big man, almost as big as you've grown in the years since I've seen you —and lifted me from my two feet and across the dike and held me so hard the Bible hurt me, and I said in a temper, 'Is

this Bible to be a thing between us, then?' He looked at me—
I'll never forget the way he looked at me—and said, 'Nothing's
between us. I love you.' "

Taraleean put her hand to her cheek, looked past Kelsey,
and murmured, "Fancy that coming from a man at first sight
of me! But the fire was in me too, and I told him right out
that I'd never been up the glen with any man but I'd go right
that minute with him." Then she turned back to Kelsey,
laughing. "But you know your father—a canny Scot if there
ever was one. He wouldn't budge an inch toward the glen, and
all that lovely night wasted—the birds calling from the haw-
thorn trees, and the breath of the sea coming up the land with
no wind behind it to hurry it. Well, he bought me my supper
and after that he courted me for weeks, following the tattie
howkers from one field to another, leaving a lad in the shop
to wait on his trade and count his money while the whole village thought he'd gone daft. And he was old for daftness—
away past thirty, and me only eighteen. But I loved him,
though all the loving he would do to me was a scanty business.
And I saw at last there was no way he'd ever have me unless
I had a ring on my finger and the Reverend McCullough saying the words over us. I had to have him, one way or another,
and so it was." She smiled at Kelsey. "And what had I to bring
him? A few belongings in a burlap sack—rose leaves to scent
my change of clothing, a broken comb, a bit of a mirror, and
the ivory beads."

"It was more than enough," Kelsey said, "and it's a story
I'll be remembering always and telling someday to my grand-
children."

Then Taraleean held out her arms to Heather. "Come to
me, wee lassie."

And when Heather cuddled against Taraleean's full breast
Kelsey said, "How are my sisters?"

"The lassies are well enough. Married, as I wrote you, and
soon to have bairns of their own. It's better they're married.

A restlessness was on them after you went to America. You'll see them at the wedding." She looked down at Heather. "What a sweet one she is! And how I've longed to have her with me. But Prim— Once Prim was pushing the pram up the road before this house. I went onto the steps and called to her, 'Will you not bring my son's child up here for me to see her face?' And she looked at me with hatred in her eyes and answered, 'If you want to see your son's child you'll come down to me, Taraleean Cameron.' "

He was saddened, hearing this, and thought, The lassie's been through hell. I saw it on her face today when I first looked at her—her eyes so big and seeming to ask if I really wanted her. All these years she's been afraid I wouldn't come for her, and fear's a vicious thing that tears us apart and makes us into strange people. Fear and love—how close they are—like the two sides of one face. Prim meant no harm to my mither. It was only someone to strike out at to relieve herself of the fear.

"And what did you do when Prim said that, Mither?"

Taraleean sighed. "I went down, of course. I got but a glimpse of her wee face when Prim pushed a cover over it and wheeled her away. It was a hard thing, I can tell you."

"But you brought it on, speaking of Crowter as you did."

"That may be true, but I was angered at the stories Big Mina and her sons put out for the village to hear, saying you ran away because you knew she was to have the child. Most folk didn't believe it, of course. But there are always the few who spread ugliness. And it was true, Kelsey, that she was along the shore with Crowter only a day or two after you left this country. I saw them myself. It was late in the night, and I had no sleep in me, thinking of you gone so far and of your father I loved and lost. I got up and walked on the shore, for the sea has aye calmed the trouble in me. I came around a turn of the braes, and they were there, standing close together. I heard them speaking. He was begging her to marry him."

"Big Mina drove her from the house with her wicked tongue. She took comfort being with an old friend like Crowter."

"No doubt, but it stayed in my mind, the sight of them there, and his arms around her."

An uneasiness stirred in Kelsey's heart. He looked at the child and thought, I must never think on such a thing. I know my own. I see myself in her, and her eyes are the eyes of Taraleean. And thank God for that!

"The future of you and Prim," Taraleean was saying, "it's to be in America. You're going back."

"Come with us, Taraleean!" His voice was eager. "It's lonely for you here."

"A foolish notion, lad. Prim and I could never live under the same roof. And it is just as well. No house is big enough to hold two women and let each be truly herself. One must give up a part of what she would like to be. This is not fair. And I would not be happy away from where I knew your father. Ah, the good years we had!" The light was on her face then, and her lips curving to fullness.

"The wee lass is asleep in your arms. Let me take her to bed."

"So she is, bless her. We can put her in the room off the kitchen there."

"No, I want her near me."

He took Heather upstairs to the big bedroom where he had slept as a boy. There were fresh sheets on the bed, and the cover was turned back. He tucked his daughter into the bed and blew out the lamp. He undressed in the darkness and crawled in beside her, holding her in the curve of his arm. And she brought back to him the times he had lain beside his father as a lad, and how he had felt there was no danger or hurt in the world as long as his father breathed beside him and sometimes spoke to him, telling a small incident of the day's work. Then there was the time, not long before his father died, when he no longer wished to sleep with his father, for there was a strangeness between them then—the strangeness of growing up, and a need to hide, even from those he loved, a part of himself, a need to have no other eyes look on his naked body except the eyes of lads his own age, who were like him. And there was a strange humility that touched him when he looked at his father and thought, I am going to be taller and stronger. There is the sign of age in him. The humility—and with it a tenderness for his father and a sadness for the times gone that could not be lived again, like the sleeping together in the long night.

A breath of wind blew over him, bringing the smell of the sea. And there was an aching in him. Had the lads and lassies of the village said unkind things to his little daughter? Had they pointed their fingers at her and asked, "Where is your father, lassie?"

How strange were the ways of living! A man never knew when he was small, like the lassie here in the curve of his arm, what was before him, the trouble he'd be in, or the singing that might waken in him when he least expected it.

But this one, this child of his, he would keep from trouble if he could. He would take her far from this village, out to where Dalt and Hilder would love her. For a moment their faces were before him in his mind, and he longed to be with Dalt again, to hear Dalt saying, "Buddy—"

He didn't care if he never saw Tommy again. Nothing had gone right between them from the moment he had brought the cow home from Vic Lundgren's.

And Monte. The hard years rose before him, flashing through his mind in a series of vivid pictures, and the big woman with the fair hair was always in them. Monte, riding with him above timberline in search of stray cattle in fall, her eyes the clean, cool blue of the sky. Monte, standing over him when he branded his first calf, saying, "Put that iron down steady, young fella. Don't smudge a brand. You'll be doing a

lot of brandin' in your day, and you learn now to do it right."
Monte, coming in from the winter snow, so muffled in clothes
she didn't look like a woman at all. Monte, sitting on the fence,
watching Dalt break out a colt, and behind her the evening
sky wild with color.

Monte hadn't wanted him to return to Scotland. Monte had
said angrily, "What kind of fool are you to go crawlin' after a
woman that don't think enough of you to come to you?"

He'd sold all his cows but Bonnie Jean. She was still at
the Red Hill Ranch. With her he would have to begin again,
trying to forget what he had lost by returning to Scotland.

And Prim? Time enough tomorrow to think of that; time
enough next week to tell Prim about Monte.

Beside him he felt the softness of his daughter, and he
drew her closer, being careful not to waken her.

                    *   *

The wedding was held in the town hall after Kelsey had
been in the village a few days. It took place early in the
morning, so they could catch the first train to Glasgow and the
waiting ship.

It was a hushed gray morning that promised rain. And it
was cold in the town hall. He stood in his new dark suit beside Prim, who wore a wedding dress the color of the drab
fall sky. The town hall was crowded; it was said that everyone
in the village was there—except Big Mina, who had taken to
her bed.

As the ceremony started Kelsey heard a murmur rise in the
hall. He turned and saw that Heather had got up from where
she was sitting between Taraleean and Thomas and was
brushing past people to the aisle. She stood for a moment,
smoothed her fine blue dress, then ran forward, her face lifted
toward Kelsey. The Reverend Mr. McCullough paused and
stared.

Kelsey held out his hand. "Leave the lass be," he said, and

Heather came and stood beside him while he married her mother. As the soft words of the minister fell in the old town hall there was a flutter of handkerchiefs and then the sound of weeping. Beyond the tall, narrow windows Kelsey could see the water, calm water with the gulls circling low over it. And he felt his daughter's hand, moist and curling warm inside his own. He heard as in a dream Prim's voice, faint and strained, taking him as her lawfully wedded husband. Over the whole scene there was an atmosphere of unreality. And when it was over he kissed his wife and his child, and the three of them walked from the hall, the people following behind them, and up the rolled stone road to Big Mina's house, where the hack was waiting and already the young men of the village were loading Prim's trunks.

Because it was a thing he must do, he went with his daughter and Prim into Big Mina's bedroom. In the dim light—for the shade was drawn—he saw her face, swollen from weeping, the wild strands of her hair sticking to her wet cheeks. Prim bent to kiss her mother and then ran from the room, sobbing. Kelsey pushed Heather forward, and she went to Big Mina. The old woman put up her arms and pulled the child to her big breasts. There was a smell of camphor in the room, and the other smell that is of old age and has an ugliness all its own.

"I'll never see you again, wee lassie," Big Mina said.

Then Heather began to cry, "Granny, Granny—"

Kelsey lifted her and carried her to the door. There he turned and looked back at Big Mina. She half raised herself on her pillows, choking over her words as she spoke. "God go with you, Kelsey Cameron—and mind the Indians."

He could not bring himself to answer her. Holding tightly to Heather, he walked out into the melancholy morning.

Taraleean was waiting by the hack. She had her shawl around her to shut away the chill. She took off the ruby brooch pinned at the neck of her good dress and fastened it on the blue serge coat of the little girl. Then she kissed Kelsey, went to Prim and kissed the cheek that was turned away from her, and stepped back to stand among the village people as Kelsey helped Prim into the hack.

That afternoon Kelsey took Prim and Heather aboard the ship, and they sailed with the evening tide. He stood close to Prim on the deck until darkness hid the Scottish landscape. "Come down below now," he said, "and forget all the trouble we knew here. We'll never see Scotland again."

"Oh, don't say it! Don't say it!" And she laid her head on the ship's rail, weeping.

He took Heather below and settled her for the night. Then he went back on deck, where Prim still stood in the windy darkness. The flashing beam of a lighthouse swept across her face, which was tired and tear-streaked and lonely. A sudden compassion moved him to put his arms around her and say gently, "Lass, come down with me now. Tomorrow, tomorrow everything will be better."

Then her face was against him and her whole body straining to him as though the years had never separated them. He held her tenderly yet awkwardly, for to him there seemed no way of returning to the time they had known before. Five years had gone out of their lives.

In the night, as the big ship moved on, lifting at last to the strong swells of the Atlantic, Kelsey took his wife in his arms. In her clinging to him he sensed her love, and his hands touched her uncertainly while a part of him cried out, Let it be as it once was with us, there on the shore, and the rocking of the sea set to our loving . . .

And as the slow warmth began to gather in him he heard the sea rising dark and strong around them, breaking harshly against the bow of the ship—this, and the cold September wind whining down around the funnels to roar away into the night.

CHAPTER X

P_{rim} saw the Park for the first time on a clear October day when the snows were shining white on the peaks, but the rolling land between lay brown and bare under the autumn sunlight. The railroad, now in construction between Laramie and the Park, had brought them part way. The rest of the trip had to be made in the spring wagon that now rocked with the gathering speed of the fresh team, moving across the flat prairie toward Walden.

"Where are the trees?" Prim asked.

Kelsey smiled; he'd felt the same way himself. "There's plenty of trees in the foothills, Prim, and a few along the rivers, if you look closely."

She drew her coat around her. It had been new when she left Scotland, but now it was wrinkled and soiled from the stage trip. Wind shook the yellow roses on her hat. She put her cold hand over Heather's warm one and drew the child close to her. And what have I come to? she thought. A bare ugly country, and with a man who's somehow a stranger to me. She saw the town rising before them now as they came down the curving hill and across the shallow river. Town? Could it be called a town? Log cabins—lonely—the bare earth around them, and the dust whirling down the width of the main street. Her voice came out, small and frightened. "Where are the shops?"

"Well," said Kelsey, "there's the one you see there to the right, with the red and white awning over the window. And

114

then there's Faun Gentry's, up at the end of the street. It's the biggest and best."

"Please take me there. I want to see it." Her hands clenched tightly in her lap. She wanted to get inside a shop, to be among familiar smells and sights, to shut out this big lonely country that sent a chill all through her.

They came to a grinding stop. Kelsey said this was Posser's Hotel, where they would be staying for a night or two, and the stage driver helped him carry the suitcases and trunks to the wooden sidewalk. Prim sat on the stage, trying to calm the feeling of upheaval within her. She was aware of Kelsey standing there, looking up at her, the questioning in his eyes.

"Aren't you going to get out, Prim?"

She moved then, holding tightly to Heather's hand. They stood by the luggage, looking up and down the empty street in the late afternoon, seeing no sign of life but a few horses tied to the hitching racks before a saloon.

"The shop," she said. "I want to go there first. And where are the women?"

"The women? They're home working. Women don't idle on the streets here as they do around the harbor. Let's go on to the store, then. I want you to meet Faun Gentry."

They went up the narrow sidewalk that tilted under their feet. Heather ran ahead, often turning and looking back, her face shining with excitement.

Inside the store Prim stared. "Oh, the mess! It's no real shop at all!"

"That's what I tried to tell you, lass," he said. "It's not like the old country."

A voice shouted then. "Kelsey! You've come back to the Park!"

"Faun!" She saw the pleasure on Kelsey's face as he shouted the name. "And here's Prim, and the lassie!" Kelsey was shaking Faun Gentry's hand.

The brown eyes of this man were warm with welcome. He

bowed to her. "Missus, it's our pleasure to have you here."
He bent to Heather and put his hand under her chin. "The
spittin' image of Kelsey Cameron! Listen, honey, I figured
you'd be showin' up soon, and I got a present for you—ordered special from Denver. Come on."

They followed him into the back room, and he rummaged
through boxes and brought out a small pair of cowpuncher's
boots. He unlaced Heather's high-top shoes, removed them,
and slipped the boots on her feet. "There. Now you tell Jake—
he's the cow boss for Monte—you tell him I said you was fixed
for business and will make him a top hand." Faun squatted
beside her. "You like 'em, honey?"

Heather put her small arms around his neck and kissed him.
Faun Gentry laughed softly. "Dolly's gonna love you. She's
plannin' on havin' you all eat supper with us tonight."

"That's kind of you," Prim said, smiling at Heather in the
strange shoes.

Faun straightened, and his face became serious as he turned
to Kelsey. He spoke in a lower tone. "You know how Monte
felt about you takin' off for Scotland with the hayin' season
on and men hard to get."

"I had to go," Kelsey said, his lips tightening.

"Sure," Faun said easily. "Monte'll get over it. You stick
around." He smiled at Prim. "See you for supper."

They went slowly down the walk toward their luggage, which
was still piled before the hotel. Prim was trying to get things
straight in her mind. "Wasn't Monte Maguire your boss, Kelsey?"

"That's right."

She wanted to ask more questions, but he hurried forward
to pick up the luggage. "We'd better get that room now. I know
you're tired, Prim."

The woman at the hotel desk was chewing on a hairpin.
"Well, Kelsey—"

"My wife, Mrs. Posser. And my daughter, Heather."

Prim felt the sharpness in the little black eyes. "Took you long enough to get here."

"Could you put up a cot for the lassie?" Kelsey asked. "In the room with us, I mean."

Mrs. Posser licked her lips. "That'll cost you twice as much, and I'd have to be paid in advance."

Kelsey's face flushed. "Isn't my credit good in this country? I always paid my bills."

She jabbed hard at her teeth with the hairpin. "They been sayin' that Monte ain't takin' you back to work for the Two-Bar outfit—not after you run off to Scotland when they needed you. And it's slack time of year now—nobody hirin' men, with winter comin' on."

Prim looked from Mrs. Posser to Kelsey's flushed face. What was the meaning of this talk? And there was something Faun Gentry had said at the store. Then it came to her with sickening clarity: Kelsey had no job.

Kelsey counted out money and said awkwardly, "It'll be a day at a time, Possy."

Their feet clattered up the bare stairway behind Mrs. Posser and into a bedroom off a dark hall. Prim looked with horror at the sagging bed, the bare dusty floor, the curtainless window, where a green blind flapped in the wind, for a pane of glass was broken.

Mrs. Posser stood watching them for a moment. "It's the cheapest," she said and closed the door.

It was quiet and cold in the room. Mrs. Posser's steps echoed away down the bare stairs. Prim walked to the window and stood still. She felt Kelsey's hand on her shoulder. "Prim—"

She couldn't answer.

"I didn't see any reason to tell you Monte was sore at me when I left. I figured it would blow over by now, anyway." He paused, drew a deep breath, and went on. "It'll come out all right."

She turned then and kissed him, her eyes bright with tears. "That horrid, ugly woman downstairs. I hated her! I was humiliated for you, so I was. And what are we going to do, Kelsey? Do we have to stay here?"

"Monte'll show up," he said. "I know."

Prim reached quickly to take off her hat. If Monte Maguire didn't come, somebody had to hire Kelsey. There were other ranchers.

*   *

That night when they went to Faun Gentry's for supper Dolly's plump hands fluttered with excitement as she put out her fine china. "Oh, your beautiful skin!" she said to Prim. "Stay out of this sun. It'll ruin it. And never put water on your face. Use buttermilk or cream. My, but you're small! Why, there's nothing to you but skin and bone."

Prim tried to enjoy the food, but she wasn't hungry. Dolly said, "Better eat more than that. You're awful frail for a mean country like this. And if you're frettin' because Monte Maguire hasn't come for you, you don't know how lucky you are to be free and—"

"Dolly!" Faun's voice was sharp. "Mrs. Cameron's tired."

"Oh, so she is. Well, God knows that trip into the Park is a killer—even with half a railroad to help out now. This place is the end of the earth. They've had railroads in Wyoming for years, and here we are just getting— When will it be finished, Faun?"

"Oh, maybe another year or two."

"About time," Dolly said. "Open that window, Faun. That cigar smoke's making me sick."

"No wonder! You got yourself laced so tight you can't breathe."

"At least I haven't let myself go like some women in this country—spreading like a sack of flour until you can't tell their middles from their laps." She glanced at Prim. "But you won't be that way. I can tell by the trim style of you."

Prim smiled. "I take pride in keeping myself up, Mrs. Gentry." She looked at Kelsey, and he was smiling too.

As they left the table, conversation shifted to people in the Park; these were only names to Prim. She sat on the floor with Heather, who had a rag doll Mrs. Gentry had given her. She was tired now, and she was glad when she heard Kelsey say, "It's time to go."

"Come again tomorrow night," Dolly said. "I always cook too much, don't I, Faun? And I hate to throw food out."

"Yes," Faun said, "you come tomorrow night—if Monte don't show up."

"No," Kelsey said, "but thanks all the same."

Dolly picked up Heather and squeezed her. "You come see me any time, and keep the rag doll. I made it for you."

Walking back to the hotel, Kelsey said, "Great people. They'd give you the shirts off their backs."

"I liked them," Prim said, and she persuaded herself that she really did.

They stayed on at the hotel day after day. Prim sat, wearing her coat, in the cold room, trying to read or knit, while Heather played with the rag doll. Each morning Prim would kiss Kelsey good-by and watch through the broken window as he walked up the street. She'd see him going in and out of saloons and stores and talking to men on the sidewalks. Each night at suppertime he would come back to her, looking tired, saying dejectedly, "I talked to everybody I could find. Maybe tomorrow somebody will need a hired man."

"I'm sure of it," she'd reply with a confidence she didn't feel, while she thought bleakly, So this is Tommy Cameron's land of opportunity. How much better off we'd be now if we'd stayed in Scotland; there was always room on my brothers' boat for Kelsey.

When the three of them ate supper in the dining room Prim was always aware of Mrs. Posser's scrutiny, and once she heard the woman say in a low tone to Heather, "Ain't your daddy found no job yet?"

They'd been at the hotel ten days when Prim asked Kelsey the question that was troubling her. "How much money have you got left?"

He looked at her, and she saw defeat in his eyes. "I had to borrow from Faun today."

And without thinking she cried out, "If my mither was here we'd never be in a mess like this!"

"I wouldn't borrow from her again if I had to starve!"

Prim felt tears coming. She was homesick and discouraged. "It's my mither I'd like to see now. I can't sit in this hotel room another day. Nothing to do, no place to go, and that woman downstairs—her food chokes me!"

"I've tried to find a job!" Kelsey waved his arms and shouted. "What more can I do? And for God's sake, stop crying, Prim."

There was a loud knock at the door. Prim wiped her eyes. "If it's Mrs. Posser snooping around to ask questions again—" She squared her shoulders and opened the door.

Her breath caught, and she stared at the big woman who stood there, a battered black hat pushed back from her brown face. Was this some tramp in these ragged clothes? "You've the wrong room," Prim said and started to close the door, but the booted foot was already thrust inside.

"Is that so?" There was laughter in the husky voice. The wide mouth curved in a smile, but Prim stepped back before the sharpness in the eyes. "If you had any manners, Mrs. Cameron, you'd ask me in."

Bewildered, Prim turned to Kelsey. He got up, and to Prim his face looked strange as he moved toward them.

The big woman said, "So you came back, eh, Kelsey?"

"Prim"—his voice was strained—"this is Monte Maguire."

Prim was shocked. She kept on staring at the rough clothes, the brown face, the large feet in the worn boots. Monte Maguire nodded and turned her attention to Kelsey. "That all your stuff in the corner, Kelsey?"

Prim waited for his answer. Monte Maguire shifted impatiently. "Well, don't stand there wastin' time. Help me carry that stuff to the buggy." She squinted at him. "Unless you got other plans."

Prim saw Kelsey's eyes harden. He reached out and took hold of her hand. "Prim, go down to the lobby—and take Heather with you. Wait there."

Prim was suddenly so angry she couldn't speak. Then she brushed past Kelsey, her head held high, grabbed Heather's hand, and pulled the child into the hall, slamming the door behind her. She walked quickly toward the stairs. What right had Kelsey to order her and Heather from their room while he talked with that brassy piece of baggage who owned a ranch?

She settled herself on a couch in the lobby, Heather at her side. Mrs. Posser looked up from behind the desk, ready for conversation. Prim gave her a cold look; the anger still churned in her. And if this one who ran the hotel expected an opinion on what was going on upstairs, she'd never get it.

*   *

When the door closed, Kelsey faced Monte Maguire. "You took your time, didn't you? Let me sit around here like a—"

"Why the hell should I hurry over to get you when you ran off and left us in the middle of haying, just because she all of a sudden took a notion she'd step off her high horse and come out, providin' you'd go after her? You beat it outta the Park like a tin-canned dog when we needed you most. You ran after a woman who didn't care enough about you to get over here when she should have, but sat back there on her butt holding the kid over your head like a whip." Monte hooked her thumbs in her belt and rocked back on her heels. "Was she worth it after you got her?"

He shouted in fury, "Keep your damn job!"

She rolled a cigarette, deliberately taking her time. There was an insolence about her that set his nerves on edge. She glanced at him through the smoke, her eyes glinting. "You know nothin's turnin' up, not this time of year—unless you want to hole out in a shack in the hills and run trap line like Jediah."

"I'm not flat busted, Monte Maguire. You've got a cow and calf of mine out there on the Red Hill."

"Cow? Are you referrin' to that bag of bones you're too damn sentimental to ship before she falls apart? Yeah, she's there. And she's got a calf." Monte shrugged. "Oh, it's a good enough calf."

"Then I've got that much to start on."

She said dryly, "You figurin' on settlin' on some ranch with one cow and one calf?"

"Damn you, Monte! Why do you like to cut me down and make me feel small? I come back here, and you start in trying to make me feel like a beggar. What's the matter with you anyhow?" He moved close to her, his fists clenched at his sides.

She let the smoke drift slowly through her nostrils. Her direct, level look never wavered from his. "All ruffled up, ain't you? What you gonna do? Take a poke at me—or kiss me?"

"Why, you cheap—" His breath caught in his throat. His hands moved up, gripped the strong shoulders, and he felt the life leap up in him, terrible and wonderful. She dropped the cigarette and ground it out, not turning away from him. Then her arms moved up with a sudden fierce motion and went around his neck. Her full breasts pressed against him. "Go on," she said with sudden harshness. "Go on! You wanted to, wanted to all the years you worked like a crazy

man before you went back for her and I prayed to God she'd
turn you down when you got there. You don't need to lie to
me. Never lie to me, Kelsey. You wanted me—but you didn't
have the guts to even lay a hand on me! What's it like now?"

Somewhere, beyond the wild throbbing in his head and
the crazy whirling of his blood, he heard light running steps
and the twist of the doorknob. He stepped back from Monte
Maguire and turned to see Heather burst into the room. She
ran to him, clung to his legs, shouting in her high, clear child's
voice, "Are we going home, Daddy? Are we going to the
ranch?"

He put a shaking hand on her silken hair. He looked at
Monte. "It didn't have anything to do with guts," he said, his
lips stiff. "My God, Monte, you ought to know that!"

He saw the flush leave her face, the quiet come over her
mouth. A dullness crowded into her eyes, and it was as if he
were watching a sunlit meadow give over to the slow graying
of rain. She said in a flat voice, "We better load the buggy now.
Night's runnin' out on us, and it's cold come daylight in this
country."

He turned away, thinking sharply, While I live I never want
anything to happen to her. I never want to know she's dead,
never want to walk the earth and her not on it—somewhere
near me.

*   *

They drove away from town in the windy starlight, going
along the narrow prairie road, the *clip-clop* of the horses'
hoofs loud in the night. Prim sat between her husband and
Monte Maguire on the front seat of the buggy. Heather dozed
in her father's arms. Prim could think of nothing but the
broad straight shoulder that touched hers. *Why didn't he tell
me about this woman? Why didn't he tell me Monte Maguire
wasn't a man?*

There was the long, dark prairie lifting under the star-

shine, and the wind blowing over them, and the endless turning of the buggy wheels. What are we but three strangers?
Prim asked herself. Where are we going this night, and for
what reasons? A numbness began to settle over her.

She stood at last in the weed-grown yard silvered with frost
and the pale starlight. Kelsey unloaded their suitcases and
trunks, and Monte Maguire drove away—Without so much as
a good-by or a look in my direction, Prim thought.

A light flickered in the house, and a man's voice called,
"That you, Kelsey?"

Heather whimpered between sleep and waking. Kelsey
lifted her in his arms and carried her across the yard. The
long weeds caught at Prim's skirt. And then they were in the
house and she was facing Tommy Cameron. He's not changed
from what he was as a lad around the harbor, she thought. He
still has the cunning look in his eyes, and I wouldn't trust him.

But Tommy was smiling at her and saying, "Been a long
time, Prim. You were only a lassie." In his eyes were other
things that added, And got yourself with bairn and a man had
to come back and marry you.

She mumbled polite words and stared at the ugly big
kitchen. She heard the rattling of the yellowed, dirty newspapers that clung to the walls. She smelled the manure and
sweat and stale food. She shut her eyes tight and opened them
again. Could such a place be, or wasn't this only a nightmare
from which she would soon waken?

"Come on into the front room," Kelsey said, lighting another lamp.

Tommy was bending over to look at Heather. "What a piece
of fancy fluff you turned out to be!" He tugged at her hair,
and she pulled away from him, thrusting out her lower lip. He
laughed. "Sulky little fox, ain't you?"

"The child's worn out," Prim said and reached to take hold
of Heather's hand. Heather pressed close to her, hiding her
face in Prim's full skirt.

"Then get her to bed," Tommy said.

They followed Kelsey into the living room. The bare, splintery floor was littered with cigarette butts and crumpled newspapers. Prim stopped in the middle of the room and wearily rubbed her forehead.

Kelsey gave her an anxious look. "It's a big house," he said, "one of the biggest in the Park. Two bedrooms here and three upstairs. We'll see to our room now, for you're tired."

"I moved my stuff upstairs," Tommy said. "You and Prim and the kid will need this part of the house."

The first bedroom was cold, stale-smelling, and with a floor as dirty as that of the kitchen. There was only one piece of furniture, a crude wooden bunk filled with hay. "When it's fixed up . . ." Kelsey's voice trailed off.

"Hell, what's wrong with it now?" Tommy said impatiently. "It's damn fine, and you're lucky to be here." He looked at Prim. "Beggars can't be choosers."

"I'm no beggar!" And she swept past him toward the second bedroom.

Paint was chipping from the green iron bedstead. There was an overturned box for a washstand. A cracked bowl and pitcher were on the box. Dead flies and dust darkened the bottom of the bowl. The wall bristled with spikes, and from these hung a few clothes—a suit of gray underwear, two pairs of pants, a torn shirt.

"Let's get the luggage," Tommy said. "Gotta hit the hay."

When they had gone Prim walked to the foot of the bed. Her hands reached out, clinging to the paint-chipped scrolls, her fingers so tight her knuckles turned white. "I mustna cry," she muttered, lapsing into the dialect of the village. Then she bent her head, pressing her forehead against the cold bedstead. "Dear God," she said, "oh, dear God!"

She had control of herself by the time Kelsey brought in the suitcases. She said, "The air's that foul in here it's like to choke me. Open a window, Kelsey. I tried and couldn't."

He went to the narrow window that faced north. He tugged and pushed at it. Sweat broke out on his forehead. He shook the frame and pounded on the sill. Then there was a tinkle of breaking glass. "Damn! You wanted fresh air. There it is, then."

But Prim didn't hear him. She was staring at the ceiling. "What's that hole above the bed?" she asked.

"Hole?" He sounded surprised. He looked up, and she saw an expression of disgust come over his face. "I'll have a talk with my cousin Tommy in the morning. I'll put an end to this."

"What do you mean? Is that where Tommy—"

"Forget it now, Prim. Let's see to Heather." And Kelsey took hold of her arm and led her back to the living room, where Heather stood with her nose pressed to the low window. The moon was up now, and Prim could see the long land sweeping to the mountains, land dark and strange and streaked with white.

Prim opened one of the trunks and took out fresh sheets and spread them over the tarp that covered the hay in the wooden bunk. Prim made her daughter's bed with fine blankets, a gift from the village people, cream-colored blankets with neat blue borders. And when at last Heather lay warm and clean in the bed, Prim knelt beside her in the crumpled suit, still wearing crookedly the hat with the yellow roses. "Now say your prayers, lassie."

Heather closed her eyes. "Now I lay me doon to sleep and pray the Lord my soul to keep. If I should die before I wake, I pray the Lord my soul to take."

"And mind our own folk across the sea," Prim said.

"God bless Granny Big Mina and Granny Taraleean and my uncles . . ."

Prim kissed her good night and carried the lamp back to the bedroom, where Kelsey was still up. She undressed and got into bed, but Kelsey took the lamp and went away. She lay in the darkness, hearing him moving restlessly in the living room. What was it troubled him? A peephole cut in the ceiling by his cousin Tommy? Or was he thinking of Monte Maguire and whatever they had said to each other?

She closed her eyes and tried to sleep. Then she heard a thin, mournful howling out in the night, and her skin rose, cold with prickles. Heather cried out, and Prim jumped from bed and stumbled in the dark to the living room. She saw that Heather's door was ajar and a faint light showed. She ran fearfully across the room, but at the threshold she paused, for Kelsey was already there beside the lassie. He was stroking her hair, saying softly, "It's only the coyotes, wee lassie. Sometimes they howl at sundown and other times in the still of early morning before the darkness lifts. Sleep now and have no fears. No harm shall come to you."

Prim took a step forward and then stopped. An ache came up in her throat, for she saw Kelsey and Heather close and such a tenderness on Kelsey's face as she had never seen before. She turned and ran back to the bedroom, got under the blankets, and began to shake with sobs. She brought her arm up, fiercely pressing the nightgown's sleeve into her mouth to shut away the sound of her crying.

CHAPTER XI

"You didn't have to come for me," Prim said. "Don't ever think you had to. I could have made out, so I could."

They were still in bed on a dark November morning. Kelsey stared up into the blackness. He said, keeping his voice patient, "Prim, I never said I didn't want to come for you. Why do you talk so?"

"Because I want you to know the truth, Kelsey Cameron. Crowter would have married me. All I had to do was say the word. Yes! He'd have married me, even when he knew the trouble I was in. That's how much he cared about me."

A dull anger stirred in Kelsey. "Will you stop talking about Crowter?"

"He'd have given the lassie his name," Prim went on, her voice rising.

"I'd have had something to say about that. What's come over you, Prim? We're here, together at last. We've work and a roof to cover us and our lassie to care for. You talk daft."

"And if I'm daft you made me so!"

"Prim!" He was torn between hurt and rage. Bitter words were on his tongue, but he held them back. He got out of bed and went into the dark kitchen, lighted the lamp, and shook down the stove—shook it hard for want of something to take care of his pent-up emotions. Red coals cascaded into the ash pan. The kitchen door slammed, and he looked up to see Hilder with the lantern in his hand.

"You shake the guts from it, eh?" Hilder said. "Now it takes

128

twice as long to heat. You don't have to build fires. I come in and do that for the missus now she bosses the kitchen. But I step mighty easy. The missus, she's young and touchy. Maybe she outgrow it, maybe not." He shrugged, put down the lantern, and came to stand with his back to the stove. "Did I hear you and Tommy fighting the other night at the barn?"

Kelsey fussed with the stove. Could you say to a hired man that there was this ugly thing in Tommy, this thing that wasn't usual in a man and shocked you and sent you flying at him in outrage? Did you tell a hired man your cousin had cut a hole in the ceiling of your bedroom so he could spy on your wife and you while there was loving going on? No, it wasn't a thing to talk about.

"He was in a sour mood, Hilder, and so was I. But that's behind us now."

Hilder grunted. "One day it comes to a head, like a boil, and things happen. You leave this ranch. I know it. And the day you leave, I leave. I stick with you, Kelsey."

Kelsey looked at Hilder and smiled. "You big Swede," he said. He turned to the wall, took his coat from the spike, and picked up the milk bucket. He walked slowly toward the barn in the dark morning, the lantern swinging an arc of light around him.

The earth had a cold smell to it now before daylight, a smell of coming winter. He went into the barn, and the air was warmer and filled with the mingled odors of cows, manure, and hay. It was early for milking, so he rolled a cigarette and smoked it, not liking the taste on an empty stomach but going on dragging at it anyhow. He heard a light step outside, and a moment later Heather came into the barn. She wore a coat over her long flannel nightgown, and the cowboy boots Faun Gentry had given her. Her hair was tousled from sleep, but her eyes were bright.

"I came to see the cows." Her voice was high and clear, making him think of the birds that ran calling across the meadows in spring. He took her hand in his, lifted the milking stool, and let her carry the bucket. They walked back to where the milk cows stood in a wide stall. The breath of the cows was steamy in the dim light from the lantern. They chewed their cuds and turned their big dark eyes toward him. Kelsey spoke to each of them, patting their flanks. "And now, my fine lassies, we've come for our milk this morning. And there'd better be no foot put in the bucket, if you please."

He sat on the milking stool, and Heather stood close to him, watching, fascinated, as the milk streamed with a thin tinny sound that deepened as it began to fill the pail. She reached out and took hold of one of the teats and smiled.

"Who's that helpin' you, Kelsey?"

Kelsey looked up and saw Long Dalton walking into the stall. His pale brown eyes twinkled. "Wind blow her in this morning?" He grabbed a braid and gave it a tug. "Not speakin' to me any more, chicken?"

Heather scowled. "You're mean. You tied the cats together by the tails. You hung them over the clothesline and let them fight. You're a mean devil, so you are!"

Dalt cocked his shaggy head to the side. "That so? Your mama tell you that?"

Heather thrust out her lower lip and didn't answer.

"You won't stay sore at me," he said. "Who made you a wagon outta those old boxes, huh?"

"You best leave the cats alone," she said.

"Won't hurt those old toms. Help 'em get it outta their systems. Did 'em good to hang on the clothesline."

"It was cruel."

"I'm a cruel man, a right mean man," he assured her, lowering his pale, heavy brows. "Come here and I'll cut off your ears." He opened his knife, rubbed it across his pants, and spat on it. Then he lifted a fistful of her hair, waved the knife, and made his eyebrows go up and down. Heather burst into laughter. "Dalt, you silly!"

Kelsey finished milking, feeling a warmth toward Dalt; Dalt would look out for Heather. When Kelsey saw him with horses or with Heather it was hard to believe what some men in the Park said of him—that he was as tough as they came and could use his knife on more than calves to be cut.

When they walked back to the house with the milk, light was breaking. A scarf of mist trailed over the hogback. There was no color left in the aspens that grew in the ravines. They were pale and naked, ghosts of trees now, stripped of all their brightness. The black and white magpies were sitting on the edge of the watering trough, their feathers fluffed against the chill.

Prim had breakfast dished up. "Hurry," she said, "or your oats will be cold."

"Oats!" Tommy gave a snort of laughter. "Oats, she says. Figures we're horses, eh, boys?"

Prim stiffened. "I'd like to know what's so funny, Tommy Cameron."

Kelsey said, "It's only a joke, Prim. In this country it's oatmeal, not oats." He saw her face flush with embarrassment as she turned her back.

"Missus," Hilder said, "you sit down and eat. You're nothin' but skin and bones, so damn thin you could wear a double-barreled shotgun for long drawers." And he laughed loudly at his own joke.

Prim whirled around. "And I'll thank you to keep your place, Mr. Larson."

"Touchy this morning, eh?" Tommy reached halfway across the table to spear a pancake with his fork.

Prim opened her mouth to reply, but just then a gust of wind struck the house, rattling the loose newspapers on the wall. She darted across the room, yanked a long paper free of the logs, and threw it on the floor. "Oh, the filth! The filth!" And she began ripping off the papers, first with one hand and then with the other, her arms in constant motion.

"Hey!" Tommy shouted. "You're stirrin' a dust! You think I want dirt in my breakfast?"

Hilder shrugged. "Looks yust like pepper, don't it?"

"I'm tearing them off," Prim cried, "every one of them!"

"It'll be cold without them newspapers on the wall this winter," Tommy warned. "And we've got nothing else to put over the logs."

"Don't care," Prim said. She raised both arms, fastened her fingers on the loose paper, and pulled. There was the scraping sound of falling chinking, and a red dust rose in the kitchen.

"My God, Prim!" Kelsey stood up. "Wait till after we eat!"

She paid no attention to him, and the men ate quickly, hurrying to leave the table. Kelsey helped Heather with her clothes. "Come on," he said. "I'll take you from this dusty place. Your mother's worked herself into a state this morning." His fingers were clumsy, braiding her thick dark hair. "Maybe we'll go down the meadow and see Bonnie Jean. She's lonesome now that her calf's been weaned."

Prim turned. A long streak of dirt made a dark finger on one cheek. "Yes, go and see the cow. *She's* important."

"Oh, hell, Prim!" Kelsey pushed his daughter toward the door.

At the barn the men were sorting the harness, getting ready to mend the breaks from haying season. Tommy turned to Kelsey, a lump of chewing tobacco in his jaw. "Better ride the fences this morning. Monte's fussy about her cows being kept in the meadows this time o' year."

Kelsey saddled Chinook, a big Roman-nosed gray with the long scar of an old wire cut across his face. He put Heather behind the saddle and told her to hang on. They rode slowly down the meadow in the still, frosty-breathed morning.

He went along, dreaming, seeing in his mind the herd of cattle that had been his a year ago—fifty head of fine cows and calves. He'd been lucky then, had lost only two calves with blackleg in spring and one the winter before with woody tongue. As soon as I get my wages, he thought, I'll buy another cow, and I'll keep on buying them. I'll trade the steer calves with Monte as I did before. It won't be long until I have cattle again.

He pulled the horse up near Bonnie Jean; the marks of age were beginning to show on her. Seven years old she was now, and one day she wouldn't be of any more use to him. He got off, helped Heather to the ground, and they walked to the cow where she stood quietly in the brown stubble of the meadow. Kelsey started rubbing her neck and ears. Bonnie Jean made a crooning sound in her throat.

"Listen," he said to the child, "she's singing to us this morning." And he touched the cow more gently. "Ah, you're the fine one—a queen of a cow! And when you're too old to have calves you needn't fear. I'll never ship you to be turned into glue and whatever else they make from a bag of bones. You'll stay here and die peacefully in the meadow or on the fine summer range where the wild pea vines grow." He swung Heather onto the cow's broad back. Bonnie Jean turned her head, her big dark eyes sizing up the little girl. Heather smiled and patted her.

"See how gentle she is?" Kelsey said. "It's because I spent so much time with her. She was the only one I had at first and even when she'd come in from summer range she remembered me and welcomed my hand on her. It was the scratching of the curry comb that started her singing. Many's the winter day when we couldn't work I had her in the corral and curried her." He sighed and added, "It was a thing angered Tommy. He'd come down and lean on the fence and scowl, muttering, 'Making a bloody fool of yourself over a cow.'"

They rode away, turning across the meadow to where the buck fences made a gray hemstitching over the land, the crossed bucks like huge Xs, the logs between them sagging and weathered silver-gray. Kelsey liked the buck fences; there was a quiet, old look about them, and at a distance they seemed to grow right out of the land, for their color blended with the sage-brush. He liked the feel of the logs under his hands and the way they looked on a morning like this, with the sun coming out of the gray clouds to melt the frost and leave wet, dark strokes on the wood. There was color in the logs too, rusty tones where rot had set in, and in places a darkened yellow that was like grass when it got overripe with fall.

"When I came here," he told Heather, "I thought fall so ugly and bare in this country, but then I began to see the color. If you look closely, lassie, you'll find a dozen shades of brown and yellow in the grass—and the weeds are on fire with orange, red, and purple. The old country has a wonderful green, but this earth has all the colors a man could ever imagine."

When they rode toward the house near noon, Kelsey noticed a pillar of smoke rising above the buildings. He kicked the horse into a lope, riding loosely behind Heather, who was now in the saddle. Her braids flopped out, and her hair blew against his face; there was a young, clean fragrance to it.

At the corral he turned the horse loose, and they hurried toward the house. As they did so men came running from the barn, racing past the watering trough, for a fire blazed in the yard.

"If wind comes up it'll take the house!" Tommy shouted. "Get the shovels, Dalt! Hilder, bring water buckets!"

Prim stood near the pile of blazing junk. "There's not a breath of wind," she said. "There's nothing to get excited about."

Kelsey brushed past her, shouting impatiently, "In this country wind can spring up any time!" He grabbed a shovel and began digging dirt and tossing it into the fire.

"My God!" Tommy shouted. "Look at that!"

Kelsey saw him pointing to the top of the burning mass. Tommy's finger shook. His jaw sagged, and a look of shock was on his face. "Our chaps!" Tommy said hoarsely. "My God, she's burnin' our chaps!"

"Oh"—Prim shrugged—"that's only those old pants I found upstairs. I'd like to know who'd want them—so worn the seats are gone from them."

"A hundred dollars' worth of chaps!" Tommy groaned.

"Prim," Kelsey said, "chaps are important. We wear them when we punch cows, and—"

"Well, they've no seats in them."

"Not supposed to have seats!" he shouted at her.

Prim's face went red. She bit her lower lip. "It's my house, so it is, and I'll not have it in a litter."

"You'll stay outta my room!" Tommy towered over her, his face ugly. "You'll leave things alone!"

"It's my house—" Prim began.

"It's Monte Maguire's house, and don't you forget it, or by God you'll go down the road talkin' to yourself!"

Prim turned and ran into the house.

Kelsey looked apologetically at the men. "I'm sorry—but you can't blame her. She just didn't know—" Then he began to laugh. "What a story this'll make for telling all over the Park!" And he laughed harder as Hilder and Dalt joined in.

"Nothin' funny about it," Tommy said sourly when they quieted down. "It's a hell of a thing to do. All that money—"

They got the fire reduced to a smoking black heap, went inside, and washed their dirty faces and hands. Prim was dishing up the noon meal, her face grim, her eyes red from crying.

"Hope you got it outta your system," Tommy muttered, sliding into his chair at the head of the table.

Prim stood very straight before the stove. "I have got it from my system. I've cleaned *Mrs. Maguire's* house. And I've fixed *Mrs. Maguire's* food for your dinner. And I'll remind you that you're eating from *Mrs. Maguire's* plates."

"Jesus Christ," Hilder said, looking around the soap-and-lye-smelling kitchen, "you tore things all to hell, Missus."

"Another thing," Prim said. "I want some dirt hauled so I can fix a flowerbed outside. The flowers will be mine, even if I do use *Mrs. Maguire's* dirt."

"Dirt?" Tommy blinked. "You mean you think we got nothin' better to do than run around shovelin' dirt for a woman?"

"So"—her voice quivered—"it's too much to ask—just a little dirt to grow something beautiful in this godforsaken country."

Kelsey cleared his throat. "Prim, you won't need it until spring. If you'll be patient I'll—"

"We got work to do," Tommy said, shoving a slice of bread in his mouth.

*   *

Prim went into the living room. She stood there until she heard the men leave and the fading voice of Heather talking to Kelsey as they walked toward the barn. She returned to the kitchen and looked at the dirty dishes. Putting her hands over her face, she began to cry.

After a while she washed the dishes, put on an old jacket, and went out to dig in the yard. If no one would fix the flowerbed she'd do it herself. The men had hauled away the trash from the fire; only an ugly stain remained in the center of the front yard.

The shovel was awkward in her hands, but she worked hard, digging, sweating, and swearing. "If a cow wanted dirt, a cow would get it," she muttered. "If a damn old cow wanted flowers they'd run their arses off getting seeds, so they would." She didn't hear the step at the side of the house.

"Say, now, you're working too hard for a pretty gal. Gimme that shovel. Shucks, that's no job for a little thing like you."

She looked up. He was a little old man, wearing clothes that clearly needed washing. As he moved closer the rank smell of

him made her want to hold her nose. Then she knew who he
was and said, "You're Jediah Walsh."

"Yep, that's me. Pleased to meetcha, Prim. I heard about
you for five years. Could have placed you anywhere if we'd
met sudden-like. And I would have been down to see you before now, but I was gettin' my trap lines strung out." He took
the shovel from her, turned over some of the red earth, and
leaned on the handle, grinning. His yellow, crooked teeth reminded her of tusks.

"How you been, honey? I come special today—just to see
you."

The smell of him was sickening, but she didn't move away.
He'd come to see her! He was the only person in this whole
ugly country who had any manners for strangers. She put out
her dirt-stained hands and touched him. "I'm so glad. Come
in. I'll fix us some tea."

The wise old eyes seemed to look right down into her heart.
"Why, honey, you've ketched yourself a good case of the blues.
Been alone too much, huh? Guess Amie hasn't had time to get
up, but she will. You won't be lonesome for long. Folks will be
comin' around any day now."

"Forget the shovel, Jediah. Come on in."

He followed her into the house and sat down with his feet
propped on the edge of the kitchen stove while she hurried to
put on the tea kettle, set the table with fine linen and silver
that hadn't been used since she came from the old country. She
polished her hand-painted dishes with a clean towel.

The fragrance of hot tea filled the kitchen. Jediah eyed the
table apprehensively. She did things up fancy, this little bit of
green-eyed stuff from Scotland. And there wasn't any use telling her how he felt about tea. A man might as well drink cat
piss.

He looked around at the old logs. He couldn't amuse himself by reading the papers now. Damn near shining, those logs.

"Now," he said, "tell me how everything's going with you. How you been gettin' along out here under the hogback?"

She poured the tea and told him about burning the chaps. "I didn't know, Jediah. I thought they were no good."

Jediah burst into loud laughter. "I'd like to have seen Tommy's face—him so damn tight he hurts when he throws away an old whisky bottle."

She talked on, words pouring out of her, and ended by telling him about the dirt for the flowerbed.

"Don't you fret about that black dirt. Sure you need it. Can't grow stuff in that red clay. Gets slick when it's rainy, and cakes worse than cement afterward. And it's a good idea to get the ground fixed up in fall if it's to be used in spring. Gives the earth time to settle and get in shape. I'll fetch you all the black dirt you want. Ravine back of the bunkhouse is full of it. And I'll work in some manure to make it better. I tell you, honey, them men been livin' out here like coyotes for so long they don't know how to treat a woman."

"Drink your tea, Jediah. It'll get cold."

His finger crooked awkwardly through the fragile handle of the cup. "Mighty pretty. I'd sure hate to break it."

"Oh, Jediah, use it! I want you to. You can break the whole set, so you can!" And she laughed.

"You oughta laugh often," he said, smiling at her. "Most delicious noise I ever heard."

"Oh, this is like being home again! Tea in the afternoon, a friend to visit with—" Then her eyes clouded. "When I think of what we put up with here, the way Tommy lords it over us like we were dirt—"

"Well," Jediah said, reaching for a cooky, "I got a cat at my cabin, and I named him Tommy. Y'know why? He's a no-good son-of-a-bitch." Jediah tilted his head back and laughed.

Prim found herself laughing too. Here was a smart man, who saw things the same way she saw them. Here was a man Tommy Cameron couldn't fool.

"Where's the little girl?" Jediah said. "I come to see her too."

"Away with her father. He takes her everywhere with him."

"Now, that's fine. Guess you know how proud he is of her— was from the very first. Told everybody in the country when she was born. And we all felt she was partly our kid too. We're gonna be mighty proud of her, and of you, Prim."

Prim stared down at the table. "It's been—a hard thing. I was over there so long, and Kelsey here, and the years between us— I've no right to be talking this way to you, a stranger."

"We're no strangers, Prim. I know it was hard, marryin' a man when you had a little kid, and coming to a far country. But that's water under the bridge. The past is done with, honey. You put your mind and your heart on the future, see?"

"It's because I've felt so hurt, knowing what people must think when they see us, when they look at Heather."

"Who the hell cares what they think? Listen, this is a big country and not standin' on any rules made by anybody any-where. We make our own. Your kid's legal. You've got a hell of a good man. Don't you ever forget what a good man you've got, Prim. He thinks the world of you. Why, once when him and me got drunk in town—"

"Drunk?"

"Why, sure. Now, get that look off your face. Didn't expect him to sit out here in this lonesome country without tippin' a bottle once in a while, did you? You take a man who don't take a drink, don't swear, don't do nothin' but act like some old maid, and you've got a man who's got one hell of a weakness some-where. In the Park, Prim, a man's just got to have some fun. If you can't laugh you sure can't live with lonesome country like this. Can't live much anyhow without laughing."

Prim's lips trembled. "It's just that— I never thought he'd be laying drunk in town while I was back there by myself and—"

"Cut out that kind of thinkin', Prim. Gimme some more of

that damn tea. It ain't half as bad as I figured it was gonna be."

She had to smile. "What did Kelsey say about me that time in town?"

Jediah took a gulp of tea, making a sucking sound. He wiped his mouth on the back of his hand. "He talked about you like you were an angel. He told me how pretty and wonderful you were, and how straight you walked, and how you could add numbers to beat anything. 'Why, hell,' he says, 'there's nobody in this whole country can figure like Prim.' "

She felt mellow now. She could lean back, smiling, while she toyed with the teacup. She could say, "Well, I won't say I'm *that* good at it, but the schoolmaster said I was the best he'd ever had in class, and he was teacher there over thirty years."

Jediah nodded. "That's the notion Kelsey gave me over town that night. 'Why, damn it,' he says to me, 'she's so far ahead of me I'm standin' still.' "

"He won't stand still," Prim said, her chin up. "I'll see to that. I'm pushing him up in the world, up where he belongs."

"Now," Jediah went on, "that's likely what you'll do. And there's lots of folks in the Park you'll enjoy, Prim—Amie Plunkett, for one. Big and warm and gen-uine—she's a real woman."

"And Monte Maguire?"

Jediah added more sugar to his tea and stirred it carefully. "Figured you'd ask me that. Far as I'm concerned, Monte and Amie are in the same class—damn fine women. You ought to have a lot in common with Monte."

"Including my husband?"

"Don't mince matters, do you? Sure, he likes Monte. And she's got a high respect for him. Anything wrong with that?"

"Not a thing," Prim said, her lips pinched in a tight smile.

"Monte had a rough time," Jediah went on. "Had two babies when she first got married, and lost 'em. Her husband was a lot older, and when he died I figured it was good riddance. Never liked Flit Maguire."

Prim put her elbows on the table. "When I was in town Dolly Gentry—"

"Yeah?" Jediah cut in. "Well, she never did see it, and what you don't see you better not go around talking about like it was gospel truth. She just didn't take a fancy to Monte, for Monte was something to see when Flit brought her in here the first time. And she got to doing some things the rest of the women didn't have guts to do. Maybe she did come outta cathouse. I don't know and care less. I say she's come a long way up in cow business, and most of the road by herself. I take my hat off to her."

"She's not the first woman had to come up in the world by herself."

"Didn't say so. Do you know something? When her little babies died not a woman showed up to help but Amie Plunkett. The men came around, though. They helped where they could, dug the grave out there in the willows over on the North Fork Ranch—that's across the hogback, and Monte used to live there. But it was Amie who got Monte out of the room where she'd locked herself in with the twin babies. Amie talked her into opening the door and took the babies from her. Monte cried for three days. I heard Amie tell about it, for Amie never left her until she stopped the crying. She just lay there and sobbed, and when she got up she was changed. She put on a man's hat and a man's boots and walked out of the house. Old Flit Maguire tried to order her back in, but she paid him no heed. When he died she had things so clear in her mind she knew more about ranching than he did. Like I said, Prim, you and Monte ought to have a lot in common."

"I don't see why. I come from decent folk, so I do, and—"

"Don't matter what you come from, good or bad. Trouble's a thing draws people closer than anything. You put outta your mind any grudge you have against Monte. She's done a lot for your husband."

"Is he to go around being beholden to her for it?" Prim asked angrily.

"You and me gonna fight the first time I come to visit?"

Prim's mouth opened and then closed. "All right," she said after a while. "Have some more cookies."

"Don't mind if I do, as Faun says when he takes another drink. Thanks." Jediah got up, stretched. "I'm gonna find that dirt while I'm still in the notion."

"I'll pack some bread for you to take home. It's fresh bread. And some cookies. You'd like that, wouldn't you?"

"Hope to tell you." He settled the greasy cap on his head. "You're a mighty good-lookin' woman when your disposition's right." And with an impudent grin he walked out.

"Well, I never!" She stood with her hands on her hips and watched him pick up the shovel. Then the gladness was in her again. I've got a friend who came to see me, she thought, smiling. His heart's that big and good, the smell of him's of no account.

CHAPTER XII

Kelsey Cameron wakened from deep sleep. Prim was quiet beside him. The little gusts of her breathing fanned his cheek, and her arm lay warm and still next to his. His ears strained, trying to place the sound that had disturbed him. He thought he heard a coyote bark from the meadow. But there was something else now—the *clip-clop* of horses' hoofs rising from the hard-packed dirt roads of late fall. Not one horse or two, but many, were traveling through the night. The sound drew closer, and with it the unmistakable thin singing of fast-turning buggy wheels. Moments later the silence was shattered by pistol shots, rattling tin cans, shouts. Rocks bounced off the roof.

He was out of bed and groping to light the lamp when Prim cried, "What's that?"

"A charivari! Quick, Prim, get up and put on your clothes." He yanked down the blind at the window. The yellow lamplight touched Prim's tangled hair and her eyes so big and green.

"It's nothing to be afraid of," he said, laughing. "It's the whole country coming to welcome you, the way they always do newly married couples."

The bedroom door opened, and Heather rushed in, jumped under the covers close to her mother, and hid her head.

"Get up, Heather," Kelsey said. "Put on your clothes. In a minute folk will be in the house. Hurry, Prim!"

She sat up. "For newly married people—is that what you said?"

"Yes, yes. I told you!" He was impatient, trying to smooth his hair.

"Oh, but we're not—I mean—" Her voice faltered. Then she looked down at the child's shape under the bed covering.

Outside he heard the sound of tin pans being beaten with sticks. Then there were loud laughter and shouts. "Open up or we'll break in!" More pistol shots went off, and there was the quick *pad-pad* of running feet around the outside of the house.

He flung back the blankets and pulled Prim from the bed. She stood shivering in his arms. "Don't be afraid, Prim," he said. "You'll have a wonderful time. It's all friendly. Do you think people haven't known all about Heather for a long time? Nobody has a secret in the Park. I told the whole damned country when I went after you. I told them because I loved you, Prim, and nothing else mattered. And now the people are here to welcome you."

He heard the front door give, and then Amie Plunkett's voice, strident and warm. "If you haven't got your pants on by now, it's too late."

He gave Prim a quick little hug. "Now for some clothes." He yanked a dress from a spike in the wall and thrust it at her.

"That's an old one. I want a nice dress, so I do."

"Then find one and be quick about it, lassie."

He waited impatiently while she dressed, hearing the stamping feet, the squeaking fiddles tuning up, the shouting of the children. Heather jumped from the bed and ran to the door. She slipped into the front room, and he heard a shout of laughter and Amie saying, "Come on, Heather-girl. Let Amie lift you, darlin', and see how heavy you are."

The fiddles began to play, and the shuffling feet beat time on the wooden floor. Pushing Prim before him, Kelsey stepped out and bowed to the people. Then he saw Heather. She was dancing by herself in the center of the floor, her nightgown held high. She whirled and bowed and smiled. The people bowed back to her, clapping their hands. Then Long Dalton picked her up and, holding her in his arms, began to waltz around and around the room.

Kelsey's heart was full. He turned to Prim in that moment before they met his friends and said, "Did you see her? Did you see how she won their hearts?"

There was love and pride on Prim's face. Her shoulders went back and her chin lifted. She moved forward to Amie Plunkett's outstretched arms. Amie kissed her and shouted, "Welcome to the Park, Prim!"

"Chap the groom! Chap the groom!" The men closed around Kelsey. He pretended to struggle violently, shouting, "Mind my weak ribs, damn you!" He scowled and flailed his arms while they lifted him on their shoulders and carried him outside. "Help! Help!" he yelled. They marched to the watering trough, bent him over, and swatted him with a pair of leather chaps. Then they dipped him in the water and carried him, dripping and shivering, back to the house. A bottle of whisky was pressed into his hand. He took a big drink and looked around, beaming at them, loving them. "Have at it, boys!" he shouted. "Let joy be unconfined!"

He saw Dalt bringing Heather out of the bedroom. Dalt had helped her with her dress, and it was on backward. Well, what did that matter? What did anything matter? They were here to dance and drink and have fun, have fun all the long night until daylight. He took another gulp from the bottle, did a little jig, and sang:

> *"Oh, gimme a gal, the first one handy.*
> *Let me kiss her fine red lips,*
> *And she'll suit me just dandy!"*

Prim danced past him, shouting, "Change your clothes or you'll catch your death of cold."

Still dancing and singing to himself, he went into the bedroom and put on his good dark suit. When he came out Dalt was calling a square. Dalt stood, jerking to the squeaky music, his yellow head thrown back, his face flushed, bawling out, "Birdie hop out and crow hop in; all join hands and circle agin!" Beside him, Heather imitated every motion, waving her arms and crying, "Bird out—crow in! Circle, circle agin!"

The women's skirts belled out and swept back as they swung in the arms of the men. The odor of sweat and sweet perfume rose to mingle with the sharper odor of whisky. The old floor trembled. The fiddles sang thin and off-key, and a tomcat howled outside.

There was such a joy in Kelsey that he ran to Amie Plunkett —big in her old black dress, with safety pins holding the ripping seams. He whirled her around and around in a dance, all by themselves, off to the side of the squaring couples. Then he left her to sweep Ellie Lundgren from Vic's arms, swing her high, set her down, and kiss her thin, pinched mouth.

"Oh, Mr. Cameron!" She squealed, and the hairs on her upper lip twitched like the whiskers of a mouse.

He moved on to Dolly Gentry, whose soft breasts jiggled against him. He came around to Prim, who was dancing with Harry Plunkett, snatched her from Harry's arms long enough to kiss her, laugh down into her flushed face, and shout, "Hooray!" He spun on to the kitchen door, where Jediah Walsh leaped upon him, putting his arms around Kelsey's neck and wriggling his hips. The smell of whisky was strong on Jediah's breath. For a few moments the two of them cavorted foolishly, going through grotesque motions of dancing.

"Let me go, you old devil!" Kelsey squirmed free. "Don't try to rape me!"

"Huh-huh-huh!" Jediah laughed, his short crooked neck sunk down between his shoulders.

The fiddles were silent for a moment. Someone flung the front door open for air. Out of the night came the sound of running horses, the squeal of buggy wheels. The men crowded through the door, Kelsey and Jediah behind.

The buggy came to a careening halt outside the fence. The team reared up, pawing the air, while the driver stood in the buggy, pulling back on the lines. "Take 'em away, boys!" she shouted.

Men moved to the horses' heads, quieted them down. Monte Maguire lifted her full skirts above her knees and jumped to the ground. She swept past Kelsey and Jediah, into the front room, and over to the fiddlers. She took off the long dark coat and stood in a blue dress with the neck so low the half-moons of her breasts were showing—not white breasts, but brown from the touch of summer sun.

Kelsey Cameron stared at her. Naked in the sun, she's been, he thought, and all the cool sweet wind going over her. She turned and looked at him, and he smiled.

She shouted at the fiddlers, "Play, boys! Play 'Dem Golden Slippers.' 'Oh, my golden slippers . . .' " And she two-stepped this way and that, and the sparkling combs in her upswept hair flickered like diamonds. She bent low before Kelsey, spreading her skirts, looking up at him, her eyes mocking him, her full mouth smiling. "Will you dance, Mr. Cameron?"

The whole room was watching. Prim was watching. The fiddlers were playing with hard, concentrated effort. He put out his arm, and she stepped closer, and he began to dance stiffly as other couples drifted onto the floor.

"What am I?" Her heavy, long brows lifted. "A fencepost? For God's sake, loosen up, Cameron! We're not two-stepping to a funeral dirge."

He was angry then, and held her closer than need be and whirled her roughly. At the first pause in the music he left her abruptly on the sidelines, hurried to the kitchen, and took a big drink. Jediah yanked the bottle from his hands, and the whisky went down Jediah's throat in a long *gurgle-gurgle*. They beamed at each other, and Kelsey whistled softly, broke into singing. He had another drink and continued: " 'Kase I don't 'spect to wear 'em till my weddin' day!' "

"Yust drunk." Hilder laughed, getting up from the kitchen table. "Drunk men always sing foolish songs." He wiped his face, which looked as round and shining as the moon outside. "I put on some coffee. If you men don't drink no coffee, this shivaree she is done for quick. All the men pass out, and all the women be sore as hell. Women, they come to dance."

"Y'know, I never could figure that out," Jediah said. "Seems there's quicker and easier ways to get next to a man. I don't dance with no women. It might give me notions, and at my age I don't want any notions."

Kelsey went back to the living room. His feet seemed to be above the floor. He felt as if he were going through the harbor water, splashing along on a fine summer day when he was a lad, and the water warm as a blanket and falling away from him like parting silk. A wave of music carried him forward to face Monte Maguire. "Want to take a walk?" he asked.

Want to take a walk? Want to take a walk? Was he saying the words, or were they only in his head?

"You're the one who needs to take a walk. The door's right ahead. Get movin', young fella."

"Full speed ahead, and the devil take the hindmost!"

He was walking in the night beside her. He was stepping high over the frost-white grass, and the hogback was rolling forward to meet him and then rolling back. They were swimming together in the starlight, her bare shoulder moving next to his.

"Shouldn't have put on that dress," he murmured. "The women'll say bad things about you."

Her hands were shoving him forward. Willows scraped his face, and he knew he was up in the grove behind the house, and the springs were there, under the red knoll that jutted out from the hogback. "Stop pushing, Monte!"

"I'm going to push your head right in that spring."

"Oh no, you're not!"

He felt the strong arm across his middle, and himself bending like a long stick of licorice candy in the heat. He was on his
knees, and the damp grass tickled his face. Then water was
over him, cold and breath-taking. He tried to shout. He choked.
His head was jerked up and, gasping, he shouted, "Damn you,
you're trying to drown me!"

He heard her laughter, and his head went under again. He
came up, gagging on water. He lay back in the willow shade
with the ground damp and cold under him and the moonlight
on his face. He put up his arms and pulled her down. For a moment she was there, and the length of her over him was a fire-
shaped replica of himself. Then she was jerking away. She
stood up, tall and proud, and smoothed her dress. "Not this
way," she said. "Never this way. The only way it could ever be
you'd be sober and remember everything about it as long as
you live." And she went away.

He lay still, and his mind slowly cleared. It wouldn't have
happened if I'd been sober, he thought. It was the drink in me
that made me want her. Drink tears a man down, making him
do things against his better judgment. I'm not like Jediah;
Jediah can have the bottle all night, fast or slow, and he stays
about the same. But a little of it gives me a madness.

He began to feel sick. After a while he went to the soda
spring. Here in this other spring in the willow grove the water
fizzed, and it took the wind from a man's stomach. It stung the
tongue and bit into the soft tissue of the mouth. He put his head
down and drank. It made him very sick, and then he felt better.
He drank some more, and this time he kept the water down.
He washed his face in it. He ran his fingers through his rough
hair. And when he went walking down the gentle slope toward
the squeaking fiddles he felt good. He was ready to dance and
drink again. Just before he reached the house he met Tommy.
Tommy stood square and black in the little path in front of
the door.

"What's eating on you, Tommy?"

"Still suckin' in with the boss, eh? Wasn't enough she's gonna let you run cattle again. You gotta take her up in the willows. Did you forget you had a wife?"

Kelsey's fist swung out. It grazed Tommy's cheek. They sprang at each other, their fists striking viciously. Kelsey tasted blood. Tommy's knee came up hard and struck him in the groin.

"Cut it out!" It was the voice of Dalt, who moved between them. Kelsey felt Dalt's big hand shoving him back. "Cut it out," Dalt said again. "This is no time for it." And he twisted Tommy's arm back until Tommy gave a yelp of pain.

The three of them turned and walked slowly to the house.

*   *

Prim was having a wonderful time. She'd never danced so much, nor with so many different partners. Every time the music started men rushed to her, jostling and shouting. "My turn!" "This one is mine, Mrs. Cameron." "Don't dance another one with that old broken-down Faun Gentry."

She found herself laughing up into the weatherbeaten faces. And she knew she was hot and flushed, and that her eyes were sparkling. Not even at the New Year celebrations in Scotland could she remember having had such fun. How foolish she had been to fear meeting these people, and how good they were to Heather!

Near midnight some of the women left the dancing to settle the smaller children for naps in the bedrooms. Prim separated Heather from Dalt and took her to her own bed. Ellie Lundgren's little daughter Mavis, who was just Heather's age, was already there, and Prim left the two children together. When she went back to the living room she was caught up again in the arms of Harry Plunkett. The momentary tiredness she'd felt as she kissed Heather good night was forgotten, and away she went, spinning from dance to dance.

Later, over a broad shoulder, Prim saw Amie Plunkett going into the kitchen. I must mind my manners, she thought, and help out there, for surely it's time to eat. She excused herself when the dance ended, and found a pretty apron to protect her dress.

Amie was at the kitchen stove, saying to Hilder, "This fire you built won't heat nothin'. It's not hot enough. I gotta have more wood." And she lifted the big woodbox to the edge of the stove.

Prim caught her arm. "Oh, no! You mustn't. It's too heavy for a woman in your condition."

Amie laughed. "Hell, honey, I couldn't miscarry if I tried. I coulda ridden a horse to this shindig tonight. Once I'm caught, I'm caught good."

Prim glanced at Hilder and felt her face turn scarlet. Amie shrugged. "He's old enough to know storks don't bring 'em."

Ellie Lundgren came into the kitchen, carrying a bleached white sack. "If there's too much food, I take home what's left. I don't eat big greasy meals like the men." And she went around, peering in all the baskets, opening boxes, licking her lips, her thin nose sniffing curiously.

"Won't likely be any left," Amie said loudly. "I'm apt to slick it all up. After all, Ellie, I'm eatin' for two, maybe three of us."

"Well, yust in case some is extra—" Ellie stuck the white sack among the boxes of food, looked around once more, and went back to the living room.

"And what'd she bring?" Amie asked angrily. "Half a dozen boiled eggs, and they're probably rotten."

Jediah and Hilder laughed loudly. Prim turned from getting dishes out of a cupboard and saw Kelsey standing in the kitchen door. She stared at him. "There's blood on your face."

"Just ran into a fencepost," he said, reaching for a cup. "Got any real hot java, Amie?"

"Man always needs coffee after drinkin'," Jediah said.

Prim began to arrange food on the table. Some of the evening's happiness had gone from her heart. Did Kelsey have to drink so much? I don't want him making a fool of himself, she thought.

It was daylight when the last buggy drove away. Kelsey walked around, looking at gifts some of the people had brought —a blue blanket, a fancy teapot, hand-embroidered pillowcases. "Hell," he said to Prim, "these will punch holes in a man's face while he sleeps." He reached in a box and pulled out a bottle of whisky. "Faun left this. Thought we might want it." He smiled foolishly and started to tug at the cork. "Let's have some, Prim."

Prim tried to take the bottle from his hands. "Oh, Kelsey, you've had enough of that tonight."

Kelsey jerked back, and the bottle fell, smashing on the floor between them. Prim jumped away with a laugh. "There," she cried. "At least you won't drink that."

He glared at her. "Damn you, Prim Munro. Don't ever do that again."

She shrank from the fury in his eyes. There had been hatred in the words. She flared back at him. "Well, I'll not have it, so I won't! I've a lassie to raise, and you'll not be drunk in my house like you were tonight."

"And I'll not be anything my lassie has to be ashamed of!" He kicked at the broken glass. "Hope you enjoyed yourself, flying into a tantrum." He walked out, banging the door behind him.

Prim felt numb. If he'd only let me tell him I didn't mean to break the bottle; it was the bottle started the trouble. Then she remembered his eyes, and the way his words had lashed out at her. She stumbled toward the bedroom. She was hurt, and it was a terrible kind of hurting that couldn't be released in tears.

CHAPTER XIII

It was the time of year when Kelsey Cameron tired of winter. Now, on this day in late March, riding over the meadow, he was weary of overshoes, weary of mittens and heavy coats. And the knowledge of Prim's distaste for the Park lay like a weight upon him. Although she had lived on the ranch only six months, she had made up her mind she'd never like it. Only that morning she had said to him, "We won't stay here. It's only for a little while; then we'll move. Don't you want to go back to the old country, Kelsey?"

"And what would we go on, Prim? Have you a magic for money?"

"My mither would send me all the money I want—to come home."

The thought of Big Mina's money revolted him, and he said angrily, "Don't mention her to me again." And because he was ready to quarrel with Prim, he hurried from the house.

It was blue twilight as he turned homeward, riding slowly among the cattle. They were rough and shabby-looking, their hides sprouting tannish hair that sometimes rainbowed when the sun touched it. Above the meadow snow curled on the razor edge of the hogback like a long line of surf breaking against the sky. He looked for a sign of bare ground showing dark amidst the white, and he listened foolishly for the note of a blackbird. It was hard for a man to bear with this waiting time between winter and the breaking of ice on the rivers. But still, he reminded himself, the clouds gave promise of better days, for

153

now and then they looked plump and white instead of thin and gray.

As he walked toward the house his overshoes made a slushy plopping in the melting snow that was crusting in the evening coolness. He could see Heather at the front window, watching him. She'd been inside for a week with a cold, and her face was thin, making her eyes bigger and grayer than before—Taraleean's eyes, he thought. He must write to his mother. He often told himself he'd do it, tomorrow or next week. But her letters came regularly. Often he read them in Amie Plunkett's warm and dirty kitchen, wanting to have a time alone with his mother's words before Prim squinted over his shoulder, saying, "Well, what's new at the harbor?" She heard from her brothers or Big Mina once a week, and he surely never asked what they might say to her. Hell with them, he thought now, stepping into the kitchen, his overshoes tracking the lye-bleached floor. Heather ran to him for a kiss.

Prim was frying potatoes for supper. "It's a hard country," she said, "and I've had enough of it, so I have." She grabbed the mop and made a quick sweep to take up the puddles of water. "There's a gunnysack tacked on the front step, and you could clean your feet, Kelsey Cameron."

He took off his overshoes and pushed them behind the kitchen stove, dragged a chair close to the heat, and sat down.

Prim turned the potatoes. They sizzled, and the smell of them made his mouth water. "What have we got here?" she demanded. "A house my folk would put cows in if they had cows. A midden of a place, that's what it is. And your big cousin Tommy lording it over us! And what's so fine about working for Monte Maguire? Maybe that half-Irish devil told her beads and got a message she was doing us a favor handing us her stinking fifty dollars a month—less than any other married couple in the Park's getting."

"I never saw the beads on her," Kelsey said curtly, "and we're getting less wages because I can run my own cattle. I've

told you that a dozen times. Can't you get it through your
head?"

"If Monte Maguire's Irish, she's a teller of beads, as with all
them that's Catholic, and to the devil with the good Presbyterians."

"What's so special about the Presbyterians? A damn dry business if you ask me, trying to take the fun from life, and a dreary
future all cut out for a man."

She turned from the stove. "I say it's good, so I do. And I
miss my church. As Dolly Gentry said when she was here last
week, the ranchers break the Sabbath every chance they get,
talking about having to fix fence or put up hay—or an old cow
having a calf."

His lips twitched in a wry smile. "And if a calf starts to be
born on Sunday is it to wait until Monday?"

"You've a way of twisting things I say to you," she retorted.
"You got it from your mother, a twisting woman if there ever
was one, gossiping every chance she got—"

"Ah, Prim, would you throw stones at my mother? You? Is
your memory so short? Is it that you can shut your mind and
heart to your own weakness and look for weakness in others?"

Her face sobered. Moisture clouded her eyes. Turning
quickly to the stove, she banged a big lid over the frying
potatoes. "Aye," she said, "a woman's to be reminded of her
fall, so she is. What kind of devil was born in me that I always
end up with the business of sin, adding it up and adding it down
like a sum I once worked at in school and couldn't get the right
answer?" Two fat tears ran down her cheeks, dropped and
sizzled on the hot stove.

He went to her quickly, put his arms around her, and said in
sudden tenderness, "It was the thing I loved most in you, the
weak thing, Prim, that brought you to my arms that night on
the shore—and oh, the sea so wonderful in its sound, and your
lips so warm on mine!"

"God, the worst is," she said, weeping loudly now, "if time

turned back I'd do the same thing again, fool that I am! A soft lassie with no stiffness in her, that's what I was, and let a lad make a fool of me. It's a stain in me, this weakness, and I tell you I'd cut it out if I could."

"No, no, Prim. Don't say that. Never think it. Be glad for what you are, and be honest. It's sometimes all a man's got, an honesty with himself. And you mustn't worry over what's past. In some it might be a stain, but not in you. In you, that night, it was"—he drew a deep breath—"in you it was lovely!"

She gave her head a little shake and muttered, "Are we to talk like this before the lassie, and her old enough to know the meaning of words?"

"Why not? She'll not be raised to be ashamed of us or what we did. Nor will I raise her not knowing what life's about. The worst and best of us, she'll know it."

"Then step clear of me now because of the hired men. What if Tommy or Long Dalton came in, or that Swede, and see us with our arms around each other in broad daylight?"

He laughed, amused at her. "Is it any different by day than by night? What is this false modesty possesses women?"

She stepped away from him, smoothing the clean apron that protected the front of her dress. "And are the cowpunchers here for supper?"

"Don't think so. Jake's at the North Fork Ranch."

"No one's been in to tell me, and I had it out with Jake last week. I said to him, 'Jake, if you're eating in this house you'd better be telling me or you'll sit down to an empty plate, so you will.' "

"They're Monte Maguire's punchers, and they have to eat, and it's understood they eat wherever they're working."

"That may be, but they'll be letting me know and not just marching in like they owned the place and I was a servant to fetch and carry when they snap their fingers."

"Prim, you'll make no friends among the men."

"I don't want them for friends. I want them to stay in the

bunkhouse, for I don't want them swearing around my lassie."

"And, if I'm not mistaken, you were swearing yourself the other day."

She bit her lip, scowling. "And if I did swear I was beside myself. Yes, I did swear. I said I'd looked at the damned snow so long I couldn't stomach it another day."

Kelsey turned to the windows filled with the last flare of sun-down red. "Take heart. It'll be spring soon—spring, and the cattle moving onto the flats to calf among the sagebrush." He lifted his daughter and sat with her in his lap. "And did you know, lassie, that the sagebrush is for a wee calf to hide in— a house of his own? Each clump's a tent that keeps the calves warm from the cold spring wind and the wet. When I first looked on this country I felt like your mother. I thought it was ugly and the gray sagebrush the ugliest thing of all and no good for man or beast. Then I learned about the calves and how it takes care of them. It's wonderful, the things nature provides."

"My God," Prim said, her eyes glinting, "he's about to go into poetry over the damn sagebrush."

"Now," Kelsey said, paying no heed to Prim, stroking Heather's fine dark hair, "when spring comes we'll ride on the flats, just you and me, and see the calves in the sagebrush. You'll ride your horse, Chinook." Turning to Prim, he added, "You should see her with that horse! It's a gift she has. She insults him with all manner of insults, and he takes it like a lamb, his eyes sleepy and his long tail with never a twitch to it."

"I talk to him," Heather said. "He knows what I say."

Prim shuddered. "As for me, I'd stay clear of him—a big, broad thing with feet like a frying pan. And heaven knows why he'll take such treatment from a lassie with the wildness in her." Prim sighed and added bleakly, "The wildness—and that's what comes from being started by the sea without the minis-ter's blessing. If I've marked her with my sin, God forgive me!" She shook her head and muttered, "You'd best be at your prayers, Prim Munro, for that's all will save you."

Kelsey watched her turn the meat, fascinated by the expression of saintliness that came over her face. At that moment Tommy walked in without taking off his overshoes, and Prim's saintly look vanished as she said tartly, "Can you not stoop to clean your feet?"

Tommy scowled. "What is this kitchen? A bloody parlor where a man can't walk without taking off his shoes like a damned Dutchman?"

"Hold up the grub," Kelsey said. "Monte just drove in."

"When food's ready it's ready," Prim retorted. "Why can't she get here on time? Ring the gong, Kelsey."

"I will not. You'll show some courtesy to Monte Maguire."

"I owe her nothing. I've been here since last fall, and she's made no effort to call on me." Prim picked up the triangular gong and started for the door.

Kelsey stepped before her and took it from her hands, "Stop it!" His voice was harsh. "Don't make a fool of yourself, Prim."

"All right! Let the food burn, then!"

Tommy shook his head. "The Munro disposition. Big Mina the second, that's what you've got yourself, Kelsey."

"God forbid!"

The door opened, and Monte Maguire came in. "Cold day," she said, shrugging out of the heavy coat. She pulled the fur-lined cap from her head, walked over to the stove, and sat down without removing her overshoes. The gunnysacks were wrapped tightly around her legs to the knee. She stretched, reached in her pocket for a match, and rolled a cigarette. "Wind been blowin' much out here?" she asked Tommy.

"Plenty. Did you ever see this time of year when it didn't? March is always the worst month for wind."

"You been able to feed?"

"All but four days. We're gettin' short of hay, though."

"It'll last," she said. "Another six weeks and we can push

the cows onto the flats." Her glance shifted to Prim. "Everything all right with you, Mrs. Cameron?"

"Oh, there's never anything wrong with me." Prim looked at Kelsey, who wasn't paying the least attention to them. There was a faraway expression in his eyes. "Off in his dreaming again," she said to Monte. "Yes, some days he hardly lives under the same roof with me. Heaven knows what he fancies himself in moments like this."

Monte put out her hand and grabbed Heather by the arm. "You're not speaking, young lady. Cat got your tongue?"

Heather gave her a shy, slow smile.

"But," Prim went on, "it's the dreamy ones of the world that get all the attention. Folk look at them and say, 'Oh, let these fine broody ones be. We'll humor them and bow before them, for they've got more color to them than ordinary folk.'" She began dishing up supper. "Ring the gong, Tommy, for Kelsey won't hear if I ask him, and you sit at the head of the table, Mrs. Maguire."

When the men were seated Prim poured the coffee, returning to her subject. "Now the lassie there beside you, Mrs. Maguire, she's like her father. I won't know what she's thinking half the time and won't be able to pry it out of her, either. But her father'll know. I see it between them already, a look passing from one to the other, and then it's like they had talked an hour and covered everything and satisfied themselves. Och aye, what is it to have a lassie, and her gone from you before she's out of her childhood?"

Heather frowned. "I'm not gone, Mama. I'm here."

"You puzzle the child," Kelsey said sharply. "Stop this talk of yours that makes no sense and eat your supper."

"Thank you, no. I'm waiting on the table."

Monte Maguire reached for a piece of bread. "Looks like the cows are in pretty good shape. Worst storms will be over soon. I noticed a big jaw on a couple. Where's Jake?"

"Over on the North Fork. Oughta be back tomorrow."

"Well, get him on those big-jawed cows. Probably foxtail back in their throats. Hell a'mighty, can't cowpunchers see past their noses?"

Heather tried to cut a piece of meat, and it skidded from her plate. "Well, hell a'mighty!" she said.

The men laughed, but Prim seized Heather by the braids, yanked her to her feet, and dragged her to the wash bench. Heather yelled and struggled while Prim washed her mouth with soap. "You don't ever talk like that again, missy, do you hear?"

Heather let out another bellow of protest. Kelsey stood up, his face flushed. "Leave her be!"

"Am I to let her grow up talking like one of the men?" Prim whirled to face Monte Maguire. "You watch your language around my lassie, Mrs. Maguire."

Monte's long, heavy brows lifted. "Didn't say a damn thing, and don't get your bowels in an uproar." She turned her attention to Tommy. "See that Jake runs the cows when the warm weather sets in. Tell him to sick the dogs on 'em. I don't know as it does much good, but some think it keeps them from gettin' blackleg—stirs up the circulation. Funny thing how blackleg always hits the best cows and the biggest calves. You can ride through the meadow on an afternoon and see a healthy cow or calf, and go out the next morning and find 'em on their sides, their legs stuck out stiff, and the blood in 'em thick and black as molasses."

Heather, still crying, climbed onto Kelsey's lap, and he stroked her hair, saying, "Hush, now. Don't cry. That's a good lass."

"You humor her!" Prim frowned at him. "And now my work's undone."

"Amie Plunkett been to see you?" Monte asked Prim.

"Yes. She's some talker, that woman."

"They don't come any better than Amie," Monte said.

Prim poured herself a cup of coffee and stood drinking it. "The day she was here her hair looked like it hadn't been washed in a month. The Lord keep me from letting myself go like some of the women in this country."

"Can't you take a friend as she is without wanting to change her?" Kelsey asked impatiently. "I thought you liked Amie."

Prim shrugged. "Never said I didn't like her."

The men started leaving the table; Hilder was humming under his breath, and Long Dalton leaned down to whisper in Heather's ear. She laughed.

In the kitchen doorway Hilder paused, jabbing at his teeth with a whittled match. "Was you comin' up to play poker with us tonight, Kelsey?"

Kelsey stared at the floor. "Don't know. I'll think about it, though."

"He's gotta ask," Tommy said, jerking a thumb toward Prim.

"And why not?" Prim set down her cup with a clatter. "He's been up there every night for the last two months, hasn't he? Every night, while I sit here alone. And comes dragging in after midnight, so he does."

Kelsey got up and moved restlessly around the kitchen. "And am I not entitled to a little fun? What happens when I stay here with you? You nag about the country and the cold and the snow, don't you? And let me tell you this: those first years I couldn't play much poker or have any fun. I'm through living that way."

Prim looked at Monte. "Where I came from it's different, I can tell you. Men walk with their women after supper, take them around the roads." She turned to Kelsey. "It's time to get the lassie ready for bed, and I'd like you to read a Bible verse to her."

"I haven't seen the Bible."

"Then I'll have to find it." She left the kitchen, and they could hear her banging drawers in another part of the house.

She returned, saying, "It's not to be found. It looks like you'd take care of it, belonging to your father as it did, and him the fine man that he was."

"I think that old hide-buyer took it with him," Kelsey said. "And why all this show about religion tonight?"

"You've slipped some in the years you've been in this country, Kelsey Cameron. Your father had prayers every night and a verse read from the Bible."

"Oh, let's get off religion and leave the lassie alone."

"Is she to be raised a heathen? Why, she won't even know who Jesus Christ is!"

"Then read her some Bobby Burns. Likely it'll do her as much good."

Monte Maguire burst into laughter. Prim glared at her and then at Kelsey. "Old drunken Burns! I'd as leave put that book out back where we use the catalogues."

Again Monte laughed. Prim said tartly, "It's not so funny, Mrs. Maguire. Maybe you'd not worry about raising a child in this country, but I do."

"It's a worry I'd be grateful to have," Monte Maguire replied.

Kelsey took off Heather's clothes. She ran for a nightgown, and he put it over her nakedness, kissed her, and said, "Are we off to bed, then?"

Heather smiled at Monte. The big woman held out her arms, and the child went to her. The tanned, wind-lined face pressed for a moment against the soft dark hair. Kelsey Cameron looked away, a queer tightness in his throat.

After the child was in bed Kelsey left the house and Prim went upstairs to make a bed for Monte. When she shook out the fine sheets with the smell of lavender to them Monte touched them and said, "Real nice."

Prim smiled. "What did you expect I had in my trunks? Rags?"

"Turn it off, Mrs. Cameron. You don't have to carry a chip on your shoulder toward me or the rest of the Park."

They finished making the bed in silence and went down to the kitchen. Monte started stacking dishes, but Prim said, "No. That's my job. You can go about your own business."

Monte put down the plates, stood by the stove, and rolled a cigarette. She smoked, watching Prim work with the dishes. After a while she said, "Mrs. Cameron, you better make up your mind to get along with me. We're going to be around each other a long time."

Prim stopped working. She carefully wiped her soapy hands and looked at Monte Maguire. "And I'll speak my mind too, Mrs. Maguire. Kelsey Cameron's a man of honor, and he'll stay that way as long as he has the lassie."

A thin smile crossed Monte's mouth. "Got it all figured out, haven't you? Got a whip to hold over him, eh?"

"Yes, and I'll crack it when I take the notion. Heather's his whole life, and you know it."

"I wouldn't be so sure, Mrs. Cameron. If you nag him like you did tonight, he might be glad to crawl in bed with any damned old thing—just so she kept her mouth shut." Monte moved toward the door. "Good night, Mrs. Cameron."

"Where are you going?"

"To the bunkhouse. I always did like poker, and I figure I'll find it more interestin' there than around here." The door closed behind her.

Prim rattled the dishes in the pan. "Well, I never! Thank God I'll not be lowering myself to sit in a bunkhouse with a bunch of hired men." She nodded her head emphatically as she went on with her work.

CHAPTER XIV

W̲here did time go? Kelsey Cameron thought, riding toward Plunketts' ranch on a fine September morning with
his daughter jogging along on Chinook beside him. It
seemed only yesterday he'd brought Prim and Heather into
the Park, and now Heather was eight years old and was
about to start school. She should have been in school last
winter, but last winter there had been no teacher on the west
side of the Park.

What schooling Heather had was a strange mixture. Prim
had taught her to add and subtract, and Kelsey had worked
with her on the reading. She'd picked up the reading easily
and quickly, and he was very proud. But the things she knew
best were not taught in a schoolroom. Jediah Walsh had
taken her on his trap lines, and she understood the finer
points of setting and baiting traps. Dalt had shown her how
horses were broken, and from Jake, the boss puncher, she
had learned something about the care of the cattle.

When they had left the ranch house that morning, Prim
had stood in the doorway, ready to cry, for Heather would
be boarding with the Plunketts through the school week and
home only for week ends.

"Don't start blubbering, now," Kelsey said. "She has to
go to school. She can't stay here and grow up like a coyote.
You know that, Prim."

"But it's the first place she's gone and me not there to look
out for her." The tears brimmed in Prim's eyes.

164

"Amie will look out for her. Stop worrying, Prim."

The schoolhouse was a log cabin that had once been an extra bunkhouse. It was built on a barren piece of ground across the wide unfenced yard, some distance from Amie Plunkett's front door.

When Heather and Kelsey rode up there were three buggies by the schoolhouse and four saddle horses in Plunketts' corral.

Ellie Lundgren came out the door as Kelsey and Heather walked toward it. Ellie was wearing a divided riding skirt and a tan shirt fastened high at the throat and a big hat to protect her face from the sun. She looked at Heather. "Well! You grow up quick, eh? My girl, Mavis, she keep you company. And the Blake girls, Doris and Fanny, they're here too. You get along fine with the Blake girls."

From the porch of the ranch house Amie Plunkett shouted, "Mornin', Kelsey! Mornin', Heather-girl! Nice we got a school-house here—three Plunketts ready, and more to come." Her laughter rang in the still morning.

Kelsey and Heather stepped inside the cabin. A thin young woman with faintly purple skin sat at the big dark desk in front of the room, facing the row of smaller desks. In one corner the potbellied stove was hot, and the smell of burning pitch-pine was in the air.

Kelsey took off his hat and pushed Heather forward. "I'm Mr. Cameron—and this is Heather."

"Oh, yes. I'm Miss Davison." She stood, shook his hand briskly, and dropped it. Her white shirtwaist was starched stiff, and it made a crackling sound when she sat down. She wore thick glasses, and the dark eyes behind them were kind. "Has your little girl had any schooling, Mr. Cameron?"

He explained what had been done. Miss Davison nodded. "I am sure she can go into second or third grade."

Kelsey looked down at Heather. "You stay here, then. On Friday night you can come home. And Hilder's bringing

your trunk this afternoon." He twisted his hat awkwardly
in his hands. "Good-by, honey." And he hurried from the
little cabin into the sunlight that blinded him. He took her
horse to the corral, unsaddled it, and turned it into Harry
Plunkett's pasture. When he closed the gate Amie was there
waiting, wearing the dirt-stained wrapper that had swept the
dusty yard on her way to the corral.

"Don't you worry," she said gently. "My Jim will look after
her. He's four years older, and he likes her. Nobody's gonna
pick on her, not with Jim around."

Kelsey nodded and said, "Oh, I'm not worrying about
it." But he was as bad as Prim, he thought, for he feared
what might happen to his daughter—not around the boys,
for she'd grown up around men, but the girls, with their whispering ways.

"You come and have coffee," Amie said.

He followed her toward the house, looking across the yard
to the squat gray cabin from which came the high, clear
voices of the children singing, " 'My country, 'tis of thee,
Sweet land of libertee . . .' " A little sour, he thought, but
beautiful all the same.

*   *

Heather thought the song was beautiful, but she wasn't
sure of the words. And when the singing ended, Miss Davison said, "Heather, don't you know this song?"

"I know 'The Campbells Are Comin'.' " Heather spoke
quickly around the lump in her throat, trying not to show
she was embarrassed at being singled out.

"Now, that's just fine. What else do you know?"

"I know the one about the girl who peddled her butt on
the Big Goose Range. Dalt sings it, and—"

The boys tittered. Miss Davison's mouth was grim. "We
won't be interested in hearing that song, Heather."

Heather's face burned. She had said the wrong thing. She

glanced fearfully around the room. Mavis Lundgren was making a face at her. Doris and Fanny Blake had handkerchiefs stuffed in their mouths. They wriggled in their seats, looked at the boys, and went off into silent shivers of mirth.

Miss Davison opened the Bible and began to read. She read slowly, pausing often to look at Heather. And as she read her voice got louder. When she had finished she said, "Isn't that wonderful?"

Heather looked around the room. Several of the children nodded. Some only continued to stare at the teacher. Heather shifted uncertainly, frowning.

"What is it, Heather? Does something bother you?" Miss Davison leaned forward. Her eyes were very big and black behind the glasses.

"It don't make sense," Heather said. She felt her heart going fast, but she hurried on. "I just don't believe Jesus walked after he was dead. Nobody does after they're dead. I don't see any calves walkin' afterward. They only stink. Ain't that right, Jim?" And she turned to Jim Plunkett, who sat across from her.

"That's right," Jim said.

"You'll both stay after school," Miss Davison said crossly, "and—"

Mavis Lundgren's voice broke in. "It's not her fault, Miss Davison. She's just ign'rant. She can't help it because she's a love child."

"No, that ain't what it's called," Doris Blake said, standing and tossing back her red braids. "My folks come from Kentucky, and back there it's a ketched colt."

Somewhere in the back of the room a boy's voice rose in a harsh whisper. "Why'nt they say 'bastard' and tell the truth?"

Jim Plunkett jumped from his seat. He walked to the towheaded boy and yanked him to his feet. "Take it back or I'll bust you!"

They flew at each other, while Heather stared and the other girls climbed on the desks and squealed. Miss Davison ran to the stove and picked up a piece of pole. "Stop it!" She whacked both of the boys across the shoulders. They backed off, glaring at each other, muttering and scowling. The tow-headed boy had a black eye. Jim Plunkett's lip was bleeding.

"Now!" Miss Davison brought the pole down on the desk with a crack. "We'll come to order. Feet on the floor and shoulders back. Attention!"

The room became very quiet, except for the soft flutter-ing of the heating stove. Mingled odors brushed against Heather's face—perfume, horses, manure, and the smell that was like old pee. Somebody needed clean clothes and a bath.

"Now," Miss Davison said, "we will divide into grades and begin our lessons."

At recess Heather sat before the schoolhouse and watched the boys playing. They had caught a cattle rustler and were going to hang him. Near her the three girls eyed her curi-ously. Finally Mavis Lundgren spoke. "Ain't you got no dresses to wear?"

Heather looked down at her tan coveralls. "Sure. They're coming tonight in my trunk, but I like pants better."

"I've got five dolls," Fanny Blake said. She was a thin girl with a behind that stuck far out, thick brown hair, and little brown eyes. "You got any dolls, Heather?"

"Dolls?" Heather frowned. "I've got a rag doll. But I'd rather have a calf. I'm gonna get one someday, and when it's old enough I'm going to breed it to Monte's best bull and get me a cow herd started."

They stared at her. "It'll be a she-calf," she explained. "I don't want any steers in my herd. I want 'em shipped. They oughta be shipped anyhow before they get too old. They just cause trouble, breakin' down fences, gettin' with the cows, and wearin' the cows out ridin' them."

The girls licked their lips. They drew away and whispered together. Then, smoothing their skirts, they went off by themselves to a far corner of the yard. Heather sat alone, chin in hand, watching the boys. Suddenly she jumped up, shouting, "Jim! You tied that knot on the noose wrong. If you're gonna hang a man, you want a slipknot. I'll show you." She darted among the boys, picked up the rope; her hands worked with it. "There. When he swings, that'll tighten and shut off his wind."

The towheaded boy's name was Billy Martin. Heather said, "He's the one gonna swing, isn't he?"

"No, I ain't," Billy said. "Let somebody else."

"Then I'll swing," Heather said. "I'm not scared. You take me down to that tree by the creek. Wait! We gotta have a horse for me to sit on under the tree. Then you hit the horse and make him jump from under me. That's how they did it. Jediah told me."

"Gee!" The boys looked at her, and she felt important.

"Get my horse, Jim," Heather said.

The three girls followed them down to the creek. Heather got in the saddle. "Jim, you got to get up here and tie my hands behind me." And she sat patiently while he clambered onto Chinook's broad rump and fastened her hands with a short piece of rope. "Now," she said, speaking loudly, making the most of her position as rustler about to be hanged, "lead the horse under that big tree and put a rope around my neck."

One of the boys shinnied up, and she felt the rough loop against her throat. "You gotta tie the other end tight to that big branch above me," she ordered.

"Now we gotta hit the horse," one of the boys on the ground said.

"Not yet," Heather said. "Wait a minute. I'll say, 'Go,' and then you do it." She was enjoying herself; she didn't want everything to be over too soon. She wriggled in the saddle, getting set. Then, as she started to open her mouth, she heard a scream.

She turned her head and saw Amie Plunkett running toward them, followed by Miss Davison. As they got closer Amie stopped and began to walk, saying, "Don't a one of you move. Don't frighten that horse." And Amie reached Chinook's head, took hold of the bridle rein, and said, "Now, you devils get that rope off her neck!" She looked at Miss Davison, breathing hard. "My God, that was close!"

Heather sat quietly all the rest of that day. She wasn't lonesome until night, when Amie tucked her into the bed in the small room that was a lean-to built onto the back of the house. There were cracks in the chinking, and the wind came in, touching her cheek with coldness. She could hear the coyotes howling in the meadow. She thought of the Red Hill, and her mother coming in to hear her prayers. Then she started to cry, pushing her face into the pillow.

The door opened, and a boy stood there, a candle in his hand. "Heather," he whispered.

She sat up, rubbing the sleeve of her nightgown across her eyes. "Yes, Jim."

"Come on out to the kitchen and have a cooky."

She got up, and they tiptoed into the kitchen. Jim set the candle on the table, found two glasses, and dumped a handful of cookies on a plate. He poured the milk, saying, "You have some milk, Heather. It tastes good if you're lonesome."

"Oh, I ain't—I'm not. Miss Davison says it's wrong to say 'ain't.' "

"Aw, hell," Jim said. "She don't know very much."

"She does so! And that poetry—I liked the poetry. 'Specially the one about the boy on the burning deck. Gee, it was good!"

"I know a better poem about him," Jim said. He took a big gulp of milk. " 'The boy stood on the burnin' deck, eatin'

peanuts by the peck; his pants caught fire, alas, alas! He had
to jump into the ocean to cool his ass!' "

They broke into hysterical giggling. When Heather quieted
she said, "My daddy knows lots of poetry. He says it to me
when we ride. I love my daddy. Jim, is that why I'm a love
child?"

"Don't know." He got up, hitched at his pajamas. "You
better go back to bed, Heather. I'll give you a light in."

The candle glow flickered and was gone. She was warm
in the blankets and she could hear the creek murmuring behind the schoolhouse. Miss Davison said a poem was words
that sang. The creek made a poem of its own; the creek made
singing words even if a person didn't know what the words
said. She closed her eyes, saying her prayers. ". . . and God
bless my own folk in the old country—my uncles, Big Mina,
and my Granny Taraleean." Her lips moved again. "Taraleean, Taraleean . . ." It sang, that word.

*   *

Kelsey Cameron had a cache in the willows by the soda
spring. The cache was under a square of sod that he had
cut so carefully he could lift it and put it down again and no
one would see that the earth had been disturbed. And on this
Sunday in September he knelt by the square of sod, eased it
up, and took the bottle from underneath. He settled himself
in the willow shade, took a big drink, feeling the warmth of
it quiet his stomach. It was always so when a man drank too
much: the next day he had to have a few snorts, as Jediah
said, to get him over the rough places.

And he'd had good reason for the Saturday drinking. That
damn toothache had driven him crazy, and he'd had to go to
town. Well, he was rid of the tooth—and two others as sound
as good apples. The dentist was a fine fellow, that was for
sure, and a man shouldn't begrudge him two extra teeth. The
dentist had understood that Kelsey was afraid to have the

tooth out, so they'd sat down and killed a bottle together. They'd both been drunk when the dentist went to work, and what matter that he'd pulled the two others first, trying to find the right tooth? It had been a painless process. "And I'm all for it," Kelsey said aloud.

He lay curled on his side now, his big, heavily muscled body relaxed, his hat tilted back, the bottle in his hand. Sunlight sifted through the willows and touched his face, which had become lean and weathered from years in the open air; around his eyes was a fine crisscrossing of wrinkles from peering into the wind and squinting at the snow; his high cheekbones stood out; and the broad nose was more prominent than in his early youth. The fingers that grasped the bottle were thick-knuckled and scarred, the nails worn down to the quick, the end of the thumb split open and smeared with black salve. But his eyes had not changed; they were still gray and young and filled with a searching light.

He didn't know what made him look up, for he heard no sound, but there was Heather's face, framed between the willow branches, a laughing, elfin face.

"Hello, lassie. Come and sit beside me. Here it's your first week end home from school, and we've had no chance to talk. Tell your daddy everything."

She sank down, cross-legged, in the brown grass, but didn't speak. Kelsey put his hand on her head, conscious of a troubled expression in her eyes. "What's the matter, lassie?"

"Daddy, what's a love child?"

He put the whisky bottle down. He heard the willows rush together in the wind with a brittle whispering, and all the years came back to him, came with pain and wonder and a haunting sadness. He took her small hand and held it tightly in his. "A love child is a child born out of love. No other lass in the whole Park is so loved as you. You are a special one, marked by the high moment of loving between your mother and myself. No preacher had married us then or set the time of your beginning. Your beginning was a natural and beautiful thing that sprang up of itself—like yon wee aster nodding purple at the spring.

"To some, lassie, it is considered a bad thing for a child to begin before a minister marries a man and woman. But remember, you didn't come from anything bad but from love, and to love is never bad—preachers or not. It is true that it is always best for men and women to marry before they have children, for then the world doesn't make any talk. We surely intended to marry before you were started, but were prevented from such a plan. Does that answer you, lassie?"

"Then I am not like other children?"

His heart felt full to breaking, and he said quietly, "You are not like other children. Our love and our sorrow are in you, for who can separate the seed from the earth that brought it into being? Or from the sun and rain that made it grow? Lassie, when you lay inside your mother, under her heart, you were a special one; no lassie was ever so loved or so wanted. Always remember that and be proud."

He rubbed at the soft skin of her cheek, and her fingers moved to cover his. Her head bent a little toward him, and he saw the red shine in the dark of her hair where the sunlight touched it. "We love you more than the world, your mother and me. And your Granny Taraleean loved you even before you were born. She said you would be a beautiful thing and we must make the world right for you. Ah, how warm and kind her words were then! In the Bible there is a passage about Jesus going before his disciples to make a place for them. Dear lass, we went before you—your mother and me and Taraleean—to prepare a place for you. And in loving you we give you the world. It is a beautiful thing to remember."

And he felt so tender and sad and loving, all at the same time, that he had another drink from the bottle. Then he said, "And what are all the days of a man's life but a long journey toward the good!" He nodded, preoccupied for a moment, not with his daughter but with his own thinking. "A fine sound those words have to them, by God! And if I had the time for it I might be a poet myself, like Burns." Then he ruffled her hair. "No, I won't make poems. But you will, Heather. We gave it to you, Taraleean and your mother and me— But I talk above your head, lassie, and my tongue thickening with whisky."

He got up and carefully replaced the bottle in the cache and put the square of sod over it, smoothing the grass with his hand and murmuring, "Let us destroy the evidence." He turned to leave, saying, "And are you coming with me, lassie?"

She shook her head. She would wait here in the willow grove until noon. It was quiet, and she wanted to be alone. After a while she got up and walked from the willows and along the narrow dusty red road that went past the bunkhouse. The men would soon be in for the noon meal, she thought, and her heart quickened, for Long Dalton would let her help unhook his team.

She went slowly on down the road until she saw the bunkhouse door standing open. It was supposed to be closed, for gophers, skunks, and porcupines could walk in. She stepped up the sloping ground to the wooden step and reached for the doorknob. A voice stopped her. "Come here, Heather. I want to see you."

She went inside, and there was Cousin Tommy, stretched out on one of the tarp-covered bunks. His face looked redder than usual, and he smelled of whisky. A gust of wind came around the corner of the bunkhouse, and the door swung half shut behind her, making a thin, creaking sound.

"Come 'ere, little Heather."

His voice was strange and hoarse. She felt uneasy and didn't know why. A weakness crept down the backs of her legs, and suddenly it was too hot in the bunkhouse. There wasn't any noise anywhere but the loud pounding of her heart. She stared at the blue fly crawling slowly up the window.

"Don't you like your Cousin Tommy?" he asked, and his voice was softer now. It made her think of the white yarn her mother used to knit a sweater. She moved slowly toward him, her feet heavy, and all the while her mind went scurrying wildly to try to define the thing that made her afraid.

"I've a dolly for you to play with," he said. "Come close, and I'll show you."

A doll? A present from Faun's store? She took a quick step forward, forgetting her fear. And then she saw, and her hands came up to cover her mouth and there was an upset feeling in the pit of her stomach.

Cousin Tommy sat up, caught her arm, pulled her roughly toward him.

"No!" she cried. "Stop that. Leave me be!" She bent her head and bit hard into the hand that held her. She tasted blood.

Cousin Tommy yelled and let her go. "Y'damn little coyote!"

She ran to the door and yanked it wide as he shouted, "If you tell, I'll kill you!"

She fled down the slope toward the house. She ran so blindly she didn't see Long Dalton until she fell against his legs and clung to him, trembling.

He lifted her up in his arms. "Whoa, chicken! What's the rush?" Then his arms tightened around her. "What happened? What scared you?"

Her mouth was dry, and she couldn't speak. She turned her head, staring at the bunkhouse. Tommy Cameron stood in the doorway. Dalt set her down carefully. "He hurt you, chicken?"

"No."

"He take hold of you?"

"My arm. I bit him."

"Uh-huh. Good for you." Holding her hand in his, Dalt walked toward the bunkhouse. Heather hung back, wanting to run, but Dalt pulled her along beside him. He took her to the front of the bunkhouse door and stopped, facing Tommy Cameron. He put his arm around her shoulders and pressed her close to him. She couldn't look at Cousin Tommy. She stared at the hogback, rising bright, where the red and yellow of the aspens blurred. Then she heard a clear *click* and looked down. The knife was long and shiny in Dalt's hand. The sun flashed on it, blinding her.

"Tommy," Dalt said, "I've had a hankering to use this on you—had it for a long time. You won't be pretty—or much use—when I get through. You say a word to the kid or lay a hand on her, and I'll cut you up so fancy nobody'll know you for a man. And you're not firin' me, either. I'm stickin' around as long as Kelsey and Prim and the kid are here. Get me? And every day I'm gonna be thinking about how I'd like to use this knife on you. It won't take but one little move that sets me against you and I'll have the pleasure of carving you up." Dalt caught his breath. The knife clicked shut. "Come on, chicken."

They crossed the road, went into the willow clump, and stopped at the spring. Dalt dipped his big dark handkerchief in the water and wiped Heather's face. The water felt cold and good, and her skin quieted until it was as if all the outside of her had been smoothed down by her mother's hand. It was only on the inside that she still shook and felt sick.

"You wanta tell me about it?" Dalt said, offering her a drink from his hatbrim.

The water made a river down her chin. She wiped it away and began talking. She stared into Dalt's eyes and said, "He looked just like my daddy."

"Why, sure." Dalt's voice was easy. "All men look that way. Thought you knew that, chicken." His hand yanked up a bunch of grass and threw it down. "Son-of-a-bitch," he muttered. "You gonna talk this over with your mother, chicken?"

Heather shook her head. She knew she wasn't ever going to talk to Prim—or to anyone. "Was he going to hurt me, Dalt?"

"Nope." Dalt spat on the grass. "That kind's got no guts. All you had to do was set your teeth in him and he was whipped. He scares easy."

She shivered. "I was the one got scared, Dalt."

"That so? Well, don't be any more. It's like the way I was about lightning. When I was a kid with my mother around I used to crawl on her knee when the lightning started. It didn't scare me when my mother was around. Then, one day, I was off walkin' by myself and this storm come up. I got so scared I ran like a crazy jackrabbit. I stuck my face in the grass so's I couldn't see the storm. Now, you meeting up with Tommy like you did today was like me and the lightning. It was something we hadn't been in before, and that's why it scared us."

Dalt looked at the willow tops, took out his knife, and flipped it. "Maybe it's just as well you don't say anything to your folks. Might worry 'em. I'll take care of Tommy from here on. You just stop worryin', chicken."

It seemed so peaceful now, Heather thought. "Maybe I just had a bad dream," she said slowly. "Maybe tomorrow I won't think about it, Dalt."

He smoothed the loose strands of her hair. "No, it wasn't any dream you had, chicken. And you won't forget it; all your life it'll be comin' back—sometimes when you least think it's around. But listen; face it and look it down. That way it won't hurt you. Don't try to keep it shut away like something in a dark closet that spooks a person. Look at it and say, 'Sure, it happened, but I wasn't hurt.' "

"Yes. It didn't hurt me none, even if it was scary."

"That's right. Say! I forgot something." He reached in the

pocket of his coat and brought out a small piece of flint. "Here. I found this out on the flats last week."

The arrowhead was cool and smooth in her hand. "Did it belong to a chief, Dalt?"

"I figure so. Man might as well figure fancy if he figures at all. I expect he was the biggest chief that ever walked through this high and away-to-hell valley."

She held the arrowhead against her nose. The smell of the earth was in it.

"Yep," Dalt went on, "this was the Indians' country, and we took it away from 'em. Jediah says that's what history is —one man takin' away from another."

The dinner gong rang, and they walked toward the house. Dalt said, "You can come in the bunkhouse and wash."

Heather stopped. She felt hot and choking again. "No, I'm not going in there again."

"Yes, you are—with me, now. You think I'm gonna let you grow up scared to step in a bunkhouse just because of what happened one morning in a lifetime? You go in, chicken, and it won't be so hard again. You back out this morning, and you'll never get over it. Come on, now. Come, or I'll carry you, and I'm tired and don't want to."

She went in, holding her breath. Tommy wasn't there, but she could see him as he had been on the tarp-covered bunk. She hurried to wash her face and dried it on the rough, smelly towel.

In the house she sat at the table and couldn't eat. There was Cousin Tommy at the head of the table, so close she could hear him breathing. Kelsey said, "Off your feed, lassie?"

She pushed back her plate and went in the living room and lay on the old couch with her cheek against the rough surface. Her mother came and stood over her.

"What is it?" Prim said. "Does your stomach hurt? Stick out your tongue." She put her hand on Heather's forehead.

"You've no fever. Have you been drinking too much soda water at the spring?"

"Go away," Heather said. "Go away and leave me alone."

"In a mood, eh? Like your father."

Heather closed her eyes. "Leave me be," she muttered.

"And if you're not sick, then what's the matter with you?"

"None of your business!" Heather said, opening her eyes to stare at her mother.

"Don't sauce me, missy!" Prim's hand flashed out and cracked against her daughter's cheek.

Heather whimpered and put her fingers over the place where Prim had struck her. Kelsey came in then, saying sharply, "It's no time to slap the lassie. Something's upset her. My God, Prim, can't you ever tell what's going on inside folk?"

"You deal with her, then, if you're so smart! You find out why she won't eat and runs off by herself and sauces me when I speak to her."

" 'Sasses,' " Kelsey corrected.

"I said 'sauces' and that's what I meant!" Prim flounced from the room, her heels clicking hard on the bare wooden floor.

Kelsey sat down beside Heather. "I'll take you fishing next week end," he said.

A spark of interest kindled in her eyes.

"And, honey, don't say things that hurt your mother. Like I told you this morning, she gave you the gift of life—and what a gift it is!"

"Didn't mean to sass her."

"I know you didn't. Don't cry about it." He patted her cheek and left her.

Later Prim came back to the couch. "Heather, the men are gone. Come out and eat, will you?"

"Yes."

"And why did you leave the table before?"

"I don't like Cousin Tommy, that's why!"

"Oh, that big, windy bugger! Why didn't you tell me? I feel the same." She kissed Heather's cheek. "Come on, now, my lassie."

They ate together at the end of the big table, Prim talking and Heather not listening. She was remembering the soda spring and what Dalt had said about the lightning.

CHAPTER XV

Heather felt older than her eleven years, for this June morning she was being treated like an adult. She stood at the corral beside Dalt and listened to the thunder on the wind, the soft thunder of running horses coming down from the upper pasture. Near them Monte Maguire's cowpunchers waited, their ropes ready, their eyes still glazed from sleep, cigarettes hanging from the corners of their mouths.

To the north she could see the red dust rising from the earth behind the running horses. Over at the chuck wagon Hilder was checking supplies, for Hilder always did the cooking on the shove-up. The chuck wagon was a canvas-covered sheep wagon with a small cookstove in the corner. There were no sheep in the Park, but it was said Monte Maguire had won the wagon from a man in Laramie during a poker game. And it suited her better than the open wagons some of the cattle ranchers used on roundups.

"Can I ride the big filly?" Heather asked Dalt.

"Maybe," he said. "But not around here where your mother might see you and worry. We'll think about it out on the flats. We might swap horses sometime today—if you're not afraid."

A little shiver went over her, partly fear and partly excitement. In the gray light before dawn the horses had come into view, and she could see the big filly leading them, chestnut-colored, slimmer and taller than the others. There was Morgan blood in that horse, Dalt said; she was one of Monte's special horses and built for speed, not sturdy and shaggy like the cowpunchers' horses. Monte had turned her over to Dalt for gentling.

Sometimes, when nobody was around to notice, Heather would go to the corral and look at her and want to ride her. The big filly always returned the look, with her small head held high, the nostrils dilating until a faint whistling came from them, the small front hoof pawing the soft ground, the delicate ears moving back and forth when Heather spoke to her, saying, "Big filly, it's me, Heather."

Heather had watched Dalt break the filly to the saddle, first by petting her and talking to her. Then one morning he let her smell the saddle blanket, and he spread it over her back for a moment. Days later he brought out the saddle and let her look it over and smell it, and after a while he set it gently on her back, talking to her all the time. The first time he mounted her the big filly reared up and made a snorting sound. Dalt stroked her neck and talked to her again, and she came down from pawing the sky and jumped lightly around the corral. She made Heather think of a deer springing over the hogback trails in October. It wasn't long until the big filly let Dalt ride her around the corral, lifting her slim legs cleanly from the manure and dust. The day Dalt took her out onto the prairie she ran, and Dalt held the bridle reins firmly but didn't try to make her stop running. "She had to get it out of her system," he said. "And her mouth is tender."

Now the horses came pounding and crowding into the corral, and Dalt moved among them to drop a rope over the big filly's head. Heather followed them into the barn, and when Dalt had saddled the filly he caught Chinook and stood looking on while Heather did the saddling, tightening the cinch with quick, sure jerks.

"That's right," Dalt said. "Let him get through puffing out his belly, and then take up the slack."

"I'm wise to that trick of his," she said. Sometimes she

thought Chinook was going to burst before he let his wind
out so she could tighten the cinch. And always he turned his
head and laid his ears flat, as though he were asking angrily,
"What did you do that for?"

She hurried toward the house, running before the men,
anxious to get breakfast over and start riding. As she stepped
in she heard Prim's angry voice. "Are you afraid to ask her?
Is a big hulk of a man like you scared to speak up to a
woman?"

"Stop bitching at me, Prim," Kelsey said. "If Monte wants
me to have a foreman's job she'll say so. A man can ask too
much. She's given me another start. That's enough."

"Well, if you won't ask Monte for a foreman's job, why
don't you get out and lease a place of your own?"

"I've told you, Prim, we haven't enough cattle. I really
haven't—not yet. And there's no point in settling on a two-
bit homestead and running forty or fifty cows. It won't pay."

"Oh, you want a big show, all right. Nothing but the biggest
and finest for a Cameron."

Heather put her hands over her ears. Not this morning, she
thought. Don't fight this morning, when the day's so clear and
fine, and the shove-up starting. Please, please don't!

Prim banged a lid on the stove. She saw Heather and said,
"And where are you off to, missy, with your boots on at this
hour?"

"I'm helping Jake on the shove-up. He's hired me. He needs
me. Two of the punchers are in bed with the summer sickness."

"Ha!" Prim snorted. "Summer sickness, indeed! Whisky
sickness, that's what they've got—drinking all last night. I
heard the noise in the bunkhouse—and your fine father up
there with them. And I'd not be surprised if some of them end
up with worse than whisky sickness. That black woman from
Laramie with her women and—"

Heather thought of the tents by the river near town. Only

last week she'd seen them when she'd gone to town for summer groceries with her father and Long Dalton. She said,
"Dalt likes Black Susie. She's a good friend of his, he says."

Prim turned to glare at Kelsey. "Hear that? Dalt tells her
about a black madam and her cheap women. What an education she's getting, your daughter!"

"All right, so she hears things," Kelsey said. "What of it?
I'd as soon have her grow up knowing about the cat wagons
by the river as not. It's part of life, isn't it? And your brothers
weren't above finding a waterfront dive, either—although
you'd have us believe they sprouted wings."

"My brothers were never loose. They never did a thing
they couldn't do before their mother, so they didn't."

"Oh, hell! Prim, why do you want to be so unreal about
some things? And get the breakfast out, will you?"

"I'll put on breakfast when I damn well please. What's in
this man's country for a woman? Cook, cook! Do men ever
really think about anything but their stomachs? Do they ever
get filled up? They stuff themselves until the sight of it
sickens me!"

Kelsey looked at Heather and winked. Then he reached
out and pinched Prim's arm. "By the look of that you've done
some stuffing yourself. Reminds me of the arm of one of the
Camerons at the smithy."

She jerked away. "And what made my arm like that? What
made me more like a blacksmith than a woman? I'll tell you:
carrying buckets of water because the men forgot to carry it
for me, packing wood from the woodpile because you promised and forgot it, and lifting the washtubs to empty them because you were in the bunkhouse or looking at your precious
cattle."

"Ring the gong for breakfast, Heather," Kelsey said, "for
your mother's off on one of her spells and won't shut up until sleep closes her eyes tonight—but I won't be here to listen, thank God!"

Heather touched her mother's skirt. "Mother—"

"Oh, never mind trying to make up to me. Ring the gong for the men!"

Heather ran to the door and rang the gong, glad for another sound than her mother's voice rising shrilly in the steak-smelling kitchen.

They rode away from the ranch at sunrise. The few riders driving the extra saddle horses headed out for the flats. A little later the other riders followed, and last came Hilder in the chuck wagon, his shoulders hunched against the cold June wind that blew steadily out of the east.

The cowpunchers spread out on the flats. Heather rode with her father and Dalt. She saw Kelsey was in a gay mood now, singing under his breath, his open coat flapping behind him in the wind.

"See that dust to the south?" Dalt said. "That's other outfits gathering their cattle off the plains. All over the Park this mornin' cattle are bein' rounded up for summer range."

They came over a little rise in the prairie and saw Jake with a cow on the end of a rope. Jake's horse backed up, taking in slack until the rope was taut. Jake dismounted and moved along the rope, teetering on his high-heeled boots.

"She's bloated," Dalt said. "Got a bellyful of larkspur."

"Well," Kelsey said, "we didn't have as much of the poison weed as usual this spring."

"No, because it wasn't a wet season."

Dalt dismounted and handed the bridle reins to Heather. "Hold her. I'll work on this one for Jake."

The cow bawled hoarsely, staggering on the end of the rope. Dalt went to her left side, placed his thumb on the hipbone, spread his fingers a full width of his hand ahead, then spread his hand another full width down. The knife gleamed. The blade sank deep, and Heather caught her breath.

"Don't hurt her none," Jake said, smiling.

Dalt yanked the knife out, and there was a sound of rushing air and a low gurgling. A few moments later spurts of green-flecked moisture bubbled at the mouth of the wound, like jets from an over-full tea kettle starting to boil.

Jake flipped up the cow's tail, and with another fast motion of the knife Dalt cut the vein. Blood gushed, running dark down the cow's legs and onto the earth between the clumps of sagebrush. Dalt grunted with satisfaction, wiped the bloody knife on his chaps, and said, "She'll make it. Got her in time."

"Come on, Heather," Kelsey said, "we'll take a look over yon little ridge while the boys push her north to join the main bunch. There's a spring over the ridge, and we might find a few cows hanging around it." He kicked his horse into an easy lope, and Heather rode beside him, her long braids flopping under the big hat.

When they came over the ridge crest and the prairie dipped sharply, Kelsey pulled up his horse and pointed. "Take a look, lassie. There's something you might never see again."

Down on the patch of green grass near a small grove of willows, Heather saw a cow standing beside a new calf. Not far from the cow, spaced at intervals, four coyotes sat on their haunches. One of the coyotes got up and trotted toward the calf. The cow swung around, facing him, her tail swinging from side to side. Then she lowered her head, gave a fierce bellow, and charged the coyote. He ran back and sat down.

"Now," Kelsey said almost in a whisper, "we'll sneak around and come through the willow grove. That way they won't see us and we can get close."

They rode along the rim of higher ground and then down the slope and slowly through the willow grove, following the narrow, dusty trail that ran past the spring.

"Stop here. Sit as quiet as a mouse. Don't move."

Through an opening in the willows she could see the coyotes plainly now, for they were close. She could see their mouths hanging open, the tongues lolling, the sharp white teeth glinting in the sunlight.

"Oh!" Her lips parted in a frightened whisper. "Stop them, Daddy! They're going to kill the wee calf. Stop them!"

He touched the rifle that hung in the scabbard bumping his knee. "No, I won't let them harm the calf. But I don't think the cow'll need any help. Just watch this, now."

From time to time the coyotes rose and ran toward the calf, and the cow drove them back, while the calf lay quietly, a dark, white-faced mound on the grass. Then the mother began to lick the calf, nudging it to its feet. Slowly she urged the calf farther from the coyotes, while it wobbled uncertainly on awkward legs.

"Why doesn't she hide it in the willows?" Heather asked anxiously. "It's sheltered there."

"That's where she's a smart one, the cow. It's best to stay clear of the willows. In the open she can see the coyotes coming from all directions, and fight them off. In the willows they could sneak up on her and get the calf. A cow always keeps her calf in the open if she has to fight coyotes."

Now the cow was pushing the calf along faster, widening the distance between her and the coyotes. The coyotes all rose at once and trotted to where the bloody afterbirth lay on the ground. They snarled and slashed at one another, their teeth clicking, making a tangled gray mass of angry sound and motion. A few moments later they ran away.

When Kelsey and Heather rode out of the willows only a pinkish stain was left on the grass. "It's the afterbirth they like," Kelsey said. "I'll pick up the calf now." He rode to the cow, dismounted, and lifted the calf to the saddle. Then he climbed up after it, and rode with it in front of him. "A wee one, isn't he? He won't travel far. We'll have to put him in the chuck wagon with Hilder. A late catch, he is."

Heather made a crooning sound in her throat and reached

to touch the calf. His hide was still damp and curling. A long silvery slobber hung from his mouth. He blinked velvety dark eyes, bawled, and nudged his head against Kelsey's knee. The mother bellowed answer, running beside the horse, sniffing Kelsey's boots, her big eyes liquid with fear.

"His mama wants to save him," Heather said. "She's trying to see nothing happens to him."

"She is that. The mother instinct—the same kind your mother has for you, lassie. She'd have run at coyotes too, if they'd been bothering you when you were wee like this laddie." And he felt a sudden tenderness for Prim, who shared his bed at night and quarreled with him during the day. "Ah, yes," he added, "she did fight for you, in a different way, and her heart breaking."

They came up over a slope, and the wind was full in their faces. The calf bawled, and the mother answered, rushing to it; her tongue came out to lick the dangling leg but could not reach it.

"Ah." Kelsey stopped and looked across the rolling prairie.

The rider came swiftly toward them, the sunlight on her pale hair, which blew loose under the wide-brimmed hat. She sat easily in the saddle, like a man, her riding a part of the motion of the horse.

Kelsey's face softened. "Did you ever see the like of that, Heather? The life that's in her! Big to match the Park—like a picture, isn't she?"

Heather felt a stab of pain deep inside. Her lips trembled. "I like my mama best," she said, her voice too high and tight. "I'll always like my mama best."

Kelsey turned quickly, reaching a big hand to touch her arm. "Of course," he said gently. "Of course, lassie, we both like your mama best."

She looked away from her father's face then, and a strange half-sick feeling swept over her. The wind shook the sagebrush until the silver undersides of the leaves turned up, and the big black horse with the tall rider came on to meet them. The rider's arm swept up in greeting, and her voice was warm and strong. "Heather! Kelsey!" The horse reared beside them and came down, crushing the sagebrush and sending up the sharp smell that was a little like turpentine. "And how goes the mornin' with you?"

"The Lord's own morning," Kelsey said, "and warming as it goes. And you, Monte?"

"I'm always happy in the mornin'," she said, smiling. "See you got a little guy there. He's well marked—outta one of the new bulls."

"Yes. And look how rich his color is."

They fell into silent admiration of the calf, while Heather shifted impatiently. Hadn't they seen thousands of calves? Did they have to get their heads that close together and look at it as if it were something special? And then she saw they had stopped looking at the calf and were staring at each other. She cleared her throat and said, "I'm not for sitting here half the day. I'm going to find Dalt, so I am."

They paid no attention to her. She stared at Monte's slim hips, the small waist caught in the broad man's belt, the swelling breasts pushing against the heavy shirt. Why did she have to come along now and spoil it? It was our day, mine and my father's, and now it's all changed.

Angrily she turned Chinook and dug her heels so sharply into him that he plunged into a run, skimming the clumps of sagebrush. Across the prairie she found Long Dalton slowly driving a small bunch of cattle north. As she moved in behind the cattle the dust blew in her eyes and the air was full of the mingled odors of sagebrush, manure, and cows.

Dalt gave her a sidelong glance. "Your lower lip's fallin' so far you'll step on it if you don't watch out. What's eatin' on you?"

"That old Monte Maguire—I hate her!"

"Shame on you, gettin' your nose outta joint over Monte."

"Don't care!" Her tongue darted out at him.

"Getting sassy, are you? Getting big for your britches. Guess I'll have to take you down a peg. Listen, chicken, no reason why you should feel mean toward Monte Maguire. She's been mighty good to your daddy. You treat her like a lady ought to be treated."

"She's no lady, so there! My mama said so. My mama said she was cheap and brassy and acted like a man because she was crazy over all men and wanted to be with them. I heard my mama tell Amie Plunkett that."

"That so? And what did Amie say?"

"Amie said she'd be just like Monte if she didn't come fresh every spring like an old cow."

Dalt burst into laughter. "Leave it to Amie to find an answer. Look, chicken, you ought to be nice to Monte. She had no mother to raise her like you have. She didn't have a fine home like yours, either."

"That's because she was a whore."

Dalt's long brows lifted. "Oh? And what's a whore?"

Heather frowned. "A woman that's bad—like them in the tent by the river."

"Is that so?"

"I heard my mama tell Amie that Monte Maguire was a whore."

"And what did Amie say to that?"

"Amie said it's what lots of women would like to be but don't have the guts."

Dalt laughed again. "And what did Prim say to that?"

"She told Amie she was shocked, and Amie said she only spoke her mind."

Dalt pulled up the horse, rolled a cigarette, licked it carefully, and stuck it in his mouth. He struck a match on the saddle horn and lit the cigarette, keeping his hands cupped against the wind. He drew hard on the cigarette, letting the smoke drift through his nose. "Heather, let me tell you something. Don't ever go around callin' people names when you don't know for sure what those names mean. And if I ever hear you call Monte Maguire a whore again I'll fan your britches so hard you won't be able to ride a horse for a month. And if I catch you being rude to Monte I'm gonna stop taking you fishing with me and swimming with me in the beaver pond across the hogback. You hear?"

Heather sat, fussing with the saddle horn, not looking at Dalt. Tears smarted in her eyes, for she liked Dalt and it hurt when he scolded her.

"Another thing," he said. "You've gotta learn not to be-lieve everything your mama says. She's a good woman, your mama, but she just don't have any sense about keeping her mouth shut at the right time. She talks first and thinks after-ward. But I'll give her credit for this, the worst she'll say to you she'll say right to your face and not behind your back. But sometimes that can be carried too far. She makes it hard on people, blatting out like she does and not bothering to back up what she says with facts."

Heather trembled. A tear ran down her cheek, and she stuck out her tongue, catching the salt taste of it. "I don't want Monte Maguire loving my daddy!"

"Why? It's not gonna hurt him. He's just a lucky son-of-a-bitch, that's all. Wish I was in his shoes. And it's not hurting you, or your mama either, as long as he don't start loving that bright-haired woman right back. And I don't figure that day will ever come."

"Someday we'll have our own ranch and never see her! My mama says we'll buy our own ranch soon."

"Why, chicken, what are you crying for? Floodin' the place with tears! I was only tryin' to set you straight on a few things." He put his hand on her bowed head and said gently, "Now, why are you crying harder?"

"I don't know, Dalt. Cross my heart, I don't."

He handed her his handkerchief, and she blew her nose

and started to return the handkerchief. "Keep it," he said. "Jake's gonna think what a hell of a cowpuncher he hired—bawlin' like a newborn calf."

But she slumped lower in the saddle. Dalt dismounted and lifted her and held her in his arms. He held her until at last she began to quiet down. Then he said, "Chicken, how old are you?"

"I'll be twelve next birthday."

He pushed back her braids, and his eyes were kind. "You're growin' up, and maybe you've got a right to cry. One day you'll be a woman." His hand cupped her chin, lifting her face to the sunlight. "Smile, now. Smile like you meant it."

She smiled through her tears, and she saw the light leap in his eyes, making them very bright. He gave a soft little whistle. "Glad you're not my age, chicken. Glad there's the years between us, or it might make a difference someday before too long—couple or three years from now."

She shivered, although she was warm. "Dalt, what's the matter?"

He looked at her for a long time and didn't answer.

"Dalt—"

"Nothing—nothing you would understand now." And he lifted her into the saddle.

"You said I could ride the big filly, Dalt."

"Did I? Yes, that's right, but not now—now when you're still riled inside. A horse senses that. He smells it on you, and if you're not feeling like yourself he'll take advantage of it. You calm down, and we'll see this afternoon. Now, let's move. Be chow time, and here we are behind all the others."

The chuck wagon was parked in a ravine at the foot of Independence Mountain. A small clear stream trickled past it, and close by was an old corral that held the extra horses.

It was hot by the chuck wagon— "Yust like hell," Hilder grunted, slapping biscuits into the Dutch oven and carrying it to a pit where the red coals waited. Carefully he heaped coals on the lid.

The tin plates on the end gate of the chuck wagon blinded Heather, for the sun set them to a wild glittering. As she walked toward the pit where Hilder was now frying steak, Monte Maguire reached from the shade of the wagon and caught her ankle. "Speak to a person, why don't you?"

"Good morning, Mrs. Maguire."

"It's not mornin', honey, it's past noon. Fill me a plate, will you, and fetch it? I need some shade today."

Heather filled two plates and returned to the wagon. "Thanks," Monte said. "You want to sit here by me?"

"Might."

"Suit yourself, then."

Heather sat beside her, self-conscious and wishing she could be among the sagebrush with Dalt and the men. She ate quickly, shoveling the food into her mouth, closing her eyes from time to time against the shine of the tin plate.

"You're eating too fast," Monte said. "Slow down or you'll have a bellyache."

Heather took a last quick gulp. She wanted to get away from this woman. She began to feel sick from bolting her food and from the look of the hot, dirty plate.

"Listen, Heather," Monte said, "I'm gonna give you a calf— let you pick it out yourself."

Heather's hands tightened on the plate. For a moment she was torn between her mother's words and the words of Long Dalton. And then she could think of nothing but the calf. A calf of her very own! She looked into Monte Maguire's face, and the blue eyes were sharp and steady and smiling. "Oh!" And before she could stop herself she had flung her arms around Monte's neck and kissed her.

"Look out!" she heard Kelsey shout. "You're spilling coffee all over her shirt. Why can't you be careful, Heather?"

"She can't hurt anything," Monte said. "What's a shirt?"

Heather jumped up and ran to Kelsey. "I'm to have a calf! I get to pick it out myself!"

She scarcely heard her father saying, "That's fine, lassie." She ran past him, dancing by herself in the sagebrush, hugging her arms across her chest and looking across the gray land toward the ranch house. She wished she could see Prim and tell her about the calf. And then she remembered what Prim had said about Monte. Well, she thought, still dancing and nodding to the distant peaks, she's a *nice* whore, so there!

All that afternoon the enchantment of knowing she'd have a calf was on her. She rode in a trance, trying out names on her tongue—"Bluebell, Daisy, Primrose, Bonnie Lass . . ."

"Listen," Dalt said, "you're not learnin' a damn thing. Now take a look at that cow and tell me what's wrong with her."

She came back to the world of red dust and bawling cattle and the thick animal smells. "She's got prickles in her nose."

"That's right—full of porcupine quills. And she can't eat, so she'll starve unless we pull 'em out." He hailed a couple of riders, and they roped the cow and threw her on the ground. Dalt took a pair of pliers from his pocket and pulled the quills from the cow's nose.

"Now come with me," Dalt said, "if you're gonna ride the big filly. Everybody's gonna be at that red hill north of us soon, and they don't need us. They'll be holding the cattle there for tomorrow's branding."

They rode over a rocky ridge and into a narrow, lonely valley. He dismounted and switched the saddles, putting hers on the big filly.

"You ready now, chicken?"

She stepped up to the tall chestnut, and a tingling ran all through her. "I'm ready."

"Then up you go!"

She was in the saddle in a swift, smooth motion, but even as she touched the hard leather seat the big filly was moving away,

and the saddle was like springs under her—springs and strength
and walking over the whole world. She felt light and small and
high in the air, and even the wind seemed cooler there.

But I couldn't stop her if she ran. I know I couldn't. She
could run forever, and it would be like I wasn't even here.

"You trust her," Dalt said. "Ride easy and don't be scared.
Don't jerk up on the reins, or she'll come right over backward
with you. Just hold the bit steady and pull easy if you want to
stop her, but never jerk. Want to take a little run? Not too far.
I'll set the pace, and you keep the steady pull on the reins. Talk
to her too—let her know you're there and want to be."

He kicked Chinook into a lope, and Heather felt the power
gather under her and flow out in the long motion of legs and
body that was so smooth it was like a dream of riding. Over
and over the sagebrush they flew, and the earth blurred. The
big filly moved out ahead of Chinook. She ran faster, and her
mane whipped up black before Heather's eyes. Heather pulled
gently on the reins. "Whoa, girl! Easy now!" She was filled with
pleasure and fear, and the ground kept slipping away and away,
and the wind brought tears to her eyes. So fast, so fast—like a
bird! So light, so light—like a cloud skimming the blue of the
sky! She pulled harder, speaking softly, and at last the big filly
eased in her stride and came gently, slowly to a long, flowing
canter, and then to a trot, and at last to her light, quick way of
walking. She pulled the big filly to a stop and sat, trembling, in
the saddle, waiting for Dalt. And when he rode up she held out
her hands and said, "Take me off now."

"Scared?"

"No, but I want to get off."

She slid down into his arms, and he laughed. "Why, you're
shakin' all over and wet with sweat."

"I know, but I wasn't really scared, Dalt. It's just—just that
it was like being on a streak of lightning and wondering what
would happen if it suddenly went crazy and struck. Oh, it was

wonderful, but I'm funny inside now, Dalt, and that's why I had to get off."

"Makes you alive, don't it? Well, maybe you can ride her again tomorrow, and after a while it'll be natural for you to sit on her. But it won't ever be like this one time again. You know that, don't you?"

"Yes." She got on Chinook and rode slowly toward camp. It's been a wonderful day, she thought—the best ever.

That night after supper she lay on a bedroll under the willows a short distance from the fire. She could hear the creek murmuring against the curving red banks. She knew all about that little creek; it watered the west side of the meadows at the ranch. There were pools where the minnows darted, shimmering in the sunlight, and places where the frogs sat on muddy ledges and where the killdeers left their thin, sharp tracks. The tall yellow-headed mustard flowers leaned over it in August, safe from the sickles of the mowing machines, and the dragonflies clung to them like pale threads of sky. Gold glittered in the gravelly bottom of the creek, but her father said it was only fool's gold and worth nothing. And sometimes when she was quiet on the bank, flat on her stomach, and put her hands softly into the water under a jutting ledge, a trout would go between her fingers, slick and cool and fast.

The creek came from Jediah's big lake in the mountains, and Jediah controlled the headgate. In her mind she could see Jediah's cabin, small and built square, and the aspen trees whispering against the windows. Jediah said the aspens were talky trees, wanting to tell all they knew, and they had so much to tell—memories of birds that lived in the green rooms of their leaves, of sunlight and rain and the wind shaking them.

She rolled over and lay on her side and wished that her father would come. He was night-herding the cattle that were bunched at the foot of the hill; the hill was like part of a corral to hold them so they couldn't stray.

Monte Maguire was there night-herding too. For a while

Heather had stayed with her father and Monte, sitting on her horse in the starlight, trying not to get sleepy so she could hear them talking, but most of the time they spoke in such low tones she had to guess about their words. Then Dalt came and told her she had to get to bed.

She wondered what they might be saying to each other, her father and Monte Maguire. She thought of getting up and creeping like an Indian through the sagebrush and not letting them know she was around. But just then there was a sound of footsteps near her bedroll.

She closed her eyes and pretended to sleep, and she felt the heavy tarp being carefully tucked around her. After a while she squinted between her eyelids and saw the man standing there close to her, looking at the sky and smoking. It was her father. When he finally went away she was very sleepy.

The woodsmoke of the campfire drifted over her. The wind had gone with sundown, and a great silence filled the night, broken now and then by the bawling of a calf.

"Now I lay me down to sleep and pray the Lord my soul to keep. . . . and God bless extra special Prim, my mother . . ."

*   *

In the cool, clean morning, just after sunrise, the branding started. Heather carried the branding irons to the fire that had been built before breakfast. The irons were long-handled and dark, and they felt cold in her hands. She handed them to Jake, saying anxiously, "It'll hurt the calves, won't it?"

"Not long. Gotta remember a brand's all a cowman's got to protect his cattle. It's his mark of ownin' 'em."

Dalt was methodically sharpening his knife, sitting cross-legged in the green grass by the fire.

"What you going to do with that, Dalt? Cut on the cows?"

"Cut the bull calves so we'll have beef for the markets, chicken."

"Then we keep the cattle here overnight," Jake added, "so

every cow gets her own calf. When they get separated, cows and calves always come back to where the calf last sucked. We gotta be sure they're paired right before we turn 'em on summer range."

"Another thing, chicken," Dalt went on, spitting on the knife and wiping it on his pants, "we picked out this clean place with fresh grass underfoot so we don't have to worry about infection."

"And dry," Jake said. "New fella in the Park last year did his cuttin' and brandin' and then run his cows and calves through a muddy creek on the way to summer range. He damn near lost half of 'em with infectin'."

Monte Maguire squinted at the sky and said, "Going to stay dry for a day or two. That's good. Can't brand to do it right in the rain. Brand cooks in when it's put on wet hide, and don't show clean like it ought to."

Heather turned to look at the cattle bunched at the foot of the hill. Her father and two cowpunchers were holding them in check. A little white-faced calf trotted from the main herd, paused, and raised his nose, sniffing the air. Heather looked at the branding irons, now glowing red in the coals. She shivered and pulled her jacket tight around her.

Monte shouted, "All set! Bring 'em on, boys!"

The cowboys rode into the bunched cattle, ropes ready; a thin drift of red dust rose behind their horses. A rope flashed, and a rider turned, dragging a calf by the hind leg. The calf bawled and bumped through the sagebrush and onto the grass near the fire.

Dalt and Jake moved in, throwing the calf. Jake thrust a knee against the neck and twisted back the front leg. Another puncher sat on the ground behind the calf, spraddling its hind legs by pulling the top leg back and setting his booted foot against the leg next to the ground.

Monte Maguire brought the branding iron. She lowered it with a deliberate motion. Heather saw the heaving side of the calf, the iron pressed against it. There was a brief sizzling sound. A small spiral of blue smoke drifted into the clear air. Then came the low, pitiful bawl, the sickening odor of burning hair and flesh. And while Heather stared, unable to look away, Dalt bent over the spraddled hind legs. The cut was quick and neat. His hand came up, tossing the bloody glands on the ground. He turned with another deft motion, bent to wipe the knifeblade clean on the grass.

Heather licked her lips. Her stomach felt queasy. She stared at the bloody glands.

"Rocky Mountain oysters," Dalt said, grinning. "Some folks like 'em rolled in egg and cracker crumbs and fried crisp, but I never been able to convince your ma to cook me some."

The men released the calf. It staggered to its feet, still bawling, and ran toward the timbered slopes. The men turned to the second calf. Again Heather heard the anguished bawling, smelled the burning hair and flesh. She turned her back, rubbed her eyes. Along the creek the willows were green blobs, the sky was a glittering, jerky blue. The grass waved in shuddering green, rose and fell, rose and fell . . .

A hand caught her shoulder, hurting her. She looked up into the face of Monte Maguire. "More wood for the fire. Hurry, kid!"

She ran then, gathered sticks from the pile, and tossed them into the blaze. The heat came up in her face. Smoke clogged her nose. A splinter speared under a fingernail, shooting little wires of pain up her arm.

"Pick your calf," Monte said. "What about this one? It's a heifer, and you want one that'll make a good cow and raise you more calves. We'll put Kelsey's KC brand on this one. It suit you, Heather?"

She came close to look carefully at the calf. She put her hand on it. "Yes," she said. And then she covered her eyes when they lowered the branding iron.

The men worked faster as the morning wore on. Calves

bawled and bumped through the sagebrush. The dust rose in a cloud over the hill. Calves writhed under the hot irons, their feeble "Maaa—baaa!" drifting away on the wind. And on the grass the stain from Dalt's knife widened into a big pinkish splotch.

"Twenty-five, Monte—steer count. The younger you cut 'em, the sooner they get over it—like kids."

"Heifer calves runnin' about the same?"

"So-so."

"Heather! Water! We're thirsty."

Heather ran for the water bag in the chuck wagon. Hilder was rolling out biscuits. "What's wrong with your face?"

She shook her head and took the cork from the water bag.

"It's pale, kiddo. You yust don't look right."

"My stomach's all twisty, Hilder."

"So. You ain't used to the brandin'. Look, I give you a little drink, only don't tell nobody I got it, see? It is for medicine only. Here, little white-face gal." He took a bottle from one of the built-in places in the chuck wagon and thrust it at her. "Yust take a big drink, like water. Then you feel strong."

The whisky burned her throat, and she coughed; tears came into her eyes. Hilder struck her sharply between the shoulder blades. "Take it like a man. No chaser or nothin'. Good! Now you take the water to the men, and pretty soon we eat, and you feel yust fine—eh?"

At the creek she filled the water bag and then lay on her stomach and dipped her hands in the creek, letting the coolness pour over her wrists. She splashed water on her forehead and tossed it on her hair.

Walking back to the fire, she felt good. Her stomach was warm and her legs were strong. She began to hum a tune, prancing and bending her head to the lilt of it.

CHAPTER XVI

"You ou sure look peaked, Prim," Amie said.

Prim turned her face away from Amie's warm but probing dark eyes. It was the Fourth of July, and they were having a picnic in the timber. She could hear the Plunkett children playing, voices raised in excitement and quarreling. And she could hear the small sucking sound as Amie nursed her baby. They sat on the ground, a distance from the men, and Amie had a shawl over her shoulder to hide her breast.

The men were gathered around the campfire, where Hilder was frying the fish they'd caught that morning in the beaver dams. Jediah, Kelsey, Dalt, and Harry Plunkett were watching Hilder work.

"I like their tails turned south," Kelsey said, "and well salted."

"I figure he's wastin' grease, cooking 'em with their heads on," Dalt said.

"That makes 'em look bigger," Jediah added. "Man's gotta protect his vanity."

The smell of hot grease made Prim's stomach fluttery. Her hand came down to rest over the sickness. She'd noticed the feeling that morning when she rode the spring wagon beside Kelsey. She'd told herself it was the jolting so early in the morning, before her breakfast had time to settle. It was a usual thing, so it was, and not anything to be frightened about.

"You been working too hard, Prim," Amie said. "I tell you, it don't pay. Scrub a floor, and in ten minutes it's tracked up again. Just as well enjoy life as you go along. House can drive a woman crazy. That's half of what's wrong with Ellie Lundgren, making her act so queer lately. As for me, I just give housework up."

Prim smiled. Amie had given it up all right. Every year Amie got a little easier-going, until now it was a struggle to find a chair to sit in at her house.

Amie shifted the baby at her breast and sighed. "I sure do hate to see hayin' time come. Everything gets plumb confused —men runnin' in and out, Harry gettin' his bowels in an uproar every time a cloud rolls over the mountains. And all that stuff we have to do—wash bunkhouse bedding, clean the damn bunkhouse, have hot dinners fixed to go to the field at eleven o'clock in the morning. Jesus, we might as well never go to bed in haying time. And it seems like I just can't get everything done at once, Prim. With all my kids, I just fall behind. Oh, well, I guess housework's like being a virgin—it will keep."

Prim laughed. You could always be easy and relaxed around Amie. Maybe a woman got that way, having one child after another. The sickness stirred in her, and she thought fearfully, No, it couldn't be—not after all these years!

"Amie," she said, "were you ever surprised about your marriage? I mean, was it different than you thought it would be?"

"I hope to tell you! I figured Harry'd settle down in his pa's store back in central Illinois and go to church every Sunday. I figured we *might* have two real smart kids that wouldn't ever say damn. Next thing I know, he drags me away out here to the Park, and we lease that ranch, and I been raisin' kids ever since. I tell you, I never thought Harry was such a fertile man. Now, he don't look it, does he?"

Prim laughed again. "Well, Amie, some things can't be judged by looks, they tell me."

"Once I told Harry if he didn't slow down I'd have Long Dalton cut on him like he cuts on Monte's calves. Everybody says Dalt's the best calf-cutter in the Park. And you know what

Harry said? 'Why, Dalt couldn't faze a good man like me!' Conceited, that's what Harry is." She covered her breast and rocked the baby gently in her arms. "I'll be glad as hell when I get through the change and can go to bed without worryin' for the next nine months."

"They're discovering things," Prim said. "Dolly Gentry told me about it. Dolly said it wouldn't be long until women get pregnant only when they really want to."

"Hmph!" Amie looked bleak. "Time they get it all figured out, I'll be too old to enjoy it. And I'll tell you this: any information old Doc Bingham puts out is just so much hogwash. He thinks anything that keeps a woman from swellin' up like a poisoned pup is contrary to nature. Too bad he can't have a few himself. Might change his notions." She lifted the baby away from her. "Wet again! Nobody in the Park's got such peein' kids as I have. Must be something wrong with their kidneys. Damn! It's all over me. Well, I better go to the wagon and change her in case she starts chappin' from it."

Prim sat alone, trying to forget the disturbance in her stomach. She heard the men's voices, Jediah's louder than the others. "I got a new sight for my gun. It's the finest sight I ever seen. It's so fine I can hit a gnat's ass at a hundred yards."

"And you know what he's up to lately?" Kelsey said. "He's painted the barrel blue so the coyotes can't see the sun shining on it and get spooked."

"Tricky, that's what I am," Jediah said, chuckling. "And you and me, Kelsey-boy, are going on top of the range this fall and get us a mountain sheep."

Men's talk, Prim thought darkly. That's all I listen to most of the time, men's talk—guns, hunting, fishing, cattle. I get sick of it, so I do. In the old country it would be different. Tears blinded her. Oh, the green land of Scotland! Would she ever see it again?

She got up unsteadily, feeling a terrible sickness in her stomach. I want to run away, she thought. I want to run away and hide in a hole where none of them can see me, where I can be sick by myself and nobody know about it.

"I declare," Amie said loudly, returning from the wagon. "You've got a white ring around your mouth, Prim." And then, lowering her voice so the men couldn't hear: "Wrong time for you to be on a picnic, maybe."

Prim's eyes moved past her to the tall pines that shimmered darkly green. I wish it was, Amie. *Oh, I wish it was!*

A hand touched her arm. "I fixed you a plate, honey," Jediah said. "You look like you could stand some waitin' on."

Always kind to her, this little trapper and ditch-walker. Always saying a soft word or doing a thoughtful thing—kinder than anybody she'd ever known. But she couldn't eat much. The food stuck in her throat, and she couldn't stand the smell of coffee.

The men finished eating and sprawled around the dying fire, smoking. Amie rolled over on her side, half asleep in the sun. And where were Heather and young Jim Plunkett? Prim thought. She'd have to speak to Heather—running off into the timber with him. She'd let Heather know there would have to be an end to that. Prim put down her plate and walked quickly away.

She went through the trees until she reached the willows, and put up her hands before her, shoving at the branches, not feeling them scratch her face and arms. It was as though she were running away from something and couldn't run fast enough. She came to a beaver pond, flat and silvery-looking in the bright sun. She sat down on the damp, shady bank and dipped her handkerchief in the water and wiped her hot face.

She did not hear him come, but suddenly knew that he was there, and turned to see Jediah settling himself on the bank beside her. She was embarrassed, thinking she might throw up right in front of him, and turned her face so he couldn't look into it.

"Time of day when things is most uninterestin', Prim. Now,

later, when the shadows come, the hills get shaped with deeps and darks, and this pond here will be fulla willow shadows. Never liked the middle of the day myself—ain't good for much but sleepin' and eatin'. I favor early mornin' or the late afternoon. And there's no better time than sundown and just after."

He stopped talking, sensing her distress as he sensed uneasiness in an animal long before there was any outward sign of it. He heard her breath catch and knew she was starting to cry. Couldn't hold herself. Wasn't made that way. All that she was showed right on the top. A devil of a woman, that's what the cowpunchers said—chewing them out for being late to meals or trackin' her floor. But they respected her. Yes, even if they didn't exactly like her, they respected her mighty highly. As for himself, he liked her the way she was. Most women didn't have enough spunk to be interesting. This one did.

She was sobbing now, tears pouring down her face. "I'm going to have a baby," she said. "I know it, so I do. Oh, Jediah, I didn't want another baby. It brings back all I went through—back there. God, a nightmare, that's what it was!"

"You ain't over there now, honey. This is different."

"I never want any part of it again—never! Jediah, the nights I walked in the dark by the sea, and her there inside me, and Kelsey in this country, and the folk all talking—talking— I wanted to die, Jediah. And in the light I held my head high, held it so when my heart was breaking. Kelsey can't ever know what it was. I don't want to remember it, Jediah, but now it keeps coming back—how I begged God to let me be free of it, to make me a lassie again with no man's mark on me, and—"

She paused, and he said, "You know this ain't the same. You've got your husband and your friends. You're married, and nothin' to worry about or be shook up over."

"That's easy for you to say, Jediah. I'm not dumb like a cow. It's not me he loves. It's Monte Maguire. Oh, I've known it a long time, so I have. He's only tied to me because of the lassie. And when she's a proper age I ought to let him go.

And I don't want another baby to raise and him going on living with me because he has to."

"Now," Jediah said, "you be reasonable, Prim. He didn't have to marry you, and he didn't have to stay stuck to you, did he?"

"Ah, you don't know him, Jediah. He stays because he thinks it's right—a noble thing. Noble, hell! I'd rather he'd loved me—God, yes—and never married me!"

"Prim, you can't say he don't love you. Things get all mixed up sometimes. And sure as shootin' nobody this side of heaven knows what love is. And here you sit, thinkin' of yourself, when you ought to be thinkin' of the little baby that's comin' and needs a mother who loves him, who's quiet and contented and will let him grow strong inside her."

"It was enough for me to go through it once, the way it was. No, no, I don't want it again! Only let us raise Heather till she can take care of herself, and then I'll be glad to be rid of him. *She* can have him, damn her!"

"Y'don't mean it, Prim. You love him, and you know it."

"By God, I'll get over loving him. I'll tear it out of myself, so I will! I'll—"

"You talk crazy—worse'n Ellie Lundgren," he said sharply. "Stop it, now. You're a strong woman, Prim, and this ain't like you. Hang on, now, and behave yourself. You hear?"

"Jediah, it was wrong for Kelsey to marry me if he didn't love me."

"Would have been worse to let the girl grow up without a name or a father, wouldn't it? And get off that stuff about him not lovin' you. And let me tell you something, Prim: sometimes it's the things people have to do because they're right before God and man that count—not what they just want to do for their own good pleasure. A right thing's not always easy, but it holds life together better'n anything else I know. It pares a man and woman down till they're whittled thin, with only the hard core of 'em showing. And it's the hard core that counts, Prim. Now you cut out that bawlin' and carryin' on and makin' an ass outta yourself."

She stood up, angry at him, as he could see. "You've got a nerve," she retorted. "A dirty old bachelor like you telling me what to do."

"I'm older than you are," he said, "and, by God, I'll tell you off if I feel like it." He shoved the willows aside for her to pass. "Now get the hell back to camp and behave yourself."

She marched past him, her chin in the air.

*   *

Farther away from the picnic, under the big pines at the mouth of a ravine where the wild columbine plants were up but not in flower, Heather lay on her stomach beside Jim Plunkett. Jim sprawled on his back, his head on his arms, a piece of grass between his teeth, as he stared up at the sky.

"Why do you keep your shirt collar fastened tight all the time?" she asked, her tanned, warm face bending close to him.

" 'Cause."

" 'Cause why?"

"You're too nosy. All girls are too nosy."

"Quit teasing me. I just asked a question."

"You want to see why I keep it closed?" His eyes, slitted against the sun that sifted through the pine branches, watched her closely.

"Yes."

His hand, big and scarred from outdoor work, moved, to open the neck of his shirt. "See?"

She looked at the tuft of soft black hair there at the base of his throat. "Oh," she said.

"Satisfied now, are you?"

"It makes me feel funny, looking at it."

"Does it?" The blue slits of his eyes were hot and bright and close. "You're a funny girl, Heather. You always were. I guess I like it, the funny part of you. I guess that's why I don't want to see any other girl in the whole Park." He put his arms around her and pulled her down against his chest. "We better get up," he said, "before somebody comes and catches us. Your pa'd raise old Ned, all right. And your ma! She'd run me plumb outta the country."

But she lay still, feeling his heart against her own, smelling the man-smell of him, her face pressed against the soft black tuft of hair.

He turned, moving them both, and held her to him more easily and kissed her mouth. "You don't know how to do it," he said in surprise. "You ain't been kissed before."

She drew back, her fingers covering her mouth. "No—no, I guess not."

"The boys said—about you been ridin' with the cowpunchers, sleepin' on roundups, swimmin' with Long Dalton when you're too old for it— And I thought— Get up, honey. We're goin' back to the picnic."

"Why? I like it here. I like you, Jim."

He shoved her from him and got to his feet. He walked away from her and then turned, saying harshly, "You be careful about Long Dalton. He's been around—all around. You got no business swimmin' in any creek with him again. You hear?"

"He's old—he's almost as old as my father."

"He was just a big bull-strong kid when your pa and him first worked together at the Red Hill. And even then he'd been around—with Black Susie's girls, with any other girl that wasn't careful with herself. And I heard way back there was a married woman here in the Park, too—and him takin' up the slack when her husband was outside on business."

Heather was laughing. "But he's old, I tell you. I've known him all my life, and he's—he's—"

"Stay way clear of him!" Jim brought his hands up in fists

and let them fall back, loose, to his sides. He walked on before her, mumbling words she couldn't hear.

Heather came slowly along behind him, reaching to break a few pine needles from a branch, squinting up at the sky, laughing to herself. Dalt could be her brother. You didn't love your brother, did you? No, not the way Jim meant.

CHAPTER XVII

Kelsey lay on the horsehair couch, a pillow under his head. His jaw was swollen to twice its normal size, and there was a hard lump under it. Outside snow hissed against the windows. Prim came from the kitchen, awkwardly carrying a basin of hot water and a thick towel, for she had got large in the last month.

"There now, darlin'," she said, "let me ease it for you. Dalt says it's the big jaw from the cows you've got. And if it doesn't break you'll have to go to the doctor."

His whole head throbbed with pain. He was afraid to move, and when Prim put the hot cloth gently against his cheek he winced. Dalt stood behind her, looking down at him, wearing his heavy coat and overshoes. "Buddy," he said, "you're in bad shape."

"Can't eat," Kelsey said thickly, the words hard to get out, for his throat felt as if it were closing.

"A piece of foxtail got in there somewhere," Dalt said. "You've got a lot of infection. Kelsey, you better get over town and let Doc Bingham look at it. It's near the jugular vein and not safe for any of us to fool with it."

Prim looked frightened. "He can't ride to town when he's so sick."

"He better get there."

There was a loud bang of the outside door, and Tommy stomped into the living room. His little mouth drew smaller. "That what I'm payin' you for?" he asked harshly. "Layin' around the house like a sick calf? Get up and get a pitchfork in your hand."

Kelsey stared at him, his head swimming in pain.

Prim turned on Tommy. "You mean bugger! You're that cruel you'd send him out to feed when he feels like this!"

"Hell, he's not bad off. Just thinks he is." Tommy took a step toward Kelsey. "Get up!"

Kelsey sat up, bright lights of pain exploding in his head. "You damn bully!" He staggered to his feet, his fist doubled.

Dalt stepped between them. "Lay off him, Tommy. He's not able to fight. And he's not feedin' any cattle. I'll take care of his work. He's goin' to town and see the doctor. You've had him out there for three days when he was too sick to hold up his head. Now, by God, you get out of here and leave him alone!"

Tommy's face was ugly. "If he goes to town, then he better not come back and work for me."

Kelsey's words came out hoarsely. "I'm not coming back, Tommy. I've taken all I can from you. I'm through. Get my coat and overshoes, Prim. Dalt, saddle a horse."

Tommy slammed the door behind him. Prim began to cry. "You'll die between here and town. You're not able to ride a horse, and you know it."

"I'll ride," Kelsey said, gritting his teeth. "Prim, stop crying and get my clothes."

She put her arms around him, sobbing. "Kelsey—Kelsey, I don't want to live if anything happens to you."

"Get hold of yourself, Prim. It's only a foxtail in my throat. It's happened before." He turned to Dalt. "Look after Prim. Sleep in the house and take care of her, will you? I don't like to leave her now."

"Don't worry," Dalt said. "I'll see that nothing happens to her." And he went out.

Dalt had the horse waiting when Kelsey got to the corral.

It was a cold morning, with a March wind blowing out of the north.

"Take it easy, buddy." Dalt helped him into the saddle. "I'll keep my eye on everything. Don't worry about the missus. And Kelsey—if you do leave the Red Hill, I'm goin' with you. So's Hilder."

"I'm leaving it, Dalt—if I have to sit in town until spring."

He rode slowly away from the ranch, each step of the horse sending the jarring pain through his head. He braced his feet against the stirrups and tried to ease the jolting of the horse. The pain made him sick, and he clung to the saddle horn. The land flowed around him, cold and blue-white in the morning. Sweat broke out on his body, and he shivered when the wind struck him.

Somewhere between the Red Hill Ranch and the Platte River he fell off the horse and lay in the snow, coming slowly out of a daze of pain, blinking at the gray sky with the scum of cloud curdled over it. I'll never get up, he thought. I'll lie here and freeze to death. And it's Tommy's fault. He never wanted me around, never from the first day I set foot in this country. And I'd have left him long ago but for Prim and my lassie. He turned in the snow, felt it cold under his cheek, struggled, and got to his feet. He saw the horse standing there with the bridle reins trailing, watching him. He began to move toward it, weaving in and out like a drunken man.

When he reached the horse he leaned against it, warming himself on the steady shoulder. He tried to get into the saddle and couldn't. Then he saw the little outcrop of rocks ahead where the land lifted out of a low ravine. Carefully he led the horse to the rocks, crawled onto them, and slid down into the saddle. He wound the reins around the horn and clung to it. The horse moved on toward the river.

At Monte Maguire's home place he turned in at the wide pole gate. Tell her, he thought, the fever high in him, tell her to take the damned job and to hell with it!

He was too weak to get off the horse. He sat there at the hitching rack, gagging and shivering, his mittened hand pressed to his swollen jaw with the bristle of whiskers covering it. He opened his mouth to shout, but the effort was too much. His jaws felt like steel traps that couldn't be pried open.

The door of the ranch house opened, and Monte stood there. He noted vaguely that she was wearing a dress instead of pants and had a shawl over her shoulders. She came quickly toward him, running through the snow. Her arms reached up, and he slid down into them and hung limply against her.

Was it night? Everything turned so black as she helped him to the house, and he heard the voice of the thin woman who was always there. "He's on fire, Monte."

They were putting him on a bed then. The pillow smelled of perfume and of Monte Maguire—a clean fragrance of healthy skin and freshly washed hair. He moved his head and said thickly, "I'm through with Tommy Cameron, the son-of-a-bitch. Go back to the old country before—I ever work with him—again."

"Get the men to hook up a team, and lay out plenty of blankets," Monte Maguire said. The bony middle-aged woman with the twisted bun of hair nodded her head and left the room.

Monte's face wasn't so clear now, but it was close. His hand trembled toward the hair that was so bright in the dim bedroom. "Lovely," he murmured, feeling it between his fingers, "lovely . . ."

"Shut up," she said curtly. "Save your strength. You'll need it."

He drank from the glass she pressed against his lips. The whisky was raw, and it spread all through him, making him sleepy. How many nights since he had slept? He tried to remember and couldn't. Dimly he was aware of men carrying him to the sled and covering him with blankets. There was the crack of the whip and Monte's voice shouting, "Move, you broomtails!" The runners squeaked, and a spray of snow touched his forehead. He slept then, and wakened when men shook him; they helped him from the sled and up the long flight of stairs to Doc Bingham's office.

He lay on a table. Doc Bingham bent over him. Doc had a wisp of white hair on top of his head and a small, moist pink mouth like a girl's. Doc said, "By God, don't move, young fella, or I'll cut your throat! Hold him, Monte. Put your weight across his legs. Cover his chest, Faun."

Kelsey was afraid. He could smell the cigar smoke on Faun Gentry, and then Faun's body was heavy on his chest and Monte was heavy over his legs. He could see all too clearly the blade in Doc's hand. It glittered like some evil thing in the shaft of sunlight that came through the window. God, my God, he thought frantically, can't they give me a drink of whisky—something?

Doc's hand was rough on his head, twisting it back and to the side. *"Don't move!"* Then the terrible thrust of agony. Kelsey heard his voice cry out, hoarse and pitiful. He gasped and shook, and tears ran from his eyes. A wetness spread from his neck down onto his shoulder, and suddenly the pain eased. He closed his eyes, wetting his dry lips. Oh, the blessed relief! The whole long length of him shuddered and then was quiet. He slept.

When he wakened he was still on the table in Doc Bingham's office above the main street. But it was night, and the yellow lamp burning. Monte Maguire moved from a chair and stood beside him. "You're fine now," she said. "I got you a clean shirt. Better put it on. Then we'll go to Possy's and eat."

He sat up, lightheaded and hungry. Doc helped him slip into the clean wool shirt. "Tough, that's what you are," he said. "Sat out there among the damned coyotes and like to died before you had sense enough to come and get help."

He went slowly down the narrow stairs with Monte, and out into the clear March night and across the deserted street to the hotel. No one was in the lobby, and they entered the wide, bare-floored dining room and sat at one of the wooden tables until Possy came from the kitchen, yawning. "It's late," she said. "I'll have to heat leftovers."

"Fry him a steak," Monte said, "a big steak, and plenty of spuds with gravy."

Possy's little eyes darted from one to the other. "Well—" She yawned again.

"Steak," Monte said. She tossed back her coat and began to roll a cigarette.

Grumbling, Possy moved away to the kitchen. "Now," Monte said, "what's this about you and Tommy?"

He told her everything then, starting at the beginning and not leaving out the part about the hole in the bedroom ceiling. "I only stayed because I had to," he added, "and nothing's worth it any more."

"You don't have to stay now," she said. "I'm firing the man across the hogback on the North Fork Ranch."

"You mean—"

"Harmon. He's no good. He's been ready to quit for six months. Between him and his slack wife, that ranch isn't what it ought to be." Her eyes became dreamy behind the screen of cigarette smoke. "That's always been my favorite ranch of the three. There's the big house there—my home once. It's closed and will stay that way. But the little house is plenty big for you and your family, Kelsey. Flit—my husband—he built the big house special for me when he thought I'd play the lady to the women in the Park. But nobody ever came—no women, I mean. Dolly Gentry saw to that. And we weren't asked any place. I couldn't stand it out there; it was a sort of prison. After Flit died I moved over to the ranch on the Platte. But I'd like to have you there on that place, Kelsey. It's such a fine ranch— the water, the meadows—"

Possy set steak before him, but he scarcely noticed it. He was seeing the North Fork Ranch—a place fit for a king.

"Take it over," Monte said. "Run it the way you like. Con-

tract it from me. Run your cattle and some of mine—you won't
have enough of your own yet. It's bigger than the Red Hill,
you know."

"Yes, I know." He reached across the table and took hold of
her hand. "Monte, why do you do all this—for me?"

"Goin' soft in my old age," she murmured. "Soft—an easy
touch. Eat your steak, man, before it gets cold."

He ate then, his mind searching into the future—more cattle,
more grass, himself his own boss. It was like a dream. He
looked at Monte, and his thoughts came back to her. "What
have you done to your hair?"

It was piled on top of her head, and a soft bang lay over her
forehead. She laughed, and her fingers went up to touch the
bang. "It's a new style; it's called 'old woman's delight.' "

"You'll never be an old woman."

"Sounds good, Kelsey, even if it isn't true."

"But it is. There's the thing in you, like is in my mother—
the music, the strong breath of living. That won't die, and because it won't you'll never be old."

She smiled. "I'll remember that someday—someday when
I'm low in my mind and thinking how foolish it is, building up a
cattle herd and ranches when there's no son or daughter to
carry them on—when there's nobody but myself."

He got up and found her coat and folded it around her shoulders. He paid Possy for their supper, and they walked up the
street to the livery stable, got the team and sled, and drove
away toward the Platte. They didn't speak all the way to her
ranch, and when they got there she said, "You better come in
and get warm before you start riding."

He stood before the rough stone fireplace, his back to the
flames. She sat in a sunken chair and looked at him, the pale
light of the little lamp flickering behind her.

"I must go soon," he said.

"Why?" It was a sharp question in the quiet room.

"If I stayed I would never leave you again."

She got up and walked to the window, and he went to stand behind her, and over her shoulder he could see the white land stretching to the west and the starlight over it. She turned abruptly and filled his arms and put her face against his.

The deep, sweet aching welled up in him, and he held her, still looking into the night and hearing the fire flutter on the hearth. "I love you, Monte."

"I didn't ask for that. And I'm not worth it."

"Whatever you're thinking, it hasn't anything to do with us. No one has loved you as I do now. You were never to any man what you are to me."

Her face was wet against his. "Then how can you leave me? What is wrong about it if you stay?"

"I told you. I would never go again. The world would be lost—"

"And what's the world? Does it matter?"

"I wish it didn't, Monte. But for me it has to—because of Heather and Prim."

She pulled away from him, her voice rough when she spoke. "What are you made of? Iron? Stone?"

"Pray God that I always will be, Monte. Help me, if I ever weaken, to know what it is I have to do."

"Only once to live—once—and then nothing. Oh, what a fool you are! There's a blindness in you, a cursed noble blindness. And sometimes—sometimes you stink with it!"

"Maybe you have no conscience. You wouldn't know what it is to feel guilty or ashamed?"

"Listen, Kelsey, I've never been ashamed of anything I felt, felt honestly—anything that was real. What I feel for you is real, and I could go to bed with you tonight and with no regret."

"But you have no lassie—and no husband."

"Oh, Christ! There it is again. Go home, then! Go, and for God's sake let's not haggle the thing to pieces!"

"Monte, Monte—" He put his arms around her and held her again. He kissed her mouth and her eyes and the hollow of her throat where the pulse beat hard under his lips. Then he put on his heavy coat and walked out.

He rode through the thin cold of the night, the snow crunching under the hoofs of the horse, the land around him bright under the moon. He rode in a strange, cool enchantment. And as the land lifted in the roll of the plains toward the mountains, his blood lifted too, making him young as he had never been young before. To keep this time always, he thought, to keep what I am and feel this moment all the days of my living— aye, to keep it in the heart where nothing can touch or change it!

In the strange way that sometimes happens in the mountain country, he came suddenly to a place where the air was less cold, drifting in warmer currents against his face, and the thought of spring was with him. Spring and the North Fork Ranch—ice breaking on the river, and the grass springing green at the edge of the melting snow, and always the mountains there so close, like a great wave of the sea rolled up and frozen against the sky. Spring and the North Fork Ranch—this was a turning point in his life, and he knew it.

And what a strangeness there was in living! A man went along, struggling with his lot, fighting it, cursing it, sometimes hoping and sometimes despairing. And then a little thing like a bit of foxtail stuck in the jaw— The little things, so unexpected, could change the whole world.

He rode into the Red Hill Ranch when the dark was thinning, and a lamp burned in the kitchen window. He unsaddled and stood by the barn, thinking of Monte, thinking too of Prim. Then, squaring his shoulders, he walked toward the house. He pushed the door open, and Prim was there by the kitchen stove, an old sweater covering her shoulders, and he knew by the look of her face that she hadn't slept.

"Kelsey!" Her green eyes widened. "You're home—and a bandage around your neck." She came to him, her lips quivering. "Are you all right?"

"Madam," he said, "prepare my breakfast and serve it to me at the head of the table."

"So!" Her mouth smiled. "You come home bossy. Well, you're better, then—coming in and giving me orders like the laird himself."

He shrugged off the coat, drew up a chair, and swelled his chest, rapping on the table with his fist while she stared at him. "Coffee, madam! At once, madam!"

"The devil with you!" she muttered, not sure whether he was serious or joking.

"I'll have you know, madam, you're talking to a foreman."

"A—" Her lips parted. "A foreman! Kelsey!" Tears filled her eyes. "I knew it! You were never any common man. I always knew it—even when you were a wee lad around the harbor."

"Well, it's good news I have. And I'm not only a foreman, I'm a contractor, my own boss. I have a lease."

She sat down beside him. "Tell me! Tell me quick!"

"I'll have a drink first. Fix it, madam. Whisky, a little hot water, and a dash"—he licked his lips—"just a dash, mind you, of sugar."

She hurried to get glasses and a bottle of whisky from the bedroom. She fixed a drink for him and one for herself and sat down.

He told her then, his eyes shining, the whisky warm in him, taking his time, drawing the story out till he got the last flavor from it. And all the time she watched him, her lips moving, saying silently part of the words after him, and the tears sliding down her cheeks. And when he finished he stared at her in surprise. "My God, Prim, you kept your mouth shut! You didn't have a word to say."

She wiped her eyes on her apron. "I couldn't. I'm so proud of you!"

"Prim—" He touched her hand, feeling a closeness he had never before known in the years he'd lived with her.

She jerked her hand away, got to her feet, and said, "Oh, the damn cooking! The men will be in, and no breakfast for them. Move, now, and set the table for me. Or are you above it, now that you're a contractor?"

"I'm above it. But I'll do it this time, seeing the shape you're in." He grinned at her.

CHAPTER XVIII

A week later they moved to the North Fork Ranch; Kelsey wanted to get settled before Prim had the baby. Heather rode her horse beside the sled, going on ahead and coming back, her face shining from the wind and the glare of sun on the slushy snow. Kelsey sat in the sled with Prim, and behind them came the hayrack with Dalt and Hilder and all their belongings. Tommy had stood over them while they packed, making certain they took only what was theirs.

North Fork Ranch was in a small valley shut off from the rest of the Park, bounded by the mountains to the west and by the hogback and neighboring hills to the east. It was lonely, but it had not the melancholy loneliness of the Red Hill country. The North Fork Valley was proud and wild and contained.

They reached the ranch buildings in late afternoon, when the shadows lay long on the mountains and the rabbits tracked through the pasture, moving like tumbling white stones, a little darker than the snow that now had the glaze from the day's melting. The damp promise of spring lay in the coming evening.

There were two dwelling houses near the river bank, the large home that Flit Maguire had built for Monte, and the smaller one into which Kelsey was moving his family. This one was narrow and low-ceilinged, with a pantry, a big kitchen, a box of a dining room, a living room the same size, and three tiny, stall-like bedrooms. A shallow porch ran all the way along the front, and a smaller, closed-in porch was tacked to

221

the south side; here were buckets, a table, shelves, and a row of spikes for hanging clothes. Compared to Red Hill it was a little house, but Prim walked into it happily, stood by the window that faced the mountains, looked at the frozen river, and said, "It's water near me at last. It'll have a good sound and a wet smell. It'll be more like the old country and the harbor."

"Yes," Kelsey said, "and like the highlands of Scotland, for the mountains are so close. It makes me remember being a lad and my folk taking me to the highlands on a holiday." He drew a deep breath, threw back his shoulders. " 'Ye crags and peaks, I'm with ye once again . . .' "

"It'll be a help to me," Prim said, unbuttoning her coat, "if you'll get off the poetry and down to work. Could you come out of your dreaming long enough to start the fire?"

But it was Hilder who started the fire and helped Prim. It was Hilder who unpacked the bedding and clumsily made the beds, while Dalt went to take care of the evening chores. Kelsey strolled down to the river and stood looking at the stems of the willows rising from the snowdrifts. They weren't black or brown, as he had expected, but some were purple and others a brilliant fuchsia, and some were pure golden with orange lights to their branches.

He turned toward the log bunkhouse there near him, closer to the river than the ranch house, and he saw that the light of the sun, now sliding behind the mountains, had put red in the bunkhouse windows, and the purple-reddish light of the willows lay over the log walls. A waterwheel, hooded with snow, was in the river directly behind the bunkhouse. On this too were the red and violet and orange lights of willows and sundown. He fell to dreaming over the colors, placing them all around the old waterwheel, and this notion so pleased him that he smiled to himself.

Heather came and stood beside him. "Were you not helping your mother, lass?"

"I wanted to see the river."

"Yes, the river is more important."

They stood in silence then, enjoying the scene around them. From time to time they could hear Prim's voice and the clatter of pans. Kelsey wished Prim would come out too, and for a moment he had a strong impulse to go to her and say, Forget the house. Come with me by the river and the willows. But instead he said to Heather, "In spring the beaver will be swimming on a misty night, and we'll hunt them, you and me. And in fall, if you want, you can run a trap line and catch muskrats and mink. And the fishing! Lassie, many a fine afternoon and evening we'll spend fishing this river."

He noticed the glint at the throat of her sweater, where a bright pin fastened the collar. "What's that at your neck, Heather?"

"A present."

"And where did you get it?"

"Jim gave it to me—Jim Plunkett. It was his own money he spent, money he saved from the coyotes he trapped."

"It's pretty fancy, isn't it, for a sixteen-year-old boy to be giving a lassie who's not yet thirteen?"

"Didn't you know my mother and give her presents when you were sixteen?"

His breath caught. "But that was different."

Her hand fingered the shining pin. Her eyes looked at him, direct and clear. A fear stirred in him. His lassie to love a Plunkett? His lassie bending over a cookstove in a ranch house, working too hard all her life?

He said carefully, "Oh, it's fine to have Jim for a friend, but you've years of education before you. Your mother and me, we want you to have the best there is. And, as God's above me, I'd rather see you dead than cooking in a kitchen for Jim Plunkett. The Plunketts—they're good people, but slack, lassie. Harry's never going to amount to any more than he does right now. And Jim will likely be through school—no more learning before him."

"I don't see it's so important," she said, "spending half your life in school."

"But you're not like the other people in the Park, Heather. You're—" He floundered, groping for words, his emotions so strong they bothered his thinking. His hands clenched tight at his sides, and he felt the sweat on them and tried to speak calmly. "We'll talk no more of it. Just remember an education's a thing worth more than all the money in the world. You're just a lassie. There's so much you must learn."

There was a faint smile in her eyes, a smile that told him she would soon be a woman. And what answer could a man ever give when the blood beat up warm, singing its own song that knew no reason for anything but loving? What of his own blood, which had never cooled over the years but was still that of a young, young man when he looked at Monte Maguire? Wasn't the same fire in his daughter as in himself?

Prim's voice rang out in the darkening evening, calling them to supper. He put his arm across Heather's shoulders and walked with her to the house.

It was that night, when the others were all settled in bed, that he crossed the yard to the second house, the big one that was always shut. Its cupolas and gingerbread trim glistened in the moonlight. He unlocked the front door and carried the lantern from room to room, wondering how Monte Maguire had looked in this house that was now without any furniture. In his mind he could see her coming down the long, curving stairway. And he found an upstairs bedroom that he was sure must have been hers, for it looked over the river and to the mountains. He knew she had wept in this room, lonely because the women of the Park shunned her and called her a whore. He wondered how she had felt, being loved by Flit Maguire, who was thirty years older than herself. And as he stood by the window he thought of what it might be like to stand there beside her in the night when spring was on the meadows and the river went by with its cargo of stars. Then he thought of be-

ing in bed with her and of having her close to him the whole
long night, while the wind sighed in the willows and there was
no one to see them or bother them at all. Surely it would be
wonderful, he thought, and I can think of nothing that would
be so lovely.

At length he went into the other two bedrooms and to the
room that held a huge wooden tank for water. There was a
bathroom too. To be sure it had been—and still was—a fancy
house, for even now one could find a bathtub only at the hotel
in town.

He walked back down the curving stairs, into the two bedrooms on the main floor, wandered through the big living room
with its neat red brick fireplace, to the wide dining room, the
large kitchen, pantry, another bathroom, and what was appar-
ently a second parlor.

Yes, it had been a house fit for a queen. Satisfied with his
looking, he locked the door, blew out the lantern, and crossed
the snow-crusted yard. He turned toward the meadows and
thought of Monte's cattle and his, there on the hard-packed
feeding ground. And he wished for the light to come soon so he
could ride through the cattle, for there was no need for sleep in
him that night.

He wandered on over to the corrals, the two barns, and the
machine shop, before he went into the house, took off his overshoes, and sat in darkness by the banked kitchen stove that
gave off a pleasant low heat.

"Kelsey—" It was Prim, a candle in her hand. "Aren't you
coming to bed, Kelsey?"

He didn't want to go to bed. And he didn't want to see Prim
or talk with her. He wanted to sit quietly by himself and with
his own thoughts.

"I'd think you'd want some sleep," Prim said, moving restlessly about the kitchen.

Could she never be quiet in her moving? Must she always
make the floors tremble when she walked and open the cup-

boards as if she would yank the doors from their hinges? But he said nothing, and after a while she sat at the kitchen table, putting herself down as though she intended to sit out the night with him. He got to his feet. "Well, then, maybe it is time for bed."

She lay awake beside him, and this disturbed him, for he felt his thoughts weren't his own, that she waited for him to talk and share them with her, and that if he didn't she would get at them in the way she had of asking, until it was easier to tell her than keep silent.

Her hand touched his arm, gentle and uncertain. "Kelsey—" And then for a moment he was distressed by what he had been thinking about her. He kissed her and rubbed his knuckles lightly across her warm cheek.

"Sleep now, lassie. It's been a long, hard day for you."

CHAPTER XIX

They were making up the bed with fresh sheets. "Tuck 'em in tight," Amie said. "It's terrible to poke your feet out, weather like this. And get 'em smooth over that place where the oilcloth is spread to protect the mattress."

"I know how to do it," Prim said irritably. "Why don't you take care of something else?"

"Nothin' else—until Doc Bingham gets here. And I want to see it's done right. A woman oughta have the best bed there is, havin' a baby."

Prim stood before the narrow bedroom window. Around the inside of the frame the nailheads were frosted until they looked like white beads. Her breath was steamy in the cool air, for even the warmth from the red-hot living-room stove hadn't made the bedroom comfortable. Out in the March morning the wind skimmed snow off the roof of Monte Maguire's big empty house. And she wished Monte would go over and stay in that house now instead of waiting around in the kitchen. Like this is going to be a show she can't miss, Prim thought bitterly. And why was it she had to arrive yesterday to ride over her land and look at her cattle? Is it that I'm never to be free of her?

The house shook under the beat of the wind, and she wondered if there had ever been such a time as spring. Surely the heart could break, remembering the sound of running water or the slow drift of green across the hills.

The pain began again; it moved down her back and into her

legs. It cramped her stomach, filling her with sickness. She went out of the bedroom to the small, low-ceilinged living room, followed by Amie.

Jediah Walsh, Kelsey, and Monte were there. They got quickly from their chairs and began to walk up and down behind her, the three of them looking haggard and frowning. She felt as though she floated before them, her swollen and distended body strangely light—or maybe it was only the pain blurring her senses. She wore no shoes, only a pair of Kelsey's wool socks, for her feet were swollen to twice their normal size.

The front door opened, and wind tore it from Dr. Bingham's grasp and banged it against the wall. He shoved it shut and looked at the three lined up behind Prim. "Well," he said, grinning, "let's see, now—which is the father?"

They glared at him. Kelsey muttered, "What took you so damn long?"

"You oughta been here two hours ago," Jediah said, squirting a stream of tobacco juice toward the stove. "We sent Hilder after you, and he's been home, had his breakfast, and gone to feed cattle. We were afraid to let Dalt go into the meadow. Figured he might have to help us if we got in a pinch."

"Lotta trouble could have caught up with her," Monte said crossly, "while you been dragging yourself out here from town."

The doctor bent to unbuckle his overshoes. "I've seen this young woman. I knew she'd be slow. And if she wasn't, birth's no stranger to those who work around cattle. Eh, Monte?"

"It's a different business, damn it! And you ought to have come right away."

And will you listen to her? Prim thought. What's she so concerned about? Not me, that's for sure. She turned to Amie, her mouth tightening. "Take the doctor's coat." Her voice was low and controlled.

"Don't you figure she oughta be in bed?" Jediah looked anxious. "She's been in terrible pain for the last two hours."

"That so?" Dr. Bingham methodically unwound the scarf from around his neck.

"There must be something you can do to help her get it over with," Monte said.

"Well, for God's sake don't just stand there," Kelsey shouted, "like you had all day!"

"Amie," said the doctor, "will you please remove these gentlemen and Mrs. Maguire to the kitchen and give them some coffee or whisky and listen to their advice. In the meantime the patient and I will adjourn to the bedroom."

*   *

Prim stared at the ceiling. The shadow of the kerosene lamp lay against it. Night and cold . . . Tired and no rest . . . When would it be over?

Amie sat beside her, wiping her forehead with a cold cloth and murmuring, "There now, honey."

Kelsey came in and stood at the foot of the bed. His face was gray and tired. "Can I get you a cup of tea or something?"

"Nothing." Prim turned her head, rubbing it wearily on the pillow. And for a moment she was back in the old country, with Big Mina sitting by her, and the strange little doctor from the big town. Big Mina was crying and muttering, "God will take care of you, lassie."

Prim ground her teeth. God was supposed to be all-powerful, loving, to have made the world and all that was in it. He wouldn't have made much, she thought bleakly, if He'd had to do it this way.

But I'm not going to die. I won't! Not while there's Heather to raise. Heather—Heather, a shame and a sorrow, a beautiful thing and a terrible thing. I'll fight. To die—maybe all right for someone else, but not for me, not for Prim Munro. I've got to live—for my lassie.

She felt Amie's hand grip hers, heard Doc Bingham's gruff voice. "Look here, Prim, you've got to stop fighting this thing.

Expect me to sit here all week waiting for a baby? When you get a hard pain you've got to work with it, not against it. I'll be damned if you're not the stubbornest female I've tried to deliver in twenty years!"

She stared at him, and he slowly came into focus—white hair, shrewd black eyes, high cheekbones, and then that wet pink mouth. Funny, that mouth. "All wrong on you, so it is," she muttered. "Should be on someone named Daisy."

Daisy—Daisy won't tell. I'll not tell whose baby it is, so I won't. Let the old women look and guess and whisper. Let them ask, "Who had Prim Munro in the heather?" Heather—ah, so sweet and warm at my breast. Mine! Mine as long as I live—

"You're a daisy," the doctor said peevishly. "Damn near two o'clock in the morning, and you're right where you were five hours ago. Want me to open you up on the kitchen table?"

"You'll do no such thing!" Prim's voice rose hysterically.

Amie bent close, and her eyes were big, too big and soft—a melting softness. . . . A hut on the shore, a girl melting away into a man, and never a thought of tomorrow . . . "Yes, Reverend McCullough, you'll baptize her now. You'll not question whose child she is, will you? To hell with the elders of the church! Will I stand before them and go over it while they lick their lips and wish to God they'd been there to see . . ."

Amie spoke softly. "Honey, try to go at it easier. Please don't fight."

"Oh, shut up, Amie!" Why had she said that? Amie was good, kind, come to help her. Sorry, Amie . . .

"Spunky as hell, isn't she?" The pink mouth opened and closed.

Ah, there it was again!—coming over her like a great black snake, writhing and writhing. Black rhythm, terrible and inescapable—outraging her mind and her body, outraging her because it took complete possession of her and pulsed and pulsed. Sweat broke out on her face. She tried to be calm, tried to think of peace and sleep and God, but instead she felt terror and anger and a need to defend her identity. She was fighting as though the end of the world had come, but she made no sound. There was only the perspiring, horrible struggle.

"Give her some more, Amie," Doc Bingham said. "Not too much—just enough to take the edge off."

"Oh, Prim, please, please!" Amie's voice was tearful. Prim felt the cloth over her face, pressing her down and down, choking her with that sickening sweetness—like spoiled honey, she thought vaguely, like rotten clover. Lucky, lucky four-leaf clover. . . . "Give it to me, Crowter. I'll wear it on my dress. No, I won't marry you, but it's good you are, and if— Bless you, Crowter! For a rag-buyer you're a prince of a man. Then pin it in my hair, if you like. . . . Kiss me if you want." What does any man matter—arms or mouth or love in the heather—when the one man I love is gone?

Lucky pink-white clover . . . I won't be crushed down by it. *I won't, I won't!* I'm Prim Munro. I know who I am. *I, I, I—*

"The forceps, Amie! Quick!"

Not that—oh, not that. "Please, doctor! They did it there. Oh God, no!"

They were tearing her apart, tearing her flesh, her heart, her very blood. Pain gathered in a great red ball and exploded in her mind, sending off streaming showers of red and blue sparks.

Suck in the rotten honey, then. Let it choke you! Nothing matters—nothing at all. Better dead than bring a bairn into the world without a name. Let us both die, my bairn and me, Prim Munro. Mina—Mother—did I tear you like this? Dinna weep, my mother—och aye, dinna weep. I'm sinking away—away. . . .

She opened her eyes, and there was Kelsey. Yes, for sure it was Kelsey. *Have you come home then? Have you come back to claim your bairn?* And the stranger beside you? Jediah—of course, Jediah. And Dalt—Long Dalton with the color and fire to him that only a woman could understand. And Monte—hair so pretty a woman could cry for wanting it. Who asked you here, Mrs. Maguire?

They were grinning, all of them. They were nothing but big shiny teeth. "Chessy cats, so you are," she muttered.

"Got one hell of a fine boy," Doc Bingham said, patting her hand.

And who cares, Mr. Pink Mouth? Who cares? She closed her eyes and slept, falling away past Scotland and the Reverend Angus McCullough, past Jinnet, his housekeeper, with her mean little mouth, past the hut in the darkness, the heather-sweet braes, and the restless, swelling sea. Past the Red Hill Ranch and the bloody meat sliding from the chopping block as she hacked it into steak for breakfast, past Heather who was all misty-gray eyes and blowing hair and a voice like a meadow lark—past all and everything, into darkness wider than the Park and deeper than the sea.

When she wakened she was sick, sick and trying to tell them it was the spoiled clover she'd eaten. "Call Dalt," she murmured. "Tell him he needs the knife now."

Why were they laughing?

Awake again. Quiet now—everything real. In what far country had she traveled and returned? So quiet—and only the faint sweetish smell still there in the bedroom.

"Fine now, aren't you, Prim?"

"No, Doctor Bingham, I am not. I hurt, so I do."

He grunted. "Sure you hurt. Why not? Been acting contrary to nature ever since I got here yesterday morning. But you're strong, Prim. Won't be long until you're on your feet and raising hell as usual."

"Look, Prim!" Amie held the small bundle. "Look at him!"

Prim raised on her elbow and stared at the puckered red face and the fuzz of fair hair. A funny ugly little thing, that's what he was. More like a rabbit a body'd see running in the pasture. Then the tiny mouth opened in a yawn, and the cleanly marked long brows lifted in a vague air of puzzled concentration. "Oh," Prim said in awe, "he—he looked just like Kelsey!"

"Somebody else you expected him to look like?" Doc Bingham asked dryly.

"Oh, don't you be smart with me! And what's that terrible racket in the other room?" For suddenly she heard shouting and arguing and swearing. Then there was loud laughter. She lay back, the baby in the curve of her arm, frowning. "I'll not have such a racket! What are they up to, anyhow?"

"Just listen," Doc Bingham said. "You'll find out." And he swung open the bedroom door.

She heard Kelsey's voice. "He's to be named for me. Kelsey Cameron, that's it."

"Now listen," Monte Maguire said, "I'd give you twenty calves—outta my best bulls—to name him Monte. Monte Cameron—it's got a fine sound to it."

"Well, I don't know." Kelsey sounded uncertain. "Twenty calves, huh?"

"Make it fifty!" Monte's voice rose. "Sixty!"

"Keep on talkin', Monte," Jediah said mildly, "and you won't have no livestock left."

"Have another drink," Dalt said. "Bottoms up, Kelsey!"

More noise, swearing and laughter. Prim's frown deepened. What did they mean, arguing about the name of her son? What did they mean when she was tired and wanted to rest? And it was plain they were all getting drunk, so it was. And hadn't they deviled her enough, hanging around the place and pacing after her and asking every five minutes how she felt? And God, how would a woman feel, not able to put on her shoes, and the front of her sticking out like the prow of a ship? A spectacle, no less. And that bold as brass woman— And now—the very idea—they were naming *her* baby!

I'm just like an old cow, she thought angrily. All they care about is the calf. "Amie," she said, "tell them to come in here—all of them. Now!"

Doc Bingham took hold of her wrist. "You take it easy. You look flushed."

Flushed indeed!

The men came, their eyes bright from drink and excitement. Monte Maguire stood with them, her hair untidy, a smudge of dirt on her cheek. They lined up at the foot of the bed like dummies.

"Now," Prim said, "I had this baby, didn't I?"

Dalt and Jediah glanced at Kelsey. He nodded vigorously. They nodded also and turned to Monte, who bowed.

"And it wouldn't be too much to ask if I'd get to name the baby, would it?"

Again they looked at Kelsey. He scratched his head. "Well, it's not the usual situation, Prim. A little while ago I didn't have any livestock offers thrown in. That makes a difference. Sixty calves—"

"Calves be damned!" Prim snapped. "I'm tired of hearing my son put up for auction, do you hear?"

"Look," Monte began, "we didn't mean— I only thought—"

"She should have had twins," Amie said. "That'd settle it."

"It's settled right now, so it is."

"Now, Prim." Kelsey shifted uneasily. "Think a minute, will you?"

"I named him months ago," Prim said. Then she looked at Jediah Walsh. "I named him for you—Jediah Cameron."

The old trapper came slowly forward. He got down on his knees by the bed and looked at the baby. Tears came into his eyes. He put one of his big hands over Prim's and said unsteadily, "Honey, this is the greatest day in the life of Jediah Walsh."

She smiled. "You think he's nice, Jediah?"

"Why, hell, honey, he's the prettiest thing this side of the pearly gates! And come to think of it, he does sort of resemble me, don't he?"

Long Dalton broke into loud laughter. "God, he's so full of whisky he's seein' things!"

"I guess that settles who counts around this place," Monte said. "Eh, Kelsey?"

"Everybody out," Doc Bingham said. "Let Prim rest now. I want it quiet around here. If there's any more drinking to be done, move to the bunkhouse." He shoved them from the bedroom, glanced at Prim, and murmured, "Damn stubborn female, that's what you were."

Prim drew the baby close and lay staring at the window. Amie had taken the lamp, and out in the white, cold morning the stars were beginning to fade and the blue-white shapes of the mountains poked sharply at the sky. The difference, she thought. Oh, God, the difference now—and what it was then.

CHAPTER XX

Jediah Cameron was not a healthy child. He had been sick most of his first two years, worrying Prim and making her even more sharp-tongued. She nagged Kelsey about the weather and the country, but it was the poker-playing that upset her most. "At the least excuse you go to town to play cards," she said. "You throw your money around in Bill Dirk's saloon."

"I had business in town. I was hiring extra men to get ready for haying. Listen, Prim, you work too hard. Why didn't you keep that niece of Possy's I got to help you?"

"Keep her! Could she boil water without the kettle going dry? And heaved enough meat out in the slop pail to feed the men for a week."

He shook his head. "Prim, you're too fussy. You'll never get a woman to help you if you stand over her and fight about little things. But you need to see people; I'm thinking you need to be around women. Why don't you ask Amie up for supper?"

"Have I time for serving guests? Oh, it's easy enough for Amie Plunkett to ask folk in to eat. The devil a care she has in her head if the house stinks and she has only warmed-over watery stew to give them. She gets worse and worse. Last time I rode in the buggy with Hilder when he went after the mail, she was in bed—in bed at two o'clock in the afternoon! And with a book, mind you!"

"What of it? Her business, isn't it?"

"You'd soon be raising hell if I lay in my bed half the day, and the house dirty. Where were you yesterday when I wanted to air the bedding and turn the mattresses?"

"Oh, after I checked the water I rode down to see Vic Lundgren's car." Kelsey burst into sudden laughter. "He drove it right through the gate, pulling back on the steering wheel and yelling, 'Whoa! Damn you, whoa!' "

Prim sniffed. "A car? Well, you don't need a car. It would only get you to town faster and oftener."

"Everybody's getting cars, Prim. And next summer I'm having one. I'll be able to ship a load of steers, collect the money for putting up Monte's hay on contract."

Prim put both hands on her hips and nodded. "Yes, the laird himself! And your daughter just like you. What does she do for me? Gives the work a lick and a promise and is out the door before I can open my mouth to call her back. Then she gets on her horse and rides all over the country like a wild Indian. And when she's fed up with that she amuses herself making sheep's eyes at Dalt."

"Dalt? What do you mean, Prim?"

"Well, look sharp and see you don't have a hired man for a son-in-law!"

"Oh, leave the lassie be! You've a queer mind that's always making something out of nothing."

He went out, slamming the door. He walked to the barn and stood by the corral. There was lots of activity this morning. Down in the lower pasture Dalt and Hilder were breaking out horses for use in the hayfield. From the machine shop came the smell of forge smoke and the clanging of the hammer on the anvil, for some of the men were shoeing horses. Kelsey walked to the shop. Through the open back door he could see one of the new men working on sweep teeth, peeling the long poles and sharpening them to points. Near him the stacker glistened, reared up in the sky, the poles ready for the loads of hay to be pushed up and over and tumble down to the ground, where the stacking crew would sort them and settle them.

He turned from the shop and went to the barn, where the swallows were making a sucking sound under the eaves, building their mud houses. The hay men would knock the houses down, for it was generally believed that the swallows carried bedbugs, and some of the men had to sleep in the barn. But every morning, when the carefully packed mud lay broken on the ground, the swallows would start over—until at last they gave up. The next year it would be the same thing; they'd return to the barns, only to be defeated.

Inside the barn, he climbed the ladder to the loft and went to the back, where a pile of last summer's hay almost reached the ceiling. Fumbling in a dark corner, he found a bottle, took a drink, and sat down, leaning back in the dry, sun-smelling hump of hay. The whisky eased him; when Prim kept at him he always got a pain in the stomach.

He reached in his pocket and pulled out a recent letter from Taraleean and read it, enjoying the warmth in her words. Then a line rose sharp before him—"I'm getting old, lad, and slower at going along the braes of an evening." Tears filled his eyes. He took another quick drink and thrust the letter back in his pocket.

Warmed with the whisky, he went down the ladder, saddled a horse, and rode up the meadow to check the irrigating water. Along the hogback water poured through the outlets in chains of silver, trailing down from the main ditch. Mosquitoes, dragonflies, butterflies were around him. Birds called from the near willows along the river. He felt an intense awareness of life all around him. He became easy and mellow inside and drifted over to the creek. Everything was fine. There was really no need to check the water after Dalt and Hilder. Maybe it was only that he wanted to be out in the open by himself on such a day.

He dismounted and tied his horse to a willow. He wandered around a bend of the river with no particular thought of anything, hearing the murmuring water, smelling the faint wild-mint fragrance that hung in the air.

This week—maybe Sunday—he'd go fishing. A man ought to take time out from his work for fishing, for in this he could lose himself, shedding his worries as if they were an outgrown coat. And he fell to musing over a time he had fished with Dalt, when he was young and new to the Park. They had no fancy flies, only bait hooks, and he had seen the fish were feeding on the surface and would take a fly. He had looked around, noticed a chipmunk, and persuaded Dalt to shoot it. Then he had fashioned a fly from the end of the chipmunk's tail, and they had caught trout to beat the band.

He chuckled aloud now, remembering, and thinking how Monte Maguire had looked at him when they rode into the Red Hill Ranch and said, "How'd you catch them?" He'd stalled her off, teasing her, until he finally had to tell her.

"Smart, ain't you, young fella?" And her eyes had glinted in quick admiration.

He stretched and stood yawning in the sun by the creek bank. A man could sleep here under the willows with the creek singing to him and the wind shaking the green leaves above his face.

Then he saw the frog. Where the water made a deep pool at the bend of the river, the frog started across. There was slow water here, and deep, partly in the shade of the willows and partly in the sunlight. The frog's legs jerked, shot out straight, and jerked again. Kelsey's eyes were held by the motion. The frog drew out of the dark water into the clear, sunlit part of the pool. Then Kelsey saw the trout come up in a flash from the deep water; it struck the bulging side of the frog like a sinuous dagger—struck and darted away.

Fascinated and surprised, Kelsey stared. Again the trout

flashed up to stab at the frog. The frog faltered in its swimming, and a blob of entrail pushed out of its side. The trout returned, streaking up through the amber, sunlit water. It took the entrail in its mouth and dragged it out, speeding down the creek. The frog sank. Water and death were upon it.

It had happened so quickly and was such a final thing that Kelsey could only stand staring at the river, living over the incredible scene. After a time he moved back through the willows toward his horse, the tall grass flattening under his feet, the soft wind fanning his face. Awareness of death in the midst of all the living wonders of summer stirred his heart and made him turn the horse quickly toward home, his ears straining for the sound of his daughter's laughter.

*   *

Late that fall, when the first November snows were scudding across the peaks, Kelsey rode the meadows with Jake. "Count's off," he said. "How many cows are you short, Jake?"

"Looks like about twenty head."

"You fellows ridden the hills thoroughly?"

Jake nodded. "Can't understand where they are. Jediah claimed he saw some way high, near Frying Pan Basin, but we looked. We floundered around up there for three days and seen nothin' but mountain sheep. Hell, even the deer have quit that country, driftin' into Wyoming, where they can rustle the plains."

"Well, they've got to be found. Tomorrow Dalt and I'll go up in the mountains. We'll make a camp and take some skis and look over that country again."

"Kelsey, I been over it. And I think sometimes Jediah imagines he sees things. He's always comin' outta the hills with some story."

"Jediah knows cows when he sees them. I'm having another look."

Jake shrugged. "I'll take your pack outfit up, but it's just a lot of work for nothin'."

They left the ranch the next morning. It was clear and cold in the North Fork Valley, but misty on top of the range. As they rode up through the foothills the snow got deep and the going was slow. Jake muttered that this was a damn-fool business. It was noon when they reached the face of the peak towering over Frying Pan Basin.

There, at timberline, the trees were stunted and twisted from the storms. Jake unpacked, and they set up a small tent in the shelter of two dwarfed pines. They put the Dutch oven and supplies inside the tent, throwing some of the bedding over the potatoes, canned beans, bacon, and coffee. Above them a heavy, swirling mist covered the peak, and the roaring of the wind grew louder as they finished snubbing down the tent.

Kelsey looked at the sky. It was murky. "Better be drifting down, Jake. It's going to snow. Get those horses out of here before it starts."

They watched Jake ride away. Dalt ran a hand over the skis. "We'll take a look after we eat," he said.

Wind whipped across the mountain and threw snow in their faces, blinding and staggering them. "Not today," Kelsey said, wiping his eyes with his mittened hand. "Might as well get inside. It's a damned blizzard starting."

They built a little fire in the mouth of the tent, gathered dead branches from the trees around them, and stacked extra wood inside. The wind was still rising.

"It's plumb foolish what a man will go through for a cow," Dalt said, fumbling for the can opener.

They ate a hastily heated can of beans and cold bread, and drank plenty of coffee. The rest of the afternoon they sat around in the tent, waiting for the wind to drop. When darkness set in, the snow was thick, going past the door of the tent in a steady, blowing stream. Soon it was too cold to keep warm from the tiny fire, which was constantly tossed by the wind. They crawled into the bedding, huddled close together, and talked as the night began. But they were not warm, for the cold crept up through the blankets and cold hung in the tent. The canvas walls shuddered and strained under the onslaught of wind.

For two days they lay in the tent and got up only to start the fire and fix food. It was impossible, even in the middle of the day, to see beyond the shaking ropes that held the tent, and when they had to relieve themselves they stepped just outside and clung to the ropes, daring to go no farther. By the afternoon of the second day they had eaten all the food and had to boil the frozen potato peelings in snow water, making a thin soup. They had boiled and reboiled the coffee grounds until the liquid they drank was the color of rain water.

"My God," Dalt said, "are we going to sit up here and starve to death?" He rubbed at the reddish-gold whiskers on his face and added, "No cow's worth it."

"It'll clear," Kelsey said hopefully.

"Well," Dalt said, drawing the blankets close and shivering, "maybe the side of a mountain's as good a place as any for a man to kick off." His eyes blinked in the dim light of the tent, for they kept the flaps shut tight when they weren't trying to cook. "Wonder if my old man ever figured I'd come to an end like this when he tried to get rid of me."

"Tried to get rid of you?"

Dalt rolled over on his belly. "I never told you, did I? When my mother died he married this woman, and they tried to ship me off to a fancy school, but I wouldn't go. He built buggies, my father, back in Philadelphia. He made plenty of money, but I got to runnin' loose and taking up with company he didn't like. The way it started, we fought all the time after he married this woman. She had her mind set on being rid of me, I guess. My brothers, now—I had two, and

I guess they're still alive—they got on with her fine, for she could push 'em around. They had good educations, too. Maybe I'd have been smart to go to school the way they planned it for me, Kelsey, but I couldn't think of nothin' except that my mother was gone and my father didn't want me around. Anyway, one day the old man tried to give me some money and send me out West; if they couldn't send me to a school, then they'd get rid of me this other way. It made me so mad I stuck some clothes in a sack and took off—left his damn money on the table. Walked all night and caught a ride with a man on his way to Kansas City. Well, then I just kept on movin' west, workin' wherever I could get it when I was broke. I hit Laramie on a freight and didn't have a dime left. Went over to a cathouse near the tracks and ran into Flit Maguire. He was there to meet a carload of Missouri bulls—figured on sellin' some and keepin' some for himself."

Dalt sat up and fished in his pockets for tobacco and cigarette papers. "Tastes like hell on an empty stomach, but a man's got to do something to pass time. Anyhow, as I was saying, Flit gave me a job driving those bulls into the Park. Another fella was helping me, and Flit came along behind us with the wagon. We walked. It was early spring, and God, but it was cold on the Laramie Plains! I kept wishin' the bulls would hurry, but you know how slow they move. It rained and sleeted and snowed, and the wind blew, and there wasn't a blade of green grass anywhere. Two of the bulls died when we reached the mountains. Flit sure bitched about losing those two bulls—acted like we were to blame for it. I was a kid and broke and hungry, or I wouldn't have taken some of the stuff he handed me. I swore when I got to the Park I'd quit him."

Dalt shoved under the blankets, smoking, keeping himself propped on one elbow. "And I would have, but Monte was so kind to me. She took me in the house one day and talked to me the way I needed talkin' to—gave me hell for getting in one of Black Susie's tents by the river. It sure did embarrass me, having her talk to me that way, but it didn't bother her. She told me about dealing faro in the house in Denver, and Flit finding her there. She came from Kentucky. Her father died, and another man moved in. She took off on her own, just the same as I did. She started west and learned about gambling on a Mississippi river boat."

Kelsey stared at the shaking walls of the tent. There was so much he wanted to ask, but he kept silent. After a while Dalt went on. "Monte told me all about the house in Denver. She wasn't any chippy there, just a dealer—and I believe her. When old Flit dropped in one night with plenty of money he took a fancy to her, and she married him. It was a fast way to come up in the world. At first he treated her fine—bought her lots of clothes and built the big house on the North Fork. Then, when the women wouldn't take to her, I think he got to worrying about what she might have been before he married her. Flit was the kind would do that. He got to leaving her home then, instead of showing her off in a fancy buggy. Oh, I think he loved her in his way."

Dalt sat up, rubbed out the cigarette butt on the floor of the tent. And you can see what it was like, living in that empty, fancy house and wearing the fine clothes, and nobody around to talk to. Then she had the twin kids and lost 'em. Amie was the only woman friend she had. You see how it must have been, don't you?"

"Yes, I know what it was like."

"Well, you can't blame her because she started playing around with Flit's hired men and getting them to take her places—dancing, riding. Then Flit turned on her and accused her of bein' a whore all the time. He stopped giving her money or clothes. She got money the easiest way she could and the quickest, and if Flit kept firing the men she used, he had to hire others, and she could use them the same way. She painted her face and was seen all over the country all hours of the day and night with men. She never was anyone to sneak around about things, and she didn't then, either. It was about that time that Flit got himself struck with lightning—happened up there along the big ditch under the hogback. By then Monte not only had some money cached away, she also knew about all there is to know about cattle and ranching. When she got a man's money she got something else along with it—what was in his head about the cow business."

Dalt rolled over, resting on both elbows, looking at Kelsey. "I never slept with her, if that's what's on your mind. She treated me like a son—and later like a brother. I sometimes think she sent me over to work for Tommy in case she might get a notion about me like she did the others. I figured she never wanted me handy on a lonesome winter night. And I never tried to be, for there was something else between us—a sort of respect. Far as Tommy's concerned, she never liked him, but she used him to get his homestead land for pasture and gave him a job for the rest of his life. She's hard in some ways, yes—but she calls a spade a spade. Tommy knew what the deal was before he got into it, so he's got no kick comin'. And she didn't ever love Flit Maguire or any of the hired men. She didn't love anybody until you came along, Kelsey."

Kelsey turned his head away. He listened to the roar of the wind, trying to forget the aching inside him. He was glad Dalt had told him the truth about Monte, but he didn't want to talk about it, not now or ever.

"I'll never forget what Monte said about the cattle business once," Dalt said. "We were riding on the flats that day, and she says to me, 'Dalt, it's like playing God, working with cattle—breeding them, watchin' the blood lines show. It's an art, and it makes up for a lot I've missed in life.' And y'know, Kelsey, after Flit died and she got interested in cattle she didn't seem to care any more about men. Maybe I've talked too long and too much, but Monte would want you to know all about her, being the kind of person she is—but I don't think she could tell you herself. It's hard to tell the truth about yourself, showin' all the bad as well as the good. It's hard because you're afraid of losing a person's feeling for you."

The silence drew out between them. Wind shook the canvas walls and whined through the stunted trees. But the mountain was old and hard and strong under them, and it gave Kelsey a sense of being cut off from the rest of the world, and all of Dalt's words seemed like a dream.

Sometime during the night the wind dropped, and the stillness caused them to waken. "Looks like we hunt cattle come mornin'," Dalt said. "I guess I'll get up and make a fire and heat that water we been drinkin'."

They sat with the blankets over their shoulders, shivering and drinking the pale liquid until daylight. The potato-peeling soup turned their stomachs now, and they didn't bother to put more snow over the mass of pulp and boil it.

They set off down the face of the peak into the canyon, skimming over the fresh snow on the skis. The world was clean and cold, and a fog lay over the top of the mountain. When the sun came through the fog banks in the east, thrusting pinkish-red in the frosty air, they could see the whole of the Frying Pan Basin below them. They sighted the lost cattle at noon, in a little park between pines and willows, the snow tramped around them and the bark chewed off the willows. The cows and calves were gaunt; the last snow was dusted in the hollows of their flanks.

"What are the crazy buggers doing piled up here in a bunch?" Kelsey said. "All they had to do was cross that little creek down there below the bank and head toward the low country."

"If water don't look right it spooks 'em," Dalt said. "We better take a peek over the edge and see what it's like."

They skirted the thin cattle that held their heads high and regarded them with mingled fear and curiosity. One or two calves gave a doleful bawl. When they came to the slope above the creek Dalt said, "They could see that trickle of dark water way down there below the snowdrifts where it hasn't frozen over, and they got scared. Couldn't tell how deep it might be or what was under it. Hell, it can't be more than four inches to bottom."

Kelsey started breaking a trail down the bank and across the narrow creek, up the opposite bank and a short distance into the timber. As soon as the trail was broken the cattle moved close to look and sniff the ground. After a while one old cow started down the bank. The others followed, and soon all of them had crossed the trickle of water that had held them prisoner and were streaming through the timber, headed for the meadows.

"Well," Dalt said, "now we gotta go up that mountain again and break camp."

It was a long, steep climb out of the canyon to the mountain's shoulder. They soon had to take off the skis, for the snow grew soft and sticky under the sun. They sank to their waists in snow, taking turns breaking the trail. Evening was settling on the peaks when they reached camp. They boiled the coffee grounds again and crawled into the blankets, too tired to talk.

In a little while they were moaning with cramps. Sweat broke out on Kelsey's cold forehead, and he rubbed frantically at the calves of his legs where the muscles had knotted in rocklike lumps. They slept fitfully, waking from time to time to massage their legs. When the light broke they took down the tent, rolled the bedding, and started down the mountain on skis. As soon as they reached a place where a horse might travel they left their burdens and went on, moving more lightly now, but so weak from lack of food that they had to stop often to rest.

It was afternoon when they came out of the timber at the edge of the meadow and saw Jake riding to meet them with horses. They took off the skis and set them against a tree and waited.

Kelsey was sick from hunger. His eyes burned like fire from the glare of sun on the snow, and his face itched from the whiskers. When Jake got there he pulled himself stiffly into the saddle, scowled at the boss puncher, and said, "We found 'em. For Christ's sake, do you hunt for cattle with your eyes closed?"

Jake blinked.

"They'll be at the edge of the timber tonight," Kelsey said, "and you see there's hay up there for 'em in the morning."

"I ain't paid to dig hay," Jake said, his voice mild but his eyes stubborn.

"Hilder will give you a hand. Get a jag on the rack this afternoon."

Jake looked at Kelsey. "You better get movin' down country. The missus is in trouble."

"Prim? What's wrong?"

"She had a loss. Doc just come when I left. I did the best I could, and Hilder helped me. Then he went for Doc. She was still bleedin' bad when I left."

Kelsey kicked the horse into a lope. Cold was settling in the valley, and the trail was turning slick. The horse kept sliding and stumbling, but Kelsey urged it on. By the time he reached the ranch dusk was on the meadows. The lamps had been lighted in the house. He dismounted by the kitchen door, tossed the reins to Dalt, and hurried inside. Hilder was cooking supper. Kelsey went past him and on to the bedroom.

Doc Bingham sat in a chair by the bed. When Kelsey walked in he nodded and went out, closing the door behind him. Kelsey pulled off his mittens, stepped to the side of the bed, and took hold of Prim's hand that lay so still on top of the blanket. "Prim, lass—"

She didn't turn her head to look at him. She lay staring at the ceiling. He had never seen her so white, and it frightened him. He leaned over her until he could see into her face, and her dull eyes stared into his.

"I did it," she said, her voice low. "I did it myself, when I was alone here."

He felt sick. "God, Prim!"

"Yes, I did it. I might as well tell you or the doctor will. I didn't want it."

"Why, Prim?" His voice was hoarse. "In God's name, why?"

"I'm tired—tired of the work that's never finished, tired of the cold and the men and the cooking. And I wanted no more strings to hold you to me. And I wouldn't have bothered a soul—but the pain—" She wet her dry, cracking lips. "When it hurt so, I cried out, and Hilder was in the kitchen and heard me. Then Jake came, and they tried to stop it. It was terrible, and I screamed at them to go away and leave me be. They tore up towels and stuffed them in me, and then Hilder went for the doctor. Everything's ruined, the mattress soaked—and the smell of it— But I'm not sorry! I'm not!" Her voice rose.

"Why do you sleep with me if you don't want my kid?" he shouted, anger blinding him.

She was crying then, and the anger left him as quickly as it had come. He knelt by the bed and put his arm over her, his face against the rough Scotch blanket that was the color of old cream. "Prim—to destroy life, to end it! Oh, Prim, how could you?"

At last he got up and went into the living room, where

Doc Bingham sat smoking. The sharp little black eyes looked at him and then away. "Too bad." The pink mouth shut firmly.

"Where's little Jediah?"

"Hilder fed him and put him in the bedroom next to the kitchen."

Kelsey found his son asleep in the small wooden bed Jediah had made for him. He held the lamp low so he could look into the thin, pale face of the little boy, and such a sadness was in him that his heart felt like breaking. He went out, closing the door softly after him. And had she felt the same way about the lad, wanting to destroy him before he lived?

In the kitchen Dalt was drinking milk while he waited for supper. "Better get something in that empty stomach," he said.

Kelsey walked on out into the night. He went to the barn, climbed the loft ladder, and found the whisky hidden in the hay. He sat there in the darkness, drinking, asking himself if it was his fault.

God forgive me, if it is.

"Buddy—" Dalt came across the loft and sat beside him, putting his hand on Kelsey's shoulder. "Come in now and eat. What's done can't be changed, and there's no use broodin' on it."

"Is the blame on me, Dalt? Is it?"

"This is Prim's trouble. She brought it on herself. Don't lay it on your own shoulders."

"But I'm mixed in it. Dalt, I've tried to do what's right." He shut his fist and pounded against the splintery floor of the loft. "I've tried so hard!"

"You've done all right, buddy. You've done nothin' a man could be ashamed of."

"All of loving's a curse, for in it's the misery of the world."

"No, in it's the best of the world, and nobody believes it

or knows it more than you. Get up, now. We'll kill that bottle."

They stood and drank what was left of the whisky. When
they got to the house Hilder had set out supper and Doc
Bingham was already at the table. Kelsey washed his face
and combed his hair, but before he sat down to eat he went
back to the bedroom.

Prim's head turned, and she looked at him. The same stillness was on her face. Then her eyes glinted with sudden life.
"Had your whisky," she said. "Can't face anything without
it, can you?"

For a moment he hated her with a terrible, shocking hatred. And then he felt only pity. "Try to get some sleep,
Prim," he said.

He returned to the kitchen and ate mechanically, lost in
the melancholy turning of his own thoughts. When he had finished he went into the middle bedroom and, without taking
off his clothes, fell across the bed and slept.

CHAPTER XXI

~ ~ ~ ~ ~ ~ ~

Heather was sixteen. She was home from school this mild spring afternoon, and she didn't especially want to walk with her mother. She would rather have spent her Saturday riding with Dalt.

They were on the dirt road at the edge of the meadow. Prim walked fast in the firm, determined way she did everything. Heather, a full head taller than Prim, came after her with a long-legged stride like that of a boy.

"I told your father," Prim said, "he could just stay in the house with little Jed a while. I said I had to get out of that place. I always liked to walk. In the old country I walked miles every evening."

Heather's mind kept slipping away from Prim's flow of talk, thinking about school and the teacher reading *A Tale of Two Cities*. She could start to cry if she let herself dwell on the ending. How noble and beautiful it was! She pictured herself going to have her head cut off, and Dalt riding in the cart with her, holding her hand. It was very satisfying to think of their dying together.

And then she remembered what Jim Plunkett had said one night when she'd tried to tell him what a wonderful story this was. Jim had been working hard and was sleepy; since he'd finished school he'd stayed on at the ranch, helping his father.

"I got more important things on my mind," he said, yawn-

ing. "All that mush about a man so in love he lets 'em cut
off his head!"

Her mind swung away from Jim and back to her mother,
who was saying, "I hope your father's not taking a nip from
the bottle while we're gone, and forgetting all about little Jed.
When he's not working he loves to sit and drink and dream
about his cattle."

"Now, Mother——"

"And what would your father be without me keeping him
in line? Thank God I'm strong!"

"Amie Plunkett says you make him sick. Amie says the
strong people often make others sick. And people we love,
she says, can make us sickest of all."

"Well, I'm glad Amie Plunkett's so smart you can take all
her words for gospel truth. It's not blaming me but praising
me Amie Plunkett should be—for making your father into
something besides another one of the riffraff of this country."

"I don't see anything wrong with him, and he'd be all
right without you nagging him."

"Don't sauce me, missy! Just because you're past sixteen
you think you know everything. Damned ungrateful, that's
what you are—just like your father." Prim walked on, muttering to herself.

Heather hurried to keep pace with her, saying nothing,
smelling the melting snow that lay in white banks on the lee
sides of the ridges; it was a fresh, wet smell that stirred her
blood.

"And another thing," Prim said. "See you're not spending
too much time with Jim Plunkett. He's there under your nose,
and Amie wouldn't turn herself to see what the two of you
were up to. Jim Plunkett's nothing, like his father. Lift yourself up in the world, that's always been my motto."

"Jim's just a friend."

Prim gave her a narrowed glance. "I fear no boy or man

will ever be just a friend to you. I can see through you like I can see the bottom of the creek when the water's clear. You've got all my strength—more than your father—but you've got my weakness too, and it's a weakness of the flesh, a damned curse, so it is. And remember this: no man ever loves a woman or respects her when he's had his pleasure of her without the marriage vows."

"Oh, for goodness' sake, Mother! You talk like—"

"I say what I know, and it was hard come by. Mind you my words, Heather Cameron!"

Heather did not believe any of it. If you loved a man and he loved you everything would always be right—no matter what happened. Of this she was sure. But who would argue with Prim?

"Heather—" There were tears in Prim's eyes. "When I say all this to you it's only—only that you mean so much to me; that I love you, and went through so much to have you—"

Love and pain mingled in Heather's heart. She put her hand on her mother's hair, so fine and dark, and no gray showing in it. "Mother—"

"Yes," Prim said softly, "I know you love me. No matter what I am or do, it's there. And I am the same to you. Oh, Heather-lass, whatever else is in us, bad as it may be, there's more love than anything."

Heather looked away, the ache tight in her throat, the mist in her eyes. How is it I love this woman with a terrible love and at other times hate her as much? Yes, it's true, at times I hate her. And I know it's the same with my father. And yet— She reached for Prim's hand and held it tight. "Will we walk home now?"

All the way back to the house Prim talked of the old country, of the goodness of her brothers and the courage and honesty of Big Mina Munro. And is all this talk to prove something to herself? Heather thought.

When they got home little Jed was running around the kitchen. He was still too small and too pale, but he smiled his strange, sweet smile and ran to Heather when she held out her arms.

Kelsey was sitting in the chair by the kitchen stove. "He got in the jam," Kelsey said to Prim.

"Then why didn't you clean him up?" Prim took the boy from Heather, murmuring, "Come on, wee thing. Let me see to you. What would happen to you if I wasn't here?"

"Did you run your trap line today, honey?" Kelsey asked Heather.

"Didn't have time this morning. I'll do it now." And she hurried to the porch, pulled on the knee-length rubber boots, and took the .22 rifle from the wall. Wearing an old jacket of Kelsey's, she went off through the willows. She had set traps for muskrat and mink along the small creeks that poured into the river. She pulled the traps every Sunday evening before she rode down to Plunketts' for school.

In the willows the air smelled of wet bark and damp earth. The small creeks were clear and fast, pouring like pale amber over the rocky beds. She had baited some of the traps with carrots, and others with the rank-smelling beaver-castor mixture that Jediah used. The smell of this was on the old jacket that Prim wouldn't let her wear in the kitchen. Two traps had been sprung but were empty, and she knelt to set them and placed them on the shallow ledges so the animals would tumble into the deeper water and drown, and not twist off their feet. Jediah had taught her this, saying, "It's kinder, so that makes it right."

She came around a bend of a narrow creek and stopped. On the bank she saw another sprung trap, and beside it a mink, slim and dark and long, one front foot held up. At once she knew it had been caught by the toe and had worked its foot loose, but the foot still hurt from the steel bite of the trap. The mink made no effort to move. It simply stood motionless on the curve of the river bank, the foot held up, the little eyes dark and bright, its fur blue-black in the sunlight.

A mink, she thought, her heart beating hard—a wild mink. The first I've ever caught—or almost caught. She pictured taking it home, and how Kelsey would praise her, and how she would tell Jediah about it. She raised the rifle, cocked it, and sighted down the barrel. The mink looked back at her, beautiful and strangely still. Slowly she brought the barrel down, staring at the animal there before her, so close it seemed she could almost hear the quick fluttering of its heart.

The long moment drew out between them, caught in the silence of the bright, quiet day. And then the mink moved, turning and sliding over the bank in one liquid, dark motion, flowing into the water and parting it with no sound at all; the amber-colored shine separated to receive the animal. It moved across the creek and around the dripping bank and out of sight. The naked willows trembled in a small breath of wind, in a brief orange-red and golden motion, and were still. Heather's hands shook, and the water murmur rose loud in the silence.

She turned and saw Long Dalton sitting on a horse, looking at her. "Couldn't—" Her breath caught. "Just couldn't shoot him." Her mouth trembled, and she jerked the shell from the gun, letting it fall in the grass.

Dalt dismounted and came to her, walking slowly by the creek. He put his hand under her chin and lifted her face, looking closely into it. "Guess you had to change sometime. Couldn't expect you to be like a boy always." And a shadow moved on his face and was gone. His hand slid down her arm in a gentle caressing motion and fell away.

"I'm pulling the traps—all of them. Had enough of it." She looked past him, staring at the willows, trying to see in them some answer to the strangeness in herself.

"If you want." And he turned, got on the horse, and rode away.

She shivered, and the sound of the little creek seemed to sing: *Neverrr—foreverrr*. Then she moved quickly, to pull the trap, to hook it impatiently to her belt, and go on, walking fast, thrusting the willow branches aside.

CHAPTER XXII

Kelsey sat at the kitchen table, figuring on a slip of paper, a whisky glass beside him. "I've got five hundred cows now," he said and stuck the pencil behind his ear. "That's real good." He stood up, smiling to himself.

Beside the stove, Prim held little Jed in her lap; he was playing with two clothespins. "It's high time we were getting on in the world," she commented.

Heather had washed her hair and was drying it in the heat from the open oven. It was a dripping day in early August. Out in the bunkhouse the haying crew played poker and read magazines. In the yard, in the rain, Hilder was doing his washing in a five-gallon can set over a small fire. Steam rose around him as he stirred with a long stick, fishing a suit of underwear from the gray water. He carried the streaming garment to the creek and dropped it in, then bent to grab it, wring it out, and carry it back to the fence to hang it up.

"That'll be the only real clean underwear he's worn in years," Kelsey said, looking out the window. "The rain will bleach it good and white. Heather-girl, mists are on the mountains. What say we go fishin' up the creek?"

"In all this wet?" Prim asked. "She ought to stay and help me. I need her. I'm turning into an old woman before my time—old from working my guts out after a bunch of men."

"Then be sure and remind us of it," Kelsey said, an edge in his tone.

"Oh!" Heather cried impatiently, running her hands

258

through her hair. "Stop it, the two of you! Every day you fight about something!"

"And who's to blame?" Prim demanded. "What does he do in wet weather while I work? Sits on his arse, countin' cows—and drinks. He's getting as much thirst for it as his fine boss, the wonderful Monte Maguire. She was drunk at the last dance at the schoolhouse!"

"She wasn't!" Kelsey said.

"Oh, have you another name for it? And don't I know whisky when I smell it? All her fancy perfume wouldn't cover that smell. And waltzing with old Tom Barnes and her cheek glued to his—disgusting, that's what it was. Everybody was talking about it. Monte Maguire's becoming a drunkard!"

"Hold your tongue. Leave Monte out of this."

"Oh, and is she so fine I'm too low to speak her name?"

"Stop it, I tell you!"

She pushed the little boy from her lap and stood up, both hands on her full hips. "Don't tell me to stop! Go and see your drunken sweetheart! She's fading—fading like a piece of poor material that can't stand weather and wear!"

"That damn tongue of yours!" He moved toward her; his arm came up, fist doubled.

"Don't lay a hand on me, Kelsey Cameron!"

Heather covered her ears. "Please! Oh, please stop!" And she began to cry.

Kelsey's hands dropped limply to his sides. "And is this what we've come to?" he asked unsteadily. "Me, my hand ready to strike a woman, and you sounding like Big Mina— yes, just like Big Mina!"

"She's my mother, and you'll not speak against her."

"Big Mina," he said wonderingly, and he stared at Prim, his face wearing an expression of shock and distaste.

She drew back, saying almost in a whisper, "You knew what I was, the kind of people I came from. You knew, and once I was good enough—before you met *her!*"

There was a sharp knock at the door. The three of them rearranged their faces. "Come on in." Kelsey strained to make his voice normal.

Vic Lundgren stood in the doorway, twisting his hat in his hands. His mouth worked, but no words came out.

"Vic!" It was Prim who spoke. "Oh, man, what is it?"

"Ellie—she's gone."

"Gone! Where?" Kelsey got up and put his hand on Vic's shoulder, urging him into the kitchen.

"She run off in the night—come this way, to the mountains." Vic looked stupidly around the room. "Never wanted to hurt Ellie—not me, Vic. And Mavis, she cries and says her mother never come back. My God, Kelsey, did I do it? The horse—at daylight I find him up back of your west meadow. But she is not near the horse. She is nowhere. I look and look. Don't know—what to do—" His big hand moved up to rub his eyes.

"Sit down, Vic. You're tired. We'll find her. We'll get all the men out. We'll send word to the other ranchers. It won't take long to find her."

"But how is she—when I find her?" Vic's voice shook.

Prim was shaking down the stove. "Heather, set out a plate for Vic. He needs something to eat."

*　　　*

The men gathered at the North Fork Ranch. They came from the far corners of the Park. They tightened the cinches on their saddles and stared at the mountains. They looked past Vic Lundgren with bleakness in their eyes and made plans to cover every hill and canyon.

On the third morning of the search, as the men got ready to ride again, Prim watched them with emptiness in her heart. They'll never find her, she thought. It's this bleak hard country—it's killed her. She looked at Heather, dressed and ready to go, the man's overalls tight on her slim hips, her hair pushed under an old hat. Get out of this country, Heather. Don't ever marry a rancher. It's no life at all; it's monotonous—eat, sleep, cook, work. Look at the young women who come here; in two years they're changed, the life gone out of them, the hard mark of the country already on their faces and bodies. And what is there to take the misery from it all? Only the dances at the schoolhouses—and the men drinking in the corners and talking cattle, while the women listen to the music and tap their feet and wait. Go get an education; never, never stay here to marry a man who'll spend the best of himself on whisky and cattle and the cards. . . .

The clouds cleared away. The sun came out and dried the cut hay in the meadows, but the machinery sat idle. The horses ran in the pastures with no mark of harness on them while the men combed the mountains for Ellie Lundgren.

*   *

Heather rode above timberline where the land was bare and clean and the wind went whispering over it. Long Dalton rode beside her, for they had met at noon near one of the high lakes. Now evening hung in the air where the trail wound over the mountaintop. The sky was pink and looked warm, but the sharpness of autumn lay in the air, and already the leaves of the wild raspberries were turning. There were no trees this high. The horses' hoofs struck bell-tones from the rocks. Blue grouse rose out of the juniper bushes with a soft whirring of wings. It was a lost and lonely country.

They stopped on the summit of the peak. More peaks ran on west, tenting the horizon. Directly below them was a small lake, catching the pink of the sky. Back toward the Park there were more small lakes, and the foothills tumbled away like dark stairs to the meadows.

"No tracks here, Heather," Dalt said. "Better get off and stretch. It's a long way down."

They stood side by side on the top of the world. The horses were quiet beside them, the bridle reins trailing. A sadness was in Heather as she thought of Ellie Lundgren. It was a spooky sadness that made her jump when one of the horses moved and a small stone bumped against another with a flat *click-clack*. Her shoulder touched Dalt. His hand reached to steady her. She turned, her hat pushed back, her hair blowing against her cheek. "What?"

"Nothing, chicken. I didn't say a word." His hand still lay on her arm, and the feeling she had about Ellie churned inside her.

Dalt said, "We're outta the world, chicken. Outta the whole damned crazy world."

Then suddenly it was as though she couldn't breathe at all, and her heart was beating so hard she could feel it in her throat. And Dalt— Her hands came up to press against his broad chest, the fingers wide, plucking at the heavy wool shirt. And all manner of strangeness blew through her like a faraway music following the wind.

"Dalt— What is it, Dalt?"

"Nothing to be scared of, girl." And his arms brought her around hard, fitting her to him.

There was something else in her now, a being afraid and excited at the same time—a helplessness and a warning and a queer aching. Not the way it had been with Jim Plunkett when he kissed her back of the barn, kissed her so hard it smashed her lips. Oh, no, not like that at all. "Dalt—please, Dalt—"

"Please, what?"

"I don't know. I'm all—mixed up." She was changing and couldn't stop herself, changing into a wild thing that was only breast and mouth and thighs. . . .

"Don't be scared," he said gently. "It had to happen sometime." And he kissed her softly, and then he kissed her again in the hard, sure way a man knows and a boy has to learn over the years. A cruelty and a tenderness were in him, for it was like holding a wild horse on a rope, a horse that was proud and beautiful and full of fear. He knew how to break a horse down with coaxing and cunning and a soft hand; it was a knowledge that had been in him always. And it flowed from him when he touched women, and there was never any haste in him, for he knew that when he was ready they would be his for the taking—a sudden, pushing eagerness in them.

Over her head he looked up at the wide blue as her body began to lose its stiffness and flow naturally and warmly against him. Above timberline, he thought, next to the sky. Did a man live here as he did on the ground below? And who would teach her the things she should know as a woman? Some soft-lipped kid with fumbling hands to make her feel uncertain and ashamed?

Jediah, what would you do now, Jediah?

Her head moved against his chest, and he could see the Park far below, with the colors of the sky hanging over it in a sort of wild glory. Distance hid the ugliness that was on the earth, showing only the softened outlines and letting a man fill the spaces to his own liking. What a man saw from here depended on how he looked at things; he could build the whole damn world to his own pattern.

"Nobody can tell a man what's right for all the time, son," Jediah had said. "Times and places and circumstances change everything—even truth. And it ain't what's preached to a man or beat into him that decides for him in a tight spot. It's a thing he listens to in himself."

He could see Jediah then, as he said those words, sitting by the bunkhouse fire on a rainy spring night, the heat of the stove making his old face shine, and his eyes narrowed away to the distance of his thinking.

"Dalt—"

"Yes, chicken."

"Kiss me again, Dalt."

A woman who knew more would have been less outspoken. A woman who knew more would act like she didn't feel anything and pull away from him, and maybe laugh a little and fuss with her clothes and hair. But this child-woman in his arms didn't know the tricks and foolishness that was part of it all, before a man went ahead and took care of what had always been the only important thing.

Her mouth was damp and cool and sweet against his. "I love you, Dalt."

"Well, now, that's fine—only it won't last. It's natural, maybe, but you've got to know it can't last, and be ready to wake up some morning and find it's not there. You see?"

"I don't see at all."

"No, I guess you can't. Y'know what I could do, chicken? I could show you some things—things that won't hurt you." He held her closer, rubbing his cheek against hers, adding, "You want me to love you a little, chicken? Or do you want to forget it?"

"I want you to love me, Dalt."

"All right, then." He stepped away from her, unsaddled the horses and led them down the mountainside to a juniper bush, where he tied them. Then, carrying the saddle blankets under his arm, he came back to her, and they walked along the bare rim of the peak until he came to where a small spring trickled from the mountain's rocky shoulder. Below it there was a patch of grass and moss. He spread the blankets on the ground. He looked at her and smiled. "Come here, chicken."

She came to him, and he held her again in his arms. Her face was pale in the dusk. He tried to see into it and couldn't. The wind moved, cold and yet gentle against his cheek. No harm in this, Jediah—no harm holding her in my arms. I can love her a little—just a little—and let her go. I can let her go because I love her, and because I'm a man and not a boy.

"Listen," he said, his hand moving over the shape of her back, "I don't want this to upset you in any way. I don't want you to cry or feel embarrassed. When you feel as you do about me, and I am like I am toward you, there's never anything to be ashamed of. Just be sure you feel right with any man you might love."

He drew her down on the blanket and held her close to him. The wind died. An enormous silence filled the world. The sky flowed over them, wide and dark, and then a star flickered, pale and uncertain in the big blackness.

"Be easy with me, chicken. Let yourself rest against me. There's the place where the bee stung you, remember?"

"Dalt—"

"Yes?"

"I'm afraid now."

"Don't be. There. That's better, isn't it?"

"Dalt, maybe I'm not sure—maybe I don't—"

He brought his mouth down on hers. He felt her stiffen in a sudden beautiful terror. He touched her with deliberate gentleness, as though it might be for the last time. And always he held tightly to a part of himself, keeping his mind hard and cold and in control of his body. In an agony, he drew her out of herself until she was all crumpled softness and yielding woman, and he could have done with her what he liked—struck or kissed her—and she would have gone on offering herself to him.

Then he knew it must be ended. He took her arms from around his neck, pushed them back, and pulled free of her. He stood up under the stars and let the wind blow over him. He thought he heard her crying. Quickly he knelt beside her, touched her face, and felt the wetness of it. "Chicken, chicken, I didn't hurt you."

"I—just can't help it, Dalt."

"Cryin' because you're sorry I loved you a little?"

"No—because I hurt in my heart, because—"

"Yes?"

"Because nothing that happens to me will ever be like this again."

He stared at the sky and felt that they rested on some outbound world, on the rim of space. "No," he said, "and not for me, either. This I won't forget."

"It makes me sad. Oh, Dalt, I don't know—"

He reached for her and held her to him, pushing her tangled hair back from her wet face, saying fiercely, "Don't ever settle for anyone who loves you less, you hear? Don't go to bed with any man unless he feels about you as I do. That way—no matter who he is or whether you're young or old, married or single, blessed by the preacher or damned by society—it won't make any difference."

"Dalt, I don't want anybody to touch me—never again— after you."

"Someday you will, and he'll know a lot of you I can't— your mind and what goes on in it, your dreamin' and thinkin' —and I hate his guts, whoever he is."

"Dalt, don't talk that way!"

"Facts, chicken. They might as well be faced. Now stop crying. And don't ever let me love you again. I might not be able to stop—and then there would be hell to pay in more ways than one. We're goin' down the mountain now, down to where the world's not like here. But someday, when you meet a man you want to marry, remember what it was like here, where everything's clean and real and above all the sneakin', bitchin' ways of the world. Let the easy loving go, chicken, for it's not worth havin'."

He got up and walked to where the horses were tied, and waited until she came along the skyline with the blankets in her arms. He saddled up and handed her the bridle reins

and stood by the horse's head while she swung to the saddle.
He let her go on down the trail, waiting for a while in that
high place that was now like no other place he had ever been.
He thought of Jediah. "You crazy old son-of-a-bitch," he
said softly.

When he rode down the mountain everything changed,
and it was only the same high country he had always known,
the trees dark-massed and the night clogged with pine smell.
An owl hooted. And the wind stirred, rising up from the
floor of the Park like something that had slept and wakened
unsatisfied from its sleeping. It moved the branches of the
pines, rubbing them together with a sound that was like
hurting.

At the ranch he unsaddled his horse. He came out of the
barn and lighted a cigarette and stood smoking, looking up
toward the high peak so sharp against the sky. Then he
heard the *scratch-scratch* of new overalls and saw a man
coming across the corral, and knew by the shape of him that
it was Kelsey Cameron.

"Find any sign of Ellie, Dalt?"

"Nothing." He drew hard on the cigarette.

"Well, they've called it off. No more searching. The hay
has to go up."

"Work goes on. Tough on Vic."

"Dalt—"

"Yes?"

"Something I've meant—something I want to speak to you
about."

"Shoot, then."

"Heather's not a lassie any longer, Dalt. When she was
young, a kid, I appreciated the way you— I never worried
about her. But now—"

The silence drew out between them. Beyond the barn
Dalt could see the curve of the river, a silver loop in the

starlight, and the dark fringe of the willows hanging over it. The water murmured on, seeming to say that what bothered men was of no importance.

Kelsey cleared his throat. "Dalt, if I thought you as much as laid a hand on her, I'd—"

"You'd what, buddy?"

"I'd kill you, Dalt."

Long Dalton's lips drew back in a thin, cruel smile. "If I set my mind on a thing, nothing would stop me. And I wouldn't kill easy, Kelsey."

"But I'd try. Remember that, Dalt." Kelsey turned and walked away. Long Dalton ground out the cigarette under the heel of his boot. He walked slowly toward the bunkhouse, and there was bitterness in him. *You might have given me the benefit of the doubt, buddy.*

He hunched his shoulders against the chill of the wind. Winter was here, speaking to a man, even in August. Did he want to stay on in this place when the friendship that had been between him and Kelsey was changed? It was spoiled now, spoiled by a few words, and nothing would bring it back, fresh and good and lasting. And Heather—how long would it be until the man in him rose with the old demanding hunger and he would have to touch her, hold her in his arms? And if he did— What was the answer then? Drift like the wind? Over the mountains and a new job?

Time enough to decide tomorrow—or the next day. Time enough to make up his mind before the snow got deep and the ice froze on the river and spring was only a dream a man held to himself in the long darkness.

CHAPTER XXIII

Jediah Walsh awakened and lay listening. It came to him after a while that he was listening because it was so quiet— no whisper of wind around the cabin, no scrape of pine branch against the west window that was covered by a snow-drift. Winter had come early to the Park this year, he thought. And here it was only November, and a man couldn't tell whether it was daybreak or past, for snow lay so deep around the cabin.

The cabin was small and with few furnishings: a bunk bed, a table made from a tree stump, a small black stove, and a wooden box tacked on the wall for a cupboard. The box was large enough to hold coffee, lard, a few dishes and cooking utensils. Traps and guns and snowshoes hung on the walls. Above his head a plank swung from the middle of the cabin, suspended from two strands of wire that were fas-tened to the ridge log. On this board, anchored out in space,. he kept his food so the pack rats couldn't get it.

He got out of bed, dressed, and built a fire. While the stove was heating he stepped to the door and pushed it open. The world was dim and gray, for light was just breaking in the east. He could see the fringe of willows sticking up from the snowdrifts south of the cabin, making a purple-dark stubble.

Again he was aware of the hushed silence of the morning. He shrugged—might be on account of no wind blowing and the way the clouds hung low and gray and thick from east to west. It was cold, but not as cold as it usually was on an early morning in November.

He stepped around to the side of the cabin; no use fighting his way to the outhouse on a trail that was drifted full. The look of the trail told him the wind had been moving in the night while he slept. When he went back inside he poured water in the tin basin, washed and dried his face. Then he made porridge and coffee and took his time with breakfast. Didn't do any good for a man to hurry in the morning; got him off cockeyed for the rest of the day. He had a smoke and washed the dishes before he got on his snowshoes and lifted the rifle with the barrel painted blue.

He started down country, the webs whispering over the snow. Wasn't but a couple of miles to where he'd dragged the horse carcass and set the traps. The smoke of his breath hung in the air before him. Never saw the morning so still, he thought again.

The sound startled him when he first heard it, made him pause and feel the hair rise on the back of his neck. It was a wailing sound, ending in short, desperate barks. Another sound followed the first, much the same but in a higher key —a thin crying out of the silence. For a crazy moment he thought of Ellie Lundgren, but Ellie couldn't have lived through the cold weather if she was running wild in the mountains. His step quickened, and his pulse hammered with excitement. "That's no coyote," he said aloud. "That's foxes bawlin' this morning."

He crossed the beaver-dam country, passing the snow-humped mounds he knew were beaver houses, walking over the dam where he had sat on the bank with Prim Cameron when she was carrying little Jed. Again the lonely sound came to him. The trees opened before him, and he stepped carefully around a clump of willows and stood still. A great sense of satisfaction swept through him as he looked at the humped red shapes, doubled in frantic motion. They were fighting the traps. He could hear their harsh breathing, see them straighten and leap in the air and come buckling back to earth as the chains of the traps tightened and held them. Like I figured, he thought; if I got one, I got both—the male and the female.

One fox was by the horse carcass, and the other on a little knoll fifty feet away. Jediah smiled, for he had set one trap at the flank of a dead horse and the second trap on the knoll, knowing that after one fox was caught the other would be wary and would go off to the nearest rise of earth. He had used plenty of beaver-castor bait on that knoll.

He leaned his rifle against a clump of willows and cut off a heavy branch. Armed with this, he went forward. They got his scent then and both turned, looking at him. As he came close to the first fox, his webs light and easy on the snow, he saw the sharp face, alert and still, the mouth open and dripping saliva. He saw the eyes, yellow-green and leaping to brightness with fear.

Jediah moved fast, bringing the club down on the small poised head. When the fox slumped to the ground, stunned, Jediah carefully put his foot on the shoulders and crushed the lungs. He saw the glaze come over the eyes and the mouth draw back in a grimace of death, the small teeth pointed and clean.

He went to the knoll and killed the second fox. I'll give 'em to Prim, he thought, to wear around her shoulders. Been wantin' to give her a present for a long time. He stood marveling at the color of the fur, the beauty of it. And then a sudden rush of regret filled him. He stooped and patted the still head. The fur was warm under his hand. "Damned if I'm sure it was worth it," he murmured.

He skinned them out where the snow was padded with their tracks, and then carried the pelts away. With the empty traps dangling at his belt, he was snowshoeing back up country to his cabin when he suddenly stopped and looked toward the North Fork Ranch.

It was like a wind, he thought, a wind that stirred against his face and then was gone, making him look to see which way it was blowing. He stood waiting to feel again that sudden breath of air, but the morning was so still, the sound of his heart was loud. And then the impulse to see Prim was strong in him. He pulled off a mitten and ran a rough hand over the red fur; the fur sprang up as his fingers moved away, as though life still throbbed under the brightness. Well, why not take the fox pelts to Prim now? Kelsey had plenty of stretchers. Nothing really pressing him to get back to the cabin, was there?

The soft *whush-whush* of the webs was a good sound. He came out of the timber west of the ranch, for he preferred to walk in the trees as long as he could. He stood, looking across the meadow, seeing the smoke rise straight up from the ranch-house chimney. And he blew through his nose like an old horse. It was so damned still a man felt like shouting to start the air moving.

When he got to the house he took off his snowshoes and leaned them against the porch, draped the fox skins around his neck, feeling coltish. He knocked hard, and finally the kitchen door opened. He grinned. "Good mornin', madam. Was wonderin' if you had a crust of bread for a poor old—" Then he saw her eyes, big and strange, and her mouth moving as though she was trying to speak and couldn't.

Kelsey came from behind her. Kelsey said, "Come in, Jediah." There was a stubble of beard on his face, and he didn't look as though he'd slept in weeks. "We've got a sick boy, Jediah."

Jediah stepped into the kitchen and dropped the red foxes by the door. He followed Kelsey to the bedroom. He looked at the boy there in the bed, and his heart suddenly squeezed up as though a big hand had closed over it. Little Jed's face was red. His eyes stared at Jediah and didn't see him at all. The old trapper heard the rattle in the breathing, put out his hand, and felt the fever on the young skin. "You sent for Doc?"

"Telephone's out again—wire's down somewhere between here and town. Dalt rode in early this morning. Doc's outside —maybe in Denver. Nobody knows when he'll be back."

Jediah nodded. "You tried mustard poultice on his chest?"

"Yes," Prim said.

"You rubbed him with goose grease and camphor?"

"Yes."

Again Jediah nodded. "You give him whisky with a little honey in it?"

"We did everything," Kelsey said. "There's nothing left I can think of."

"Well—" Jediah brushed the damp hair back from the boy's forehead. His hand trembled, and he tried to steady it. "I'll think of something—must be something, if it would just come to me."

Prim sat by the bed, holding little Jed's hand. Tears slipped down her cheeks, but she made no sound. Jediah walked back to the kitchen. He stood by the window and stared at the mountains. Wind was beginning to lick their summits. Not quiet up there—only here in the lower country.

A man might pray if he knew what to pray to; a man might pray if he knew how. He tried to close his eyes and didn't feel natural or comfortable that way, so he opened them again. Must be something a man could think of besides the bigness of the Park and how cold it looked.

Jesus Christ, he said in his mind, don't let him die. Seemed strange to say it that way, and not the easy, natural way, like when a man was mad or happy. He tried to say the words again and couldn't. He went to the stove, pushed on the coffee pot, and stuck more wood in the firebox. You could say life was stinking mean sometimes—now, for instance, with the little fella in there, and the gurgling in his throat, and the sick smell of him hanging all through the house.

Hilder and Dalt came in from feeding the cattle. They took off their overshoes and poured the bitter coffee and drank it.

"He is bad," Hilder said. "I see it coming."

"How?" Dalt looked at him.

"Last summer when he come to the bunkhouse one day—and a blackbird fly in with him. I know then it is death. The blackbird in the house, it is the worst sign I know."

"Christ," Jediah muttered, "nothin' but superstition."

"T'ink what you like," Hilder said. "Me—I know."

Jediah went back to the bedroom. Prim was sobbing now. "I knew it, so I did! I always knew it. I didn't want him, and now he's to be taken from me! God's punishing me!"

"Stop that!" Kelsey's voice was harsh. "You don't know what you're saying. He's only got a bad cold, and it's a common thing among children. The fever will break soon. And you wanted little Jed—of course you wanted him."

"I didn't! I didn't! I told Jediah—a baby was only another reason to make you stay with me when you didn't want to."

"I never said such a thing. By God, I never did!"

Her face, flushed and splotched from weeping, turned toward Kelsey. "You think I don't know? You think when you go off in your broody spells I don't know you dream about that woman? And her riding the country like a wild thing, fretting herself half daft over you! Haven't you heard about the day she was seen on top of Independence Mountain, naked to the waist, riding in the wind and sun?"

"Shut up, Prim! You're out of your head."

"No, I'm not. He'll die, the lad, and Heather's only got this year and she's through school here—and then you're free!"

Kelsey brushed past her and put his hand on the child's forehead. He looked at Jediah.

Prim tore a piece from a towel, blew her nose, and stuffed the rag in the pocket of her apron. "You never noticed how sick he was early this morning. I went to the corral and got Dalt to ride for the doctor. You were busy with one of your damn cows!"

"If you'd told me, Prim— I was trying to help the cow, to save her."

"Find an excuse. God, yes, squirm out of it, the way you always get out of things. You never paid any heed to the lad, anyhow. You never really did."

"Prim—" His voice choked. "Damn you, Prim! You've got the meanest tongue. Give me a rag. I'll dip it in cold water and cool his head."

"You get the hell out of here!"

"All right, Prim. But don't shout. Please don't shout at me." He turned blindly away and walked past Jediah.

*   *

Kelsey stood by the kitchen stove. A numbness filled him. The wee lad—surely nothing would happen to such a wee lad who hadn't begun to live.

Pictures of the child tossed up in his mind—the boy running to the corral in the summer morning when the wrangler was driving in the horses for haying, and all their manes tossing black in the wind; the boy jumping over a stick Kelsey had placed for him on the floor, laughing; and the morning Kelsey had skinned the coyote, showing the child the fleas and shouting, "Catch a flea, Jed! Catch him!"

Kelsey walked to the window and looked out, seeing nothing. In his mind echoed so many of Prim's words: "You never take time for him. . . . Just like a man . . . come home, tease him, toss him up and squeeze him and hand him back to me. What's a son? Only a plaything for Prim to raise!"

He bowed his head, pressing it against the rough window-sill. A man's work was out-of-doors, wasn't it? A man's work was to make money, pay the bills, feed his family. Children were a woman's chore. Prim, it isn't true! I did notice him. I loved him. He was mine—ours.

He heard a step and Jediah's voice. "Bring the tea kettle. Find a sheet. We'll steam him. We can try that."

*   *

In the dark November morning, at four o'clock, Jediah Cameron died. He died while Prim held him in her arms, making a moaning sound in the still ranch house. Hilder saddled a horse and rode toward Plunketts' to tell Heather and Amie and Harry to start for town. Long Dalton and Jediah went out to the woodshed and started making a casket by lantern light. A cat howled in the darkness. Dalt threw a stick at it. "Whinin' son-of-a-bitch!"

In the gray light they rode in the sled toward town—Jediah, Prim, Kelsey, and Long Dalton. Hilder stayed home to feed the cattle. The two fox pelts lay at Jediah's feet, covered with the hay in the bottom of the sled.

To Kelsey Cameron it was all unreal, a thing happening in a dream from which he must surely waken. There was the long time in Faun Gentry's store—the waiting time while only Faun worked in the back room, and Amie Plunkett took Prim to Dolly Gentry's house, while Dalt went with Heather to the hotel and saw to it that she ate some breakfast. And there was the time when they went to the graveyard—the wind whistling over the snow-hooded sagebrush, wind springing up in the middle of the day with a strange fierceness, and, somewhere close by, a playing child shouting in a glad, brief sound.

When they got ready to lower the casket into the earth Jediah Walsh stepped forward. A grayness hung over him; it was in his face and voice. He stroked the red fox skins and said gently, "Don't seem right he should go so far away—and nothin' with him that's part of me." And he laid the two red pelts over the casket. "Little Jed, them foxes are the color of life. Them foxes will keep you warm."

Kelsey saw the earth fall on the bright red fur. He heard the sound of Prim's weeping, muffled against Amie Plunkett's breast. And he saw Heather shivering, Long Dalton's arms around her. The minister stood, the wind flapping his long overcoat, the book open. " 'I am the Resurrection and the life . . .' "

Near them in the graveyard a little group of people had gathered. The wind sighed around their feet, kicking up a mist of loose snow.

Kelsey shut his eyes. A time that went on forever, he thought, and to get through it—oh, somehow to get through it! My lad, my lad, his days ended in their beginning . . . *Taraleean, my mother, be with me now.*

And he turned, stumbling blindly. Lifting his head, he saw the blurred face of Heather coming quickly to him, and in a moment her arms pressed around him, holding him hard and close.

CHAPTER XXIV

~ ~ ~ ~ ~ ~ ~

Winter had never been so hard, Kelsey thought, walking through the deep snow between the barn and the ranch house. It was late January. The icy wind brought a drip to his nose, and he brushed it away as it started freezing.

Prim was by the kitchen stove, rocking back and forth, her hands busy with knitting. It hurt him to see her knitting day after day; there was something so mute and futile about the movements of her hands, for he knew that all this show of occupation was only on the outside. Inside she fretted, alone and grieving and tortured by her thoughts. She had built a high fence around herself, shutting him out.

She had not slept in the room with him since Jed's death. Sometimes she was in the middle bedroom, sometimes on the lounge in the living room, and often here in the rocking chair, sitting wide-eyed through all the long night. The first week after the funeral she had cried every day; there seemed no end to the tears that spilled from her. But now she never cried or mentioned the child's name, and this frightened him.

"Prim, old lass, how are you?"

"I'm all right. Is it time for supper?"

"No. I finished the feeding. Dalt and Hilder are hauling an extra jag for the barn. It's only three o'clock. No hurry about supper."

Her hands moved again at the knitting. The needles click-clicked. A gust of wind flung snow against the windows. The roof creaked.

He touched her hair in an awkward gesture. If she would put out her arms to him . . . If she would rise and come to him . . . If she would cling to him, a part of him would answer out of physical need and loneliness. And was this a kind of loving? Could it be love that made his body want her now as he had never wanted her before? Or was it only because he was a man and needed the ways of the living to ease the blow of death? But his hand lay as harmless as a leaf on her hair. She was away in a far country where he couldn't follow or find her.

She said, not stopping the knitting, "When Hilder brought the mail yesterday there was a letter from my brothers. They want me to come home. My mother is bad off. And they think it will do me good to leave this country after losing my son."

He stared at the snow that swirled past the window on the wind. Every night more snow fell, and every day the wind tossed it from one part of the earth to another. "And what is it you want to do, Prim?"

The needles flashed. "I think I'll go." *Click-click.* The yarn was so blue, like thin loops of summer sky over her fingers. "And what about Heather? I'd like to have her with me."

"No. The lassie stays with me."

"I'm her mother. She's not a woman yet and needs me."

"Prim, for God's sake quit knitting!"

"Why?" She looked up in surprise.

"It drives me to screaming inside."

Her fingers tightened on the blue yarn, holding the needles stiff and silent. "And why shouldn't Heather go with me?"

"She'll not stop in the midst of her last year at school to run off to Scotland with you. And I want her here with me."

"Her place is with me," Prim said firmly. "And I'll be writing about the passage this week. I've my own money to go on, and I won't be asking anything from you."

He stared at her. It was a while before he could speak. "I suppose Big Mina or your fine brothers saw to that."

"I got the money from Jediah. Oh, I was leaving you right after the funeral, but I changed my mind."

"And who's Jediah Walsh," he asked angrily, "that you get money from him instead of your husband?"

She got up, shook the stove, and pushed the tea kettle to where it would boil. "I'm going to town tomorrow and have them book passage for Heather and me."

He walked across the kitchen and stood behind her while she fussed with the kitchen stove. "Heather stays with me. And if you go, when will you be back?"

She kept her face turned away and didn't answer.

After a while he shrugged into his coat, went to the corral, got a horse, and rode up the meadow. He looked anxiously at the cows, seeing they were still fat. Feeding had been cut to a minimum the past two weeks, for when he'd last talked with Monte they'd decided it was going to take more hay than usual to get through the hard winter.

"Won't hurt 'em to shorten their rations a little," she had said, looking at the cows and then at the snow-covered haystacks. "We've got to make the feed last, Kelsey. There's none to be bought."

He had known fear then, but he'd tried to hide it. He'd said casually, "Well, it's not like it used to be in the Park. We've got the railroad. A man could always ship his cattle if things got too tough."

"It's no time to ship," Monte had replied. "Bloom's gone from our cows and steers. I figure we'll get 'em through the winter. It may pinch, but we'll make it."

And now Kelsey began to count the haystacks that hadn't been broken. It was a thing he'd done often recently. Surely there was still plenty of feed if the weather only quieted. Jediah said it wasn't normal to have such continuous wind and snow. Any day now the weather was bound to break.

Wind slapped sharply at his cheek, and he saw the light falling off toward dusk. Days were too short now, and the nights seemed endless, and a man's thoughts rising big in the sleepless hours. He wondered if Vic Lundgren looked at the mountains now in winter and thought about Ellie. But of course he did. Poor Vic, he had kept on searching, riding the hills alone, until the snows got too deep. It was as though a madness drove him to find a scrap of clothing, something that would point the way to what might have happened. And sometime in the Park, when a man heard a mountain lion scream, he would say it was the ghost of Ellie Lundgren.

He turned back toward the ranch house, where he could see the blue smoke from the kitchen stove streaming in the wind. He thought of Heather. Prim couldn't take her to Scotland. She must finish her last year of high school. And then he would send her outside, beyond the mountains, as Monte Maguire had suggested. Monte had said, "Get her outta the Park. You want her to hang around this country and marry a damned Swede?"

He had no objection to Swedes, for he knew many fine ones —such as Vic Lundgren and Hilder. He didn't worry about Swedes. But a man like Long Dalton . . . Twice he'd been on the verge of firing Dalt, giving some poor excuse to be rid of him. He would look at Dalt sprawled on the bunk, reading a magazine, and he would think of a big tawny mountain cat waiting to rise up and strike. Then Dalt would lift his head and look into Kelsey's eyes and smile a strange, thin smile. "Something on your mind, Cameron?"

"No, Dalt. Nothing." When he wanted to cry out, Yes! My daughter. Damn you, Dalt, what are you doing to her?

And he'd watch when Heather was home on the week ends, trying to see something between her and Dalt that he might make an issue of, bring the whole thing into the open and end it. But there was nothing, at least nothing so real a man could put a finger on it. There was only a fine tension in the air, flowing through the room when the two of them were together, a tension that rose when they avoided even looking at each other.

He unsaddled the horse and stood quietly in the dim barn, making himself face the idea of Dalt having his daughter. And he wanted to bow his head and weep like a woman. No, not that, not a man with no fine education and only a job as a hired ranch hand. The wind whimpered around the barn in the blue chill of falling evening. *But your father was an educated man, and he married an Irish potato picker.* Taraleean— but she was different. Yes, she was.

CHAPTER XXV

It was the third week in February. In the kitchen of the North Fork Ranch, Monte Maguire paced the floor, rubbing a hand wearily across her forehead. She was thin, and worry lines showed around her eyes. "How did I know things would get so tough the railroad would close and no trains comin' into the Park?" she said. "And I kept figurin' on a thaw. What are we goin' to do? We can't keep on cuttin' down on the feeding. It shows on the cattle now."

Kelsey stared at the oilcloth-covered table. Yes, he had seen the mark on the cattle; they were beginning to shrink. It was a thing that haunted his sleep, sending him from his bed to walk the floors and smoke too many cigarettes and drink too much bitter coffee. It was a thing that sent him out into the cold winter nights to stand in the darkness and look at the clouded-over sky, hoping for stars, hoping for silence instead of the never-ending roar of wind at timberline. Wasn't it enough that a man had lost his son, that his wife was a stranger, that he fretted over his daughter and a hired man? Did he have to be nagged every waking hour by the fear for his cattle?

Beside him Vic Lundgren, Harry Plunkett, and Jake went on drinking coffee. Amie Plunkett and Prim had gone to the front room, for Amie had said, "I've had all the cow talk I can stand. Let's get out of here, Prim."

"One thing sure," Monte continued. "We can't go on like this. As I see it, there's only one thing left to do—rustle the ridges on the flats between here and town. Let the strong cattle find what little feed there is."

"Rustlin'," Vic said sourly. "That business, she is for Wyoming plains ranchers. When did a Park rancher ever kick his cattle onto the flats, weather like this? And look what you gotta do; snow's getting deeper every day, and you'll have to break trail from ridge to ridge so the cattle can get through. And don't forget, when things get as tough as they are now it weakens cattle to rustle."

"They're not in the best shape anyhow," Monte retorted. "And we've got to make the hay stretch farther."

"Any grass a cow brute or steer can find will help to keep 'em alive," Jake said, "even if it is slim pickin's."

"How long can they last on what you'd find on ridgetops of the flats?" Harry Plunkett demanded, his face gloomy.

"A damned short time," Vic said.

"We still gotta rustle," Monte said. She sucked hard on her cigarette, dropped the butt to the floor, and crushed it. "We gotta move the strong cows, the big steers, and the range horses onto the flats. If we do that, what hay we've got left will carry weak cows, calves, and bulls until spring."

"Yes," Kelsey said, "it's the only answer."

"God, what a mess!" Harry Plunkett shook his head. "Nope, not for me. I'm holdin' what cattle I've got on the feed ground where they belong. And what'll you do with your cattle on the flats if it just keeps on snowin'? Trail 'em back to the meadows?"

"Don't talk like a fathead," Monte said impatiently. "You know we can't bring them back to the meadows where there's only hay enough for the cattle we've left behind. When we trail to the flats, our cattle stay there till spring."

"Where they die if the weather don't break."

"It's a chance we've got to take," Kelsey said. "We've got to gamble on the weather break and on an early spring."

"It'll be a hell of a long time before you see spring on the flats this year," Vic said. "Trouble is, Kelsey, you and Monte are in the worst fix of any ranchers in the Park. And you know why? Because you didn't ship those yearling steers last fall. Monte, she gets foxy and figures on holding her steers over another year and making more money on 'em. Monte, you are foolish this time; you yust get caught with your pants down, yup, yup."

"The hell you say! If we got a decent winter, everything was under control. How did I know the sky was gonna spit snow day after day?"

"You learn, Monte," Vic went on, his tone gentler now. "A man can figure out lots of things, but not the weather. Nature, she fools us when we least expect. Is too bad." He spread his big hands in a futile gesture.

"I don't want any damn sympathy!" Monte's eyes blazed.

"Take it easy, Monte. We all get hurt before this is over. We all break our hearts over cattle. Not a rancher in the Park who sleeps well these nights."

Kelsey knocked his doubled fists together. His stomach hurt; his head ached. He looked at Monte. "I told you last year we ought to be putting up more hay."

"What are you?" she shouted angrily. "A cowman or a farmer?"

"You sound like a woman. You don't think what you're saying."

"When I need your advice, Kelsey Cameron, I'll ask for it!"

"Get sore, then." His voice rose, and he couldn't keep from shouting. "It's our fault, isn't it? Didn't we look around us and see this could happen? Monte, two years ago we almost got caught, and I told you then that the whole business of balancing feed and cattle was getting out of hand."

"By God, we got by, didn't we? We got by until right now."

"Right now is what counts, Monte. Right now can break us."

Her mouth quivered. Her eyes were desperate as she looked

at the men. Then her shoulders went back, and she laughed, a harsh, rude sound in the quiet kitchen. "You can all do what you damn well please, but I'm rustling the ridges. Jake, you start here today, and work the Red Hill meadows as soon as you're through with this outfit." She put on her coat and walked to the door. She turned, her lips drawn thin and tight in a bitter smile. "The Park will never see the day that Monte Maguire goes broke." The door slammed behind her.

Kelsey got to his feet and followed her out into the windy winter day. "Monte! Just a minute—"

She had untied her saddle horse from the yard fence and was ready to mount. "We've nothing more to say to each other," she said, her eyes hard and angry.

"I only wanted to tell you—no matter what happens, no matter what we have to do, I'm behind you, Monte. I always have been. You must know that."

She turned her face away, and when she looked at him again he was shocked to see tears in her eyes. In that moment he felt a terrible need to take her in his arms, to hold her hard and strong against him, to tell her that together they could lick the world. But instead he stood, awkward and hurting, finally managing to say, "Better stay for dinner. Dalt and Hilder will be in from feeding soon. Prim's got a roast in the oven."

"I'm not hungry; I couldn't eat if I tried." She swung to the saddle and kicked the horse into a fast singlefoot gait.

He stood looking after her until she was out of sight. Going back into the house, he found Amie setting the table and Prim busy at the stove.

Vic said, "Don't set no place for me, Amie. I drift on home now. Maybe the weather, she is better tomorrow." Vic settled his cap low over his ears and walked out.

"Fat chance of good weather," Harry Plunkett said. "Creek's startin' to overflow, water pushin' up and runnin' on top of the ice. Always means a storm's coming when the creeks overflow."

"Oh, the damned country!" Amie cried. "I want to leave it forever. I'm gettin' out of here come spring."

"We won't be able to," Harry said. "We won't have anything left to start over in another place."

"Then we'll start broke, Harry Plunkett. I'm telling you, this winter's given me my fill of the Park."

"Now, Amie—"

Her face hardened. The softness went out of her big brown eyes. To Kelsey she wasn't the same easy-going Amie he had known over the years he'd lived in the Park. "Harry," she said, "if you won't go with me I'll go alone."

Harry's jaw sagged. He stared at his wife. After a long silence he spoke quietly. "Amie, I'm not leavin' the Park. It's home to me. It may be a hell of a country, but I don't want to live anywhere else. What was I back in Illinois? Nothin'— nothin' to be proud of. Then I come to the Park, and right away people treated me special, made me feel as important as any man that walked the face of the earth. Long as you live half decent, pay your bills and keep your word, the Park's ready to respect you. Amie, I'd starve to death here before I'd go back to Illinois!"

Amie turned away. There was a rough sound from her throat, and Kelsey saw her shoulders shaking. Harry went to her, brought her around to fill his arms, and held her as though there were only the two of them in the kitchen.

"Amie, you won't leave me. We've had too much livin' together."

He drew a deep breath, put his face down against her hair, and went on, "From the first time I saw you, Amie, I knew I couldn't get along without you. You were young then, and runnin' up the street, barefooted—dust squirtin' under your toes— and the sun was shinin' on your hair. There was something about you, Amie. You'll always be that to me, a girl runnin' in the summer day, and your thin dress blowin' back against you, and all of me wantin' to take right after you."

She pulled away from him, blew her nose hard, wiped her eyes, and looked around the kitchen. "Some fancy speech! Took him half a lifetime to say it, and maybe it was worth a hard winter."

Kelsey smiled. Tonight would be the best night Harry had ever known in Amie's arms. And even as he thought this Amie's hand went up to touch her hair, and in the motion of her arm was all the magic of a young girl going through a sweet, calculated gesture before a boy who loved her.

"Get the grub on, Prim," Kelsey said. "We've got to work the cattle this afternoon."

*   *

In the cold afternoon Hilder gathered the horses from the lower pasture and drove them toward the flats. Jake and one of the punchers headed the steers along the same trail where Hilder had gone before them. Across the pasture lay the prairie between the ranch and town. Here the ridgetops had been bared by the wind. And to the north, on Independence Mountain, bare ground was on the south slopes.

Dalt and Kelsey worked the cow herd in the big meadow, cutting out the strong cows and shoving them toward the flats.

"There's one we got to get in the corral," Dalt said, riding up beside Kelsey.

Kelsey squinted into the wind and saw the young cow with the bloody length of afterbirth hanging from her. It was a short afterbirth, only about a foot long, and he knew she had aborted her calf. When that happened the afterbirth never came away clean; in abortion there wasn't enough weight to pull it out, and half of it stayed inside the cow.

"Yes," he said, "we'll take her in and tie a weight on it. About two pounds will do. Can't be too heavy. It's the steady pull that straightens things out, brings it away." A man could use most anything handy for a weight—a rock, an old piece of iron, or even wood.

"If a man leaves it till it rots away," Dalt said, "he's got a sterile cow."

"You think the shortened feeding had anything to do with this, Dalt?"

"Maybe, maybe not. She coulda slipped on the ice around the water hole."

"I know, but this is the fifth in a week. We've got to be careful. Any of these cows that look weak can't be moved to the flats. They'll abort sure as hell." He looked bleakly at Dalt. "Just one more worry to add to all the rest."

"Buddy, don't ever figure on the worst," Dalt said. "It might not come—and if it does, then a man's got to face it."

It was the first time Dalt had called him buddy in months, and a warmth filled Kelsey's heart. In a moment he would have reached to take hold of Dalt's arm and said, Let's forget anything that might be troubling us. Let's talk things over like we used to. But Dalt was already wheeling the cowpony and moving toward another cow, cutting her deftly from the main herd, and driving her toward the bunch they would push to the flats.

They all worked until long after dark. Prim had gone to bed when they got home, but there was warm food waiting on the edge of the stove. It was nine o'clock when they sat down to eat. Hilder carefully washed the dishes and set the leftover food in the pantry. Kelsey got into bed and lay, weary but wide-eyed, in the darkness.

He heard the creak of the floor as steps came from the adjoining bedroom. For a moment his heart beat large in his throat. Prim sat on the edge of the bed and said, "Are you going to lose the cattle, Kelsey?"

"Don't know, Prim. A man doesn't know anything."

She got up and left him, and he felt empty and lonely. He wanted her close to him. Prim was so strong. And if she would only say a word, one small word of understanding. He turned restlessly, pushing his face into the cool, clean-smelling pillow.

*   *

The weather held for a week, and in that time they rode the flats every day, breaking trail from ridgetop to ridgetop where the brittle brown grass stood up stiff to the wind. The cattle ate the tops of sagebrush as well as the meager grass. They got their water from the snow on the ground. And there was less thirst in them now that they no longer fed on hay.

"They're shrinking more," Kelsey said to Jake. "They're not as strong as they were a week ago when we brought them out here." And he looked around the open country, where cattle from the Red Hill Ranch, the North Fork, and Monte's home place were clustered on all the available bare ground. How long would the grass hold them?

As though Jake read his mind, Jake said, "There's feed for another week. Then we better get a thaw, by God."

"And if we don't, Jake?"

Jake, his back to the wind, cupped his hands around a match to light a cigarette. It hung in his mouth, sticking to his chapped lips. His eyes, dulled and narrowed from squinting at the glare of sun on snow, looked past Kelsey toward the east.

"Don't look like a man can do much, Kelsey. If the train was runnin' we could ship and get out from under, even if we did take a big loss. But it don't look like the train will be tootin' across this country for another three-four weeks."

Snowflakes were sailing out of the air when they turned toward home. Kelsey had seen the storm growing in the west that morning, but he had told himself it was only a flurry. Now, as the snow thickened with every passing moment, he knew it was going to mean six or eight inches of added depth. As soon as it cleared, new trails would have to be broken. And, worse than that, the bared places where the cattle now rustled would be covered, and the cattle would go hungry until wind and sun bared the earth again.

Hilder met them at the barn. "Vic, he come up early this

afternoon," he said. "Cattlemen are meetin' in town soon as it stops snowin', wantin' to talk over the trouble. Told me to pass on the word to you, Kelsey."

That night, after supper, Prim took up her knitting again. Kelsey went to the bunkhouse and sat late with Dalt and Jake while Hilder slept.

From time to time Kelsey went to the door, opened it, looked out at the blowing snow, and came back to sit by the round, red-hot stove. After a while they drank whisky from a bottle Dalt had quietly got from under Hilder's bunk.

Whisky and heat brought out the sweat on Jake's face and on his shining bald head. He began to nod, half in sleep, a foolish smile on his mouth. "Look, Kelsey," he said thickly, "you might as well take it easy. Cattle on the flats can't last. Kiss 'em good-by and get your belly full of whisky and go to bed."

Dalt said nothing. He sat tilted back in a chair, his feet resting on the scarred wooden table with its litter of Wild-West magazines, matches, sacks of tobacco, and mittens.

"Can't bring the cattle back to the meadows," Kelsey muttered to himself.

"God, no!" Dalt's feet came down on the floor with a crash. "Go to bed, buddy. Empty the bottle. It'll make you sleep."

But Kelsey wanted no more whisky. He felt sick, sick and old and beaten. He went out into the night and waded through the snow to the dark house. He sat in the old rocker by the kitchen stove until daylight.

Prim came in, looked at him, shook down the fire, and put in fresh wood. She brought bacon from the pantry and began to slice it with a sharp butcher knife. "Snow's stopped," she said. "Didn't last as long as I thought it would this time."

"I'll start for town after breakfast," he said. "Pick up Harry Plunkett and go on in to the stockmen's meeting."

"And I'll go with you," Prim said, shoving a frying pan onto the hot part of the stove. "I'm not staying stuck out here in the snowdrifts."

He closed his eyes, feeling suddenly sleepy from the heat of the stove. There was nothing for Prim in town—or for any woman; they couldn't be like men, ganging up in Bill Dirk's for talk and drink and poker. But he wouldn't argue with her. He was too tired to argue; he was too tired for anything.

*　　　*

Kelsey and Prim sat at Plunketts' kitchen table, drinking Amie's thick warmed-over coffee.

"There's no use goin' to town," Harry said. "What good's to come of a bunch of cattlemen sittin' and talkin' about the weather?"

"A lot of the cattlemen have been in this country longer than I have," Kelsey said. "I want to hear what they have to say."

"They won't say nothin' important," Harry replied. "They'll just hash the whole thing over and tell you what you've known all along—we've got too damn much snow and too little hay."

"You can stay home if you want," Amie said, "but I'm going to town with Prim. I'm gonna shove my feet under one of Possy's tables and let her wait on me."

Harry shrugged. "Go ahead. It's all right with me. I can batch."

Amie looked at Prim. "You get word about when you sail for the old country yet?"

"Last of March."

"How'll you get to Laramie? Fly? No train. But come to think of it, you might go out on one of the sleds they been sendin' for freight—if they're still runnin'."

Kelsey glanced at his watch. "Get yourself dressed, Amie. I want to make town before dark."

Prim turned to Harry. "And see that Heather stays here while we're in town. I don't want her at the ranch."

Amie swung around in the kitchen doorway, a little smile on her mouth. "What do you want him to do, Prim? Hogtie

her? You think you can go on treating her like a little kid the
rest of her life?"

"You raise your kids, I'll raise mine," Prim retorted.

Harry Plunkett went to the stove and stuck in more wood.
"You want those rocks taken outta the oven, Prim?" he asked.
"They're plenty hot now."

"Yes. There's gunnysacks and old blankets in the sled.
Wrap them around the rocks. Amie and I will keep our feet
warm, even if the rest of us freezes."

They left the Plunkett ranch at noon, Amie and Prim
bundled in wraps so that they appeared twice their normal sizes.
The women fell into conversation, damning the country and
the weather, while Kelsey's thoughts drifted toward town.
Jediah had gone in ten days ago and hadn't returned to his
cabin on the west side of the Park. Even Jediah had wea-
ried of the wind and snow. Jediah would be eager for a poker
game and good whisky, Kelsey thought now, and a poker game
would be a relief from all this worry. And likely Prim wouldn't
say a word. She hadn't mentioned cards and whisky for weeks.

Prim—her body had spread, becoming round and sturdy
until it reminded him of a tough cowpony with its coat shagged
out for winter. Sometimes he tried to picture the other Prim
he'd known as a lad, the light-stepping Prim, slim as a willow
shoot in spring, and with a waist so small it delighted a man to
look at it. Had she really been like that, or was it only a
dream he carried in his mind? It was a queer thing about life,
that often a man couldn't separate the dreaming from what was
real.

He saw at last the width of white land and the low spread of
blue smoke that marked the town. The air was heavy, holding
the smoke close to earth. That meant more snow.

He got Prim and Amie settled at the hotel, saying to his
wife, "Don't wait for me. I don't know when I'll be back. You
and Amie go ahead and eat supper."

"We can take care of ourselves," Prim said.

He hurried out to the chill winter afternoon, got in the sled, and drove to the livery stable.

"Sol," Kelsey said to the tall, lean man who ran the place, "I want to put my team up. I'll be here tonight—maybe tomorrow night too."

Sol scratched under one arm. "All right, Kelsey. How's everything on the west side? Got lots of snow?"

"God, man, you ought to see it!" Kelsey hurried to unharness the team, wanting to get away from Sol, who was always full of gossip.

"Possy," Sol said, "she got the hotel sold to some fella outside, but he ain't been able to come in. Y'know her old man can't live in the Park no more. Country's too high for him. She acts like she's rarin' to leave, but they say Vic's been hangin' around there and—"

Kelsey backed out the door. "Thanks, Sol. I'll be getting about my business."

"Sure. I'll grain your horses before I go to bed. Still got a little grain left. And y'know," Sol went on quickly, "Monte Maguire's been hittin' the bottle pretty hard. Somebody said that ain't all, either. She's got a new cowpuncher at the home place, and they say he don't use the bunkhouse bed long enough to get it warmed up. And she's been in town every afternoon lately, and—"

Kelsey started down the street. Sol's voice floated after him: "—she's been sittin' in Bill Dirk's, drinkin' like a man."

Kelsey walked fast in the sharp evening air toward Bill Dirk's. There was a crowd of ranchers drinking at the bar. He pushed through them until he came face to face with Bill Dirk. "Where is she?"

Dirk jerked a thumb toward the back room. "She's all right. You leave her alone, Kelsey. It's not anything that's gonna last—not with Monte. It's just that she's worrying too much about the cattle. Don't you jaw at her."

But he went directly to the back room and quickly closed

the door behind him. Monte was sitting alone at one of the worn slab tables, a bottle and glass before her.

"Hello, young fella!" She gave him an impudent grin, and the same glinting sharpness was in her eyes that he remembered from long ago, the first time he saw her, in the kitchen of the Red Hill Ranch.

"You—" His voice choked. "A common cowpuncher! My God, Monte, how can you do it?"

"Been listenin' to the tongues wag, eh? Didn't figure you'd ever be the kind of man who'd do that. Well, suppose it is true? What difference does it make? Long as it's not someone you love, it isn't a thing—not a damn thing."

"It's cheap! It's ugly and—"

"Cheap, eh? Well, it wouldn't have cost *you* a thing, young fella. But you turned it down. Sit and take a load off your feet. Have a drink. Don't be gettin' riled up over my business." She shoved the bottle across the table.

"Monte—" He drew a deep breath. "When I look at you and think— I could cry!"

"Save it for spring," she said briefly. "Then we'll cry together. There'll be something to cry over then—the fine cows dead, and their calves dead inside 'em, and the maggots workin' them over."

"I'd rather lose the cattle than see you—"

"No, you wouldn't. You only think that now and have to say it. Sounds noble and good, but it ain't so, young fella. Listen, a man can forget any woman when he loves cattle as much as you do. And don't think I won't know how you feel come spring when you walk among the dead ones. Take a drink. It won't do much for your mind, but it warms the belly."

He took a swallow of the whisky. It burned his throat. "Monte, you're too fine a person to—"

She shook her head. "Don't preach. I been worked on by experts, and it didn't do any good." Then she leaned forward, staring at him. "You're gettin' a streak of gray in that red hair. Well, we're all comin' to it—bein' old, and the best years behind us. I've got it too. See?" And she touched the side of her head, where the smooth hair swept back.

When he saw the small splash of silver it shocked him. In his mind he had never thought of her as changing; the rest of the world could change, and men and women with it, but not Monte Maguire. He realized now that foolishly he had assumed she would always be as he had known her in those early years—her big body straight and strong, her hair bright as captured sunlight, and her eyes so sharp and clear.

His heart filled with an aching tenderness, and he got up and went around the table to her. He pressed her head against the hardness of his thigh, and his hand shook as he touched the graying hair with gentle fingers. Ah, he thought, what a fool I am!—softer in the heart than a woman. But he felt more tender than before, and he wanted to stroke away that grim reminder of age.

"It doesn't matter," he said, his throat tight. "Nothing you do matters, either. I forgive you everything, Monte darling. I forgive you because I love you."

She started to speak, but there was a sound at the door and he stepped away from her.

Vic Lundgren came into the room, followed by Tommy Cameron, Jediah Walsh, and Bill Dirk. Other ranchers crowded through the narrow doorway, and soon the room was filled. They pulled tables together, sat down, and began drinking.

"After this round the drinks are on me," Vic Lundgren said.

"What we oughta do is forget about cattle and play poker," Tommy Cameron said.

"Y'know, Monte," Vic said, leaning toward her, "we're gonna have a war. We're gonna get in that mess across the ocean. Cattle prices are gonna be up pretty soon."

"Sure. I see it comin', Vic." Her mouth quirked. "If we got any cattle by then."

"Well," Vic said, "they won't draft me."

"Shucks," Jediah said mildly, "they won't get many soldiers outta this country. Most of the men in the Park are flat-footed from wearin' rubber boots, or got their guts pulled loose from diggin' hay."

"I'm a good man," Tommy said, wiping his mouth on the back of his hand. "Nothing's busted loose on me yet."

"Then you'll get in the army," Jediah said, lifting a bottle. "Here's to you, Colonel!"

"Aw, go to hell!"

"Don't get too drunk, Tommy," Vic said. "Man don't play good poker when he's drunk."

Monte Maguire stood up. "I didn't come here to play poker. I came to talk about the cattle business."

A heavy silence settled over the room. Monte looked from one face to another. Some of the ranchers stared at the floor. Others went on drinking or concentrated on rolling cigarettes.

"We're on the flats with our strong cows, steers, and horses now," she went on. "We've rustled about all there is to get."

"Wasn't much to begin with," Vic said. "I kept my cattle home. Figured it wasn't worth the effort for all they'd find on the flats."

"I didn't have any choice," Monte said shortly. "But now what are you figuring on doing—watch 'em starve to death on your meadows?"

There was a murmur among the men. A south-end rancher said loudly, "We might get a chinook."

"Chinook!" Tommy Cameron laughed. "You forget you're living in the Park? Did you ever see a real chinook in this country?"

"Well," Jediah spoke up, "sometimes it does blow warm —or kinda warm for this country. Sun comes out and we get a big thaw. But I never did see a chinook like they get in other parts of the country—in Wyoming, for instance."

"That's right," Vic said. "Only place close to here that

gets bare ground in March is Wyoming. Laramie Plains will bare off in March. Snow never does stay long on the Laramie Plains."

Kelsey jumped to his feet, his face brightening. "That's it! The Laramie Plains! We'll take our cattle to the plains!"

The ranchers stared at him. One or two laughed uncertainly. Vic cleared his throat. "No trains runnin'. Did you forget that, Scotty?"

"Trains? Who said anything about trains? We'll trail the cattle over the mountain."

Several ranchers began to talk at once. There was swearing and nervous laughter.

"You talk crazy, Scotty," Vic said sharply, "and you ain't had that much to drink."

"Why is it crazy? Because it hasn't been done before?"

"It's been tried," Vic said. "A winter like this hit the Park in eighteen-ninety. In March the hay run out, and it was down to thirty-one below zero. Ranchers tried to trail cattle to Laramie. Christ, you could walk on dead cows from here to the plains!"

"I don't care what happened in eighteen-ninety," Kelsey retorted. "I'm going to try and save my cattle."

"Big talk," Tommy said. "Just like you, Kelsey Cameron. What in hell we gonna do? Freeze to death along with the cattle somewhere between here and the Laramie Plains? And how could we ever find a trail over the mountain? We can't travel the stage trail they been usin' for freight sleds. It's packed hard under the loose snow that's fallen fresh. Cattle can't straddle it; it'd wear 'em down and beat 'em to pieces. For God's sake, Kelsey, talk sense."

"He's talking sense!" Monte Maguire thumped on the table with a whisky bottle to quiet the men.

Kelsey, staring into space, saw in his mind the long line of cows stringing over the mountain to grass and safety. "We'll break a new trail," he said. "We won't follow the stage road."

"Yes!" Monte's voice rang out. "Break trail with our range horses. Let the cattle follow."

"Monte," Vic said, "you gone crazy too? Who's to find a trail over a mountain in wind and snow, huh? Maybe in a blizzard. Who's to show you the way? Who can cross that mountain and know where the hell he goes?"

Kelsey turned and looked at Jediah. The old trapper was smiling. "Jediah can go anywhere in the mountains. Jediah's been all over the mountains that circle the Park. He can do anything."

Jediah's eyes glinted. "That's a right smart compliment, son."

"Would you take us over the mountain, Jediah?"

"Why, sure. There's an old trail they cut years ago, wide enough for a big sled and wider in some places. Goes straight across the back of the mountain and drops off to the plains. You get cattle started on that trail, and it's likely they'd just follow it. Trees would hold 'em to it. Now, there's a couple of forks—cut-offs—in that trail, but I figure I can spot 'em and keep us headed in the right direction."

Vic shook his head. "Not for me. If my cattle die I yust as soon they die at home in my meadows and not on any damned mountaintop between here and the Laramie Plains."

Arguments began again. One of the ranchers finally got the floor. "I'm stayin', like Vic. It's too big a risk."

"It's a risk either way," Kelsey said. "Your cattle will die on the meadows. If we cross the mountain, we might save them."

"I'm for it," Monte Maguire said. "The plains are the closest feed. Tommy, you're goin' with us."

Tommy looked down at the table. He sucked in his cheeks and puckered his thin mouth as though he might whistle. Then his head came up, and he stared at Kelsey. There was hatred and defiance in his look. "I'll last as long as you do, kiddo—any old place, any old time."

"Good!" Monte stood up, hands thrust deep in the pockets of the worn trousers. "The sooner we start, the better—and that means tomorrow morning."

She said to Tommy, "Get that old sheep wagon we been usin' for a chuck wagon on spring shove-ups. Set the wagon box on sled runners. Tear out the built-in bunk and table at the end; it's a big sheep wagon, but we might need extra room for shelter. Take it down to the North Fork Ranch and let Prim load it with groceries. She can figure better than any of you men what oughta go and how much. That has to be done tomorrow, Tommy."

He nodded. She looked at Kelsey. "You take a wagon box at the North Fork and put it on runners. Load it with a little hay, grain, and extra bedding. Throw in a big tent—anything else you think we might need, Kelsey. We'll put a four-horse team on the sheep wagon and hook the other wagon on behind. When you get ready to go, start across the flats."

"It'll take twenty or thirty range horses to break trail," Jediah said.

"We got more than that on the flats now." Monte drew on a cigarette. "We'll need another man—at least one more man. I can't count on the cowboys. They'll be spooked when we talk about crossin' that mountain."

"Dalt will go," Kelsey said. "Dalt will try anything."

"Good. I figure Dalt's a fine man to have around any time things get tough. Well, that takes care of everything, don't it?" She looked at the ranchers. "Any of you have the same notion we have, you can start movin' cattle tomorrow. We'll go first and clear the trail."

No one spoke. Vic Lundgren poured himself another glass of whisky.

Monte put on her heavy coat and went to the door. She turned, and her eyes had a hot, bright look in them. "Vic Lundgren and the rest of you can sit on your butts till spring. We're crossin' that mountain."

CHAPTER XXVI

Heather wasn't sleepy. She lay in the back bedroom at the Plunkett ranch and listened to the house crack with the cold. It was late, but she hadn't shut her eyes; she kept fretting about the cattle, and wondering what the ranchers were saying in town. Tomorrow was Saturday and no school, but Prim had told her to stay at Plunketts'. Now she thought how easy it would be to get up and ride to the ranch and be back before any of the Plunketts were out of bed. She wanted to see Dalt, for in the past months she had found no opportunity to be alone with him. Prim and her father had seen to that.

Heather got out of bed, moving quietly in the darkness, and groped to find her clothes. Thrusting her hair under a cap, she moved out the door, carrying a sheepskin coat over her arm. On the sagging front porch she slipped into the heavy sheepskin and walked cautiously toward the barn. A dog stirred and came toward her in the starlight. She spoke its name, stroked its head, and let it smell her hands.

She saddled a horse, led it from the barn, and was about to mount when a sound stopped her. It was the unmistakable *crunch-crunch* of footsteps. She turned toward the house and saw a tall figure hurrying toward her.

"Where are you going?" Jim Plunkett's voice was harsh.

"My business."

"You don't fool me any," he said, close to her now. "You're going to see Long Dalton."

She didn't answer, trying to think of some way to persuade
Jim he was wrong. She liked Jim, and she felt embarrassed,
as though he had caught her doing something she was ashamed
of.

"You don't need to go around spying on me," she said peevishly.

"I won't tell on you. But I want you to know I'm not dumb.
I figured you'd do this."

"So you stayed awake, listening." She was angry now. "Well,
you can't stop me from going home if I want to—nobody can
stop me!"

"I'm not tryin' to, Heather. It's your funeral. But I know
what it means when a girl sneaks off in the night to meet Long
Dalton, and her folks gone, and old Hilder sleeping like a hog
in the bunkhouse."

"You make it pretty plain what you think of me, Jim
Plunkett."

"I aim to. I been crazy over you ever since you were a little
girl, but I'm not any more—not after tonight. You're not worth
it. But before you go to him, there's a few things you oughta
know. Where do you figure he's been on winter afternoons
when he said he was going coyote huntin'?"

"I know where he's been—at Jediah's cabin."

"Yeah? What a laugh Monte Maguire's got on you! Him and
her being cozy over there at the home place while you sit
around thinking about him! Hell, you're just a kid! Did you
think you could run competition to a woman like Monte
Maguire? They're two of a kind, Long Dalton and Monte
Maguire—both of 'em slick and smart. Go on up and see him
now, and when he starts lovin' you don't forget that he's had
Monte all winter, and nobody catching on—not even your
dad, smart as he is."

"It's a lie!" Heather's voice shook.

"That so? Happens I've seen him when I been out huntin'

coyotes. Happens I followed him once, and he didn't leave her till damn near daylight. What do you think they were doing over in her house by the river—talking about the weather?"

"I don't believe it!"

"Suit yourself. I'm only telling you facts. Listen, some men chase women for the hell of it, and some men chase them once in a while, but Long Dalton works at it. Let him add you to his list. Go on up to the ranch and let him make a cheap thing outta you too!"

She climbed to the saddle and kicked the horse into a lope, sending him skidding and slipping up the sled trail toward the North Fork Ranch. Jealous, that's what Jim Plunkett was, jealous because he'd kissed her once or twice and figured she was his girl. She wouldn't let herself think on what Jim had said. Besides, all those things weren't true.

The night was clear and cold. The far-off sound of the wind roaring on top of the range was like the sea and brought back blurred images of her childhood. There were voices and faces that went with that sound, but most of them had no names. For I was only four years old then, she thought. Four, the same age as—Jediah, my brother. Tears blinded her, and there was an ache in her heart. How lonely it was here between the hills. The sadness inside her began to push up and fill her mind. What did it all mean—the dim memories of years ago, the sharp longing for little Jed, on this cold winter night when the hills were so dark and not even a coyote barking at the stars?

Midway up the draw that led to the ranch the silence seemed deeper and she no longer heard the wind roaring at timberline. The stillness made her think of the morning Hilder had come for her at school when little Jed died, and how lonely it had been between these hills then—and how sad the earth at daybreak that morning. Jediah, my brother . . .

Again the sorrow was in her, curling into words in a slow, gray motion, like the mists she'd seen on the mountains. The words shaped themselves into meaning: "I sing the earth and the leaves of autumn. . . . And my brother gone down with the green still in him . . ."

Yes, that's surely how it was: Jed, a little green thing, and dying too soon, before the autumn of his living. The words went around and around in her head, drawing other words to them, rising and falling to their own cadence as she rode on.

The ranch buildings came into view, dark and silent, and the willows, black along the creek and reaching narrow fingers up the meadows. She unsaddled the horse and walked slowly to the house, not wanting to hurry, taking her time in starlight and snow, listening to the words that moved in her head.

In the house she lighted the lamp and built up the banked fire. She took off her heavy coat and cap and wandered into the pantry, putting her hands on shelves where all things were exactly in place, as Prim always kept them. It was strange, Heather thought, how Prim set these things in perfect pattern, while often Prim's mind had no order to it at all.

She padded in her stocking feet through the rooms, pausing by windows to scratch thumbnail designs on the coating of frost. In her parents' bedroom she paused. This was never a place for them to sleep, not where my father could look out the window and see the house old Flit Maguire built for Monte. Monte—Monte and Dalt.

She thought how she could go out to the bunkhouse and bend over Dalt's bed and put her hand against his cheek, and how he would waken and cover her fingers with his, pressing them closer. A warm tingling ran through her. But with it came the words in her mind again, rising large, singing their strange music, as though the thought of loving Dalt had provoked them into sharpness.

She found a stubby pencil and a sheet of lined paper and sat at the kitchen table, writing about the mountains in fall and her brother's dying. She put the words down with tears in her eyes and an ache in her heart, but when they were there on paper she began to laugh and cry at the same time, for the words stood apart from her and had a life of their own. *But I made them—I, Heather Cameron!* And she fell into astonished wondering at herself.

The kitchen door opened, and Long Dalton stood there, blinking in the light. "Chicken! You came home!"

She saw him distantly, far across the wide plain of her thinking. She smiled, and it was as though she watched herself smiling. "Make us some coffee, will you, Dalt?"

He put his hand on the back of her neck, under the dark, loose hair, then pushed the hair up and kissed the place where his hand had been. This pleased her, and she smiled again, but it seemed she stood off and looked at herself, being two people instead of one.

She forgot Dalt until she heard him go to the stove and set on the coffee pot. Then he was moving in the pantry, where Prim kept the big jar of coffee. And in that instant Heather could smell the freshly ground beans and see Prim's arm, brown and strong, moving with the hard motion of turning the grinder.

"What's that you're doing?" Dalt asked, returning to the stove. "Your lessons?"

"No. A poem. Listen!" She was nervous and read too fast, her chest tight with excitement. Then she looked anxiously at him. "You like it?"

There was a queer light in his pale brown eyes. The long lips drew back in a strained smile. "I like you."

"That's not what I'm talking about!" She shouted at him, loud in her impatience.

He came to her quickly, jerked her from the chair, and held her hard; his hands hurt her. Her breath caught, and the physical warmth of him beat over her, draining her strength until she felt limp and shaken. "No, Dalt," she said, pushing the words out. "No!"

He let her go then and stepped back, staring at her, and she saw passion and cruelty on his face. She said, half crying, "Is that how you treat Monte Maguire?"

He deliberately turned his back, taking two long steps to the cupboard to bring out cups for their coffee.

"Is it?" she asked again. And then she flew to him, pressed her face on his broad chest, putting her arms around him, clinging to him and saying, "I don't believe it—about you and Monte. Kiss me, Dalt. Put your arms around me."

"No."

"Why?"

"You're all wrapped up in that damn piece of paper and a bunch of words. You can't fool me, chicken, and, by God, don't ever try!"

She moved away from him. "Why—you're jealous! Jealous of a little thing like a poem."

"It's damned silly." He reached for the coffee pot and poured their coffee.

"What's the matter with you? Why do you hate things like poems? I've heard you talk as though even an education was a waste of time. Dalt, what makes you like that?"

He sat drinking his coffee, not answering. Silence drew out between them. The coals shifted in the stove, falling to the ash pan with a soft, shuffling sound.

"Why do you sulk?" she asked peevishly. "Why don't you say something?"

He got up and walked out. She sat staring at the table, and then, like a magnet, the sheet of paper drew her. She forgot Dalt, forgot Jim Plunkett, forgot what he had said about Monte Maguire. She forgot everything but the words she wrote, crossed out, and wrote again.

It was there at the kitchen table that Prim and Kelsey found her when they walked in at daylight. Kelsey bent over her, staring at the sheet of paper. "Read it," he said, and he sat down.

Prim moved to the stove and stood quietly, spreading her cold hands to the heat, never taking her eyes from her daughter.

The words came out in the clear lilting voice that trembled.

"I sing of the earth and my brother gone down
With the green still in him;
I sing of the leaf that has fallen before its time
And the autumn hills in mourning. . . ."

Kelsey Cameron shoved the heavy cap back and cocked his red head to one side. "Oh, my God," he said, "it's fine! It's wonderful! Read it again, lassie."

And when she had read it over and over to suit him, and he had read it as many times himself, he took off his heavy clothes and said he'd scramble them some eggs, by God. "It's a rare occasion when I cook," he added, grinning at Prim, "for, to tell the truth, I consider myself above it. Prim, look sharp and get us a white tablecloth, for we'll dine in style, the three of us."

"Orders to the scullery maid," she muttered, but she was smiling as she went to get the linen.

Kelsey worked carefully, beating the eggs until they were frothy, prowling through the pantry and examining this and that, adding a dash of nutmeg and pepper. And finally, when he had thoroughly browned the eggs, he took sweet pickles from a little round keg, cut them in neat squares, and sprinkled them on top of the eggs.

As they ate, and drank the cups of strong coffee, warm, happy silence was upon them. Then he told Heather of the trip to be made over the mountain. "I'll ask you to stay here at the ranch while I'm gone," he concluded.

"And you'll have to help Hilder cook and see he doesn't ruin the stove with grease," Prim said. "I'm going over the mountain with your father."

Kelsey stared at her. "And what would you be doing on a cattle drive, Prim Munro?"

"I can sit in the wagon and drive the team. You'll need me. The cowpunchers won't cross that mountain. Monte Maguire's right about that."

"And is this noble act on your part only a scheme to get to Laramie, so you'll be ready to sail to the old country next week?"

"Think what you like," she retorted. Then she looked at Heather and said unsteadily, "Maybe the poetry comes from the Camerons, lass, but I was the one who brought you into this world." And she got quickly to her feet and left them alone in the gray kitchen where the kerosene lamp burned a shabby yellow in the morning light.

CHAPTER XXVII

From the doorway of the chuck wagon Prim looked over the backs of the four horses into the gray afternoon. She didn't have far to drive now; at dark they would camp between the low hills up ahead. Near her were the cattle, a wavering dark line that wound around the slopes; the range horses moved before them, trampling the snow. "Got to make the neck of the Park by night," Jediah had said. "Better be startin' through that canyon tomorrow at daybreak." Then he had looked at the sagging sky that hovered over them like a great smothering paw. "No wind, Prim—be spittin' snow before long."

Above the occasional squeak of the sled runners she could hear the bawling of the cattle. Hungry, she thought, hungry and tired, and a mountain to cross. She had seen them chewing at the naked willow tops along the North Platte River; they had milled and bawled, their mouths slobbering.

Behind the group were three days of moving slowly so that the cattle could feed. They had to let the cows rustle all they could get, Kelsey said, before they reached the mountain. When they started over the mountain they would have to push the cattle, forcing the crossing in the least possible time.

Over Prim's head the canvas roof arched, stretched tight across the wooden bows, for the old sheep wagon was a small replica of the Conestogas that had crossed the plains. In a front corner of the wagon was the little black stove, with its pipe stuck through the canvas roof.

Inside the wagon were low, narrow chestlike cupboards built

309

to the floor; these were used for storage and seating space. Prim was sure there was plenty of food there—salt pork, bacon, beans, bread, coffee, sugar, and butter. Chained to the back of the sheep wagon was the tarp-covered bed wagon, containing hay, grain, wood, the big tent, and extra bedding.

Soon now, when they made camp, Dalt would fill the big coffee pot with water from one of the kegs that were near the stove, and the smell of boiling coffee would be fragrant—a high moment in the long day. She stirred, stretching a cramped leg, and saw Kelsey riding toward her. She pulled up the team when he reached her. He sat loosely in the saddle, rolling a cigarette.

"How are the cows?" she said.

"Not so bad. Hungry, but they could be worse off. We've let them take it easy, but tomorrow—" He looked at the sky. "If it snows— Maybe we should never have started this, Prim."

"We had to, didn't we? Did you get a count on the cattle?"

"There's close to two thousand—mostly Monte's, of course." He looked at her and then away. "Prim, you can still go back. I've been thinking—there's Heather, and if anything should happen she's—" His words trailed off.

"Heather will be all right," Prim said.

"Well, then, there's yourself. And if we run into trouble—"

For a moment her lips quivered. "When was trouble a stranger to me, Kelsey Cameron?"

"All right, then."

"I'm as strong a woman as Monte Maguire, and I don't see you sending her home or trying to."

"Monte's—well, she's lived an outdoor life, and she's used to hard weather."

Prim's eyes glinted. "So now I'm to be thought delicate, so I am!" And she laughed, the sound of it ringing out in the silence. She watched Kelsey ride away, big and settled in the saddle, and thought, He's like a mountain, so he is, and I wonder that I never noticed it before.

She spoke to the team, and the wagon moved on. Around
her the Park was quiet; the grayness of the day was running
into dusk. And a sense of timelessness came over her, as
though she had been here long before, in this same place, driving the same shabby-coated horses.

That night she lay in the wagon and listened for the wind,
but there was no rattling of the canvas roof, no whisper of
snow. Only the intermittent bawling of the cattle rose in the
silence and seemed to fill the world. Monte Maguire lay beside
her, wrapped in her own blankets, and Prim knew Monte also
was awake and listening for the wind. The men took turns at
night herding, coming in from time to time to drink coffee. No
one slept much.

When the cold dawn came Dalt struggled with breakfast on
the little stove and swore.

"Get outta the way," Monte said crossly. "You're burnin' the
damn bacon."

Tommy Cameron looked at Prim. "Figured you'd be the
chief cook," he said.

"I'm driving the wagon," she said. "That's my job."

While they ate, Prim looked past them through the open door
of the wagon. She saw the strip of gray sky, and beyond it
the canyon, where the trail was drifted deep with snow.

"There it is," Jediah said, smiling at her, "and the going
gets tough. We break trail through that canyon. At the far end,
to the north, there's a valley. Part of it will be badly drifted,
but we can follow the slopes where the snow ain't so deep.
After that, it's over the top."

Monte said, "Kelsey, you and Dalt start breaking trail with
the horses. Tommy, you and I and Jediah can bring the cattle.
Prim will come after us with the wagons. Let's get movin'!"

Prim watched Kelsey and Dalt ride into the canyon. Soon
the two saddle horses were floundering belly-deep in snow.
They reared and plunged and broke through the drifts. Then
Kelsey and Dalt dismounted and waded waist-deep ahead of

the horses. Slowly, foot by foot, a narrow trail was broken. Following behind, Tommy drove the range horses, which bucked and fell and rose again, widening the narrow pathway. The men came back and started the cows through the canyon. The leaders moved cautiously, sniffing the snow and bawling, some trying to turn back. After a while Kelsey took a small bundle of hay and scattered it in front of the cows, and they began to go forward, fanning out until the mass of them looked like a dark V shoving between the high white canyon walls.

Prim swung the wagon in behind the cattle, bumping slowly along the choppy trail.

It took them all that day to get through the valley north of the canyon and reach the heavy timber where the broad back of the mountain began. At dark they had left the lower slopes and were on high ground. The wind, which had not troubled them during the day, came up in the night. Prim lay huddled on the floor of the wagon, a tarp and blankets around her. She heard the wind pluck the canvas roof, heard it moan through the pines.

Kelsey's voice came from outside. Then he was in the wagon, muttering and fumbling in the darkness to light the lantern. She saw him shove the big coffee pot on the stove, poke wood in the narrow firebox. Then Jediah came in too, and Monte Maguire got up. Prim turned her face from the light and tried to sleep. She dozed and wakened to the sound of their voices.

Kelsey asked, "You think it's going to snow, Jediah?"

"Can't tell yet. Sky was heavy at dark."

"Wind's been comin' up the last two hours," Monte said. "I don't like it, Jediah."

"Nothin' to do but go on, Monte. Can't turn back now. Two or three days oughta see us on the plains."

Toward morning Prim wakened again. She sat up, startled,

for all the men had moved into the wagon. The roar of wind filled the night. The door of the wagon rattled, and a fine spume of snow was sifting across the floor. Monte Maguire was sitting by the stove, her head down on her knees, which were drawn up with her arms folded around them.

"Blew the damn tent down," Dalt muttered.

Prim threw back the bedding and got to her feet. "What is it?" she asked, shivering.

Jediah looked at her. His face was old and grave. "Blizzard," he said.

A gust of wind struck the wagon, and it rocked. From outside came the desolate and lost sound of bawling cattle. Prim's hand went to her throat. She closed her eyes. We've got to reach the plains. *Dear God, let us find bare ground.*

The men crouched on the floor near the stove. Dalt went out and brought armloads of wood from the bed wagon. Only the little space around the stove was warm.

"The trees will hold the cows up there in front of us," Jediah said. "And we're camped here at this end of the trail. Only way they can move is ahead."

"Some of 'em won't go any farther," Dalt muttered gloomily. "You're gonna see dead cows in the morning. We might as well face it."

"I told you it was crazy!" Tommy shouted, turning on Monte. "I told you it couldn't be done!"

"Nothin' crazy about it," Jediah said quietly. "I figure I can start off soon as it's light. You follow me with the range horses. We're headed in the right direction, and we're on the trail, and I reckon I can keep us that way."

"Like hell!" Tommy's voice shook. "You'll be lost in this blizzard, Jediah, lost before you get a mile from this wagon."

"Scared, Tommy?" Dalt's voice was soft.

"You're goddamned right I'm scared—and so are you!"

"Go back to the ranch, then," Monte said impatiently.

"Seems there's a lot of fuss and talk about a little wind and snow," Jediah said mildly. "Could we have some fresh coffee, Monte?"

"You betcha can, fella. I'm glad to have something to do."

Tommy grunted and moved closer to the stove, and Monte had to step over his legs. The men became silent.

After they'd finished the coffee Monte crawled close to Prim and shivered. Prim buried her face under the tarp and tried to shut out the sound of wind and cattle. It seemed a long time until morning, and when the light broke the men ate quickly and left the wagon, stumbling through the snow to their horses, which were tied to trees. Monte Maguire followed them, going to the extra teams and saddle horses that were picketed in a little pocket of pines.

When Prim got out of the wagon she stepped into a whirling mist. The wind staggered her.

"I'll hook the team," Monte said, wading through snow to her side. "Stay in the wagon. No woman belongs out in this."

"See to yourself," Prim said shortly, and she stumbled forward, grasped a tug, and made it fast to the singletree. Columns of snow went past her like tall, spinning dancers. The snow stung her face, and her hands were cold in the heavy mittens. She got back into the wagon, sat in the doorway, braced her feet below her, and shouted at the four horses. They strained forward, heads bowed, tails whipping in the wind, and the wagon began to move.

"Keep 'em humping till we catch the cattle!" Monte shouted. "We'll be right ahead of you."

She looked down at Monte. Monte's eyes were two narrowed slits, her nose like a red bulb turning purple on the end, and her face ugly with splotches of red. "Use the whip if you gotta," Monte said. Prim nodded and shoved her head down until her chin was protected by her wool scarf.

Between gusts of wind she caught glimpses of the white

corridor that stretched between the dark pines. Then the storm would close down, and she could barely see the backs of the horses. The wagon rocked from side to side, jolting her back and forth, and her breasts began to ache from the cold and the rough motion.

To the left of the horses a dark heap lay on the ground, a heap like a mound of earth spilled on the snow. And then she saw the stiff legs and the white face, the snow half-drifted over the gaunt flank. She swallowed and looked ahead, wanting to pass the dead cow quickly, wanting to pretend it wasn't there. More dark mounds came into view as the slow morning drew toward noon. She wondered how many dead cattle lay closer to the fringe of trees, beyond her narrow range of vision. And still the wagon lurched on, and still the wind blew and the snow fell, twisting and tossing.

At noon the men and Monte didn't come for food, and Prim forced the tired horses to keep moving, using the whip and shouting above the roar of wind. At length she saw a rider ahead. She stood up, clinging to the doorway of the wagon, and recognized Kelsey. He dismounted and bent over a fallen cow. He tugged at the cow and pounded her with his quirt. The cow struggled and then fell back on her side, her neck outstretched, her head thrust in a drift. A cloud of flying snow shut out the scene, and when Prim saw Kelsey again he was standing there, the quirt limp in his hand.

She pulled up beside him and shouted, "Let her go! Move the others!"

He took an uncertain step toward her. Snow clung to the whiskers on his face. His lips were blue from cold. "It's Bonnie Jean," he said. "Prim, it's Bonnie Jean!"

She got out of the wagon then and grabbed his arms and tried to shake him. "Kelsey! You're going daft! Bonnie Jean's dead—years back!"

His eyes blinked, and his big mittened hand came up to rub across them. Prim pounded at him with her fist. "Think, man!

We've got to reach the plains! You can't stand and break your heart over one cow."

He looked at her blankly. Slowly he turned away, mounted his horse, and disappeared into the swirling whiteness ahead.

At dark the riders came back, and Prim stopped the team. She sat shivering, too tired to move, too tired to think of eating. Kelsey climbed over the wagon tongue and up beside her to lift her and set her inside. She leaned against him in the darkness. "It's the end of us, the end of all of us," she said.

He shook her hard and began to unfasten her heavy coat. Monte Maguire thrust a bottle into her cold hand. "Take a drink," Monte said curtly, "a big one." The bottle was cold and slick. She coughed and gagged. "Take another," Monte said.

Prim rested against the side of the wagon while Monte lighted the kerosene lantern. In the dim light she watched Kelsey start the fire and saw how tired he was; his gray eyes were dulled with exhaustion.

She got awkwardly to her feet. "Kelsey, there's something I've got to tell you, so I have. Got to." She staggered, and he put her down on a pile of bedding in the corner. "You stay there," he said. "We'll manage. What'd you do with the bacon, Monte?"

"Damned if I know. It's there—somewhere." Monte's hair lay loose on her shoulders. She drew hard on a cigarette and looked at Prim. "Take it easy, girl," she said.

The men came in then. "Did you grain the horses?" Kelsey asked.

"Yes."

After that they said nothing, and Prim saw the whole scene sharply and yet with a sense of unreality: the wagon floor cluttered with chaps, ropes, rolled-up bedding; the men slapping hunks of cheese between thick slices of bread and standing while they ate, drinking coffee from cups that hadn't been washed. And all the time there was the wind roaring, shaking the canvas roof in small muffled explosions.

Monte brought her a sandwich, and she ate mechanically, licked her fingers clean, and crawled under the blankets, not caring that she was dirty and smelled and still wore her over-shoes. Sometime in the night she wakened briefly and knew vaguely that they all were sleeping close together. And it didn't bother her that when she burrowed her head against a shoulder she didn't know whether it was her husband's or another man's. It didn't even bother her that Monte Maguire might be close to Kelsey. Privacy no longer mattered; nothing mattered, for she was sure now they were all going to die. Again she thought, I must talk to Kelsey. I don't want to die without telling the truth.

In the morning, driving the team again, Prim thought the day moved more slowly than the one before. The mounds of dead cattle were all along the trail, a few showing dark, and others partly white, and some completely covered with snow. Ahead, when the storm lifted briefly, she saw the phantom-like shapes of the riders, and before them the dark, bobbing mass of cattle. Cows that were not too feeble chewed at the few aspen branches that waved light against the darkness of the pines; other cows floundered and fell; some got up, and some only lay, their hollowed-out flanks heaving in last great gasps of life as the wagon dragged past. And she remembered that once Kelsey had tried to tell her how it was with life and death, that both began with a gasp for breath, and how, when the new calves came, the gasp to one meant living and to another dying.

But this is only death, she thought. I can't stand it another day, so I can't. I can't look at the cows and see them dying. I can't face the wind, the cold, the snow.

The pattern went on and on, and she was a part of it, driving the horses, hoping desperately for a glimpse of clear sky. At night in the wagon she sensed a rising tension; it lurked among them all like an evil force that might spring up at the slightest provocation. Dalt had grown short-tempered. Tommy was sullen and kept licking his lips and talking about the dwindling food supply. Monte was cross, her eyes sunk back in her head. Kelsey said nothing, but kept to himself and brooded. Only Jediah seemed natural.

Dalt started supper, fumbling with the stove, slamming a thin end of salt pork on a board and slicing it with a butcher knife.

"Like to know where we are," Tommy muttered. "I coulda sworn I saw the same bunch of fallen timber I passed yesterday."

No one answered. Kelsey went on rolling a cigarette. Jediah looked straight ahead, staring at nothing. Dalt examined the thin strips of salt pork. Monte worked at trying to get a comb through her tangled hair. Prim felt a tightness in her throat.

"You're lost, Jediah!" Tommy's words came out loud in the wind-rocked wagon.

Jediah turned his head and looked calmly at Tommy. "Reckon I am," he said quietly. "But I been lost before and always found myself again. Took the wrong turn back there a ways, I figure, but I'll come back to the trail. I know which way we're movin' now, and we're likely to end up on the trail again. Worst is behind us, anyhow, and if we don't find the trail we're bound to drop off to the plains soon."

Tommy began to laugh. It was a hoarse, broken sound that sent goose pimples up the back of Prim's neck.

Dalt said, "Well, there it is—one slice of salt pork apiece. We got to go easy on this grub. Storm's held us up. We've got no grain left for the horses, and what hay's in the bed wagon wouldn't make a bird's nest."

"I used all the hay," Kelsey said. "Had to. Cows got so they wouldn't move any farther. I gathered what there was and strung it along in front of them to keep them on their feet."

Dalt turned to Tommy. "Don't snitch on the grub, Cameron. You're always stuffin' yourself."

Tommy got to his feet, his face flushed and strange. "God damn it, leave me alone! I'm fed up with you and the whole deal. I've had enough! I'm riding for a ranch. To hell with this!"

"Stick another day, Tommy," Kelsey said quietly. "Tomorrow we might see the plains."

"See the plains! Christ a'mighty, Kelsey, don't try to stuff that down my throat! We're lost! Jediah can't lead us any farther. I'm startin' on my own. I'm findin' a ranch—a decent bed and food. I'm not gonna—gonna die in this asshole of creation for a bunch of cows!"

"Let him go, Kelsey," Dalt said, his eyes ugly in his whiskered face. "I always knew he'd run when the going got rough. I always knew the yellow was in him."

Tommy grabbed a stick of wood and hurled it savagely at Dalt. Dalt ducked, and the wood struck against the canvas wall. Kelsey moved between them, one hand shoving Dalt back and the other grasping the front of Tommy's shirt. "Cut it out," he said.

Prim lay on the bedding and watched the men with an odd sense of detachment. Her eyelids drooped wearily. Let them fight. Who cared? She heard their voices raised again, and then Tommy shouting, "We've lost over half the cows now, and the rest will never see grass. I've spent my last night in this damned stinking wagon! Get up, Monte! We're riding!"

"Way below zero out there," Kelsey said in a level tone. "Do you want to freeze to death?"

"Tommy." Jediah spoke curtly. "You can't find a ranch. They're a long way from here. Closest one is at the edge of the plains, and you'd be lost before you got twenty feet from this wagon."

Monte Maguire spoke, her voice thin and strange.

"Tommy, you can't quit now. You can't let the cattle go, not after what we've all been through. You can't run out on your friends. Jediah will lead us off the mountain. I know he will."

Tommy took a step toward her, his face twisting. "Monte! You're comin' with me. You gotta come with me!"

"Don't be a damn fool. Nobody's leaving this wagon." Kelsey's words were cold and steady.

Tommy swung around then, his hand darting behind him to grab the butcher knife that lay by the slices of salt pork. "You ain't gonna have her, Kelsey! I had her first—before you ever come to the damned country. Why do you think I stuck in that snow-hole all my life? I'll tell you! Waitin' for her to come around, to be to me what she once was. Who got my first bunch of cows? She did! Who got my homestead? She did! And, by God, I'm takin' her with me now. Not one of you bastards will ever reach the plains. But I'm not gonna die, and she's not, either. You got a wife, you son-of-a-bitch! Get outta my way!" He lunged at Kelsey with the butcher knife.

Monte Maguire screamed. Prim stared in horror, and in that instant Dalt threw himself between the two men. She saw him leap on Tommy, his arm sweeping up and the smaller knife gleaming in the yellow lantern light. They went down together, crashing on the floor, and then there was a hollow clatter as the big butcher knife struck the edge of the stove leg. Over and over they rolled, and came to rest against the woodbox. She heard grunting animal sounds— the rasp of breath, the strange gurgling. And then Dalt was rising slowly, the small knife still in his hand, the blood dripping, and behind him, on the floor, a small thump, a rustle —then silence.

Jediah took hold of Monte Maguire's shoulders and swung her around to face the wall. "Don't look, honey." He came to Prim and lifted her in his arms. "Lean against me and get hold of yourself, Prim." She felt his hard old arms pulling her tight to his chest, heard the quickness of his breathing against her ear. "You men see to him. Quick!"

Prim's legs shook violently. Her stomach cringed. She heard Monte Maguire sobbing, and then Kelsey's voice, flat and empty. "He's dead, Jediah."

"Oh, Jesus!" It was Dalt who spoke, his voice shaking.

"Calm down, Dalt!" Jediah said. "Get a tight rein on yourself. Nobody's gonna blame you. He'd killed Kelsey and maybe the rest of us. Plumb outta his head, he was. I seen it comin' a coupla days ago. Now take care of things, you men. Put him in the bed wagon and cover him with a tarp. When we reach the plains we'll take him on into Laramie. And I want that floor cleaned. If there's any whisky left, bring it here. Now!"

Jediah left Prim and went to Monte Maguire. Prim had her hands over her face, and when she looked between her fingers she saw that Monte had her head down and was still sobbing. On the other side of the wagon, she heard the thump and thud of the body being moved. She closed her eyes tight and felt the rush of cold air from the opened door.

"Now," Jediah said to Monte, "you just sit here on the bedroll beside me. That's it. Rest your back against me, honey. Sit easy and drink this whisky. I'll hold the bottle. You just drink. There. Mighty terrible thing when a man gets his throat cut. Mighty rough thing to happen, but no way to prevent it tonight. We won't talk about it again, but it's always best to say it out and have done with it."

Prim got up, shaking and sick. She moved slowly to the water keg, found a kettle, and drew water. After taking a blackened dishtowel from the storage space, she began to clean the floor. Jediah's voice went on, talking soothingly between Monte's muffled sobs. "Now Monte, you pull yourself together. You're here, and we need you. You hang on tight."

"My fault," Monte said. "If I hadn't been the way I was —back there when I didn't care for nothing or nobody— maybe it wouldn't have happened."

"Can't look back," Jediah said. "And it would have happened. A crazy man don't need no excuses for tryin' to kill. Drink some more whisky, honey. Won't hurt you."

The men came back into the wagon, and Kelsey knelt to take the wet rag from Prim's hand. "I'll finish it." He rubbed at the floor. "Prim, go and rest."

"I can't. Kelsey, I want to tell you something." She stood up in the wagon, twisting her hands, the big sheepskin coat hanging clumsily about her. "Kelsey, when I went on about my people, how fine they were—" Her breath caught and she started to cry. "I knew they weren't! I knew what my mother was, so I did, and me—just common, like Crowter the rag-buyer. But you, you Camerons were different, and I —I tried to hide it, to hide the way I felt inside me, so I did."

"Prim—" Kelsey got up from the floor. "Don't try to talk now, Prim. It's all right. You don't have to tell yourself all this now—or me, either."

Prim pressed her doubled fist into her mouth. "I was afraid —always afraid you wouldn't really want me or love me. And Heather—I used her to get you, Kelsey. Yes, I did!" She turned and looked at Monte Maguire, who had stopped sobbing and was staring at her. "I'm worse than you, Monte Maguire. You don't know how much worse."

"Prim." Jediah was urging her toward the bedroll. "Stop thinkin' about yourself. Here. Rest and let me talk to you."

She sank onto the bedroll, and he took her hand and held it in his. "I never sat in no church, Prim, and I guess I only tried to pray once—that was the night your little boy died. But I come close to prayin' today. Wasn't askin' anythin' for myself—I'm old and had a fine time livin'. But I was thinkin' of you and Kelsey, of Dalt and Monte—all of you, with the good years to come. I was thinkin' there was a way to get you off this mountain. I don't rightly know what God is, Prim, but I'm mighty sure the hills and creeks couldn't have come into being without somebody behind 'em—somebody a heap smarter than Jediah Walsh. I've got no ax to grind with Him; I count it a favor to have been around this old world long as I have, and whatever's to come after, I won't worry about. But tomorrow—tomorrow I'd like to get straight with myself again so I won't be fumblin' like a blind bear, not knowing east from west. We need to pray, Prim. You think on that. It ain't hard for me to be humble, and I never felt more that way than I do right now. I think maybe you and Monte feel the same way—Dalt and Kelsey too."

Jediah paused. The wind came up in the trees with a long whimpering. "When it comes to a time like this," Jediah said slowly, "we all think about our mistakes—sin, some people call it. Maybe we can't forgive ourselves, for there's things we gotta live with as long as breath's in us, but we can forgive each other. You pray, Prim. Pray for all of us the way you learned to do it back there in your own country."

She put out her free hand and took hold of Kelsey's and bowed her head.

*   *

"You gotta get up, Prim," Jediah said. It was morning again.

She saw that his bloodshot eyes were anxious as he bent over her. She sat up and ran her hands through her hair, which fell in a loose, tangled mass. Then she saw Monte and Kelsey and Dalt. They were grave and quiet, standing there in front of the little stove, where a mist of steam rose from the coffee pot. In the morning light their faces looked haggard and old.

Her glance shifted to the floor by the woodbox. The stain still showed. Dalt said, "Coffee's weak but hot. And there's a piece of bread I toasted for you."

She got to her feet. She grabbed the bread and stuffed it into her mouth, gulping it down. Then she felt sudden shame. "Like an animal, so I am!"

"Don't need to be ashamed of being hungry," Dalt said.

"Come take a look at the weather, honey." Jediah put his arm around her. "Maybe I'm crazy, but I don't think it's snowin' as much as it was yesterday."

She felt weak, and her thinking was fuzzy. The sky looked just the same. But she put her hand in his and said, "You'll take us off this mountain, Jediah."

Monte Maguire smiled at her. "That's what I like to hear."

Later that morning Prim sat grimly in the doorway of the wagon, holding tight to the lines. The trail stretched before her. She tried to see far ahead, tried to look beyond the dead cows that marked the way the herd had gone, cows she had to drive around and sometimes over, the wagon rising and then falling back with a bump. She felt drained of everything but the bitter need to keep moving on, on to where the blue sky would show and the ground be bare under the sun. On either side the pines looked as though they had been dipped in a thick white frosting and set up like decorations along the way.

Before noon the snow stopped and the wind slackened, coming in slow gusts to shower snow from the trees. She kept staring ahead for a glimpse of the riders, but the trail wound on and on.

It was in the afternoon that she started down a hill and came to a little point where the land dropped sharply. Before her the trail wound down and down, following the curve of the hill. And suddenly she stared, unbelieving, for a shaft of sun had touched the backs of the horses. She raised her throbbing head and saw the rifted clouds and the river of blue sky running between.

She drove on, her eyes looking hungrily to the east, and at length the hills opened and she saw the flat land stretching into distance. A little cry broke from her throat, for the land was brown, brown and warm under the sun.

She held the lines hard now, leaning forward, her lips parted, driving the wagon down and down. And when the first splotch of bared ground showed on the slope above the trail she stopped the horses and got out. She pulled off her heavy cap and threw it down, and walked unsteadily to the brown bank that was dark-creased where small trickles of moisture ran from the melting snowdrift above. With a great sigh she leaned against the bank, her arms outspread, digging her fingers into the dirt. The bank was higher than her head, and she pressed her cheek hard to the earth. Then she began to cry.

She didn't hear the rider come up the trail. She didn't know Kelsey was there until his hands touched her shoulders. "I came back to tell you—" He turned her around and lifted her face toward him.

"Kelsey—"

Carefully he wiped away the dirt and tears. He smoothed her hair. "It's all right now," he said. "You mustn't cry. We did our best, and it's all right." He took her chapped, dirt-lined hands in his, looked at them, and lifted one to press it against his cheek. "You were brave, Prim. You were strong," he murmured.

"The cattle—" Her mouth trembled. "We didn't save many, did we?"

He led her forward and around the shoulder of the hill to where Dalt and Monte and Jediah sat on their horses. "Look," he said.

Below them she saw the cows moving slowly toward the long brown grass that bowed and bowed in the steady east-blowing wind. A mist was over her eyes.

"We saved some—not many, but some."

"Enough to start over in the spring," Monte Maguire said, looking down at her. "We'll split them, Prim—half for me, and half for you and Kelsey."

Prim's throat felt dry and hurting. She shook her head. "I— Kelsey, there's something I must tell you."

"Save it," he said. He turned back up the trail, and while she waited he brought his horse and boosted her into the saddle and climbed up behind her. "Dalt will bring the wagons," he said.

She kept staring down at the brown earth. She felt the strength of his shoulder there like a mountain at her back.

He said, "I guess you can still make that boat to the old country."

She wet her lips. "Not now. I won't let you go back alone to start over. Maybe in the fall, after the hay's up—maybe I'll go then, but not now. And I want to see Heather again. I have to see her, so I do."

CHAPTER XXVIII

There was water everywhere, Kelsey thought, riding in from the meadow on a warm June evening. Creeks were out of their beds, flooding the bottomlands; water glistened on the flats, for every natural hollow of the earth had become a reservoir. And the peaks were still shining and white, promising more water to come. No Park rancher would run short of water this irrigating season. And he thought how ironic it was that in haying time the ranchers would put up more feed than ever before, but there wouldn't be cattle to eat it. All over the big valley were the dead cows; the new grass grew lushly around the rotting carcasses.

Mosquitoes rose around him in silvery clouds, their sound like the humming of thousands of tiny motors. They were on his face and his ears, and the black horse was gray with them. He rubbed them from his wrists, and his skin was covered with blood. Damned pests! He kicked the horse into a lope, splashing through the water that flooded the meadow.

When he reached the corral he was surprised to see Dalt waiting for him. Dalt had gone to town for rock salt and groceries, and Kelsey hadn't expected him home so soon. He'd figured a few days in town would do Dalt good, for Dalt had stayed close to the ranch after the business about killing Tommy had been settled in the Laramie court. No one had blamed Dalt, and the whole thing had been taken care of quickly and easily with Monte, Jediah, Prim, and himself

327

to serve as witnesses on Dalt's behalf. There was no reason why Dalt should want to stay away from people; the killing was a thing he must face and live down.

"You ought to have hung around town and got wet up, fella," Kelsey said as he unsaddled and turned the horse into the pasture.

"Kelsey—" Dalt cleared his throat and looked away.

"Yes?"

"I've had an offer to move on—to a foreman's job. I'm gonna take it."

For a moment Kelsey was too surprised to speak. Dalt leaving him? Going to work for someone else? And he thought how close they had been since the cattle drive. The ranch wouldn't seem the same without Dalt.

"A man oughta move up in the world if he gets the chance," Dalt went on, still not looking at him. "And chances won't come my way very often."

Impulsively Kelsey put his hand on Dalt's shoulder. "I'm glad for you. Even when I hate to see you go I'm glad, Dalt." And then he wondered curiously who could afford to hire a new foreman with times so hard and money so scarce in the Park. "Who you going to work for, Dalt?"

And then Dalt looked at him, the pale brown eyes glinting to brilliance. "For Monte," he said.

"Monte!" Kelsey stared at him.

"I'm taking over as foreman of the Red Hill Ranch."

A surge of wild emotions swept over Kelsey. "Why, damn her! Hiring you from under my nose—not even talking it over with me! She's got her guts!"

"I worked for her before I worked for you, Kelsey. I told her last winter if a chance came up for me to get ahead I'd take it. Don't blame her. I put the notion in her head. And she needs me on the Red Hill. Hired men been runnin' the place ever since we crossed the mountain, and things are fallin' to pieces."

"Things looked fine to me when I was there last week. Water was spread evenly on the meadows, fences were in good shape, barns were clean—"

"Haying time's comin'," Dalt cut in sharply, "and a ranch needs a boss to get things lined out."

Kelsey clenched his hands to stop their trembling. Was Dalt leaving because he really wanted to get ahead in the world, or because he had fallen in love with Monte? Or had all this something to do with Heather and the fact that she was going away to college in September and Dalt wouldn't see her around when winter came? He tried to reason with himself, to realize that Dalt had a right to work for Monte, no matter what lay behind his accepting the job, but the anger was too strong. "She could have talked it over with me," he said harshly. "She didn't have to sneak around behind my back."

"I told her I was planning on leaving," Dalt said. "I let her know I wanted another job. Look, Kelsey, we've known each other a long time. Let's not part with hard feelings."

"Do as you please. It's nothing to me." Kelsey started away.

"Just a minute, Cameron." Dalt's voice stopped him. Dalt's eyes were cold, and the thin, familiar smile was on his lips. "You can't have everything, Cameron—your wife, your daughter, and Monte Maguire."

"What do you mean?" And Kelsey felt a stab of jealousy, thinking of Dalt and Monte together, talking ranch business, riding through the cattle.

"How long do you figure you've got a right to go on fillin' her life, Cameron, and givin' her nothin'? You want her to keep eatin' her heart out over you until she's an old woman?"

Kelsey took a step toward Dalt, his fists clenched. "I could go to her tonight, and you wouldn't matter at all."

"You're takin' a lot for granted. And you won't go to her —at least, not now."

"And," Kelsey went on, confused and angry, "you and Heather—"

Dalt's laughter was brittle. "You gonna throw out your daughter as bait to keep me from shinin' up to Monte?"

"No, damn you! Get your stuff packed, and I'll write your time." And then he saw pity in Dalt's eyes and he was suddenly ashamed. "Dalt, we're talking crazy. I'm sorry." And he walked quickly toward the house, thinking painfully, A man like Dalt couldn't really matter to Monte—or could he? And what right have I to care if she should someday love him? And he thought of Prim, who had said she would stick with him until haying was over and Heather off to school. Then Prim would go back to Scotland as she had wanted to go in March. And if Prim left him . . .

He went into the kitchen, hurrying past Prim and Heather to take his time book from its place on the shelf. He sat down at the kitchen table and began to figure how much he owed Dalt, working fast, trying to shut away Monte's face, which came between him and his work.

"What's wrong?" Prim said. "You look sick, Kelsey."

"Dalt's quit." He looked up and saw Heather standing behind Prim, and Heather's face began to crumple. In a moment she would be crying.

"He's going to run the Red Hill for Monte," Kelsey added.

Prim nodded her head. "That's good. He deserves a better job than what he's had all these years. He'll make a fine foreman."

Heather made a broken sound in her throat. She came to the table and stared at Kelsey. "That woman! I hate her! I've always hated her. Does she have to put her spell on both of you?"

"Heather! That's enough!"

"Don't lie to me. You've always been in love with her, and now Dalt—"

Kelsey jumped up and grabbed Heather's shoulders, shaking her. "Stop it! You'll keep your wild notions to yourself, Heather Cameron."

"Leave the lassie alone," Prim said calmly. "Step back from her and cool off or I'll put a pitcher of cold water over your head. Now, Heather, you get the table set and stop making a show of yourself."

But Heather darted past her and ran from the house toward the barn.

*   *

In the twilight Heather rode the top of the hogback, seeing below her on one side the meadows and buildings of the North Fork Ranch, and on the other side, to the north, the Red Hill. In her mind rose the picture of Dalt now in the Red Hill house, sitting at the table where she had sat beside him as a child. And a flood of memories washed over her— Dalt tugging her hair on a cold morning, Dalt boosting her onto Chinook's broad back, Dalt washing her face at the soda spring and telling her about the lightning.

An aching sadness filled her. She could see dusk creeping in across the Park, and far out on the flats the twinkle of the lights of town. She didn't understand Dalt—and she didn't understand her parents. A great loneliness swept over her. Surely Dalt had never really loved her, or he wouldn't be going to Monte Maguire's ranch and leaving her father. She thought of Jim Plunkett's words and pounded her fist against the saddle. "Cheap, cheap! How could he have done that? Ugly and cheap and easy—and me believing in him!"

Her words sounded small and foolish in the still night air. She rode on toward the north, bowing her head, letting the horse choose its own way of going. And her father— Didn't he ever love my mother? Did he marry her only because of me—stay with her years and years when he wanted Monte Maguire? Is all this my fault?

She began to cry softly, rocking back and forth with the

motion of the horse. But I love them both, my mother and
my father. I love them so it's terrible . . .

It was very dark when she pulled the horse to a stop and
saw the light in the Red Hill house directly below her. And
the need to see Dalt rose strong in her. She went down the
slope and past the soda spring and the bunkhouse. When she
saw Monte Maguire's car parked outside the buck fence that
surrounded the yard she hesitated for a moment, and then
dismounted and walked boldly toward the house, her heart
thumping. She pushed open the kitchen door without knock-
ing and saw them sitting close together at the table, a sheet
of paper before them.

It was Monte who spoke first. "Come on in, Heather."

Dalt got awkwardly to his feet. "What is it, chicken?" His
voice was gentle but strained.

Heather looked at Monte's strong brown hand holding the
stubby pencil, and she thought with childish passion, Someday her hair won't have such a shine to it. Someday she'll
be old and ugly. And if he ever does try to love her, maybe
he'll remember the mountain the way he said he always
would, and she won't be anything that could really matter
to him—

Monte's voice was soft. "Heather, dear, there's nothing to
worry about. Everything's going to be fine. You're going away
to school—new friends, new experiences—and it's best that
way."

She stared at Monte, hating her, and yet feeling awkward
and small before the kindness in Monte's eyes. How could a
woman so wicked look at you as though she loved you?

Heather looked at Dalt, and his face was grave. "You go
on home, honey," he said. "Your folks will be worryin' about
you."

She wanted to cry out, What do you think I am—a child?
But she could only stand before them, wishing now she
hadn't come, feeling no defense against their age and their

wisdom that reduced her to dumbness and embarrassment.

At last she managed to say, her voice too high and breaking, "Dalt, I won't ever come to see you again. And I'm going away—in September. If you—if there's anything you have to say to me, you'll have to come and say it." She turned and stepped blindly into the night.

A sliver of moon came over the east range of the Park as she rode toward home. The sound of the horse's hoofs was hard and rhythmic on the packed dirt road that ran along the base of the hogback. September, September—the words echoed in her head. Maybe Dalt would come then to tell her there wasn't anything, and never could be, between him and Monte Maguire.

CHAPTER XXIX

On a September morning Prim had been up since three o'clock. She had scrubbed the kitchen floor, and when Kelsey came in to ask what she was doing her face twisted and tears began to pour down her cheeks.

"The lassie isn't going forever," he said. "It's only to college, that's all. She'll be back."

"It won't be the same," Prim said, wiping her eyes on her apron. "She belonged to us, but now she'll belong to herself. And when she comes back it'll only be for a little while. We —we've lost her."

"Stop that blubbering, Prim! Get up off the floor and make us some coffee. Are you going to send the lassie off on a sour note? Her heart aches enough, with Dalt not coming down to say good-by to her."

"And it's just as well he stayed at the Red Hill. Oh, he was crazy about her. I knew it all the time, and only the good Lord has protected her from him."

"You might give Dalt some of the credit," Kelsey said. "And will you please stop crying, Prim?"

"But when I think of her—a wee thing at my breast, and her eyes first opening to look at me!"

"My God, the dramatics again!"

"To hell with you, Kelsey Cameron—double to hell with you!"

He stared at her. The wet skirt clung to her plump middle, slapped like a piece of paper across the round hill of her belly. Her sturdy legs were braced wide apart. Her arms were muscled and deeply tanned. Her black hair was twisted tight, pulled back from her face until it tugged at the corners of her eyes.

"Like a damn chinky," he said.

"What?"

"You look like a Chinaman with your hair about to be pulled from the roots."

"Well, I'm clean. I've no stain of gravy on the front of me like you. And I take a bath before I get to stinking. If I didn't get after you your clothes would rot and fall off, so they would."

He was amused and grinned. "But my soul's that pure it's like a lily, and my disposition so sweet folk flock around me."

She threw up her hands. "Oh, yes! They hover around you like flies at a dish of honey. It's all right to have a harsh word for Prim, the old workhorse, but for the outside world —oh, my, sweety-sweety in the mouth! And the big smile spread all over you, and your chest out like a great crowing rooster." Prim thrust out her full bosom and pounded it with both fists. "He says, 'My daughter is going to study poetry and music. My daughter is going to college.'" She glared at him, putting both hands on her plump hips. "Your daughter —shit!"

He burst into laughter. "Your tongue, Prim! Think shame of yourself!"

There was a rush of steps, and they turned as Heather came into the kitchen. Prim's face became tender. "Well, honey, you didn't have to get up so early."

Kelsey made her an exaggerated bow. "Good morning, sweetheart, and a lovely morning it is."

She kissed them and went to the window for a long look at the land.

"Set the table, old mealy-mouth," Prim said to Kelsey.

"Did you want us eating before the hired men are out of bed?"

"Maybe I'd like to sit down with my daughter one morning of my life without hired men looking down my throat." She turned to Heather. "Wouldn't you like to wear my pearls, honey?"

"No, no, Mother. I don't want your pearls. You keep them."

"A fine way your mother treats the pearls I gave her," Kelsey said. "Wants to give them away the first chance she gets. Damned if I'm going to spend any money on her from this day on."

"And you know why I got the pearls, Heather? This summer, when we had to be close with our money, he goes over town and sits in a poker game. Then he comes home when the sun's up and has to give me something to pacify me. Some gift, so it was!"

Heather smiled at her father. A wink passed between them. Then Prim said, sudden tears in her eyes, "Oh, I know what goes on between you two. You've always loved him best."

"Mother—" Heather went to Prim quickly and put her hand awkwardly on her mother's shoulder. "Mother, don't ever say that again."

Prim's face quivered. "It's the truth—the truth!" And a great gush of tears spilled over her face. She wiped them away on her broad arm. "Oh, hell! Not a stick of wood in the woodbox. Can you go to the woodpile, Kelsey Cameron, or is it beneath you?"

"It's beneath me," he said.

"My God, you fancy yourself!" And she swept past him and past Heather, threw open the door, banged it after her, and returned with an armload of wood. "Thank the Lord I'm not that helpless that I'm afraid to bend myself down to get a stick of wood."

"You've the shape for it," Kelsey said. "For the bending,

I mean. Did you notice, Heather, how her south end pointed north—like a new hill up against the morning sky?"

"Shut up!" Prim banged the big skillet on the stove.

"Her mood's foul this morning, Heather. Be thankful you're going where it's peaceful and quiet, and no loud voice ringing in your ears from morning until night."

"But I'll miss it," Heather said gently. "I'll wish to hear it."

Prim nodded, her chin quivering as she turned the frying bacon.

They sat down to breakfast. Prim had thought it would be a time when they had lots to say to one another, but silence came over them, and after a while Kelsey said loudly, "Why do we act like it's a bloody funeral?"

Heather left the table, and they could hear her moving in her bedroom, closing drawers and opening the closet. Kelsey looked at his big watch. "Well," he said, "I'll get the lass to town in time to catch the stage. You're sure she's got everything she needs?"

"A fine time to think of that now! Could I buy her clothes out here, miles from everything, and nothing around me but cows and hired men waiting to be fed?"

"Well, I just wondered. I wouldn't want her to feel strange —her dresses not right, or—"

"And have I been sitting with my hands folded all summer and not seeing to her needs? Use your head, Kelsey Cameron!" She picked up a clean dishtowel and spread it over the sugar and cream and butter in the center of the table, protecting them from dust until the hired men came for breakfast. "Now you help her get her stuff to the car."

Kelsey looked down at the floor. "You do it, Prim."

"Are you helpless?"

"Prim, I'd rather have you."

"And who'll feed the men if they come in?"

"I will." He walked to the window and stared at the mountains. The thought of carrying the new suitcases from the small bedroom to the car was almost unbearable. He heard the hard click of Prim's heels as she left the kitchen. Prim would take care of it; Prim could take care of anything.

The men came in. The new man, Shorty, took the milk pails and went to the barn. Hilder stood with his back to the stove. He's getting old, Kelsey thought, old like Jediah. Jediah would never be quite the same again, for the trip over the mountain had taken something out of him. And now Hilder was stooped, and his hands were unsteady, making the cigarette. Was this the same man, strong and ruddy-faced, that Kelsey had known on the Red Hill so many years ago?

"Fine mornin', huh?" Hilder paused and licked the cigarette paper. "Hell of a fine mornin'. Where's the missus?"

"Helping Heather get her suitcases ready."

"Maybe I cook breakfast for me and Shorty, eh?"

"For God's sake, don't spill any grease on that stove, Hilder."

"This mornin' the missus won't mind no grease. Maybe I spill it on purpose, give her something to think about. Ya, I think I do that." And, whistling, Hilder shoved the frying pan into place. "I make pancakes for me and Shorty. You eaten?"

"Prim's been up all night. So help me, I don't think she shut her eyes."

Hilder mixed pancakes, scattering flour in clouds, using extra eggs. When Prim came back to the kitchen the men were eating. She looked around and said, "What a mess! Flour everywhere! The stove smoking with grease!" And she ran to lift an old rag and polish the stove.

"Good for you," Hilder murmured. "Always a woman with too much energies."

Kelsey stood up and began pacing. "Well, it's time we started. Stage leaves at eight, and we could have a flat tire. Aren't you going to change your clothes, Prim?"

She turned then, the stove rag still in her hand. Her mouth

drew into a tight line. "No. You take her to town. I'll stay here."

"You don't want to go?"

"No, Kelsey."

Hilder looked up as Heather came into the room. "Well, Heather-girl! You are fancy dressed, eh?"

She was wearing a neat gray suit, a little red hat, and carrying new gloves. "Morning, Hilder." She smiled at him.

"You don't look like my little girl who used to ride horses and fish and trap. You look city-like and grown up." There was a sad gentleness in his tone. "Jesus Christ, honey, you ain't a little girl any more." He reached in his pocket and pulled out a crumpled bill. "Here's ten dollars. Buy yourself something nice for college, something make you look pretty, huh?"

"Hilder—" Her gray eyes had the misty look. She leaned forward, caught his head in her hands, and kissed him. He left the kitchen.

"I put in the suitcases. You better be going." Prim did not look at them when she spoke.

"Mother—" Heather stood, holding a shiny red purse against her heart.

"Well, let's not stand around all day," Kelsey said gruffly.

Prim straightened. She walked to her daughter, put her rough red hands on the slim shoulders, and looked into Heather's eyes. "Good-by, honey. Write us sometimes."

"I love you." Heather kissed her.

Kelsey held open the door, and Heather brushed past him. He saw her fumble for her handkerchief, and he closed the kitchen door softly, knowing that behind it Prim would sink weeping into the old rocker by the kitchen stove. And he swallowed the lump in his throat, opened the car door for Heather, and said lightly, "Hop in, m'lady."

They didn't say much on the way to town. When they spoke, the words were ones they might have spoken any day in the past years. "Cattle look good this fall. Creek's runnin' low."

"Yes, the way it always does in fall."

"See Sam Ellis has those little doodles of stacks again. Meadow looks like it was covered with pimples."

As the land flowed past and the car chugged slowly toward town, the fresh morning wind blew over them. Kelsey noted the land with a sharpness that had become a habit; there was a ditch that needed cleaning, a fence that would fall with the first weight of winter snow, a cow that was roughly marked, a bunch of goldenrod where there had been only a few stalks before. A rider waved from a meadow as he rode through the white-faced cattle. Cattle were scarce in the Park this year; many ranchers had gone broke, and the carcasses of dead cows were still heaped in the willows, a bleak reminder of the winter.

The town was quiet. Faun Gentry was just opening his store, and shouted at them as they drove down to the hotel that had once belonged to the Possers. The stage was waiting. A few passengers had gone aboard, and the driver was settling their suitcases. Not like the one I came into the Park on, Kelsey thought, remembering the rough spring wagon and all his bones aching.

He got out of the car and carried Heather's suitcases to the stage. "Morning, Charlie," he said to the driver. "How's tricks this morning?"

"So-so, Kelsey. See you brought a good-looker to ride up front with me."

Time was going too quickly now; it was running away from Kelsey while his heart ached to stop it, to hold Heather there beside him a little longer. She took hold of his hand, pressing a paper into it. "A poem—for you and Mother." His fingers closed over it, thrusting it deep in his pocket. He looked at his daughter, and it was like looking into the eyes of Taraleean. And from across the years he heard his mother's voice, warm and deep: "Make a beautiful thing of it, lad. A mistake can be a beautiful thing. . . ."

"Well, lassie—" His voice broke, for all the fine good-bys he had intended to say to her were gone. He was awkward and hurting. He blinked, staring at her with fierce pride. She *was* a beautiful thing, his and Prim's. They had built a life to make right a mistake, and they had done a good job. Now it was over; Heather stood apart from them, clean and strong, and all her life before her.

"Ta-ta," she whispered, pressing close to him. Her mouth touched his cheek, and her hand gripped hard to his. Then she was moving away. She was climbing into the stage. Her legs were slim and lovely, and one day a man would look at them and have the thoughts that men have. Kelsey resented that man, whoever he was, wherever he might be. He hated him. The sky and the earth ran together as though in a great wash of rain. But he lifted his hand in a gay salute as the stage moved away and dust rose behind it, and the face of his daughter was gone.

Kelsey turned slowly back to his car. A dog stirred and yawned in front of the drugstore. Somewhere up the street a door slammed. He got in the car and sat for a moment, trying to ease the sense of loss that filled him. The years of his living rushed over him in memories bitter and bright, and it seemed to him then that all his days had been a hard journey toward some distant green where all things were good. He brought his big hand up and drew it across his eyes.

His glance shifted to Bill Dirk's saloon, where the door stood open, letting in the morning air. A shabby gray cat rubbed against the doorjamb. He could go in and drink with Dirk, and in a little while they would be loud and laughing, and nothing in him hurting. Then he remembered the crumpled piece of paper in his pocket. A poem, God bless her! Well, he wouldn't read that with a head foggy from drink.

He'd take it somewhere on the prairie where it was quiet and nobody around to bother him. Then there flashed in his mind the picture of Prim weeping in the lonely ranch house, and he knew he would not open the paper until he could share it with her.

The car bounced along the narrow prairie road. When he dipped into the valley where the Platte moved north, he saw Vic Lundgren out riding through his lower pasture, stopped the car, and shouted, "Hey, Vic!"

Vic rode over and lounged in the saddle, rolling a cigarette. "You got the girl off, yup, yup. How you think my cows look? Ain't many left. I sell out one day. You and Monte did best. The rest of us was hurt more. You and Monte are the ones who'll come out."

Kelsey squinted at a cow, shading his eyes against the sun. "You'll come too, if all your cattle are like that one."

Vic shrugged. "Cattle don't mean much to me any more. I like this country when it was young, like you see it when you first come, Scotty. I like cow business like it was then. The old days, they go." His eyes were sad. "You grow with it, Kelsey. You understand the changes, but not me, not Vic Lundgren. I leave it when I find a buyer."

"This is your country, Vic."

"No. I'm getting old. It's a young man's country—always was and always will be. And you grow with it. One day you have lots of cows and own the North Fork Ranch. One day you have plenty money. Then she is not so much fun, the livin'. You wish to God you had less cows and was a young man startin' over when anything can happen."

Kelsey wanted to get away from Vic now. The droning voice disturbed him. The emptiness in Vic's eyes made him uneasy. "So long, Vic."

When he reached home he got out of the car and stood for a moment, listening to the sound of the river. He thought of how it was in spring—the beaver swimming, and the fine mist of rain against his cheek as Heather walked beside him in the evening. He could never go back to that time.

He went into the house. Prim was sitting by the kitchen stove, her mending in her lap. Her face was composed, but he saw the swollen eyelids and the splotches on her skin. He looked at her a long moment, thinking he had never seen her so ugly from weeping. He had given her the years she needed to raise a child they had conceived in a wild moment on a dark night by the sea. He still had good years before him. He had a right to go now. Nothing held him to Prim Munro.

She lifted her head and looked at him, and he stared back at her. If it's to be settled between us, he thought, it should be done now; I must speak of it and be done with it. But instead his hand moved to his pocket, and he said, "Something the lassie wrote for us. I waited to read it. For both of us, she said."

Her face showed no emotion. "Sit down, Kelsey. I must tell you now what I should have told you years ago—what I tried to tell you when we crossed the mountain." Her glance wavered from his, and he saw her hands clench tightly in her lap. "Heather—she may not be your child, Kelsey. I—" Her voice faltered.

A stillness came over him. "Go on, Prim."

Her head drooped. "I can't face you—and tell you. After you left, Crowter and I— I was—so lonely. I thought you had gone forever, and I—"

The silence drew out in the kitchen. Through the window he saw the sunlight on the shoulder of the mountain, lighting the face of the peak. Now, at noon, everything was flat and bright, and no shadows. The men would be in soon from work, and Prim had no dinner ready.

"Yes?" he said. "Go on."

"I've taken your life, the best of it," she said, her voice almost a whisper, "and I had no right. I'm not sure—about Heather. She could be Crowter's child."

He waited to feel anger or regret or disgust, but he felt only a quietness in himself. Prim's voice came again, so low he could scarcely hear it. "I've done so much that's wrong, but this was the worst thing I did—to you, to you that I love."

He remembered the mountain then, the fear and the hunger and cold. He remembered the dead cattle and the blowing snow and the waiting for death that seemed just around the corner— As it is always, he thought now. And he saw again Jediah's face on the night when Dalt killed Tommy—a face compassionate and still.

Prim said, "I—I can never forgive myself."

He found words at last. "But I can forgive you, Prim. And Heather is my child. That I know. Even if it could be proved she is Crowter's child, it would make no difference now."

Prim's head bent lower. "You're free, Kelsey. Go to Monte. It's right you should; maybe it was always right. I've been a burden to your life—a bitter, twisted thing." Her breath caught, and she said, "I would die, so I would, to make up for it."

He put his hand in his pocket and drew out the crumpled paper and smoothed it until he could see the words that were written in Heather's bold, clear hand. "I'll read this now, Prim."

She lifted her head, and he saw the pain and glory on her face. He cleared his throat and looked at the first line, and it seemed in that moment that the brief words held all the meaning of himself and of Prim and of the world. The page blurred and then cleared as he slowly spoke the words aloud.

"This is for my people, dearly beloved . . ."